T

All the portents say so. Those of us with the proper gifts can see it in the shape of the clouds, or hear it in the murmur of the rivers. Every divination points to it. Many of you can feel it in your restlessness and ill temper, in the vile pictures that rise unbidden in your mind. I witness it in my dreams, whenever I can bear to sleep.

A Rage is surely coming, the greatest ever, a madness that will overwhelm every one of us as completely as it will our evil kindred.

We must protect the small folk from our fury.

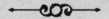

THE YEAR OF ROGUE DRAGONS

Richard Lee Byers

Book 1
The Rage

Book 11
The Rite
January 2005

Book 111
The Ruin
May 2006

Realms of the Dragons
Edited by Philip Athans
December 2004

Other FORGOTTEN REALMS Titles by Richard Lee Byers

R.A. Salvatore's War of the Spider Queen, Book I
Dissolution

The Rogues
The Black Bouquet

Sembia
The Shattered Mask

FORGOTTEN REALMS

THE RAGE

THE YEAR OF ROGUE DRAGONS

book *1*

Richard Lee Byers

Wizards OF THE COAST

THE RAGE
The Year of Rogue Dragons, Book 1
2004 Wizards of the Coast, Inc.

Distributed in the United States by Holtzbrinck Publishing. Distributed in Canada by Fenn Ltd.

Distributed to the hobby, toy, and comic trade in the United States and Canada by regional distributors.

Distributed worldwide by Wizards of the Coast, Inc. and regional distributors.

Cover art by Matt Stawicki
Map by Dennis Kauth
First Printing: April 2004
Library of Congress Catalog Card Number: 2003111912

9 8 7 6 5 4 3

US ISBN: 0-7869-3187-6
UK ISBN: 0-7869-3188-4
620- 96536-001-EN

U.S., CANADA,
ASIA, PACIFIC, & LATIN AMERICA
Wizards of the Coast, Inc.
P.O. Box 707
Renton, WA 98057-0707
+1-800-324-6496

EUROPEAN HEADQUARTERS
Wizards of the Coast, Belgium
T Hofveld 6d
1702 Groot-Bijgaarden
Belgium
+322 467 3360

Visit our web site at **www.wizards.com**

For John

Acknowledgments
Thanks to Phil Athans, my editor,
and to Ed Greenwood for his help and inspiration.

PROLOGUE

12 Flamerule, the Year of Moonfall
(1344 DR)

The world changed in an instant.

Before that moment, it seemed to Dorn Graybrook that life was perfect. The nine-year-old boy rarely escaped his round of chores in the master's cheerless house, and it was only to run errands through the city with its surly crowds and high gray walls that blocked the sun. Today, though . . .

Open expanses of tall grass, shimmering in the summer heat, rolled away on either side of the dusty road. The snow-crowned Dragonspine Mountains rose far ahead, and sometimes Dorn caught a glimpse of the purple-blue waters of the Moonsea to the north. He was outside, truly outside, and he loved it.

The best thing of all, though, was the change the journey evoked in his parents. At home, they often seemed sad and weary, worn down by their years of servitude.

Mother, who'd opted to walk for a time among the half dozen guards, sang songs. As Father drove the wagon, he joked with the boy seated beside him and told him things about the countryside. Sometimes the balding bondsman with the wry, intelligent face even let Dorn take the reins and guide the two dappled horses himself.

Priam said, "Look!"

He pointed up at the western sky. The leader of the guards, Priam was a lanky mercenary with a fierce trap of a mouth. He'd slain many a bandit and goblin in defense of the master's trade goods, and everyone admired his courage. But his voice was subtly different, as if he had to struggle to keep it steady.

Dorn peered upward. At first he couldn't see what the fuss was all about. Then he spotted the specks streaking along against the blue. When he squinted, he could make out the long tails, serpentine necks, and beating wings.

"Are they dragons?" Father asked, reining in the team. His voice was different, too, quavering, higher-pitched, and though he was a clerk, not a warrior like Priam, somehow his fear alarmed Dorn even more than the mercenary's had.

"Yes," Priam said.

The other guards startled babbling all at once.

"Weeping Ilmater," Father said. "What do we do?"

"Get off the road," Mother suggested, her braided red hair glowing like flame. She seemed a little calmer than the men. "Hide in the tall grass, and keep quiet."

"The grass isn't likely to hide us from something soaring overhead," Priam replied. "Still, it's worth a try. The Storm Lord knows, we can't outrun the things." He cast about, then gestured with the broad steel head of his spear. "That spot looks as good as any. Everybody, move!"

They moved, and Dorn saw that Priam was right. It was a bad hiding place. People could crouch down in the grass, but the horses and wagon stuck up over the top.

Father applied the brake, then climbed down to stand with the team. He stroked them and crooned to them, trying to keep them calm. Every few seconds, he fingered the hilt of the broadsword hanging at his side. He always wore it when he traveled, but Dorn had never seen him practice with it or even draw it from its bronze scabbard.

Mother led Dorn away from the wagon to hunker down on the ground.

"Now," she said to Dorn, "you just have to be very still."

The boy's heart pounded in his chest, and his mouth was dry. He had to swallow before he could speak.

"Are we going to die?"

"No," she said. "The dragons may not come this way. Even if they do, they probably won't notice us or take any interest in us. We're just being safe."

"All right," he said, though he could tell she was acting more confident than she felt.

"One of them's swinging this way," said a black-bearded spearman.

"Bugger this," said another guard, a sharp-featured young man named Janx. "Let's scatter. It can't catch all of us."

"Yes, it can," Priam said. "It's fast enough. So, would you rather fight it by yourself or with your comrades beside you?"

"I'll wind up just as dead either way," said Janx, but he stayed put.

The next minute or two crawled by, and everything started happening very fast, or at least it felt that way. The approaching dragon changed course again to fly directly at the travelers. It swooped lower. Shivering despite the hot sun, Dorn could make out the color of its glinting scales—red like blood.

"When I tell you," Mother said, "I want you to run away through the grass, and whatever happens, don't look back."

"Priam said—"

"That we mustn't scatter. But you're small, and you'll have a head start. The creature could easily overlook you."

"What about you and Father?"

"We'll be fine," she lied. He thought she'd never lied to him before that day, and suddenly she was doing it over and over. "We'll find you when the trouble's over."

"You aren't guards. You could run, too."

"Just do what I tell you."

Like some terrible shooting star, the dragon plunged down to just a few yards above the ground.

Until then, Dorn hadn't been able to tell how huge it actually was—huge enough to make the humans before it look like mice scurrying about below a scarlet lion. Its amber eyes shone like molten lava, and its neck frills and wings were ash blue at the edges. It stank of sulfur and burning.

Despite Father's efforts, the horses went mad. They wrenched themselves free of his hold and nearly knocked him over as they wheeled to flee, dragging the wagon with its locked front wheels jolting along behind them. He let them go and unsheathed his sword.

A couple of the guards panicked and likewise tried to run. The red dragon turned its wedge-shaped head almost lazily, regarded them, then puffed out a jet of yellow flame at them. They dropped instantly, without so much as a scream, to lie withered and black among the beginnings of a crackling grass fire.

Priam threw his spear. It bounced off the scales on the wyrm's neck.

"Bring it down!" he shouted to the other guards, and they started casting their own lances.

"Now!" Mother said. "Run!"

She gave Dorn a shove, and he obeyed her. He was too scared to do anything else.

Yet he didn't run far. Perhaps he didn't have it in him to abandon the only people he loved in the whole world, the only people who loved him. In any event, after a few strides, panting and shaking, he turned back around to see what was happening.

The scarlet dragon was on the ground, but not, as best Dorn could tell, because anyone had "brought it down." No one had yet succeeded in hurting it at all. It had simply chosen to land. It slashed with its claws and pulled Janx's insides out of his belly. Its gigantic jaws bit Priam's head off.

After that, there weren't any more guards. Just Father, holding his sword in an awkward two-handed grip, and Mother, sprinting to join him without any weapon at all— spending their lives to buy their son another moment to run.

Dorn couldn't bear such a sacrifice on his behalf. He had to stand with them, die with them. He ran back toward his parents and the dragon.

He was a fast runner, but not fast enough. Before he could close the distance, the wyrm caught Father in its fangs. It chewed him up and swallowed him down, spitting out the broadsword a moment later, the blade bent from the pressure of its jaws.

Mother snatched up the ruined weapon and hacked at the dragon with it. The reptile puffed malodorous flame into her face. She staggered a step and collapsed, her hair burning, the flesh of her head and shoulders running like melted candle wax.

Fists clenched, Dorn hurled himself at the wyrm. He never got a chance to hit it. It met him with a flick of its talons and hurled him to the ground.

To his surprise, he wasn't dead, but when he tried to get up, he couldn't. The throbbing pain started a second later.

He'd fallen with his face pointed toward his mother. He watched the dragon eat her, not gobbling her all at once as it had his father, but rather picking her apart and devouring her a piece at a time.

He could have shut his eyes. He still had that much control over his damaged body. But he chose to watch.

Something had changed in him. Agony and grief wracked him, but he wasn't afraid of the dragon anymore. Terror had given way to hatred, and he glared at it as if in the hope that his malice alone could kill it.

When it finished with his mother, it pivoted toward him.

ONE

16 Hammer, the Year of Rogue Dragons
(1373 DR)

Kara jerked upright, and her wounded arm and shoulder throbbed. How long had she dozed? Long enough for the air to grow cold despite the miserly fire dying in the fieldstone hearth. Or perhaps it was the bleeding that made her feel a chill. Blood had soaked her tattered velvet sleeve and dripped down to spatter the sawdust strewn around the floor. The smell of it mixed with the ambient odors of eye-stinging smoke and stale beer.

Hoping to discover some sign of imminent assistance, the willowy woman with the flowing silver-blond hair peered around the taproom. No one was there but the same six surly-looking men she'd observed before, sipping their ale and watching her from the shadows. Alarmed, she raised a numb, trembling hand. Mandal, the taverner, a gaunt man with spiky, grizzled hair, ambled to her table. He gave her a smile that didn't quite reach his shifty eyes.

"Patience, maid," he said. "The healer is surely on his way."

Well, he ought to be, Kara thought.

She'd promised Mandal a ruby brooch from her pouch if he would find help for her. Still, she was starting to wonder.

"Are you certain?" she asked.

"You saw the messenger leave to fetch him."

"But it's been a long while. Perhaps I should seek the temple myself."

She tried to rise, and dizziness assailed her. She might not have made it to her feet even if Mandal hadn't gripped her shoulder and held her down.

"You're too weak to walk anywhere," he said, "you don't know your way around Ylraphon, and these dark streets are freezing cold. Just wait. It will be all right."

"Very well."

In her dazed, depleted condition, acquiescence was easier than resistance, and in any case, maybe he'd offered good advice. Perhaps it was simply fear that made her feel it was folly to stay there. Though she'd suffered serious injury before, she had little experience of dread and the way it could unsettle one's judgment. Many things were changing, and none of them for the better.

"More mulled wine?" he asked.

She shook her head. The drink might warm her and ease her pain, but she was reluctant to dull her senses any further. Mandal shrugged and wandered off to huddle and whisper with his friends.

Then, at last, the door creaked open.

Kara wrenched herself around so quickly it gave her torn flesh an excruciating twinge. An instant later, she felt an even crueler pang of disappointment.

Two strangers stood framed in the doorway. The halfling, no larger than a human child, his heart-shaped face framed by curly black lovelocks, wore leather armor and carried a warsling and a curved, broad-bladed hunting sword. The tall and brawny man behind him sported what amounted to half a suit of iron plate armor affixed to the left side of his body. The uppermost portion conformed to the contours of his head, but lower down, the sleeves of metal encasing his arm and leg were so massive it was a wonder even such a giant could bear the weight. It made him look lopsided, with the knuckle spikes and claws jutting from his gauntlet further contributing to the appearance of grotesque asymmetry.

They looked around the grubby, cheerless tavern as if inclined to turn up their noses and go elsewhere. Then, however, the halfling noticed Kara, and frowning, hurried toward her.

"What happened?" he asked, concern evident in his clear tenor voice.

"I was attacked on the road just outside of town," she said.

She hoped he wouldn't press for details. She felt too weak and muddled to weave any more lies.

"You need help," he said, "and right now."

"We already took care of it," said the taverner. "A priest is on the way."

"You're sure? I have a friend—"

"We're sure," Mandal said.

"Well, even so, it will do no harm to fetch Pavel, also."

"I told you," the taverner said, "she's going to be fine, so why don't you run along and let her rest?"

"I'm not keen on being told to 'run along,'" the small stranger replied as his hand eased toward the staghorn hilt of his sword.

"What I'm telling you is this place is closed, to give the poor injured maid some peace and quiet."

Chairs scraped and squeaked as the tavern's other patrons pushed back from their tables. Plainly, if the halfling opted to defy the host, he'd have to reckon with the rest of the men as well.

The halfling looked to his companion and asked, "What do you think?"

"Plainly, they're lying," the man in the iron armor said. "They mean the lass ill. Which is none of our affair, but I reckon you want to make it so."

"Well, up to now it's been a dull night." The halfling turned back to the denizens of the tavern and said, "If you choose, you can turn the lass, along with her coin and belongings, over to us and live."

For a moment the knaves were silent then they whooped with laughter—and why not? The huge man presented a bizarre, daunting appearance, but it didn't change the fact that the outlaws outnumbered the intruders seven to two.

"You really should think about it," the halfling said. "My friend is Dorn Graybrook, and I'm Will Turnstone."

Mandal sneered and said, "Never heard of you."

Will glanced at Dorn.

"I told you we should have bribed a few bards to spread tales of our exploits," said the halfling.

"If you insist on doing this," Dorn rasped, "let's do it."

Dorn yanked his bastard sword from its pewter scabbard. The blade was long and heavy, designed so a strong warrior could wield it with two hands or one. Dorn opted for the latter tactic, using the arm that merely wore leather to cock the weapon behind him. The one sheathed in iron he extended toward his foes.

Meanwhile, Will pulled his warsling from his belt. It seemed a poor weapon with which to fight long odds at close quarters, just as the halfling himself looked puny compared to the human scoundrels, but if Will was frightened, Kara couldn't tell it. He grinned as if relishing the chance to prove his mettle.

"Kill them," Mandal said.

The outlaws charged, and as they scrambled forward, they changed.

The transformation happened fast. Still, Kara glimpsed thin, black-gray fur spreading over skin, faces jutting into bestial snouts, front teeth swelling into chisel-like incisors, whiskers and thin, hairless tails springing into being. In an instant, her captors, though still scuttling on two legs and capable of gripping weapons, had cast off a goodly portion of their humanity to become a mix of man and rodent.

The transformation from man to wererat dispelled any lingering doubts Kara might have had as to whether Mandal and his cronies truly did mean to hurt her. She had to help the strangers fight on her behalf. She groggily heaved herself to her feet, called a spell to mind, and an earthen jug smashed against her forehead.

One of the ratmen had seen her rise and had thrown the missile at her. She collapsed to the floor in a shower of shards and pungent spirit. Stunned, she tried to flounder onto all fours, but her limbs wouldn't obey her. She could only lie and watch the fight unfold.

Her would-be rescuers looked unfazed by the ratmen's metamorphosis. Dorn stood motionless as the shapeshifters rushed him, then, just as they were about to close, he sprang forward. It was remarkable that such a hulking, heavily-armored man could pounce so quickly, and it caught the wererats by surprise. He swung his fist in a backhand blow, and the knuckle spikes on the gauntlet crunched into a lycan-thrope's skull. Evidently the iron glove was enchanted, for the creature's normal resistance to any but silver weapons did nothing to protect it. Flung backward, it sprawled inert, its head bloody and battered out of shape.

Three more shapeshifters hacked and stabbed at Dorn. It seemed inevitable that one of them would penetrate the big man's guard, but he swept the gauntlet back and forth, blocking and parrying the attacks, for as long as it took to bull his way out of the center of his remaining foes. That accomplished, he came back on guard as he had before, armored hand extended before him, sword poised behind.

Kara peered to see if Will was faring as well. For a moment, she failed to spot the little halfling himself, just the three ratmen scrambling in pursuit. That was because he was taking evasive action, dodging behind or ducking under furniture, using his size to his advantage, making it difficult for his screeching, chattering, manifestly frustrated foes to close with him. Indeed, he was so adept at the tactic that for a moment, they lost track of him all together. As they crouched to look under one table, he leaped on top of another, then gave a piercing whistle. They lifted their heads, and he spun the warsling. Kara didn't see the stone fly, but it was obvious from the way two of the lycanthropes jerked that the missile had hit one, then skipped to strike the other.

Swords raised, beady scarlet eyes blazing, the ratmen rushed forward. Will stood his ground long enough to hurl another rock, which made a double crack as it impacted not just one skull but two. Evidently, like Dorn's gauntlet, the stones were enchanted, for one shapeshifter swayed and crumpled sideways, overturning a rickety chair as it fell.

Alas, that still left two assailants who finally lunged close enough to strike. Will, however, somersaulted off the edge of the table before the leaping blades could touch him. He landed on the floor as neatly as a tumbler in a carnival, then ran. Tails dragging through the sawdust, the ratmen scuttled after.

By then, Dorn's gauntlet was bloody from claw-tips to wrist, evidence of the vicious efficiency with which he employed it. He snatched, and a ratman with a gashed, gory chest frantically sidestepped, only to discover that the mauling grab had merely been a feint. The human swung his hand-and-a-half sword at the creature's shoulder and sheared its long, skinny arm off. The ratman went down, gore pumping from the stump.

One of its comrades pounced, desperate to drive its dagger into Dorn's back before the human could come back on guard. Dorn somehow sensed the attack coming and snapped his elbow backward into the creature's ribs. Weighted with iron, the blow caved in the wererat's chest. That left the biggest of the pack, who snarled and drove in hard, foam flying from its gaping jaws.

Will was down to a single opponent, too, but that one had finally managed to push him into a corner. Still smiling, the halfling drew his hunting sword. The weapon seemed sized for a human, and Kara assumed a smaller fighter would have to wield it two-handed, but it wasn't so. Apparently the sword was one of the small folk's enchanted "hornblades," so light and exquisitely balanced that its relative largeness was no impediment.

But the ratman's broadsword was longer still, as were its limbs. It poised itself at just the proper distance to exploit its advantage in reach, then began rather cautiously cutting and slashing. Will parried but couldn't reach the shapeshifter with a riposte. After a moment, he darted forward.

It was what the wererat wanted him to do. The creature hopped backward and swung its blade in a low, murderous stop cut. Will dived under the blow, rolled back to his feet, and raced on into striking range before his amazed opponent could recover. The hornblade ripped open the shapechanger's belly.

At almost the same instant, Dorn caught his remaining opponent's blade in his armored fingers, gave it a cunning squeeze and twist, and snapped it in two. Disarmed, the lycanthrope recoiled. Dorn bounded after it and gripped the long, wire-wrapped hilt of his sword with both hands. His final stroke flung the wererat's severed head tumbling through the air.

Both Dorn and Will took a look around, evidently making sure all their foes were dead or incapacitated. Then they came to check on Kara, and she goggled in amazement.

She recognized that Dorn wasn't really wearing plate on the left side of his body. Rather, someone had replaced his limbs of flesh and bone with appendages of iron, cast all in a single piece and granted mobility by enchantment. Below the neck, it was impossible to tell precisely where artifice ended and nature began. His dun leather brigandine and breeches hid the joins. But his square, heavy-jawed, green-eyed face displayed the vaguely sickening dividing line where metal fused to skin.

Noticing Kara's astonishment, he scowled. Or maybe that was simply his habitual expression.

Will knelt beside her and asked, "How are you holding up?"

She tried to answer but slid into darkness instead.

As Gorstag Helder stepped out into the night, freshly fallen snow crunched beneath his soles. Soon enough, his feet would be cold, for his thin, cheap boots wouldn't keep out the chill. He hadn't possessed enough silver to pay for both warmth and the latest style.

He wouldn't mind chilled feet if he could finally slip out of town. His report was more than a tenday overdue. He let the salle door swing shut behind him, sealing in the clatter of practice blades, the babble of conversation, the music of glaur, longhorn, and hand drum, and the shrill laughter of a whore, and surveyed the benighted street. His heart sank, because Firvimdol Eastmere was sitting on the edge of a frozen horse trough, awaiting him. Gorstag couldn't figure out whether his "brothers" thought they needed to keep an eye on him or were simply making an effort to bring the newest initiate fully into the fold. Either way, the effect was the same. They sought him out so relentlessly he could scarcely visit the jakes unsupervised, let alone sneak out into the countryside.

Well, he mustn't let his frustration show. He arranged his narrow, long-nosed features into a smile and hurried toward his comrade, who rose and met him with a mushy hand clasp. Both men were young and wore their capes thrown back, defying the cold to display their fashionable slashed doublets, and their equally modish rapiers canted at just the proper angle, but in other ways, they made a contrast. Firvimdol had a plump frame, waxed, curling mustachios, and flaunted genuine velvets and gems. Gorstag was thin—he hoped it made him look athletic, rather than like someone who periodically starved for want of funds—clean-shaven, and a creature of cheaply woven tripe and paste.

"Well met," Gorstag said.

"How was the fencing?" Firvimdol replied.

"Fine."

"Did you and Taegan Nightwind have a chance to talk?"

"Yes." They'd spoken at some length, in fact, but Gorstag would rather have cut out his own tongue than attempt to entice his teacher into the same corruption he himself had seemingly embraced. "I felt him out again, and I must tell you, he simply isn't interested. Why should he be? He's already prosperous and renowned."

"Notorious, anyway."

Inwardly, Gorstag bristled, even though he had to concede that Firvimdol had a point. In recent years, a new breed of fencing master had sprung up in Impiltur to teach swordplay to anyone with coin, and a good many commoners proved eager to learn and to lionize their instructors. The knights and paladins who constituted the kingdom's traditional martial elite, however, disdained the maestros as a source of public disorder, fomenters of duels, brawls, and blood feuds. It perhaps didn't help that a good many of the salles shared space with taverns, gambling halls, ratting pits, or, as in Taegan's case, bawdyhouses.

"Still," Firvimdol continued, "why wouldn't he jump at the chance to be a lord in the Impiltur to come? Are you sure there's no hope of him joining us?"

"I'm sure."

Firvimdol's mouth tightened and he said, "So be it, then. Stroll with me, why don't you?"

They set off wandering the broad, cobbled, elm-lined avenues of Lyrabar, Queen Sambryl's city. Though it was late, many a shop shone bright with lamplight to lure customers. Laughing and singing, sometimes racing one another, revelers traveled from one entertainment to the next in ornately carved, brilliantly painted carriages and sleighs. Signs of wealth and bustling commerce abounded on every side, as if in mockery of those who lived in need.

"I fear," said Firvimdol, while fat snowflakes started

drifting down, just as they had in fits and starts all day, "that you aren't making a very impressive start."

"I can't reach inside Maestro Taegan's head and change the way his brain works. By the Nine Hells, I've accomplished every other task you gave me."

Firvimdol shrugged and said, "Routine chores. Not really enough to prove your commitment or usefulness."

Gorstag felt a pang of anxiety, drew a calming breath, and replied, "I have the feeling you're about to set me a test."

"Not me—the Wearer of Purple. She said that if you could make no headway with your mentor, I was to give you a different errand."

"Whatever the job is, if it will prove my loyalty, I welcome it. I'm tired of being the new man, mistrusted and kept in the dark."

"Good. You know Hezza, the pawnbroker on Lutemaker Street?"

"Vaguely."

In truth, he knew Hezza, and others like him, depressingly well. He'd often pawned one or another of his meager belongings to put bread on his table.

"We've learned he took possession of an emerald pendant just a few hours ago," said Firvimdol. "The stone's of the highest quality."

Gorstag saw where Firvimdol was going. The cult had been procuring jewels "of the highest quality" for some tendays.

"You want me to steal it," Gorstag said.

"Yes, we do. It's rare luck that such a prize is sitting in Hezza's shop. The place isn't nearly as secure as it ought to be to protect such a treasure."

"It's surely locked, though, and I'm no burglar."

"With a light and a crowbar, you'll do fine."

"What does the brotherhood need with all these gems anyway?"

"You'll find out at the proper time. Will you do it?"

The spy nodded and said, "Anything for the cause."

So it was that Gorstag made his way to a neighborhood displaying little sign of Lyrabar's general affluence, a district of crumbling brick tenements and rookeries like the one where he'd grown up, and where, to his shame, he still resided. Nearing the scene of his intended misdeed, he abandoned the customary swagger of a rake to skulk through the shadows. He had a certain practiced knack for it. Over the years, as legitimate ways of bettering himself had eluded him, he'd occasionally resorted to petty thieving to make ends meet. He suspected his employer somehow knew, and that was why he'd sought him out to be his agent.

Grateful to find it deserted, Gorstag crept down a narrow, twisting alleyway to the rear entrance of the pawnshop. He pulled his hood up to shadow his features, took another look around, then brought the hooked iron pry bar Firvimdol had provided out from under his cloak. He stuck the end between door and jamb then threw his weight against it.

The lock held for a moment then broke with a snap. To Gorstag, the noise seemed hellishly loud, and when he pushed the door open he half expected to hear Hezza rushing to investigate. But the dark space beyond the threshold was silent.

Gorstag slipped through the door, pushed it shut behind him, and removed Firvimdol's other gift from its black cloth bag. Strung on a leather thong, it was a wooden bead enchanted to shed a pale luminescence, and Gorstag couldn't help thinking that by itself, it was a niggardly sort of help for the cultists to provide, in view of the potent magic they claimed to command. But apparently it was all an unproven recruit could expect.

The ghostly light revealed a large room cluttered with tools, furniture, flutes, porcelain dolls, display cases full of cameos, bracelets, and tortoiseshell combs, and countless other dusty objects. The pawnshop took up the entire first floor of the house. Hezza lived upstairs.

Holding the bead aloft like a lantern, Gorstag cast about. Where would Hezza stow a valuable emerald? Surely he wouldn't leave it sitting out with the junk. He'd stash it somewhere safer.

Gorstag found a strongbox under the counter. It was harder to pry open than the door had been, because his crowbar was too big for the job. Finally he managed to open it, to discover only an assortment of coins.

At that, it was coin that could feed and clothe him and pay his rent, and for a second he considering pocketing it. But he was better than that, or at least he aspired to be, and he left the gold and silver where it lay.

Where was the emerald? It occurred him to that Hezza might have taken such a valuable item upstairs with him, but he flinched at the prospect of looking for it in such close proximity to its keeper. He'd conduct a thorough search of the shop first.

He found the second strongbox built into the wall behind a grubby hanging. The steel hatch yielded grudgingly, bending a fraction of an inch at a time. Every metallic rasp and groan jangled his nerves and made him glance over his shoulder. But still Hezza failed to appear, and finally Gorstag widened the gap enough to work his hand inside. He groped about, found something that felt like a pendant, and drew it forth. Even in the dim illumination, the emerald seemed brilliant. Flawless.

It was far more enticing than the coins had been, but that temptation, too, he would resist. He'd keep faith with his employer, hand the gem over to Firvimdol, and better himself in an honorable way.

He turned, and Hezza was there. Barrel-chested, tufts of his curly brown hair sticking up every which way, the pawnbroker was still in his nightshirt, but had taken the time to equip himself with a falchion. He used it to chop at Gorstag's head.

Gorstag avoided the stroke by leaping backward. Irrationally, perhaps, in that moment, he was less worried about the threat of the curved sword than that Hezza would recognize him. But the pawnbroker didn't seem to. Evidently Gorstag's hood provided sufficient disguise in the feeble light.

He tossed the bead away and dodged around a display case, interposing it between Hezza and himself. That gave him time to draw his rapier, though the gods knew he didn't want to use it. He couldn't use it as it was meant to be used, not against a tradesman who was only trying to protect what was rightfully his.

"Please stop," he said. "You don't understand."

"No?" Hezza grunted as he kept maneuvering, trying to work in close enough for another attack.

Gorstag wasn't supposed to babble his employer's private business, but it would be better than killing an innocent man, wouldn't it?

"I serve the Harpers." He didn't actually know for a fact that his contact was a member of that altruistic secret society, but he suspected it. "They set me the task of infiltrating a nest of traitors to the queen. I have to borrow the emerald to do that. I swear, you'll get it back."

"Oh," said Hezza, "that's fine, then. Would you like me to wrap it up for you? Or give it a polish?"

He faked a shift to the right, dodged left instead, and there was nothing between him and Gorstag. He rushed in cutting and slashing.

Hezza was no expert swordsman like Maestro Taegan, but he was competent. Gorstag had to parry and retreat frantically to preserve himself from harm. He saw openings for ripostes and counterattacks, but he couldn't bring himself to exploit them.

He had to do something. Hezza was rapidly taking his measure. Figuring out how to penetrate his defense. The pawnbroker's cuts only fell short by a finger breadth, or else Gorstag only managed to block them at the last possible moment. If he didn't do something soon, Hezza would surely cut him down.

He waited for Hezza to lift the falchion for a head cut, then sprang forward. It was a risky to plunge straight into an opponent's attack, but he proved quick enough to leap safely inside the arc of the stroke. He bashed his surprised opponent in the jaw with the rapier's bell guard, then hammered his forehead with the pommel. The pawnbroker fell, unconscious.

"I'm sorry," Gorstag panted, "but it was necessary."

Maybe the Wearer of Purple, Firvimdol, and the other madmen, Gorstag thought, will finally tell me about their grand design.

Pavel Shemov fanned out his cards to see what the dealer had wrought. When he found the Sun, the King and Queen of Staves, and the Knights of Staves, Coins, and Blades, it was a struggle to keep his tawny, handsome, brown-eyed face from breaking into a grin.

Ever since he'd sat down at the table, he'd drawn one dismal hand after another and watched his stakes dwindle until he could almost have wished he was a priest of Tymora, goddess of luck, instead of his own beloved Lathander. The cards he held, however, constituted an excellent hand headed, moreover, by the Morninglord's own emblem. It was inconceivable that he could lose.

The trick was to make the most of it. It wouldn't do to scare the other gamblers out. When the dour, shaggy-bearded ruffian on his right opened for ten gold pieces, Sembian nobles and Cormyrean lions mostly, the cleric made a show of pondering, then contented himself with a modest raise.

At which point, Will burst through the inn door, admitting a gust of frigid air in the process.

He spotted his comrade and shouted, "Pretty boy! I need you."

"I'm busy," Pavel replied.

The halfling strode across the hard-packed earthen floor, peered at his comrade's cards, and announced, "He's got a royal marriage under favorable aspect, with a full honor guard."

The other players threw in their hands.

Pavel rounded on Will and grumbled, "You poxy son of a—" Then he registered the honest urgency in the halfling's face. It wasn't just the usual game of insults and pranks they played with one another. "What's wrong?"

"A human lass, wounded and in need of healing. Dorn's standing watch over her, in case any more ratmen show up."

"Wererats wounded her?" Pavel asked. "If so, she might have contracted lycanthropy herself."

"No. At least, I don't think so. Just get off your festering arse and come with me, all right?"

"Very well."

He raked what remained of his coin off the table, then picked up his mace. By the time he finished, Raryn Snow-stealer had come to join them.

As far as superficial appearances were concerned, Will and Pavel were the "normal" members of their small fellowship. Raryn, like Dorn, turned heads wherever they went, for in the lands surrounding the Moonsea, arctic dwarves were as rare as half-golems. Scarcely taller than the halfling, Raryn was squat and burly, almost as broad as he was tall. His goatee and unbound, waist-length hair were white, and it was hard for the eye to separate them from the polar bear fur of his tunic. In contrast, the sun had burned his exposed skin to what, for a human, would have been an excruciating red. He carried his ice-axe in one stubby-fingered hand.

"Let's go," the dwarf said.

Will led them out into the muddy streets of a town that, even in the dark, presented the raw, unfinished appearance of an outpost newly carved from the wilderness. A good many settlements in the region had the same air. It was, in a sense, misleading. Civilized folk—humans, mostly—had dwelled around the Moonsea for untold centuries, as countless weathered standing stones and crumbling ruins attested. Unfortunately, wars and rampaging beasts had time and again obliterated the works of man, requiring him to erect new habitations on the rubble of the old.

Of course, Ylraphon was rough even by local standards. Standing on the eastern shore of the Dragon Reach, the channel linking the Moonsea with the Sea of Fallen Stars, it was an important way station for freighters and caravans moving in either direction, but also notorious as a haunt of brigands and pirates. A number of knavish-looking characters were prowling about in the dark, but none who cared to give Pavel, Will, and Raryn any trouble. The slim, long-legged priest supposed they looked too formidable, himself included.

When he'd left Damara, he'd naturally worn his red and yellow priestly vestments, but piece by piece, they'd worn out over the years, until only the gold-plated sun amulet set with garnets remained. He'd come to affect the sturdy wool and leather garments of one who roamed the wild. He thought he'd changed in other ways, too. He moved like the hunter he'd become, wary and confident at the same time, with his weapons always ready to hand.

As they hurried along, Will explained what was afoot in more coherent fashion.

"I don't understand" said Pavel at the story's end. "If the wererats meant her harm, why not just stick a knife in her? Why sit around waiting for her to bleed out?"

"My guess," said Will, "is they really did send for someone, but it wasn't a priest. It was their leader. They were waiting on him to decide whether to kill and rob her and be done with it, ransom her, or sell her into slavery."

The three companions came to a disreputable-looking tavern at the edge of inhabited Ylraphon. Beyond stood only charred, gutted shells of buildings—destroyed in whatever calamity had last befallen the port—that no one had yet bothered to raze or restore. When Pavel stepped inside, he found more or less what he'd expected: dead wererats; a wounded and unconscious young woman, uncommonly lovely even with her face ashen and her gown soaked with blood; and Dorn, glowering at him.

"What kept you?" the big man snapped.

"I set forth as soon as the halfwit bothered to come and tell me I was needed," Pavel replied.

He crouched over his patient, tore away her shredded sleeve, then winced. The gashes were even deeper than he'd expected. Still, by Lathander's grace, he could save her, though it was likely to take the most potent healing magic at his command. He recited the incantation, and his hands glowed golden. He pressed them to the lass's gory wounds.

His own flesh seemed to burn, albeit painlessly, as the spell did its work. When the sensation ebbed, the wounds had closed, halting the flow of blood. Indeed, they'd dwindled to mere pink lines on her ivory skin, as if they'd been healing for tendays, and a blush of color had returned to her lips and cheeks.

"She'll be all right," he said.

"So you were finally good for something," said Will.

Given their perpetual mock feud, it was as close as he could come to commendation.

The woman's eyes fluttered open. Large, lustrous, and a unique shade of violet, they were as striking as the rest of her. They gazed up at Pavel's face for a moment, then shifted to the sacred pendant dangling from his neck.

"Did you heal me?" she asked. Even after her travail, when her throat must have been dry as dust, her soprano voice was clear and sweet. "Thank you, and Lathander too."

Will grinned and said, "Don't bother thanking the charlatan there. Generally he botches the curing and kills the sick folk, and anyway, Dorn and I did the real work. You remember, I'm Will Turnstone. Well, Wilimac, really, but Will to my friends."

"Thank you, too, Will Turnstone," she said. Pavel helped her up off the floor and into a chair. "And you, Goodman Graybrook."

As Pavel might have predicted, Dorn merely grunted and averted his eyes. The stranger looked puzzled at the seeming rebuff, but didn't question it.

She said, "My name is Kara . . . well, that will do. It's been a while and many a mile since I bothered with the rest of it."

Raryn and Pavel completed the round of introductions, and the cleric moved to investigate the stock behind the bar and fetch Kara a restorative drink.

The dwarf said, "Good to meet you, lass. How, may I ask, did you fall among vermin such as these?"

He tipped his bone-handled axe toward a couple of the dead shapeshifters.

"I was attacked on the road just outside of town," Kara replied. "Wounded, I fled to the first place that seemed to offer refuge. I imagine Will told you the rest of it."

"More or less," Raryn said, clambering up to perch atop a stool, his stubby legs in their knee-high deerskin boots dangling. "But he didn't know who attacked you."

"I don't either, really. Men with spears and swords. Bandits, I suppose."

Pavel felt a pang of mingled surprise and curiosity. He appropriated a bottle of what appeared to be the best vintage the tavern had to offer—something red from Sembia—an armful of dusty pewter goblets, a rag to wipe them, and headed back toward Kara and his friends.

"Did the outlaws kill your companions?" Raryn asked.

"No. I mean, I was traveling alone."

The dwarf arched a shaggy white eyebrow and asked, "In these lands, in the dead of winter? You're brave. And lucky, to have escaped those who waylaid you."

"I'm a bard," she said. "I have my songs to protect me, as they would have saved me from the robbers if they hadn't taken me by surprise. As it was, I still drove them off, but not before they hurt me. I wanted to use magic to help Dorn and Will against the ratmen, but once I took that final blow to the head. . . ."

"It's all right," the halfling said. He plainly liked her. Well, Pavel could sympathize. He too found her charming, despite what he knew. "I've seen the toughest warriors fall helpless after taking the wrong sort of wound. It's no reflection on your courage."

"Enough chitchat," Dorn growled. "Maid, if you're up to

it, we can all clear out of here. My friends and I should go to the council of merchants and explain what happened before somebody else stumbles on all these bodies. Especially since they look to be melting back into human shape. We'll take you as far as a safe inn."

"Easy," Pavel said. "The lass was injured nigh unto death a moment ago." He set his burden on the table between Kara and Raryn, then drew his knife to dig the cork out of the bottle. "Give her a little time to recover."

"I'm sure she needs it," Will said, "considering that we didn't have a real healer to tend her."

"I do need it," Kara said. She straightened her arm and hissed in pain. "It's far better than it was. I'm sure it will be all right eventually, but it's still weak and sore."

"Most likely," Pavel said, "it will remain so for a while."

"Well, perhaps it's no worse than I deserve. For you're right, Goodman Snowstealer, even if you were too tactful to state your opinion in so many words. I was a fool to travel alone. Yet it's urgent I reach Lyrabar as soon as possible, and so I wonder: You four have the look of wandering sellswords. Could I hire you to escort me?"

"No," said Dorn.

"I can pay," she said.

She opened the pouch on her belt and removed a slim silver bracelet set with pearls. After a moment of silence, Will whistled. Once again, Pavel understood how his comrade felt. The exquisitely crafted ornament was plainly worth hundreds if not thousands of gold pieces, and he glimpsed more gems and pieces of precious metal glittering in her purse, so many that he surmised the pouch was one of those enchanted receptacles larger inside than out.

"Is this enough?" Kara asked.

"I told you," said the half-golem, "we're not interested."

"Speak for yourself," Will said.

"We're hunters," said Dorn, "not bodyguards."

The halfling snorted and said, "We've done all kinds of work when times were tough."

"They aren't tough now. We have a job. The one the council of merchants hired us to do."

"Accompanying the lass on her journey strikes me as pleasanter work than slogging around in a frozen swamp looking to get our heads bitten off."

"I gave my word," said Dorn, "that we'd help Ylraphon."

Pavel handed him a goblet. The half-golem took a token sip then set the cup aside. He often pushed pleasure away, as if it might somehow weaken him.

"What about afterward?" Kara asked.

"We're not bodyguards," Dorn reiterated, "nor inclined to journey all the way to Impiltur under winter skies. We resolved to spend the season in Thentia."

"Yet you left there to come here," said the bard.

Dorn shrugged.

Had he so chosen, Pavel could have explained. They'd forsaken their winter quarters because the city fathers of Ylraphon wanted them to kill a dragon. And Dorn would have crawled ten thousand miles naked through incessant blizzards for that.

Raryn tossed back a mouthful of wine, then smacked his lips in appreciation and said, "It's all right, maid, you don't need us anyway. Even at this time of year, ships and caravans occasionally travel east. Find one with an honest reputation, book passage, and you'll be fine."

"I might do that," Kara said, "but I'd still prefer to make the journey with protectors who've already proved their courage and integrity."

"We're sorry," Pavel said, "we're simply not at liberty to say yes."

Will looked up at the faces of his comrades then sighed, shook his head, and grumbled, "You're a trio of idiots, stupid as stones in a ditch."

Pavel was certain he'd hear variations on the same theme for days to come.

TWO

21 Hammer, the Year of Rogue Dragons

At some point, the cultists had discovered a system of ancient catacombs beneath Lyrabar and adapted them for their own use, equipping many of the vaults for the supplication of infernal powers and the practice of necromancy. The dank crypt Gorstag and Firvimdol currently occupied, however, they'd merely furnished to create a space where conspirators could palaver in relative comfort or relax when they had nothing else in particular to do.

Gorstag was trying to wheedle secrets out of his companion when he sensed a presence. He turned in his chair, beheld a stranger standing in the doorway, and felt a pang of terror, which made no sense.

Revealed by the greenish light of the ever-burning torches, the newcomer was just a man, albeit one the spy hadn't seen before. Tall and pale, he wore a woolen robe and mantle, and he carried a blackwood staff. Unruly strands of dark hair flopped over his high fore-head, and his narrow-shouldered frame was gaunt enough to make even a scarecrow like Gorstag feel momentarily well-fed. His face, with its sharp planes and blade of a nose, bespoke intelligence and fervor, and all in all, he appeared to be another of the cult's wizards, little different than the half dozen such folk Gorstag had already met. A person to be reckoned with, certainly, but no immediate threat.

Yet something about him inspired dread. Or maybe it was just Gorstag's jitters that were to blame. The gods knew, the dangers and necessities of his deception were taking a toll on him. He took a deep breath, and the fear ebbed.

"Hello," said the stranger in a strangely accented baritone voice.

Evidently realizing the newcomer's presence for the first time, Firvimdol spun toward the door. He scrambled to his feet, pressed his palms together, bowed deeply, and held the position, separating his hands just long enough to gesture frantically, presumably for Gorstag to rise and make the same obeisance.

The spy obeyed. Though his moment of irrational panic had passed, he was eager to ingratiate himself with anyone who commanded such deference from his normally arrogant comrade.

During his indoctrination, Gorstag had learned that Lyrabar's traitorous fraternity was only one of many such cabals scattered across Faerûn. In general, the cells labored in ignorance of one another, so that even if their enemies destroyed or infiltrated one, its downfall posed little threat to the cult as a whole. But plainly, the conspiracy must possess at least a few commanders who possessed knowledge of the entire enterprise and thus could formulate an overall strategy to achieve its goals. He suspected that such a leader stood before him. If so, then the whoreson could supply the answers to Gorstag's every question.

"Rise," the stranger said. "It's nice to see you, Firvimdol. Been practicing those spells I taught you?"

"Yes, sir," Firvimdol replied. "Have you met with the Wearer of Purple?"

The stranger shook his head. "I just arrived."

"I know where she lives," Firvimdol said. "I can fetch her."

"Later. I have an errand to run, and an itch to get it done before I sit down for a lengthy conference with your chief. I just need a couple trustworthy fellows to watch my back. Are you game?"

"Of course!" Firvimdol beamed as if he was a small child, and the gaunt man the father who had just invited him on some fascinating outing. "But ... I don't know how much use I'll be. What can I do for you that your magic couldn't do better?"

"Perhaps you can do it more discreetly. When a person wishes to pass unnoticed, it's often counterproductive to fling thunderbolts about."

"Well, I'll do my best for you."

"No doubt." The mage's dark eyes shifted to Gorstag. For an instant, the spy felt a renewed surge of fear, or maybe simply recalled the panic of before. Either way, it only lasted an instant, and he managed to bear the stranger's gaze without cringing. "I don't know you. A recent convert?"

"Yes, sir. My name is Gorstag Helder."

"Are you a full initiate?"

"He's proved himself," Firvimdol said.

"Then you can tag along, too."

Gorstag knew a thrill of exhilaration. For the first time since he'd stolen the emerald, he felt he was making some actual progress toward the completion of his assignment.

"Yes, sir. I'm honored." He hesitated. "May I know your name?"

The wizard smiled and said, "That's a more difficult question than it seems. I've used many. It would be reasonable enough to call me Scorned, Forsaken, or Betrayed. But perhaps Seer would be best. Or Speaker."

Gorstag blinked. Like every initiate, he knew who the

First-Speaker had been: the founder of the cult and the author of the deranged prophecies it sought to fulfill. But that "Speaker" had perished long ago, and if by some evil miracle he yet survived, he wouldn't much resemble a common human being.

Then again, if the tales were true, the prophet had returned from the dead before and had almost certainly commanded magic that would have allowed him to look like whatever he wanted.

But no. Gorstag refused to entertain the notion. He was tense enough already without allowing such an unlikely fancy to rattle his nerves.

"Speaker it is, then."

"Get ready," the wizard said, "and we'll go. For once, you gallants might consider flouting fashion and wearing your capes closed. It's quite chilly tonight. Or perhaps it only seems that way to me. This morning, I was in Tethyr, a thousand miles to the south."

Gorstag and Firvimdol strapped on their rapiers, donned their cloaks, then accompanied Speaker out of the tunnels and the derelict tannery above. As the mage had warned, the temperature had plummeted. The membranes inside Gorstag's nose crackled when he drew a breath. Yet Speaker himself bore the chill without the slightest sign of discomfort.

They walked quietly for a time, on a hike that took them from one of the city's poorest precincts to one of its wealthiest, where grand and ostentatious structures stood tall against the starry sky. A good many were imposing cathedrals, one adorned with gonfalons bearing the bound-hands sign of Ilmater, another marked by the eyes-and-stars emblem of Selûne rendered in stained glass above the entrance. For that was the other face of Lyrabar. It was a pious city, its devotion paradoxically existing cheek-by-jowl with the burghers' frantic pursuit of gold and the countless luxuries and entertainment the coin bought.

Speaker looked at the temples and made a spitting sound,

as if the gods were poor and contemptible things for men to worship.

A little farther on, he peered down the wide, straight avenue ahead and exclaimed, "Aha! Behold our objective, and about time, too. You lads need to get in out of the cold before you catch your deaths."

When Gorstag realized where Speaker was looking, he felt a stab of dismay. The boulevard led up to a castle on a hill, a bewildering tangle of keeps and spires rising above massive walls. It was, in fact, Queen Sambryl's residence within the city.

Firvimdol swallowed and started, "I . . ."

"Oh, don't worry," Speaker chuckled, "we're not going to try to invade the royal bedchamber and strangle Her Majesty. She's just a figurehead anyway. The Council of Lords makes all the decisions. We're going to call on someone more interesting, if less well guarded."

Feigning a confidence he was far from feeling, Gorstag said, "Sir, if you say you can sneak us in, that's good enough for me."

"Good man," Speaker said, eliciting a momentary scowl of jealousy from Firvimdol.

The mage led his minions on into the pocket of shadow between two buildings. The frigid snow was almost knee-high there; no one had bothered to shovel or sweep it away.

"Now, keep watch," said the mage. "If someone happens by and notices what I'm doing, kill him with as little commotion as possible."

Gorstag prayed it wouldn't come to that, for he'd have no choice but to disobey Speaker if it did. For his part, Firvimdol looked nervous but excited too, as if he'd welcome the chance to spill some blood and prove that he too was a "good man."

Speaker extracted a roll of parchment from a pocket in the lining of his cloak.

"Ordinarily this can take hours, even for me," he said, "but when you have the spell on a scroll, you can cast it quickly."

Seemingly unhindered by the gloom, he read a short trigger phrase. The air shimmered, and Gorstag felt a prickling on his face.

Speaker stood and stared at the palace for a time. Finally he swayed and grabbed Gorstag's shoulder for support. The spy thought the wizard's fingers felt . . . wrong somehow. Too hard, perhaps, But Gorstag's layers of clothing made it difficult to be sure.

"Are you all right?" he asked.

"Yes," Speaker said, releasing him. "It's just that that particular bit of magic takes a toll on a fellow's stamina, even if it comes off a sheet of vellum."

"What did it do?"

"It showed me all the wards intended to keep intruders like us out. Having noted them, I should be able to suppress them."

Gazing at the castle, he muttered an incantation and swirled his hands in a complex pattern. The air around him made a grinding sound.

"That's got it. Now . . ."

Lashing his hands back and forth, he rattled off another spell, and on the final percussive word, grabbed hold of both his comrades. Firvimdol let out a yelp, and they were falling.

Or hurtling in some direction, anyway, flashing through a void of writhing shadows. An instant later, that dark emptiness spat them out in a courtyard paved with hexagonal flagstones. Walls and towers loomed on every side, proof they were inside the fortress.

"Now I understand" Gorstag whispered, shaking, "how you could start the day in the South and end in the North."

"I'm sorry I didn't warn you," Speaker said, sounding, if anything, amused by their discomfiture, "but I had to get us in quickly, before the wards reasserted themselves."

"What now?" Firvimdol asked.

"Now," said Speaker, "we skulk on cat's feet. Our destination isn't far, and most of Sambryl's servants are surely indoors, huddled up to their fires, so with luck, no one will spot us. When we get where we're going, I'll palaver, and you'll stand guard as you did before."

They crept onward, down the passages that ran between the keeps and along the shadowy edges of the baileys that lay between them. At first, they encountered no one, and Gorstag dared to hope their errand whatever in Mask's name it was, would come off without a hitch. He thought the sentries on the battlements posed little threat. Their job was to look outward, not in, and even if they did happen to notice three men prowling in the murk below, they might well mistake them for more of the queen's retainers.

But just as he was starting to relax, an adolescent girl, bundled up in a fleece-lined cloak with an upturned collar, stepped through a door with an embroidery basket in her hand. From her disgruntled frown, it seemed likely she was some lady's maid, sent forth into the freezing night to fetch the needles and thread her mistress used to pass the time. She peered at the trespassers and frowned.

Gorstag said, "Good evening."

As he commenced, he didn't yet know what lie he was going to tell, but plainly, someone needed to say something quickly to set the maid's mind at ease.

Snarling words that surely had their origin in some demonic language, Speaker swept his hand up from his hip as if pretending to draw a sword. A shaft of utter darkness as long as a rapier blade seethed into existence in the air before him. The girl opened her mouth to scream but never had the chance. The manifestation leaped across the intervening space and plunged into her breast. Her knees crumpled, her form grew cloudy and vague, and she vanished.

Gorstag stared in horror. He'd seen people slain before, sometimes for the basest and stupidest of reasons, but that was the most cold-blooded slaughter of his experience. And somehow, the fact that even the lass's body was gone, scoured from existence like a sand painting in a gale, made it even worse. He shivered with the desire to draw his rapier and drive it into Speaker's heart.

But it was an impulse he had to resist. The poor girl was gone; he couldn't help her anymore. If he lashed out, it would only preclude any possibility of his ever completing his mission. Besides, he was reasonably certain Speaker could annihilate him as easily as he had the maid.

Firvimdol had his rapier halfway out of the scabbard, and he shoved it, scraping, back inside.

"I would have killed her for you."

"I know," Speaker said. "But with luck, no one sensed my spell contorting space, and I thought it better to silence her without leaving a corpse behind. This way, folk may well assume she simply ran away. Come along, we're almost there."

They sneaked onward. The black blade drifted along before them for a few seconds then faded out of existence.

After another minute, they came upon several domes, each possessed of a chimney fuming smoke and a doorway high and broad enough to pass the largest wagon in or out. Inside those openings, saddles, their girths longer than any horse required, dangled from the high ceilings, suspended by ropes and pulleys. From their presence, another trespasser might have concluded that the complex was a sort of stable, but Gorstag, who realized precisely where Speaker had led him, knew that wasn't really so. For the occupants of the domes were no mere beasts of burden. They were personages, dignitaries of the realm no less than the knights and paladins they deigned to carry on their backs.

They were also likely to attack Speaker, Firvimdol, and their ilk as soon as they recognized them for what they were. Gorstag couldn't imagine what the wizard hoped to accomplish there. Surely even a madman would have better sense than to attack all the Queen's Bronzes at the same time and on their home ground.

The intruders slipped through one of the doorways. The corridor on the other side curved, following the outer edge of the dome partway around, no doubt to protect the inhabitant's privacy. At the end of the arc, gold and silver coins littered the floor, and the inconstant light of a fire gilded the wall.

The fire's heat warmed the air in the passage. His heart hammering, Gorstag had to concede that Speaker had kept his promise. He'd gotten his henchmen in out of the cold. The only catch was that death by freezing seemed a kinder fate than the one that likely awaited them instead.

"You lads keep watch here," Speaker said, "while I conduct my business."

He ambled on to the far end of the hall, and something came to meet him. Gorstag couldn't see the creature itself. The inner wall of the passage blocked his view. But the fire abruptly cast the gigantic shadow of a horned reptilian head with a jagged ruff and a long, flexible neck with a finlike protrusion on the dorsal side. A musky scent tinged the air. Gorstag clenched himself against his fear. Firvimdol actually whimpered, and fearful the cultist would bolt, the spy gripped his shoulder to steady him.

"Quelsandas," Speaker said.

"You," the creature's voice rumbled, deeper than any human's, yet it possessed a sibilant quality as well. "The lurker from my dreams."

"Dreams I sent, to prepare you for this parley."

"Why would you wish such a thing? Do you chase your own death? I'm a bronze!"

Speaker shrugged and replied, "Metal, color, gem. Once it didn't matter, and in a new guise, that time is coming around again."

"I don't believe you."

"Of course you do. You feel change nibbling away at everything you are. But you can endure. I'll help you if you earn it."

"Why must I earn it when others need not?" Quelsandas said.

"You may imagine, to make up for all the trouble your kind has given me in the past, but that's not really it. I have an important venture underway in Impiltur. Most likely, the lords will never learn of it. But if they should. I need an agent in place to stymie any attempt they make to interfere."

"Why choose me?"

"Because I've looked into your soul, and I know you're different than the others."

The shadow reared and curled, cocking its head backward like a serpent poising itself to strike.

"You think me cowardly?" asked the dragon. "Or disloyal?"

"Merely sensible. Sensible enough to want to survive as something better than a beast."

"Who are you?" Quelsandas said. "Show me your true face."

"You've already determined who I am," Speaker replied. "However, if you wish it. . . ."

The mage waved his hand and his features shriveled.

THREE

23 & 24 Hammer, the Year of Rogue Dragons

In Dorn's estimation, the Flooded Forest had proved to be a particularly unpleasant swamp, a place of dead trees, spotted toadstools, grimy drifts of snow, sluggish channels of murky water, and boggy, treacherous earth, all of it stinking of decay. Unfortunately, it was where the dragon menacing wayfarers in the vicinity of Ylraphon made its lair, and so the hunters had to seek it there.

That simple truth failed to keep Will from complaining as they slogged along tracking their quarry as best one could track a flying creature.

Swiping at a fat, buzzing fly that evidently thrived on winter's chill, the halfling said, "We could be lounging on the quarterdeck of a nice galley, munching grapes, drinking beer, and listening to a comely maiden sing sweet songs, but no, not us. We're too manly for such soft work. We live to flounder through filthy, freezing, bug-ridden quicksand bogs—"

"Enough," Pavel said. "At first it was amusing to hear you gripe and grouse with never a clue as to why the rest of us decided as we did. But it's become annoying, so listen up: Kara lied to us. She said it was bandits armed with swords and spears who hurt her. The truth is, her wounds were claw marks, with some singes and blisters thrown in."

Will snorted and said, "As if you could tell the difference."

"He's right," Raryn said. The dwarf was wearing all his armor and carrying much of his gear, including a number of magical implements supplied by the company's business partners among the wizards of Thentia. Indeed, he bore such an arsenal—harpoon with coiled rope attached, bow, quiver, fighting knife, and ice-axe—that the small hunter was nearly lost behind the weapons. Still, he moved with the lithe, sure-footed tread of a born ranger. "I noticed, too."

"That wasn't the only strange thing," Pavel said. "Why wouldn't she give her surname, and why would anyone travel these lands alone in Deepwinter, particularly with a fortune in jewels in her purse? Why was she plainly so afraid someone would attack her again?"

"Well," said the halfling, "I don't know, but say she is a shady character. Her treasure would still spend like anybody else's. By the Mother's smile, we've even worked for Zhents a time or two, when they had a beastie that needed killing."

"At least then," Raryn said, "we knew what we were getting into. We have no idea what kind of trouble hides in Kara's cloak."

"But we could have made a bundle finding out," said Will. "Maybe we still can."

"No," said Dorn.

"Aren't you even—"

"No."

That pretty much quashed any further conversation for several hours thereafter, and Dorn was just as glad. Hunters didn't catch their quarry by chattering their way through the wild. That was how they became prey in their turn.

Perhaps an hour before dusk, as Dorn was considering halting to make camp, they came upon another open space sufficiently large for an enormous flying beast to light. At the edge of the clearing stood a willow with a section of its bark charred away and the wound still bubbling and steaming. Slimy gray-green scales littered the ground beneath it.

"It set down to scratch," whispered Raryn, "and recently."

"Did it take flight again?" asked Dorn.

The ranger studied the marks on the ground then said, "No. It scuttled off that way."

He pointed with the barbed head of his harpoon.

"We could be close," said Will, "so I guess I'd better stroll ahead and take a look."

He pulled off his calfskin glove, wet a finger, and held it up to ascertain which way the breeze was blowing. If at all possible, he wanted to approach their quarry from downwind.

After the halfling vanished into the undergrowth, his companions had nothing to do but watch and wait. The passing minutes gnawed at Dorn's nerves.

Finally Will came scurrying back.

"It's there," he said. "Just a bowshot from where we're standing. I mean, if all the trees weren't in the way."

"What's it doing?" asked Dorn.

"That's the strange part. Muttering to itself like a cranky old granny."

"What's it saying?" Pavel asked.

"Since when do I speak Draconic? That's you, or so you claim. Do you want to sneak up and have a listen?"

"As long as it didn't seem to be casting spells," said Dorn, "it doesn't matter what it's grumbling about. It's on the ground and within reach. Let's get ready."

They shrugged off their packs. They didn't want their gear weighing them down in combat. They drank the elixirs intended to protect them from the acidic secretion slathering the dragon's hide. Then it was time for Pavel, brandishing his sun-shaped pendant, to work magic.

From past experience, Dorn knew the first prayer was a blessing to brace and invigorate the four of them. It cleansed the fleshly part of him of the aches and heaviness of fatigue even as it cleared and sharpened his mind. The second invocation engendered no such sensations, but in some subtle fashion he didn't pretend to understand would make it more difficult for the wyrm to strike them.

The third spell was for Dorn alone. The world fell silent as Pavel shrouded him in stillness. In theory, the rest of his comrades might have benefited from the same treatment. But Will was too vain of his thief-craft to admit the magic might be of use to him, and neither Pavel nor Raryn wanted to dispense with their voices and thus their ability to recite incantations. The latter possessed his own store of cantrips, wilderness lore handed down from ranger to ranger, not as formidable or versatile as the cleric's divinely granted powers, but useful enough in certain situations.

After that, they were ready. Dorn nodded, signaling it was time to go.

They crept in single file, Will in the lead, Raryn second, Dorn third, and Pavel, currently the noisiest as well as the least adept with mundane weapons, bringing up the rear. Each kept several yards back from the hunter in front of him. Even if a dragon had no breath weapon—and if they were right about its species, the one they were stalking didn't—it was good tactics not to bunch up. That way, the creature couldn't rear up and fling itself down on the whole hunting party, pinning and crushing everyone with a single hop.

As he drew nearer to the quarry, Dorn's eyes started to water and sting. It hardly inspired confidence in the efficacy of the potion he'd just consumed. He wondered if old Firefingers had brewed up a weak batch.

Then he caught his first glimpse of the wyrm, hunkered down among the trees. As expected, it was one of the bog-dwelling creatures called ooze drakes. Smeared with a vile-looking whitish slime, its dull green body was lanky and serpentine, and even the idiots who claimed to consider other breeds of dragon beautiful would have found nothing fair or graceful in its proportions. Its claws were gray, and Dorn knew that when he saw them, its fangs would be the same. As usual, the sight of the thing gave him a pang of dread, but he reminded himself why he hated them, and he was all right.

The ooze drake jerked, and a stone rebounded from its flank, leaving a bloody pock behind. It seemed miraculous that such a small missile could penetrate the creature's scales. But Will was a master of the warsling, knew the spots where the dragon's hide was thinnest, and had hurled an enchanted missile. All in all, it was sufficient to give the beast a sting.

The creature whirled in the direction of its attacker. Pale yellow eyes blazing, it opened its jaws, roaring, surely, though Dorn couldn't hear it. Another stone caught it on the end of its snout, and it charged.

Dorn drew back his composite longbow and sent an arrow streaking through the trees. He too knew where to aim, and the shaft plunged deep into the base of the dragon's neck. It stumbled, then, its sweeping tail obliterating a stand of blue-spotted mushrooms, lurched around in the archer's direction. Will immediately hit it in the shoulder with another stone.

The ooze drake spread its batlike wings. If it took to the air, that might give it a crucial advantage, even against foes who took care to remain beneath the sheltering trees. Or if it was feeling timid, it could simply soar away and leave its attackers behind. It was Raryn's job to keep that from happening. He scrambled out from behind a stand of brush and threw his harpoon. Trailing rope behind it, the lance drove into the wyrm's belly.

Most dragons were at least as intelligent as men. This one clearly had the wit to surmise that the white-bearded dwarf had knotted the other end of the line to a tree. Perhaps it even realized the harpoon was barbed, and that if it simply yanked it out, it risked giving itself a far more serious wound than it had taken hitherto. In any case, it made the right move. Twisting its neck, it reached to bite the rope.

If Dorn was lucky, he could prevent that, but not by sniping away with his bow. He gripped his bastard sword and charged out into the open. Had it been possible, he would have shouted a war cry to attract the ooze drake's attention

Not that he needed to. The reptile could hardly miss such a hulk of a man, body half made of iron and long, straight blade in hand sprinting to engage it. And it obviously realized that if it simply ignored him, he was likely to drive the sword into its eye while it chewed at the rope, because it swung around and pounced.

Dorn sprang aside, just avoiding the scaly foot and talons that would otherwise have eviscerated him and smashed his mangled body to the ground. He cut at its foreleg but scarcely nicked it. The creature spun around to face him.

When Dorn had nightmares, they were about dragons, and conducted in utter silence as it was, the duel that commenced had something of the same eerie quality. Certainly, seen up close, the ooze drake was nightmare incarnate. Its gnashing, slate-colored teeth were like swords, while the citrine, slit-pupiled eyes shone with demonic rage. Its body, long as a tree and big as a house, coiled and struck with appalling speed. So far, its wounds weren't slowing it at all.

Dorn fought as he generally did, the almost indestructible iron portion of his body forward to parry, or when unavoidable, bear an enemy's attacks; the soft, human half behind. The ooze drake caught his metal arm in its fangs, bore down, realized it couldn't bite through, and settled for whipping him up and down. The action slammed him to the ground. Instantly the reptile raked at him. He thrust, and the point of his sword drove into the flesh between two of the creature's claws. The wyrm snatched its foot back, away from the pain, and for an instant, the pressure of its jaws slackened. Fortunately, Dorn's artificial limbs had sensation of a sort, though it wasn't like a normal human sense of touch. His master had seen no reason to make a tool meant purely for killing susceptible to pain. The half-golem felt the loosening and wrenched his fist free. The knuckle spikes caught on one of the drake's lower fangs and ripped it from the gum. He heaved himself to his feet, and the reptile lunged at him once more.

As they fought, drops of the drake's corrosive slime spattered him. They stung his face, and he wondered again how well the potion was protecting him. Smoking and smoldering, the pasty stuff burned holes in his brigandine and even pitted the blade of the hand-and-a-half sword, enchanted though it was. Only the iron parts of him proved entirely resistant.

Finally, after what felt like an hour of frenzied struggle even though it had only been a few seconds, Raryn charged in on the dragon's flank and chopped at it with his ice-axe. From that point forward, though his attention stayed focused on the wyrm, Dorn nonetheless caught glimpses of his comrades.

Raryn drove the axe into the creature's body. It pivoted, jerking the weapon from his grip, and clawed at him. He jumped back, avoiding that attack, but the reptile wasn't done. It kept turning, and its tail lashed the dwarf across his barrel chest. Raryn flew through the air and slammed down hard, hard enough, by the look of it, to break his bones. But he scrambled up and grabbed for the hilt of his dagger.

Will darted under the reptile's belly and jammed his curved sword through the scales, making a long incision as if he was gutting a deer. The wyrm slammed its stomach flat on the ground, sending a jolt through the earth. Its weight would have pulverized anyone caught beneath, but the half-ling flung himself clear.

A translucent mace sprang into existence, and as if wielded by an invisible warrior, battered the ruff of jagged, bony plates behind the dragon's blazing eyes and snapping jaws. Having seen the trick before, Dorn knew Pavel had conjured the effect. A few seconds later, the priest himself advanced on the creature, the mace of steel and wood in his own fist shining like the sun.

Dorn did his best to stay in front of the drake and attack relentlessly, trying to keep the reptile's attention fixed on him while his friends hacked, bashed, and stabbed it from the sides and rear. He gradually cut its mask into a crosshatch of bloody gashes. Still, the wyrm wouldn't even falter, much less go down.

Eaten away by acid, the bastard sword snapped in two. As he fumbled for the long knife he carried as backup or for fighting in close quarters, a column of dazzling yellow fire hurtled down from the darkening sky to strike the drake between the wings. Dorn knew Pavel wasn't sufficiently learned—or wise, or saintly, however it worked—to cast such a powerful spell from his own innate capabilities. He'd used a precious scroll, divine magic the arcanists of Thentia couldn't replace, because in his estimation it was the only way to put the dragon down.

The ooze drake convulsed, but only for a second. Then it rounded on the man it had plainly identified as the principal spellcaster among its opponents. Its head shot forward and caught Pavel in its jaws. Teeth gnashing, it reared high, on the brink of chewing him up and swallowing him down.

No time for the knife now, Dorn thought as he lunged in and ripped with his iron claws.

Heedless of their own safety, Raryn and Will attacked just as furiously.

At last, reeking of burned flesh, the wyrm collapsed. The three hunters scrambled backward to keep it from landing on top of them, then rushed to its head to determine if Pavel was still alive.

They couldn't tell until they pried the fangs apart and pulled him free. Then they saw he was breathing shallowly, but might not be for long. His wounds were deep, bleeding profusely, and he was the healer. Who, then, would heal him?

Well, they had restorative potions, if he wasn't too far gone to swallow. Dorn grabbed the one he carried in his belt pouch, pulled the priest's jaws apart, and poured clear liquid into his mouth.

Pavel coughed most of it back out, but a little evidently went down, because his brown eyes flickered open, and he guzzled the rest of the pewter vial. It served to stanch the worst of the bleeding. Afterward, he gestured weakly for Dorn to step back.

For a moment, Dorn didn't understand why his friend was shooing him away. Then he recalled the bubble of silence. Pavel couldn't recite any incantations while Dorn was crouching over him.

Once he withdrew a few yards, the cleric cast one healing spell after another until his wounds closed, and he was able to stand upright. Then he wiped away the enchantment he'd cast on Dorn, and sound popped back into the world.

"You know," panted Will to Dorn and Raryn, "if we'd moved just a little slower, we would have been rid of the charlatan's useless arse."

"You all have acid burns on your faces," Pavel said. "They don't look serious, but I have a few spells left. I might as well see if I can fix them." He grinned at the halfling. "Though regrettably, I've no cure for simple ugliness. Or ugly simpleness."

Once the priest had eased the sting of their blisters, Raryn said, "What do you say we make camp and chop up the wyrm in the morning? A few teeth and talons should suffice to prove we killed it."

"Fine," said Dorn.

It occurred to him that he ought to be elated at the death of another dragon, but as was often the case, the feeling eluded him. Instead, he felt a glum mood settling in.

"What I want to know," Will said, "is why we never catch the wyrms in their lairs. Seize one treasure horde and we could live like kings for the rest of our days."

"They hide the lairs so folk like us won't find them," Raryn replied. "They build snares, too, and arrange the ground so that if they do have to fight, any intruders will find themselves at a serious disadvantage. Trust me, it's better this way."

"You say that because you have humble tastes," said Will.

"A mug of lager, a bowl of stew, and you're happy as a crow in a cherry tree. I suppose it looks like luxury compared to the way you lived on the Great Ice. But I was meant for finer—"

Off to the north, something roared. An instant later, elsewhere in the swamp, another voice answered with a similar harsh, sibilant cry. A third responded, and a fourth. Startled, the hunters peered wildly about.

"What is this?" Pavel asked. "We knew other dragons lived in the Flooded Forest, but what could make them all screech like that, when judging by the sound of it, they're nowhere near one another, or to us, for that matter? I've never heard the like."

"I have," snapped Dorn. "Listen to it carefully. See if you can make out any words in it."

Just as the clamor was subsiding, the priest's eyes opened wide.

"Oh, no," he said. "The town."

Dorn turned to Raryn and asked, "How far are we from Ylraphon?"

He thought he knew, but the dwarf's sense of direction was infallible.

"A few hours out," Raryn said. "As we trailed the ooze drake, we looped back around. I take it we're going now?"

He plainly understood the gravity of the situation, for he didn't question the wisdom of setting out when they were already so weary, or point out the hazards of marching over such treacherous ground at night.

"Yes," Dorn answered.

"I don't understand" said Will. "What about the fangs and claws?"

"Leave them. They don't matter anymore."

The apprentice scurried up a staircase, leaving the hunters in a workroom that took up the entire ground floor. On their left were piles of crates and bags of salt for packing fish, on their right, screw presses and amphorae for rendering them into oil.

After a time, Esvelle Greengate, wrapped in a quilted dressing gown, a nightcap askew on her graying curls, descended the stairs with the apprentice in tow. At first glance, she looked motherly, a plump, harmless dumpling of a woman. Then one noticed the hardness in her eyes.

"Goodman Graybrook," she said, "what's all this? If you killed the dragon, I'm happy, of course, but you didn't need to haul me out of bed to tell me. I certainly can't pay your fee until the whole council approves it in the morning."

"The ooze drake is dead," said Dorn, "but you've got a bigger problem. Do you know what a dragon flight is?"

Her eyes narrowed and she said, "I've heard of them. Once in a while, a pack of wyrms assembles and goes on the rampage all together. Why?"

"It's happening. The rest of the drakes in the Flooded Forest are uniting to descend upon Ylraphon."

Esvelle frowned and said, "If this is some ploy to inflate your price . . ."

"Forget our price," Dorn snapped. "Keep every copper we've got coming." From the corner of his eye, he saw Will throw up his hands in mock despair. "Before they gather, the wyrms of a flight call out to one another. They're doing it now. Can't you hear it, even here in town?"

"I heard something," she said. "I didn't know what to make of it. Are you sure you do?"

"Yes. I've made a study of such matters. It's why you hired me."

"True, but even if the dragons are becoming aggressive, who's to say they'll come here?"

"I am," said Pavel. "I speak Draconic, and I heard them declare their intentions. It makes sense, doesn't it? They go on these rampages to kill people, and Ylraphon is the town closest to their territory."

"Well," said Esvelle, "say they do attack. How much would you charge to protect us from them all?"

"You don't understand" said Dorn. "When my friends and I are fresh and have a chance to make the necessary preparations, we can kill one dragon. One. How many men-at-arms can you muster?"

"Ten on the town payroll. Then, depending on the nature of their wares, some traders employ guards to ward off thieves. And some folk will volunteer. Maybe fifty?"

"It isn't enough. You have to evacuate everyone who can't fight. Send some out on the Reach in boats. The rest can hike south and east. Those folk who can brace a spear or draw a bow will stay behind as rearguard. If we're lucky, all the non-warriors will get clear before the wyrms come. Then the rest of us can run away, too."

"Just abandon the town? Surely there's another way."

"If this was a great city, with a standing army and stone fortifications, maybe. As it is, your only other option is to die."

"But . . ." She shook her head. "Won't the dragons just chase us down?"

"Even if they do, some folk are likely to escape. It's a better chance than staying here. And the dragons may not pursue. They might linger to level the houses or tear off in another direction all together. Ordinarily, they're sensible in their way, but when this fit takes them, it's difficult to guess what exactly they'll do."

Esvelle turned to the apprentice and said, "Run to the other members of the council, then to the captain of the watch. Tell them I need them here immediately." She glanced back at the hunting party and added, "You'd better be right about this, or we're all going to look like idiots."

The next two hours offered up a little taste of the Hells as Dorn and his comrades made the same arguments over and over again, often to merchants more skeptical than Esvelle. Gradually, though, the bullying and pleading had an effect. A ragtag little militia gathered. Other folk began to flee the town, though far too many remained, either because they disbelieved, were wasting precious time packing their valuables, or simply hadn't yet heard that anything was amiss. Up until that point, Dorn had thought of Ylraphon as a hardscrabble outpost populated by rugged men—loggers, trappers, and outlaws—but it gave him a pang to see how many frightened, bewildered women and children were scurrying through the frigid dark.

Finally, after he'd talked himself hoarse, he wound up leading a band of what an optimist might call men-at-arms with Will at his side to serve as his lieutenant. Raryn and Pavel were commanding another squad to the west, closer to the harbor. Dorn had considered assigning each member of his band to direct a different troupe of militiamen. The hunters were, after all, the only people there who knew anything much about dragons, but he was loath to order any of his friends into peril without even one trusted, seasoned comrade to watch his back. They didn't owe Ylraphon that much valor.

Come to think of it, having slaughtered the ooze drake as per their contract, they didn't owe the place anything. They could have hidden safe in the Flooded Forest while the dragon flight had its bloody way with the town. No one, not even Will, had so much as suggested the possibility.

Warsling dangling in his hand the halfling studied the sky above the swamp, looking for the bat-winged shapes that, as they beat their way south, might momentarily cut across Selûne's silvery crescent or block the light of one or another star.

"I don't see anything yet," Will said.

"Nor do I," said Ailon Finch. The balding, heavyset cloth merchant's voice sounded a little strangled. He'd squeezed himself into a cuirass a couple sizes too small, a family heirloom, perhaps, and his neck and arms fairly bulged out the openings. "I think this is all foolishness. We're going to catch our deaths standing in the cold waiting for dragons that never appear."

"They'll appear," said Will. "We explained, that's why the ooze drake was acting strangely. It was slipping into frenzy. It's also why the other wyrms called out."

"They're not roaring anymore."

"Because they don't need to. They've already found one another."

Just then Dorn saw a shadow blotting out a section of the sparkling motes trailing the moon, the bright haze people called her Tears.

He pointed and said, "Get ready."

It was dark, and the onrushing wyrms were still some distance away. Human eyes could barely make them out. Still, the sight panicked some of Dorn's command. Screaming, they broke from the blind they'd built at his direction, a makeshift fortress of stacked crates, timbers, barrels, and empty carts.

Their terrified flight caught the notice of a wyrm, which swooped after them. As Dorn might have guessed, it was a black dragon, another marsh-dweller like the ooze drake. Even in the dark, he could tell the species from the bony, almost skull-like appearance of the head, and the spikes jutting from the lower jaw.

The black spat a stream of liquid. The targets shrieked as the acid seared the flesh from their bones. Some of the men clustered behind Dorn moaned and sobbed in horror.

"Shoot it!" the half-golem yelled.

The wyrm was still moving, still on the wing, but had dived low and close enough that Dorn hoped his remaining troops had some slight chance of hurting it. Some of them obeyed his order. Others stood frozen.

The volley of crossbow quarrels, arrows, and sling stones hurtled upward. Dorn loosed a shaft he'd carried in his quiver for five years, just as Pavel had saved the scroll that called flame from the sky.

The black wyrm lurched as the missiles struck it. Dorn prayed it would plummet. He was sure he'd hit it, and if so, that one injury might be enough to kill it all by itself, for that was what the arrow had been enchanted to accomplish. But no such luck. The reptile was evidently too hearty to succumb. The great wings kept beating as it wheeled and lit on a rooftop. Something in the way the creature crouched and wove its leprous-looking head warned Dorn that it was casting a spell.

He loosed another arrow, and Will slung another stone. Those among their frightened troops who'd managed to ready a second missile followed suit. Dorn's instincts warned him the stinging barrage hadn't been enough to shake the black's concentration. It was going to complete the conjuration.

"Get down!" Dorn shouted.

He and the others crouched behind their improvised ramparts. Will noticed one idiot still standing paralyzed with fear. The halfling grabbed him by the belt and pulled him down.

Alas, it didn't help. The black had opted for magic that barricades didn't hinder, at least if the spellcaster had the high ground and the fortifications were open at the top. Dorn's vision blurred, and he felt faint. But only for a second, and the effect lost its grip on him.

Others were less fortunate.

"I'm blind!" wailed Ailon Finch.

Dorn peered over the top of the barricade just in time to see the dragon launch itself into the air. Having blinded its foes, or many of them, at any rate, it likely meant to plunge into their midst and slaughter them with tooth and claw. It wouldn't waste any more sorcery, or another blast of corrosive breath, on men it had already incapacitated.

"If you can't see," Dorn bellowed, "run!"

The gods only knew how sightless men were supposed to manage that, but there was nothing more he could do for them. He barely had time to snatch up the new hand-and-a-half sword he'd commandeered from the watch's little armory. It was a lackluster weapon compared to the enchanted blade he'd lost to the ooze drake, but there was nothing to be done about that either.

The black wyrm crashed down in the midst of its adversaries' defenses, its pounding wings and lashing tail scattering the component parts in an instant. Men screamed, crushed and impaled beneath its talons. Up close, like the ooze drake, the black gave off a vapor that burned the eyes and nose, and Dorn had no potion to shield him from the worst of the discomfort. Bearing it as best he could, he hacked at the dragon's ribs then, when it spun toward him, came on guard in his usual manner, iron limbs forward.

The black struck. He leaped backward, just out of range, and clawed furrows across its snout. It hissed and raked at him with its right forefoot. Horribly, it had the still-living Ailon Finch jammed on the talons of the left one. The wretch shrieked every time the reptile took a scuttling step.

Dorn didn't dodge quickly enough. The strike shredded his brigandine but failed to breach or even scratch the iron underneath. It slammed the wind out of him, though, and flung him reeling backward. The dragon's jaws surged forward, reaching to snap his head from his shoulders. The fangs might not penetrate the metal armoring the left side of his neck, but they'd have no difficulty cutting everything else.

He struggled to recover his balance, got his feet planted, and swung the sword with all his strength if little skill. The blade sheared deep into the wyrm's lower jaw. The pain made it recoil, and Will was underneath it, thrusting his own newly acquired short sword repeatedly into its chest. It screamed and went into convulsions, thrashing and rolling, shaking the earth, crushing crippled and dying men.

It nearly flattened Will, too, before he scrambled clear.

"We won!" the halfling gasped

Dorn supposed they had. Yet the judgment seemed a mockery, an obscenity, for the dead lay everywhere. There was, however, neither time to mourn them nor berate himself for leading them to their doom. He glared at the survivors who were still fit to fight.

"Form a column," he said. "This wyrm's finished. Now we have to find the next."

They stared back at him as if he was insane.

"Surely," one of them quavered, "we've done enough."

"While we were killing this drake, the rest of them entered the town. Some of your women, children, and old folk are still there, or so close it makes no difference. We have to buy them more time to get clear."

A man with a pox-scarred face shook his head and grumbled, "Not me, metal man. I'm done."

He turned and ran toward the edge of the swamp. Two others followed, leaving half a dozen. Dorn supposed he ought to be grateful that any of them were still brave—or foolish—enough to remain.

Will gave them a grin and said, "Thanks be to Brandobaris! Now that we're rid of the weak and gutless, the rest of us can really have some fun."

With the halfling ranging ahead, the company skulked through streets reverberating to a cacophony of roaring, screaming, and crashing. Dorn felt alert—he was so tense it could scarcely be otherwise—but under the frazzled tautness lay grinding fatigue. How many more battles would he have to fight? How many more wyrms were there? He'd made out four separate dragon's voices screeching across the Flooded Forest, but there could be even more. A lot more.

He told himself to forget such questions, to concentrate on meeting the requirements of one moment at a time. He'd fight the cursed drakes as he came to them, and if he died doing it, well, what did it matter? It was how he'd always expected to perish.

The sounds of destruction and terror grew louder. Will peeked around the next corner then raised his hand signaling a halt. He crept back to join his human comrades, who clustered around to hear what the halfling had to say.

"Another black," he whispered, "bigger and older than the last." Which meant even more powerful. "It's hunkered down outside a temple of Tyr. From the sound of it, some fools tried to hole up inside instead of running away like we told them."

"Has the wyrm broken through the wall?" asked Dorn.

"No. Maybe the priest said a prayer to hold it back for a moment."

Dorn turned to his militiamen and said, "We're going to sneak up on the thing and do our level best to be quiet. It doesn't matter that it can't see us around the corner or that the folk inside the shrine are making a racket. The drake could still hear us if we're not careful. When we get up there, we'll spread out so it can't target us all at once, then start shooting."

"Our arrows didn't kill the last one," a man armed with a crossbow and a boar spear said.

"They softened it up," Dorn replied, "and that's usually what it takes. It's hard to slay a wyrm the way you'd kill a man with one solid stroke to a vital spot. You have to chip away at them."

"But you can kill them," said Will, brushing one of his love-locks away from his eye. "As you lads ought to know, since you've done it once already. So, shall we go bag another?"

The militiamen's eyes were wide with fear, but the cowards had either perished or fled already, and those who remained muttered their assent. The hunters led them creeping forward.

When Dorn peered around the corner, he winced. The black was even bigger than he'd expected, so huge it filled the street like a stopper in a drain. He tried to find a shred of comfort in the thought that its size made it virtually impossible for it to take flight swiftly from its present position. The surrounding walls would prevent it from spreading its wings.

The skull-faced wyrm lifted its foreleg and batted at the face of the temple, an unassuming structure built of logs chinked with mud, with the god of justice's scales-and-war-hammer emblem painted on the door. The wall shattered.

"Go!" said Dorn.

He and his comrades scrambled forth, formed a ragged line, and as fast as they were able, started shooting at the behemoth.

The skull dragon rounded on them, and the darkness deepened around it, cloaking it in murk to spoil their aim. Fortunately, Will was ready for that particular ploy. He whirled his sling and hurled a stone Pavel had enchanted for him, a pellet shining as bright as a tiny sun.

The missile landed at the reptile's feet, where its radiance countered the unnatural gloom.

The black glared, however, and a second obscuring haze rose between it and its attackers. For a second, Dorn imagined it was simply more conjured darkness. Then he heard the buzz and felt the first stab of pain, as a swarm of stinging flies enveloped his little band.

Once engulfed, Dorn could scarcely think for the relentless harassment and could see no farther than his arm could reach. As he stumbled forward to escape the cloud, he was certain the dragon was poised to deliver a follow-up attack to whoever emerged.

Sure enough, the instant he, Will, and a couple of others blundered into the clear, the black hissed and snarled an incantation. On the final word, the surface of the dirt street convulsed, crumbling away beneath Dorn's feet and shooting up before him, plunging him and his comrades into a steep-walled trench. Long neck arcing, the dragon peered over the top of it. The half-golem could tell from the black's attitude that it was about to spit acid, and floundering in the loose earth at the bottom of the hole, its targets would find it all but impossible to dodge.

Somewhere up above, a soprano voice sang. The sound was clear and sweet, utterly unlike the skull drake's rumbling, sibilant conjuration. Yet Dorn sensed that it too was spellcasting, and when the black spread its jaws wide, nothing jetted out. It simply made a retching sound, as if the corrosive spew had caught in its gullet.

Its head spun around, clearly seeking the impudent soul who'd robbed it of one of its greatest weapons. The other sang a lilting arpeggio, and a barrage of snowballs streaked up and battered the black dragon. It seemed too puny an attack to affect such a horror, but the wyrm roared, stung or perhaps simply even angrier than before.

Dorn and Will sent an arrow and a stone hurtling up out of the pit. They each hit the dragon, but probably fortunately, failed to draw its attention back to themselves. It wrenched itself around, its tail sweeping across the top of the ditch and spilling loose dirt over their heads. Then they couldn't see it anymore.

"Up!" said Dorn, and he and his comrades started climbing the side of the pit.

Will, his burglar's skills standing him in good stead, reached the top in advance of the others. Dorn crawled out second. His iron claws had proved useful for scooping handholds.

He scrambled to his feet and peered down the street. Forked tongue flicking in and out, the dragon was casting about, twisting this way and that, seemingly still seeking the spellcaster who'd attacked it. By some chance, Dorn saw her instantly. It was Kara, crouching low inside the window of a post-and-beam house.

Uselessly, Dorn suspected. If he'd spotted her, the wyrm likely had, too. It was simply making a show of searching while it eased into striking range, at which point it would try to pounce and take her by surprise. He opened his mouth to shout a warning but was too late. The black dragon pivoted and hurled itself against the facade of the house. The impact smashed the wall and brought a goodly portion of the roof tumbling down. Kara vanished, buried in clattering rubble. The reptile scrabbled at the wreckage.

Dorn readied his sword and dashed forward, bellowing to draw the dragon away. Will charged, too, half-pausing every few strides to sling another rock.

The wyrm wheeled and sprang to meet them. No one could simply stand and receive that charge. The creature's momentum would bull him over. But as Dorn had already noted, the black was so huge, it virtually filled the street. He scarcely had anyplace to dodge to. He flattened himself against a wall then flailed at the dragon, first a backhand blow with the knuckle spikes, then a cut from the bastard sword. Meanwhile, Will dived and rolled past its stamping forefeet and under it belly, reared up, and thrust his blade in.

The dragon spun around toward Dorn. It didn't seem fair that something so gigantic could turn so fast in such close quarters, but almost as nimble and flexible as a serpent, it managed. Its jaws snapped at him, and he met them with iron and steel.

He managed to cut it three times, while arrows and crossbow bolts slammed into its scales. A couple even penetrated instead of glancing off. The militiamen were still fighting, albeit from a distance. He didn't blame them for that. Given a choice, he wouldn't have closed with the leviathan, either.

It bit at him, and he sidestepped, then sensed the attack was a feint. He tried to avoid the true attack, but it was hopeless. He'd already dodged right into it. The wyrm reached around the metal part of him to slash at the vulnerable flesh behind. Its talons jerked him to his knees before ripping free. It didn't hurt, not yet, but he knew the drake had cut him deep. .

Possibly so deep that he had only a few heartbeats left before he lost the ability to fight. So he'd better make them count. No longer bothering to shield himself, gripping his blade with both hands, he threw himself forward in an all-out attack. Maybe the dragon didn't expect such savagery from someone it had just mauled, for it failed to snatch its head back quickly enough, and the hand-and-a-half sword bit deep into its neck.

The wyrm's eyes opened very wide. Then its legs slowly gave way, laying it down with a sort of ponderous softness. His strength slipping away, Dorn collapsed alongside it.

Will scurried up to him. Gritting his jaw with pain, the halfling cradled what was usually his sword arm against his chest but still carried his blade in his off hand. The weapon was bloody from point to guard.

Bruised and filthy yet still lovely, Kara limped along behind the small hunter. A poniard made of crimson flame burned in her hand. Evidently she'd dragged herself clear of the half-demolished house and resumed attacking the dragon with her magic.

Will crouched over Dorn, inspected his wounds, then awkwardly uncorked and held a flask of healing elixir to his lips. The half-golem gulped the bitter, lukewarm liquid down. He didn't feel the surge of renewed vitality he sometimes did, but presumed the stuff was doing him some good.

"You're cut bad," Will said, "but Pavel will fix you up. We just have to reach him."

Dorn heaved himself to his feet. The world spun for a second, but he found his balance.

"We've still got dragons to kill," the half-golem said.

"Don't be a jackass," said Will. "We're in no shape for another fight, and we barely have any men left. When the bugs swarmed on us, half of them ran off in the wrong direction."

"Listen to him," Kara said. "You saved some of the towns-folk at least. Now it's time to save yourselves."

"All right," Dorn said as he turned to the militiamen. "We're done fighting. Drag yonder imbeciles out of Tyr's house and chivvy them out of town. Hide in the Flooded Forest if you think it wise. It's probably as safe as anyplace, now that the wyrms have passed through."

"Right," an archer said, "and thanks."

Dorn turned to Kara and said, "Stick with us if you want."

The hunters had agreed that once they'd done what they could to help the folk of Ylraphon, they'd rendezvous at the harbor, where Will had appropriated and hidden a skiff to use in their own escape. Alternately creeping and scurrying, he, the bard, and Dorn made it close enough to catch a whiff of saltwater. For folk who'd spent their last while breathing air tinged with acidic dragon breath, the smell was as sweet as nectar, sweet as the hope of actually making it out of the settlement alive. Dorn filled his lungs, and another drake crawled into the street just a few yards behind them.

It was the biggest yet, larger than any building in town, an immense, lumpish, wingless thing with webbed claws and a mottled hide. Its head snapped around toward Dorn and his companions, the pale yellow eyes shone, and the three allies froze. The landwyrm, as such reptiles were called, crawled in their direction.

Dorn still understood what was happening, and that he, Will, and Kara were all going to die if he didn't do something about it. But he couldn't, as if the dragon's gaze had severed some essential link between his mind and his limbs.

Then Kara sang three vibrant words, and the paralysis was gone. His was, anyway. When he looked down, Will still stood slack-jawed and trembling. In desperation, he grabbed the halfling's injured arm and gave it a vicious jerk.

Will yelped. "Ow! Demons take you, you oaf!"

Dorn spun back toward the swamp-dwelling landwyrm. It was close, so close it seemed to fill the world.

"I have a few songs left," Kara said. "I'll hold it here while—"

"Don't be stupid," Dorn snarled.

He grabbed her and manhandled her into an alley. Will scurried after them.

They sprinted down the narrow passage, and the dragon pursued, its tread jolting the earth and making them stumble. It advanced with a constant crashing sound, for it was far too huge to negotiate the path, and one could only make headway by plowing through the shacks on either side. That was precisely why Dorn had opted to flee in that direction, but when he glanced over his shoulder, it didn't look as if the tactic had done any good. Obliterating walls as easily as a man could swipe away a cobweb, the landwyrm was still gaining on its wounded, exhausted prey.

Then, however, it roared. He looked back. The dragon had caught fast between a pair of houses evidently sturdier than the ones it had already destroyed. It threw itself forward, and the buildings shattered, but in so doing strewed heaps of tangled, broken planks around its feet. It took another stride, then slipped and floundered in the litter.

The mishap slowed it down enough for Dorn and his comrades to reach the far end of the alley then bolt down a winding side street. After a time, it became clear the reptile was no longer pursuing them.

"Onward," panted Dorn.

By the time they reached the rickety little dock, Pavel and Raryn were already in the long, narrow skiff, ready to cast off. It must have surprised them to see Kara, but neither wasted time saying so.

"Hurry," said the dwarf. "There's a wyrm just to the south of us. It could turn this way any time."

Dorn, Kara, and Will scrambled aboard, and Raryn shoved off.

"Everybody grab an oar," the dwarf said.

"My arm's broken," said Will.

"The little shirker always has an excuse," Pavel said. He crouched beside Dorn, inspected his wounds, and frowned in dismay. "I only have one spell left. It'll just have to hold you until I can pray for more."

He murmured the sacred words, and his hand glowed as if the bones were made of fire. The healing touch didn't ease Dorn's pain or flush away his fatigue, but as with the potion, he assumed it had had some effect. With luck, he wouldn't go into shock or bleed out. He sat upright on the bench and grabbed a sweep.

"You should rest," Pavel said.

Dorn shook his head. "We have to get clear."

They rowed as quietly as they could, out onto the rippling black waters of the Dragon Reach, and Ylraphon, or what remained of it, gradually fell away behind them. First the shanties and wattle huts faded into the murk, and the roars, hisses, crashes, and shrieks dimmed away to nothing.

Raryn lifted his sweep out of the water and said, "We have a little wind. I'm going to raise the sail."

Pavel commenced a prayer, giving thanks for their escape. Dorn reluctantly turned to Kara.

"So," he said, "you need us to take you to Lyrabar."

FOUR

Midwinter, the Year of Rogue Dragons

For worshipers of Lathander, god of the dawn, Midwinter was an important feast, a declaration of faith that in time, warmth and green leaves would return to the frozen north. Accordingly, on that day, Pavel always performed his sunrise rituals with considerable panache. With Kara helping out on the hymns, they were especially evocative. Many of the hard-bitten sailors who'd gathered for the observance watched raptly or even blinked back tears.

For his part, Dorn felt morose and left out. The Morninglord's message of optimism and fresh beginnings had never seemed relevant to his own bitter trudge from womb to grave. Yet he stood with the rest of the assembly out of respect for his friend, and to give the god his due for granting Pavel the powers he exercised on the band's behalf.

The ceremony concluded with impeccable timing, the scarlet edge of the sun appearing over the horizon just as Kara reached the climactic notes of the final anthem. Taking it for a good omen, the worshipers cheered. The first mate permitted the crew a final moment of reverence, then started barking orders. The hands scattered to take up their duties, and Dorn wondered how best to pass another cold, tedious day at sea.

Neither he nor any of his comrades was mariner enough to relish the prospect of sailing a small boat all the way down the Dragon Reach and east across the Sea of Fallen Stars, especially in winter. Fortunately, it hadn't come to that. Two days after their flight from Ylraphon, a merchant galley overtook them, whereupon they hailed it and negotiated passage.

As usual, the others seemed to enjoy shipboard life. Pavel divided his time between ministering to the crew's spiritual needs and striving to fleece them at cards. Raryn fished over the side with bow and harpoon, and Will, rather to the sailors' annoyance, displayed a penchant for climbing to the top of the mast, where he'd perch for hours, taking in the view. But Dorn, who rarely felt much inclination to trivial amusements in any case, had never found any comparable pastimes to divert himself. Maybe, he thought, he should just try to find a quiet spot on deck and see how much of the morning he could sleep away. Then Kara resumed singing, and he lingered to listen.

It wasn't a sacred song, but the rollicking tale of a good-wife, the clever mouse who filched food from her pantry, and her fanatical efforts to catch the thief—increasingly mad, elaborate schemes that always ended badly. Kara milked every drop of humor from the story, and Dorn realized he was grinning. It made him feel strange, self-conscious, and he scowled the expression away.

Next the bard sang about flying and beholding all the rivers, mountains, forests, and cities of Faerûn spread out beneath her. It was a children's song, devised to teach them their geography, but no less charming for its pedantic intent. Kara's sweet, throbbing voice truly conveyed the exultation of soaring like an eagle on the wind.

She'd continued singing on the fo'c'sle, where Pavel had performed his observance. Dorn was loitering just below the elevated deck by the first of the rowers' benches, vacant since a favorable wind was blowing. He didn't think she knew he was there, but when she finished, she surprised him by peering down and giving him a smile.

"Sorry," he said, turning to go aft.

She laughed and said, "You don't have to slink away. Do you think you were eavesdropping on something you weren't meant to hear? Everyone on board could hear, or at least I hope so. Otherwise my voice has grown puny."

"Still. . . ." he said, and started to limp away, the timbers groaning beneath his iron foot.

"It saddens me that you dislike me."

Dorn thought it would be better simply to ignore her, but for some reason, he turned back around and said, "You're mistaken."

Kara descended the steep little companionway.

"You didn't want to escort me to Lyrabar when I first asked," she said, "and you'd still rather not. It's just that after I helped you, you felt an obligation. Even though you saved me first, when the ratmen wanted to kill me."

"My refusal wasn't based on dislike. It was just that you smelled like trouble, because you kept things back . . . things you still haven't told us. Raryn and Pavel had the same worries."

"But they also liked the shimmer of my jewels. Ultimately, they looked to you to decide, and you said no. Was it because you dislike all women?"

"Of course not."

"I suspect," Kara murmured, "you avoid women because you fear they find you ugly, and that pains you."

She was exactly right, and pretty ones bothered him the worst. Saying so, however, would only encourage her to keep on chattering, and that was the last thing he wanted. Though he still couldn't quite muster the rudeness to tramp away.

"I've been ugly for a long time," he said. "I'm used to it."

"How did it happen?"

None of your business, was what he thought he should have said.

"My parents were the indentured servants of a wizard in Hillsfar," Dorn replied instead. "When I was nine, he sent them on an errand to Yulash. They took me along. Bad luck for all of us. We wandered right into the path of a dragon flight, reds out of the mountains to the west. One of them spotted our wagon and tore us apart. It ate my mother and father and my severed arm and leg, too, but then it flew away. I guess it wasn't quite hungry enough to finish me.

"Well, I would have bled out soon enough, except that the mage knew a spell for jumping from place to place in an instant. I guess he also had a way of keeping track of us, maybe to make sure we wouldn't run away. At any rate, he knew when the drake attacked, though he had better sense than to come immediately and encounter the creature himself. He waited until it cleared off. But then he showed up to salvage as much of his property as possible."

"Property," Kara repeated. "Meaning you?"

"Partly. My parents still owed him many years of service. By the laws of Hillsfar, if they couldn't pay the debt, it became their child's responsibility. The wizard just had to figure out a way to turn a one-armed, one-legged cripple into something useful."

"So he made you a pair of enchanted iron limbs."

"Several pairs before he was done. I was still a child, remember. Whenever I outgrew a set, he had to slice it off and graft on a new one."

And weeping Ilmater, it had hurt.

"Then he invested a fortune in conjuring time and spell components to make you as you are," said Kara. The bard's tone was matter-of-fact. Perhaps she sensed he wouldn't welcome a show of pity. "Either he loved you, or he saw a way of making a great deal of gold from you. From the way you speak of him, I gather it was the latter."

"In Hillsfar, they're mad for the arena. People wager huge sums on the fights. As the mage once told me, he'd already picked me out as a likely gladiator, because I used to get in a lot of fights with other boys, and would take any stupid dare they tossed my way. He figured that with iron claws, I'd fare even better, so he fitted me out and found me a trainer. The teacher decided I'd do best as a bestiarius, a killer of wild animals and abominations, so he steered me in that direction. Before long, he declared me ready for my first match. When the spectators saw I was still a stripling, they gave long odds against me. The mage cleaned up."

She shook her head and whispered, "To force a child to battle for his life . . ."

"Well, I liked the fighting," he said with a crooked smile. "What I didn't like was doing it on command to enrich somebody else. Unfortunately, it took years before I could make a change. It's not easy to murder a wizard if he's cautious. But eventually I found a way, then fled the city."

"I wouldn't call it murder."

Dorn shrugged and said, "You can probably guess the rest of the tale. Once I was free, I had to earn a living, and slaughtering beasts was the only thing I knew. So I set up shop as a hunter for hire. It wasn't long before I figured out that being able to kill a creature did no good if I couldn't find it, so I joined forces with a tracker. After one or the other of us got mauled a few times, we decided we needed a healer. A couple years later, we met Will and realized he'd make a useful addition, too. And here the four of us are."

"Plying a trade that lets you slay dragons."

"I don't deny hating them. In my place, wouldn't you? I hunt for coin, I'll bring down any brute a client wants dead, but it does please me when the quarry's a drake."

"Any drake?" she asked.

Behind her, the sky was brightening. The sun floated round and complete above the hills on the eastern shore.

"You mean, have I ever gone after one of the metal-colored variety? The ones people claim are kindly and wise? No, but only because nobody ever hired me to. A wyrm's a wyrm to me."

"You know, hate can be as cruel a master as the one you left behind in Hillsfar."

He scowled and said, "If I want moral instruction, I have a priest who can dish it up to order. Good morning to you, maid."

"Please," she said, "don't walk away. I'm sorry. I didn't mean to preach. I simply want to be your friend."

"Why? Because you feel sorry for me? Don't bother."

"Because I like you."

"Don't bother about that, either," he said.

"You're right about me," she said. "I do have secrets I mustn't share. But I'll tell you this: I'm terrified, and I see something in you . . . I'd just like your companionship is all."

Spurn her, he told himself. Otherwise, you might grow fond of her and say so. Then you'll have to endure her replying that yes, she likes you, too, but not in the way a maid fancies a man.

Will shouted from the top of the mast, "Those huts on the beach! Can anybody else make them out?"

"Barely," said Dorn, squinting. "What about them?"

"I'd like Raryn to climb up here and take a look at them. Captain, maybe you could lend him your spyglass."

The master of the vessel, a squat man with sigils of good fortune and fair weather tattooed above his eyes, frowned, for the brass instrument was valuable. Still, something in Will's tone must have persuaded him that important matters were afoot, because he handed it over.

"Be careful with it," he said.

"I promise."

The dwarf stowed the telescope in his belt pouch, then clambered upward.

He studied the specks on the shore for half a minute, then said, "Will's right."

"Right about what?" demanded Dorn.

"The village is dead, torn apart. Dragons killed it. At least three of them. I see the tracks."

Dorn tried to wrap his mind around the idea. It was possible the wyrms of the Flooded Forest had laid waste to the tiny hamlet, without the hunters or mariners noticing the creatures making their way south, but it seemed unlikely.

The alternative, however, would appear to be two dragon flights occurring simultaneously, and if that was the case, might there be even more? The flights were rare events, but history told of calamities rarer still, seasons of madness when all the wyrms in Faerûn ran amok at once. Such Rages, as they were called, could result in the slaughter of countless thousands, annihilate entire kingdoms, and scar the world for generations to come.

The prospect was horrifying, yet likewise filled Dorn with a guilty sort of eagerness. Naturally he didn't want folk to die, but the thought of all the dragons in the world rushing recklessly forth into reach of his arrows and sword. . . .

He gave his head a shake and told himself to rein in his imagination. Even if the Rages were something more than a myth, it didn't mean one was happening without so much as a comet or some other portent to herald it. Surely there was another explanation.

He glanced at Kara. As she stared at the ravaged village, tears slid from her lavender eyes. She'd seemed so bold and cool-headed during the fracas in Ylraphon that the open display of sorrow rather surprised him. But evidently she had a tender nature, and no compunction about indulging it when she wasn't fighting for her life.

Dorn resented her weeping, because somehow it meant he couldn't rebuff her after all. It condemned him to be her friend. He awkwardly put his human hand on her shoulder.

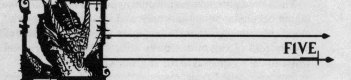

FIVE

8 Alturiak, the Year of Rogue Dragons

Nervous as on the night he'd stolen the emerald, Gorstag skulked through the chilly, torchlit catacombs. He had been given free run of the entire complex ever since he'd accompanied Speaker into Queen Sambryl's castle. But the spellcasters were performing a necromantic ritual, their chanting echoing through the tunnels, and the Wearer of Purple expected everyone who wasn't busy elsewhere to attend. It wouldn't do for Gorstag to be caught skipping. Someone might suspect— correctly—that he was up to no good.

He'd learned a great deal during the past couple of tendays, from both Speaker himself and the cabal's lesser officers, who assumed that if the great man had seen fit to trust him, he must be all right. Yet he still feared he didn't know enough. He had some notion of what was happening, but not how to stop it, if indeed that was possible. He didn't even have any proof of what he'd discovered, and wondered if his employer would believe such a wild tale without it.

So he lingered to find some. The cult kept him so busy aiding in various jewel thefts that it would have been difficult to disappear in any case. But how he wanted to! From the first, he'd known the brothers were dangerous men, but at least it had been easy to dismiss their beliefs as mad delusions. He'd come to fear that the nightmarish tomorrow of their ambitions might truly come to pass unless he himself prevented it. At times he felt as if the responsibility would crush his mind into a lunacy as profound as theirs.

Since Gorstag had discovered who the wizard actually was, the worst moments were those he spent in Speaker's company. He couldn't shake the feeling that the cult leader would have absolutely no trouble reading an underling's thoughts if it simply occurred to him to make the effort. In which case, he'd find it equally easy to destroy a spy a heartbeat later, or more likely, incapacitate him for interrogation and torture.

The day had started particularly bad, not because anything special had happened, but simply because Gorstag's nerves were fraying fast. He'd been certain he was on the verge of making a slip and giving himself away. Then he'd learned Speaker had set forth on another journey. The mage seemed to like Lyrabar but spent only a fraction of his time there. He had affairs to manage in cult enclaves across Faerûn.

Gorstag decided his chance had come. He'd search Speaker's quarters to see what he could find, and whether he turned up anything or not, flee the city to make his long-overdue report to his employer.

It seemed as good a plan as he was likely to hit upon, but when he reached Speaker's chamber, he hesitated. As far as he could tell, the spacious crypt with the tunnel-vaulted ceiling harbored no threats, simply the ornately carved cherry desk, chairs, bookshelves, and tapestries the brothers had fetched down into the tunnels to furnish it. But as everybody knew, spellcasters liked to set magical snares to catch intruders. Gorstag might summon a devil or set himself on fire simply by stepping across the threshold.

But maybe not. Speaker was busy, and regarding himself as the wisest and noblest of leaders, clearly assumed his followers shared his opinion. It seemed likely he simply counted on their awe and devotion to protect his privacy.

In any case, Gorstag wasn't making himself any safer or less scared by hovering at the entrance worrying about it. He took a deep breath, calming himself as Maestro Taegan had taught him, then he stepped through the basket arch.

Nothing happened. Breathing a sigh of relief, he turned and peered about. The shelves were full of tomes, loose documents, and rolled-up sheets of parchment, so many the smell of old paper threatened to make him sneeze. He was going to need luck to find what he needed in a reasonable amount of time. He just hoped he'd recognize it when he saw it.

Then he spotted a volume with the flame-and-claws sigil of the cult stamped in gold leaf on the spine standing in the middle of a shelf. The sickly greenish light of the ever-burning torch in the wall sconce made it difficult to distinguish color, but the rich purple of the leather binding was unmistakable.

The book was the *Tome of the Dragon*, the compendium of arcane secrets and apocalyptic prophecies that had guided the conspiracy since its inception. Steal that—

And Gorstag realized, he would accomplish relatively little. The Harpers and their allies had waged war against the cult for centuries. Surely somebody had seized a copy of the *Tome* already. Besides, the spy had learned that several months back, when Speaker first revealed his current plan, it had come as a surprise even to Lyrabar's Wearer of Purple. That plainly meant the book didn't cover the scheme.

Gorstag had to keep searching. He turned his attention to the desk. If any of the papers littering the writing surface or stuffed into the cubbyholes was of critical importance, he was too thick to realize it. But one drawer, the top one on the left, was locked.

As he drew his main gauche, he thought again of magical traps, and the conjured blade of darkness that had, with a single stroke, erased the maid from existence. Refusing to let such reflections deter him, he worked the dagger into the crack between the drawer and the rest of the woodwork, then pried.

The action failed to bring any hellish spirits leaping forth, or to rot his flesh on the bone. The sturdy lock simply resisted him until he feared the parrying blade would snap or break loose from the hilt. Finally, though, the drawer lurched open.

He slid it all the way out. Inside was a battered brown leather folio. He turned back the cover and flipped through leaves covered in tiny script. Having looked on while Speaker scribbled a note or two, he recognized the wizard's handwriting.

That had to be it. He started to pick it up, then heard a tiny rustle of cloth at his back. Instinct prompted him to fling himself sideways out of Speaker's chair. As he slammed down on the cold stone floor, he saw the out-thrust rapier that had nearly pierced his back. Firvimdol was at the other end of it.

"Are you mad?" Gorstag said. "The Wearer of Purple sent me—"

"Liar!"

Firvimdol pounced after him and thrust. Gorstag rolled, and the point missed him to rasp against the floor.

"Traitor!"

Another stab.

"Unbeliever!"

Another.

Fortunately, the fat youth wasn't agile. Gorstag managed to dodge every attack and eventually heave himself to his feet. His back was to the wall, and his main gauche was still on the desk where he'd set it down, but at least he had his rapier. He jerked it from the scabbard, put it in line, and Firvimdol hastily backed away from the threat.

That was bad. If the merchant's son had kept on rushing forward, Gorstag could probably have spitted him. As it was, the spy thought he could still kill Firvimdol, but probably not before he called out for help.

"Calm down," Gorstag panted. "I swear to you, the Wearer of Purple sent me here."

"Do you think I'm an imbecile?" Firvimdol asked, his double-chinned face mottled and sweaty. "I guess you must, since I'm the one you picked to flatter and befriend, to persuade me to sponsor you in the brotherhood. But I'm not stupid! I saw how hard you worked to win the prophet's trust, and something about it troubled me."

"We all try to serve Speaker however we can," said Gorstag. "You know that. It just irked you that he took a liking to me when I was only a neophyte. It made you jealous, and that affected your judgment."

"Nonsense. I spotted you for a spy. I just couldn't denounce you right away, not without proof, not when I'd vouched for you myself. How would that have looked? So I bided my time. When you didn't show up for the ceremony tonight, I came searching to see if you were getting into mischief. And now I have you."

"Maybe you do," said the spy, "but have you really thought about what you're doing? Your father's rich. Everything the cult promises, you already have. It makes no sense for someone like you to conspire against the Crown."

"My family is rich, and deserves to be, for it's the merchants who bring prosperity to Impiltur. That's why we ought to be the masters. Yet the old chivalry, the paladins and cavaliers, make the laws and turn up their noses at us, as if we were no better than the rabble. The brotherhood will change that."

"Weeping Ilmater, man, you'd still have rulers set above you, even if the prophecies came true."

"At least we'll be first among human beings."

"Not really, because it's never going to happen. Every time the cult puts some grand scheme into motion, people like the knights step in and break it up."

"It's different this time. Don't you see that?"

"I see it's time for you to think about practicalities," Gorstag said, "like how you yourself can survive the next few minutes. You fluffed your chance to murder me, and now I've got a rapier in my hand and I'm the better duelist. You can scream for help, and probably it will come, but not in time to keep me from killing you. If you want to live, you'll have to creep quietly along with me while I make my escape. Once we reach the street, I'll let you go."

Firvimdol hesitated then said, "You . . . you wouldn't dare harm me."

"If you think that, you really are stupid. At this point, what do I have to lose? One thing's for sure, I can't afford to stand here arguing until somebody else happens by. So this is how it will be. I'm going to give you to the count of three to be sensible, and after that, I'll kill you. Who knows, maybe I can drive my point into your heart before you even get off a yell, or maybe that wretched chanting will cover the noise. One . . . two . . ."

"All right!" Firvimdol yelped. "I surrender!"

"Throw away your sword and poniard," Gorstag commanded.

The weapons clanked on the floor.

"Now go stand in that corner."

Once he had Firvimdol where he wanted him, Gorstag grabbed and sheathed his main gauche, then stooped to collect the folio. It was big and bulky, and the papers were loose inside it. It was going to make an awkward burden, but—

He realized Firvimdol was whispering.

Gorstag jerked his head up just in time to see the cultist spin his hand through a complex figure like a wizard casting a spell. Only then did he recall that Speaker had alluded to teaching Firvimdol magic. Gorstag threw himself forward, intent on killing the pudgy youth before he could finish the incantation.

Too late.

Like a wave rearing from the surface of the sea, a pale luminescence shot up and raced across the floor. It smashed into Gorstag like a giant's fist, bore him backward, and slammed him against a bookshelf before blinking out of existence. Jolted loose by the impact, volumes tumbled down around him. One banged him squarely on the head, and he fumbled his grip on the folio. It fell and bumped open, scattering the pages inside.

As Taegan had taught him, he refused to let the shock of being hit paralyze him. He charged once more.

Firvimdol jabbered words of power and stuck out his hand. A crackling tendril of white light leaped from his fingertips to Gorstag's blade. The power burned down the length of the weapon into the spy's hand. His whole body shuddered spastically.

Only for a moment, but that was all the time it took for Firvimdol to recover his own rapier. He lunged and thrust at his adversary's chest. Off balance, Gorstag nonetheless managed a parry but didn't trust himself to stand and fight. After taking two hurts in a matter of seconds, he needed a moment to gather his strength. He jumped backward, grabbed a chair, and threw it. It didn't hit Firvimdol, but the pudgy rake had to dodge, and that kept him from chasing right after his foe.

Gorstag struggled to control his breathing, came on guard, and did his best to quell the fear shrilling through his mind. He told himself that Firvimdol was no wizard, not really. He'd simply mastered a few rudimentary spells and was surely incapable of casting many more before he ran out of power. He was no swordsman, either. That ought to mean Gorstag was still more than a match for him.

The problem was that the spy's back ached fiercely, and something inside his torso throbbed every time he inhaled. His rapier trembled no matter how he struggled to hold it steady. Firvimdol's magic had genuinely hurt him, impairing his ability to fight.

Maybe the fat youth knew it, too. Maybe that was why he

was so confident he hadn't seized the opportunity to run or cry for help. Or maybe it was just that his blood was up.

Either way, Firvimdol stood his ground, hitching from side to side and back and forth, looking for an opening. Gorstag decided to give him one. When Firvimdol faked a step to the right, then immediately hopped left, Gorstag pretended the clumsy deception had fooled him. He pivoted in the direction the cultist wanted, giving Firvimdol his flank.

Firvimdol charged. Gorstag whirled, spinning his sword to sweep his foe's weapon out of line and riposte, until another spasm, perhaps a residual effect of Firvimdol's miniature lightning bolt, shook him uncontrollably. It made him miss the parry.

Firvimdol's point drove into Gorstag's chest. Grinning, oblivious to the possibility that his foe might still pose a threat, the cultist yanked his rapier free and cocked it back for another thrust. That was when Gorstag's own desperate attack rammed into Firvimdol's torso.

Firvimdol gaped stupidly, then collapsed. Because Gorstag was still holding the blade buried in Firvimdol's flesh, the cultist's weight dragged the spy to his knees.

The abrupt drop made the crypt spin and darken, and Gorstag realized he was on the verge of passing out. He fought to cling to consciousness, and finally the feeling of faintness abated. Though that had the unfortunate consequence of intensifying the pain.

Gorstag couldn't permit it to cripple him. He had to flee. Trying not to bleed on them, he gathered the leaves from the folio. It took time. The wretched papers had flown everywhere.

He tried to pull his rapier out of Firvimdol's corpse, but it stuck fast. He planted his foot on the body, gripped the hilt with both hands, and it slid free with a nasty little sucking sound. Alas, the process proved so taxing as to convince him he no longer had the strength to wield a sword. He couldn't bear to abandon it, however, and despite the handicap of shaking hands, managed to slip it back into its scabbard.

Was there any way to hide what he'd done? Gorstag couldn't keep the cult from discovering Firvimdol's body. He was too weak to move it. But maybe he could prevent their realizing he'd stolen the folio, at least for a while. He pushed the desk drawer shut, then grabbed the purple-bound copy of the *Tome of the Dragon*, leaving an obvious gap on the shelf. With luck, the brothers would assume he'd come to steal the sacred text and not investigate any further.

Time to flee. But where? His employer had charged him to tell no one of his mission. The cult had agents everywhere, perhaps even among the officers of the queen, and in any case, the Harpers kept their affairs a secret. Yet Gorstag had to seek help somewhere. Otherwise, he'd never make it out of town alive.

He smiled, for the answer was obvious. Maestro Taegan would succor him, if his numb legs could carry him that far.

They bore him to the stairs leading up to the tannery, anyway. Then the chanting ended in a ragged fashion, as over the course of a couple seconds the cultists fell silent. Someone had apparently burst in and interrupted them. Probably someone who'd discovered Firvimdol's corpse.

In Lyrabar, a salle was more than a school for instruction in the science of fencing. It was a social club, where the duelists often lingered long after the practice was through, and the maestro presided over their revels as he had their training. For he had to prove himself the epitome of everything the city's young hellions aspired to be, knowledgeable not merely about swordplay but also wine, gambling, clothes, horses, hawking, and venery. Moreover, he had to render his judgments on such matters with eloquence and wit. Otherwise, no matter how well he taught combat, his academy would go out of fashion, and his pupils would desert him.

Accordingly, Taegan Nightwind often found himself the center of attention from morning until late into the night.

Finally, however, a moment arrived when one or another distraction—the whores, a drinking contest, or the snowball battle in the garden out back—had lured every one of the winged elf's admirers away. He seized the opportunity to slip off to his office on the top floor, where another sort of work awaited him.

Corkaury Mindle was there too, sitting in a circle of lamplight at a worktable sized for halflings. Stooped and wizened, Corkaury was small even by the standards of his own diminutive race, which never prevented him from projecting an air of firm authority over the provosts, maids, cooks, and bawds who made up the rest of the staff.

"You should have gone home hours ago," Taegan said. "Your family will be worried."

"I knew you wanted to review the accounts," Corkaury replied.

"I could have puzzled them out by myself."

Corkaury made a derisive spitting sound.

Taegan chuckled and said, "I could, and you know it very well. You probably fear that if you give me an hour alone with the ledgers, I'll realize you're embezzling."

"You've found me out."

Taegan pulled one of his specially made chairs up to the table. When necessary, he could manage a human seat with impeccable grace, but he much preferred furniture crafted to provide room for his black-feathered pinions.

"Well," he said, "let's have at it, and try to get you out of here by midnight."

As the crackling fire in the hearth burned lower and chill crept into the room, the avariel, as winged elves were called, and his assistant went over the entries line by line. Like every other aspect of city life, coin had been a mystery to Taegan when he'd first come to the human world. He'd made a point of learning all about it because that, too, was necessary if he was to make his way in the city. The alternative was to slink back to the dismal circumstances of his birth.

Eventually the discussion drifted down a familiar path.

"You realize," Corkaury said, "Cormyrean brandy's doubled in price since the troubles there."

"Good. If the other maestros are too miserly to pour it, I look all the more munificent."

"I suppose munificence is also the excuse for this yacht you're having built."

"Of course. I have to toss coin around to attract wealthy patrons."

"But you yourself aren't wealthy. The salle brings in plenty of gold, but it flows right out again, to service your debts and pay for each new extravagance . . ."

"Answer me this: So long as the coin keeps coming, will I stay afloat?"

The elderly halfling scowled and said, "Probably, barring disaster."

"There you are then. You're fretting over mist and dewdrops."

"If you say so," said Corkaury. "Let's at least make sure we take in as much gold as possible. Some of the students are behind on their fees."

"They always are. The names, if you would be so kind."

"Odoth Amblecrown."

"He's just absentminded," said the maestro. "He'll ante up if I drop him a hint, provided it's not too subtle."

"Nalian Fisher."

"Bugger. His family's too prominent, and he's too much of a brat. If we squeeze him, he'll leave in a snit and take his sycophants—who do pay—with him. Let it go for now."

"Gorstag Helder."

"Still?" Taegan asked. "Chuck him out."

"I'll tell the porter not to admit him."

Taegan arched an eyebrow. He'd cultivated that particular mannerism, like many of his gestures, to make himself over into a perfect Impilturan rake.

"That's it?" he asked.

"What else is there?" Corkaury replied.

"On previous occasions, you had more to say."

"True. I pleaded poverty on Goodman Helder's behalf, whereupon you grudgingly granted him an extension. I don't feel like covering the same ground again. If he really can't afford to live like a swell, with fencing lessons, fancy clothes, and all the rest of it, that's his problem. Let him take up a trade like everybody else."

"Oh, to the Abyss with it," said Taegan, "give him another month. Maybe Tymora will blow on his dice."

The corners of Corkaury's mouth quirked upward.

"Why the smirk?" Taegan asked.

"I just wanted you to acknowledge that actually, we keep Helder on the rolls because *you're* fond of him. As you ought to be. He idolizes you."

"All the sheep idolize me. That's what enables me to shear them. Are we done?"

"I suppose."

"Then take a sedan chair home, and don't feel you have to scurry back at the crack of dawn. Stay in bed, and wake Olpara in the way a wench likes best."

"I'll thank you not to refer to my wife as a wench," said the halfling. "Anyway, at her age, she likes to wake to griddle-cakes smothered in butter and cherry syrup."

"Spare me the lurid details."

"Are you going to turn in?"

"No," Taegan answered simply. Avariels didn't sleep, and though they had their own sort of rest, a trance-like meditation, they only needed about four hours a night. "I have an itch to get out of this place of a while. I believe I'll find out what Selûne and the Sea of Night are doing."

With his wings protruding in the back, an avariel couldn't wear ordinary cloaks, but Taegan possessed a number of specially tailored tabards that went a long way toward staving off the chill. He opened an armoire, selected a deep blue velvet outer garment trimmed with scarlet satin, and pulled it on. Thus protected, he strode to the casement with its panes of pebbled, milky glass, threw it open, and sprang out into the night. His wings spread and hammered up and down, swiftly carrying him above the level of the gabled rooftops. After a time, they caught an updraft that hurled him higher still, until he could gaze down on the entirety of Lyrabar at once.

Glittering with enough lights to rival the starry sky above, Queen Sambryl's capital sprawled along the shore for nearly a mile. Supposedly it was the largest city for hundreds of miles. Certainly it was the greatest Taegan had ever seen, and the sight of it stretched out beneath him could inspire a variety of emotions, depending on his mood. Often he felt wonder, joy, and gratitude that he had come to dwell here. Other times, though he would never have admitted it to another, Lyrabar made him feel ashamed and unworthy of its grandeur.

Fortunately, the humans whose city it truly was rarely behaved as if he didn't belong. Elves of any sort were a rarity in Impiltur and the surrounding lands. Avariels were virtually unheard of, and because of their wings, slender frames, porcelain skin, fine-boned features, and large, luminous eyes, many folk in Lyrabar regarded them as marvelous and exotic. Taegan had recognized that fascination early on and turned it to his advantage. It had played a considerable part in making him one of the most popular masters-of-arms in town.

Tonight, the spectacle of the benighted port, with its host of warships and merchant vessels either moored at the piers or sitting at anchor in the harbor, lifted his spirits and made him want to play. He climbed and plummeted, swooped through the boulevards and alleys, testing his ability to level out of a dive or make a turn at the last possible instant. It was exhilarating, and if people saw, so much the better. The gossip would bring in new students.

Avariels weren't like dwarves or goblinkin, able to see in the utter absence of light. But their vision was sharper than that of men. Midway through another ascent, Taegan noticed the lanky man weaving and stumbling his way across a plaza at the intersection of five avenues. It was obvious he was hurt and just as clear that the shadowy figures tailing him intended to finish him off. He was probably leaving a trail of blood spatters for them to follow.

It was unfortunate, but none of Taegan's business. He resolved to fly elsewhere and leave the distasteful scene behind. Then the human lifted his face as if praying to Selûne to save him. It was Gorstag, his long, narrow countenance pale as the moon herself.

Curse you, Taegan thought. I already did you one favor tonight, isn't that enough?

He furled his wings and dropped like a stone. As a result, he landed hard, but not hard enough to hurt himself. Up close, Gorstag reeked of blood. He gave Taegan a dazed smile.

"I was coming to find you," the student said.

"Lucky me," the maestro grumbled. "Get down and stay there."

Taegan shoved Gorstag down into the dirty, much-trodden snow to make a smaller target. It was the only way. An adult human was too heavy to fly to safety.

The maestro pivoted, whipped his rapier from its scabbard, and reviewed the spells he currently carried ready for the casting in his memory. Most of Lyrabar knew him only as a duelist, for the simple use of weapons was the only art he imparted to his pupils. It was all he had to teach that non-elves seemed capable of learning. But during his youth, he'd also mastered bladesong, a technique for combining swordplay and magic to lethal effect, and he suspected he was going to need it very soon.

The question was, which spell to cast first in the final moments before Gorstag's hunters rushed into the plaza. Taegan decided to armor himself specifically against ranged attacks. He trusted his fencing to protect him from foes bold enough to advance within reach of his rapier, but even the greatest swordsman could fall prey to enemies who kept their distance and shot him full of arrows.

He rattled off the incantation, swept a scrap of turtle shell through the proper pass, and the first two of his foes darted into plain view. He smiled, because he'd guessed right. They carried crossbows. They faltered for an instant, surprised to see him waiting there, then lifted the weapons. They knew how to use them, too. Despite their excitement, they took a moment to aim. Then the crossbows clacked, and the quarrels leaped forth.

One shaft missed. The other struck Taegan in the chest, only to snap in two without penetrating. It had, however, chipped away at the magic. A few more such impacts and the protection would be gone. It was a good reason not to give his attackers a chance to ready the crossbows for a second volley.

Taegan charged them, his wings beating, augmenting the strength of his legs to close the distance in several prodigious bounds. His opponents tossed away the crossbows and reached for their blades. He killed the curly-bearded one on the right before his falchion cleared the scabbard. The other, a thin man in a high-crowned hat, rushed in stabbing with a dirk in either hand. The avariel saw that he wouldn't quite have time to yank the rapier free and swing it around to present the point. So he sidestepped, and as the knife-fighter blundered past, bashed him in the head with the heavy steel pommel. The human lurched off balance. Taegan thrust his sword into his back.

That was two foes down, but Taegan had glimpsed more. He turned to meet the next ones, and a nauseating stench assailed him as withered, gray-faced figures shuffled out of the dark. He cursed in surprise. He'd assumed Gorstag had simply run afoul of footpads or come out the loser in a brawl. Yet that wouldn't explain someone setting zombies on his track. It was astonishing that a spellcaster would even dare to create undead in Lyrabar, crawling with paladins and priests of the gods of light as it was.

Taegan had never fought zombies, but he had some notion of their weaknesses and capabilities, They were slow and clumsy, but strong, fearless, and difficult to slay. The best way to deal with them would be to keep maneuvering so that only one or at the most two could come at him at a time. And make his rapier a more potent weapon, to let the animating force out of the walking cadavers that much more quickly.

He circled, sidestepped, advanced, retreated, and dodged, thrust, counterattacked, parried, and riposted. Meanwhile, he recited a rhyme and swept his off hand through a pass, managing the swordplay and spellcasting simultaneously as only a bladesinger could. At the conclusion of the incantation, he tossed a pinch of powdered lime and coal dust onto his blade. Magic groaned through the air, and for an instant, the weapon flared as if white hot.

He made faster progress after that. Every hit plunged the rapier deep into a zombie's body, and a single such attack generally sufficed to dispatch it. He disposed of a woman's corpse with the nose and jaw all black and mushy, a broad-shouldered husk swinging a battle-axe, and a skinny old fellow's cadaver with bits of bare bone peeking through its flaking skin. Then another living man intent on creeping in on his flank.

Taegan grinned. Only a fool risked his life except for profit—which made him a fool at that particular moment—but even so, no one could deny the satisfaction of mastering an adversary or better still a pack of them. For a few seconds, the fight seemed an amusing game, then the situation altered once again.

A human might not have noticed, but a flying warrior learned to keep track of what was happening above and below him, not just in front and behind, even when he himself was battling on the ground. Thus, Taegan's ears caught the whisper of wings. Glancing upward, he saw a huge, dragonlike silhouette, the wings fifty feet from tip to tip, with a crooked stinger at the end of its long, skinny tail and a rider straddling its back. The beast was swooping at Gorstag, who held his rapier aloft in both trembling hands in a pathetic effort at self-defense.

A wyvern lacked the intelligence, sorcery, and breath weapon of a true dragon. Yet even so, the reptile was far more formidable than any of Taegan's other foes, and he was accordingly surprised it hadn't revealed itself before. But perhaps the rider was the sort of leader who'd rather send dozens of underlings to their destruction than face danger unnecessarily himself. In any case, since the bastard assumed his minions had the bladesinger tied up, he was racing to finish off the man he actually wanted to kill.

Taegan spun and wings beating, leaped into the air. A blade bit into his calf. He snarled against the shock, flew onward, and saw he couldn't intercept the wyvern in time, not by flying anyway. He rattled off words of power.

Transported instantly through the intervening distance, he was directly in the plummeting reptile's path. He drove his rapier into its scaly chest, then tried to dodge out of its way. He was an instant too slow, and the wyvern slammed into him.

The collision stunned him, and he dropped tumbling toward the snowy cobbles waiting to smash his bones. Somehow he shook off the daze and struggled to beat his wings. To his relief, they still worked. The impact must not have broken any critically important bones. As he leveled off, then climbed, he peered about to see how the wyvern was faring.

The unexpected injury had caused it to veer off short of rending Gorstag with its talons, but that was the only good news. Despite the flower of fresh gore blooming on its breast, it was still airborne, its master still perched atop its back. It wheeled toward Taegan, leathery wings snapping and rattling, gaining altitude all the while. The rider, clad in a dark robe, shoulder cape, and cowl, swept a staff through mystic passes. The shaft was made of jet-black wood, while the silver knob on top was shaped like a skull.

Essentially, it was the same situation Taegan had already faced with the crossbowmen. He had no intention of hanging back while the spellcaster hurled one curse after another. Rather, he meant to close with the immense two-legged reptile and send it and its rider plunging to earth as soon as possible. Wings pounding and rapier extended like a lance, he streaked toward it.

Even as he flew his fastest, bladesong enabled him to weave another defensive enchantment. For an instant, the words of power sent rainbows rippling through the air around him. The subtle illusion he'd called into being would make him look as if he was a foot or two away from his actual position. It ought to hinder the wyvern's efforts to rip him to shreds. Whether it would hamper the rider's magic depended on which particular spell the whoreson chose to cast.

A clawed, shadowy, and disembodied hand erupted from the silver skull and streaked at Taegan. He veered, dodging. The hand raked at empty air, then withered out of existence.

So far, so good, but he might not be as lucky next time. He had to get into sword range but realized that, his shield of illusion notwithstanding, it would be suicide to approach the wyvern at any but the proper attitude. So he zigzagged back and forth, making the reptile struggle to match him shift for shift. The dragonlike brutes could fly faster than avariels but were less agile in the air.

Even so, he'd nearly closed with it before he maneuvered it into the proper posture. He put on a final burst of speed and fetched up under its belly, where he grabbed a loose handful of scaly hide to anchor himself in place. While he clung there, it would have difficulty twisting its neck far enough around to snap at him or its tail to sting. The man perched on its back wouldn't be able to target him at all.

Still, his position could scarcely have been more perilous. The huge, three-taloned feet scrabbled at him. The great jaws with the slit-pupiled eyes glaring rage behind them bit repeatedly, and the crooked, venomous stinger thrust and thrust. The wyvern thrashed to shake him loose. Meanwhile he struggled to hang on, twist out of the way of each new attack, and drive the rapier home over and over again.

At last the reptile shuddered and rolled over. It was falling, and Taegan had to get clear or it would carry him to the ground along with it. He leaped away from it, wings pounding, and either by dint of a final murderous effort or simply because the wyvern was convulsing in its death throes, the stinger leaped directly at him. He twisted away from it. The bony point came close enough to tear a feather or two from his left pinion but failed to pierce flesh or pump poison into his veins.

After that, the reptile was too far away to threaten him. The rider shrieked, and for a moment, Taegan took a cold satisfaction in the doomed man's terror. Then he glanced down and saw the men and zombies closing in on Gorstag. Ilmater's wounds, was this fight never going to end? He dived.

Luckily, when the wyvern crashed down with an earthshaking jolt, it startled the ordinary humans, freezing them in their tracks. The undead took no notice, but they were lurching along more slowly than their living counterparts. Thus Taegan reached the ground in time to interpose himself between Gorstag and his would-be assassins. He drove his rapier into a zombie's face and out the back of its head, jerked the weapon free, deflected a short sword with a thrust in opposition, and pierced his attacker's solar plexus. An instant later, a mace whipped at his head. He ducked and extended simultaneously, and another animate corpse went down.

The surviving humans bolted, leaving the last two zombies behind to cover their retreat. Taegan destroyed the creatures, took a wary look around to check for other dangers, then crouched over Gorstag.

"You'll be all right now," the maestro said.

Gorstag shook his head.

"I don't think so," the student murmured.

Actually, Taegan marked the precise location of his pupil's wound, and he didn't think so, either.

Nonetheless, he insisted, "We'll find a priest to mend you."

"No time. Just listen."

Gorstag fumbled at his side. After a moment, Taegan realized the wounded man was trying to produce something from inside his blood-soaked cloak but was too weak to bring it forth.

The elf folded back the cape to reveal a book with an odd sigil stamped on the spine and a folio stuffed with loose pages.

"What are these?"

"The tome," said Gorstag, "and Speaker's notes."

"What speaker?"

Gorstag made a little rhythmic wheezing sound. It took Taegan a second to realize it was laughter.

"You're right," said the dying student. "I kept calling him Speaker even after I found out. It scared me to use his real name, even in my private thoughts. But you need to know. It's Sammaster."

Taegan wondered if his student was slipping into delirium. Sammaster was a villain in old stories. Perhaps such a human had really lived once upon a time, but even if so, he was surely dust.

"I don't understand" the maestro said. "Has some knave taken to calling himself by the monster's name?"

"No," Gorstag replied. "He came back. He's leading the cult again, and this time the prophecies are going to come true. He's found the way to make them all do what he wants."

Taegan felt lost. He dimly recalled that Sammaster had founded a secret society known as the Cult of the Dragon, which by some accounts still existed, but beyond that, he could make little of what Gorstag was straining to tell him.

"Make *who* do what he wants?"

"It's why we had to steal all the gems," Gorstag replied.

"That was you?"

"With the others. I had to, to keep them from suspecting I was a spy." He panted out his ghastly crippled laugh. Blood ran from the corners of his mouth, but he continued, "Not a good spy, though. They caught me in the end. I thought I could pull it off. Thought I'd finally found a way to make something of myself, but . . . Never mind. It's not important anymore. Keep the notes safe until the Harpers come for them. They'll find you. Somehow. Don't trust anybody else. Even a paladin. Even the queen."

"If the folio's supposed to pass to someone else, tell me how to find him."

Gorstag didn't answer, simply stared up at the heavens. Gazing after his ascending soul, perhaps.

At that moment, had it lain in his power, Taegan might have consigned the young idiot's spirit to the infernal realms instead. It was true, the avariel encouraged his students to revere him as a mentor and prize him as a boon companion. It was good for business. But that didn't mean he was keen to fulfill their perilous, inconvenient dying requests. He most emphatically was not.

"Curse you," he said, "you didn't understand. I only liked you in a casual sort of way, and I certainly don't care about your wretched batch of papers. You should have sought the aid of a knight. I'm just an avariel."

Gorstag had nothing to say to that either.

Taegan sighed, gathered up the book and folio, and his leg gave him a twinge. Thus reminded of the gash he'd received, he checked it and was relieved to find it shallow.

He decided to heed Gorstag's instructions in one regard anyway. He wouldn't trust paladins or any of the other royal officers likely to discover him if he lingered there. He'd rather not try to justify his slaughter of several humans. The carcasses of the wyvern and zombies might serve to vindicate him, but it was by no means a certainty, not when the authorities held his profession in such disdain. He spread his wings and soared upward.

As he fled toward the salle, he wondered if he could find a way to turn the burden Gorstag had foisted upon him into coin. The possibility blunted his resentment, but only a little.

SIX

11 Alturiak, the Year of Rogue Dragons

Will was no mariner, but he and his fellow hunters had spent enough time sailing around the Moonsea, traveling from one job to the next, for him to learn that many captains preferred to hug the coast during winter. It gave them a fighting chance of finding shelter in a harbor or cove if a gale blew up. Nonetheless, after sailing past the third ravaged village, the skipper of the merchant galley had ordered his crew to the benches to row out into the center of the Reach. Evidently he feared running up on a dragon flight more than getting caught in a blizzard.

As a result of his caution, the rolling grasslands of the Vast were simply a line on the eastern horizon, and the Earthfast Mountains just a bump. That didn't stop Dorn from spending hours in the bow staring at them.

The gray, breezy afternoon of the eleventh was no exception. Dorn had stood like a statue at the port rail since the midday meal of rock-hard biscuits and pickled cod. Eventually Kara wandered up to join him.

Will had made it a point to keep abreast of the progress of their friendship. Someone should, shouldn't he, considering that back in the Flooded Forest, his comrades had proclaimed the bard a duplicitous and possibly sinister figure. Besides, it intrigued him to see a softer side of Dorn emerging, no matter how the big man himself struggled against it, and while some folk affected to resent eavesdroppers, the practice didn't bother them unless they caught you at it.

They rarely caught Will. The skills that had once made him the ablest guild thief in Saerloon saw to that. He descended the mast and sauntered forward. Fortunately, the galley carried some of its cargo on deck, including half a dozen crates, stacked two high and lashed down to keep them from sliding just aft of the bow. The metallic contents clinked and rattled when the ship rolled. The pile offered plenty of cover for a skulker as small as a halfling. Will sat down with his back against it, yawned, and pretended to doze.

He picked up Kara's rich soprano voice in midsentence: "—wish you were ashore, don't you? Hunting them."

"We'll see you safely to Lyrabar," Dorn said, "as promised."

"That's not what I asked."

"The voyage is . . . pleasanter than I thought it might be. Light work for good wages. But I like killing dragons. We talked about that already."

"The previous dragon flight almost killed you, your friends, and me. We were lucky to escape with our lives."

"Yes. It's stupid to want to face another one. But if you could find a way to split the wyrms up, pick one off, slip away, regroup, and return for the next. . . ." He chuckled. It was a sound Will had rarely heard. "Easier said than done, I know."

"I imagine that if anyone could figure it out, it would be you," Kara said.

That killed the conversation dead, at least for a moment. Dorn had never known how to respond to a compliment, or a simple expression of gratitude, for that matter.

"I've spent a lot of times studying drakes," he managed at last, "questioning folk who've seen them up close and lived to tell the tale."

"Yet you have no idea why they slip into frenzy?"

"Apparently nobody does, not even wizards, sages, or priests."

"It must be horrible for them."

Dorn spat and said, "More like the kind of drunk where hurting people and breaking things seems like the grandest sport in the world. But even if it was awful, who could pity them? Dragons slaughter and pillage even when their minds are clear."

"I know. You'd slay them all if you could, and considering what they took from you, who could blame you? I just wonder what you'd do afterward."

Will peeked out in time to see Dorn shrug.

"Since it's not going to happen, why even think about it?" the former gladiator said, his iron half-mask gleaming dully in the pale winter sunlight.

"I know you'd find something to do, because I know there's more to you than hate."

"I suppose I'd just go on hunting. Faerûn would still have plenty of dangerous beasts, and I'd still need to earn a living."

"Suppose you found one of the great dragon hoards Will is always going on about. Then you wouldn't have to worry about coin."

"I'd still hunt."

"To help others?"

"Because it's all I know."

"Oh, nonsense. You're clever enough to learn another way of living. If you wanted to, you could settle down and have the things most people want. A home, perhaps, and someone to share it."

His rough bass voice grew colder when he said, "You're mocking me."

"No."

"I've known only two sorts of women in that way. Those I paid, and those who were curious to find out what it would be like, or if I even could. To discover whether the red drake left me my manhood."

"Some people think that different is the same as ugly and frightening, but not everyone. I don't. How could I, when I'm different myself?"

"Because your eyes and hair are unusual colors? Spare me. You're shaking the tree for compliments, and you need to try your luck elsewhere. I never learned to play such games."

"I've offended you," Kara said. "I'm sorry. I'll leave you alone."

Will looked out from his hiding place and saw the slender bard, her cheeks ruddy with the cold and her long, straight white-blond hair whipping in the wind, turn to go.

Dorn reached out with his human hand to stay her, almost touching but not quite.

"Please," he said. "I'm the one who should be sorry. I don't understand why you say some of the things you do, but I know it isn't out of meanness."

"I often don't know why I say them either," she said with a smile. "Perhaps simply because I'm afraid, and it makes me babble."

Once again, Dorn didn't appear to know what to say.

Just kiss her, thought Will impatiently. You'll both enjoy it, and with any luck, it'll gripe Pavel's arse.

Pavel had an amorous nature, and since he served Lathander, who was, among his other attributes, a god of love, nothing in his creed or vows constrained him from indulging it. At the start of the voyage, he'd spent several days making subtle romantic overtures to Kara, hints and invitations she'd ignored. Will hoped it would irk him to learn that where the handsome, loquacious priest had failed to strike a spark, his scarred, surly comrade had succeeded.

The moment stretched out, the two humans standing close together, gazing into one another's faces.

Then Raryn bellowed, "Got you!"

Naturally, everyone, the half-golem and singer included, turned to see what was happening.

Bare from the waist up, his skin sunburned the angry-looking red that evidently caused his kind no more discomfort than did the winter chill, the arctic dwarf was standing on one of the rower's benches a short distance aft. The muscles in his burly arms bulged and knotted as he hauled in a line. At the end was a harpoon embedded in the plump, glistening gray body of a tuna nearly as big as himself. The fish thrashed and flopped about the deck until he pounded its head with the butt of his bone-hafted ice axe, fitted with a new blade since the ooze drake's corrosive slime had ruined the old one.

Afterward the dwarf recited the prayerlike formula he intoned after killing any game animal, apologizing to its departing spirit and promising its body wouldn't go to waste. Then he gave his shipmates a grin, the flash of teeth almost indistinguishable inside the tangle of white beard.

"Fresh tuna filets for our supper," said Raryn. "There's nothing tastier."

He wrenched the harpoon from his catch, drew his knife, and crouched down to clean it.

Having determined what the fuss had been about, the sailors went back to their duties. Will peered up at Dorn and Kara, then frowned, perplexed. Unlike everyone else, the bard wasn't turning away. She stared as Raryn's blood-smeared fist hitched the knife along, shearing away slabs of moist pink flesh.

It didn't make sense. Surely she'd seen someone dress out a freshly killed animal before, so why the fascination? Will couldn't believe she was squeamish and thus transfixed with horror. Back in Ylraphon, she'd maintained her composure with smashed, shredded human corpses scattered all around. Yet she still couldn't take her violet eyes off the tuna.

Dorn saw it, too.

"Kara?" he said. "Kara?"

She didn't answer. She took a step toward the companion-way leading down from the bow, paused, then took another. Will had a sudden premonition that he didn't want to see what she'd do if she made it all the way to Raryn and his catch. It would be . . . disturbing. Maybe worse than that.

Kara wrenched herself around, and staggered to the very front of the bow, seemingly putting as much distance between herself and the dwarf as possible. Panting, she clutched the rail as if she lacked the strength to stand without a prop. Or maybe as if to anchor herself in place.

Dorn followed her.

"What's wrong?" he asked.

Shaking her head, Kara replied, "Nothing. I felt faint for a moment, but it's passing. Perhaps it was just hunger. Maybe I should have eaten my share of the cod, repulsive as it looked."

Dorn peered down the length of the ship then shouted, "Pavel!"

The shout brought the priest hurrying forward. Will fell in behind him, and they clambered up into the bow.

"She's ill," said Dorn.

"I'm not," Kara replied.

"I'll tell you whether you are or not," said Pavel.

His tone must have convinced her resistance was useless, for she submitted to an examination without further protest. He gazed into her eyes and mouth, held her dainty wrist between thumb and forefinger to take her pulse, and cast a divination. Apparently it revealed nothing helpful, for he then proceeded to ask the usual questions physicians trotted out when they hadn't a clue what ailed the patient, and lastly to inspect the wounds he'd first treated in the wererats' lair. As far as Will could tell, she'd healed up nicely, with only faint scars remaining.

"Well?" asked Dorn.

Pavel directed his answer at Kara. "You seem fine."

"I told you so." She adjusted her mantle and gown to cover her shoulder and added. "I would like to find a spot to lie down, though."

"I'll walk with y—" Dorn began.

"Don't trouble yourself. I'm all right."

Once she was out of earshot, Will sneered up at Pavel.

"Baffled and useless as ever," the halfling said.

"Go eat a toadstool," Pavel replied. "If she is sick, no other healer could have diagnosed the problem, either."

"Do you think she is?" asked Dorn.

"I don't know," the cleric answered with a shrug, "but I find myself remembering that when we first met her, we mistrusted her. Now we like her. Considering that she risked her life to cover the retreat from Ylraphon the same as we did, how could we not? The problem is, our fondness doesn't make her any less of a mystery."

After that, no one else had much to say. In time, Will climbed back up the mast, where he remained while the sun sank toward the horizon. The elevation should have allowed him to see farther than anyone else onboard. Still, it was Raryn's keen eyes that first spotted the threat, and Raryn who raised the alarm.

"Dragons!" the tracker shouted. "Flying out of the west!"

⸎

Raryn's cry jolted Dorn out of his out of his fretting over Kara and made him snatch for his bow. The problem was he didn't have it. Like most of the rest of his gear, it was packed away to protect it from the damp salt air.

He hesitated, torn between the desire to rush to his baggage and the equally compelling urge to find out more about what was going on. Then, yielding to the latter impulse, he leaped from the bow and scrambled down the deck, through the jabbering crewmen, to join Raryn at the rail.

"Show me," he said.

The dwarf pointed. The setting sun burned in the western sky, and Dorn had to squint against the glare. Finally, though, he made out two specks. They were still far enough away that it was amazing even Raryn had spotted them.

The captain tramped up, his tattooed face twisted in a scowl of concern, and said, "You claim to know about dragons."

"We do," Raryn said.

"Are those two chasing us?"

"It's too early to tell," said the dwarf.

"Suppose I order all hands to the oars?"

"It wouldn't help," Raryn said. "You can't outrun dragons, and I guarantee you, if we've spotted them, they've already seen us as well. My advice is to break out whatever weapons you've got stashed away. My friends and I will tell you how to use them to best effect. Though I hope it won't come to that. A ship under sail is a poor place to fight wyrms. You can only maneuver the length and breadth of the deck, and if they feel like it, they can drown you just by knocking a hole below the waterline."

The captain frowned and said, "Surely we can do something."

"We told you what to do," said Dorn. "Loan us your spyglass, and go do it. We may only have a few minutes left. When Raryn and I know more about the wyrms, we'll tell you."

From the way the mariner glared, he plainly didn't like being ordered around on his own vessel. Still, he surrendered the telescope, strode off, and started barking commands in his turn. The crew scrambled to obey him.

Dorn peered through the spyglass, then cursed.

"With the sun behind them," he said, "I still can't make out the color."

"It could be the swamp dragons again," Raryn said, "except there were more than two."

"Considering that it may have been a whole different bunch of wyrms raiding along the eastern shore, the gods only know what's coming," Dorn replied. "We'd better arm ourselves while we still have time."

Kara found Dorn when he was fastening up his acid-scarred brigandine, buckling the flaps that made it possible for him to don the reinforced leather armor despite the girth and protrusions of his metal arm. He felt a twinge of relief that she looked tense but composed, not strange and entranced as she had before. Maybe she really had just needed a nap.

"Do you have spells prepared?" he asked.

"Always," she replied.

"Good, but if we have to fight, wait for the proper moment to throw them. Wyrms will almost always target a spellcaster if you give them a chance."

"I know," she said. "You be careful, too. You look more dangerous than the average sailor. The drakes will want to eliminate you quickly, also."

"Maybe so . . ." Dorn faltered.

He had more he wanted to say to her, but didn't know what, and in any case, they were running out of time. He turned to the mariners who'd lined up to take spears and bows from the mate who was passing them out.

It turned out the majority had seen combat before, fending off the raiders of the Pirate Isles, which put them one up on the militiamen Dorn had led in Ylraphon. Marginally encouraged, he divided them into squads and gave them their battle orders.

When he finished, he climbed up into the bow to resume surveying the sky. The wyrms were much closer. Even without the spyglass, he could clearly make out the batlike wings, wedge-shaped heads, and serpentine tails silhouetted against the bright golden clouds. But still, not the color of the scales.

As he strung his longbow, the captain approached him.

"What's happening?" the captain asked.

"We've come a bit farther south, and the wyrms have turned to follow. It's possible they just want a closer look at us. If so, we mustn't provoke them."

"But if they do mean to attack," said the man with the tattooed face, "I don't want to give them the first move. That could be all it takes for them to sink us."

"You're right," said Dorn. "Have the archers stand ready. As soon as any of us hunters sees the least indication the wyrms mean us ill, we'll let everybody know."

The captain gave a brusque nod and bustled off toward the quarterdeck.

Once Dorn readied his bow and selected an arrow for his first shot, he had nothing to do but watch. The waiting gnawed at his nerves. Eventually Pavel came to join him.

"Stand over there," the cleric said, motioning him a couple paces toward the stern.

Pavel then positioned himself farther forward than anyone else. He chanted a prayer and brandished his sun amulet, blessing everyone within range. Dorn felt the usual surge of vigor and confidence, though the latter couldn't truly banish his apprehension, just muffle it a little.

Once Pavel had finished all the spellcasting he deemed useful for the time being, he stood and peered out over the rippling, lead-gray water as everyone else was doing.

"What's the color?" he muttered under his breath. "Curse it, show us—there!"

One wing dipping low and the other angling high, the drakes turned to keep the merchant vessel directly in front of them, and at last their position was such that they weren't flying directly out of the sun. Their long bodies gleamed a silver bright as newly minted Sembian ravens, and Dorn could make out the broad, kite-shaped plates on their heads that inspired some folk to call their species "shield dragons." A number of the sailors cheered, called out thanks to Tymora and Umberlee or simply slumped in relief. Others still held their weapons ready and snapped at their shipmates to be silent.

Dorn was one of those who kept his arrow nocked. The fact that the wyrms had metal-colored scales wasn't enough to make him drop his guard. Maybe such creatures were less purely malevolent than the rest of their kind, but he'd heard of instances when they, too, raided for treasure or harmed folk who failed to pay them the deference they considered their due. Anyway, if this pair had slipped into frenzy, their normal inclinations didn't matter anymore.

They soared overhead and on past the bow.

"That's it, then," a sailor said, sounding almost disappointed.

"Not yet," Pavel told him. He'd noticed the first telltale tail switching, and the enormous, serpentine bodies beginning to twist. "They're wheeling for another pass."

They swooped lower as well, and stupid as it was, Dorn realized he was glad. Eager to see if he could bring the wretched things tumbling down into the sea.

He was about to give the warning that would start the battle, when Pavel, evidently sensing his intention, said, "No. Wait. We still don't know they're hostile."

"By the time we're absolutely sure, it could be too late."

"They're metal dragons, born of light the same as humans."

"How do you know?" asked Dorn. "We've never even seen a silver before."

"Be that as it may, we can't lash out at them just because we fear they might be hostile."

"Is that what the Morninglord teaches?" Dorn snapped. "Bugger him and you, too."

Harsh words, but just bluster. Dorn realized he wasn't going to give the signal to attack after all, not yet, not with his trusted comrade so set against it.

The reptiles hurtled over the ship, lower still, so close Dorn's nerves sang with the impulse to send an arrow streaking upward. Again, the silvers didn't attack. What did they want then? Were they really just curious after all?

They circled. The smaller of the pair climbed higher, while the larger dropped even lower. Leveling off, it then glided in an almost stately fashion across the surface of the waves, straight toward the galley. Crewmen yammered in terror and raised their weapons.

"No!" Dorn shouted.

He hated stopping them, but it was the only sane thing to do. He could tell the silver meant no immediate harm. No dragon, even a deranged one, would approach a ship it intended to attack in such a manner. First it would rake the decks with its breath and magic, and when it did decide to fight with fang and claw, it would dive as fast as it was able and smash into the massed defenders like a boulder flung from a catapult.

Apparently the wyrm wanted to come aboard peacefully, by lighting on the quarterdeck. Dorn could only hope that alone wouldn't bring disaster. It was easy to imagine the huge reptile's weight shoving the stern all the way down under the water.

But it didn't come to that. As the shield dragon drew near, it dwindled, its body drawing in on itself so quickly that for a second, Dorn lost track of it. Then he noticed the ordinary-looking white gull at the center of the space the wyrm had occupied.

Wings fluttering, the seabird set down in the center of the quarterdeck, which the captain and everyone else had hastily vacated to make room for a gigantic drake. There the creature shifted shape again, swelling upward into the guise of a skinny old man clad in a shabby brown robe and buskins. He had a genial sort of face, seemingly made for smiles and laughter, in which the eyes looked out of place. Pale and piercing, the gray orbs, set deep under scraggly white brows, peered out at the world with the cold, imperious regard of a magistrate or warlord.

The silver gazed down the length of the ship, then said, "Do you think I didn't spot you from the air, Karasendrieth? That I can't taste your scent? Show yourself."

Kara stepped from behind a bundle of burlap sacks bound together in a net.

"Hello, Azhaq," she said.

"That's the first sensible thing you've done," Azhaq said. "Now come along. It's time to go."

Dorn leaped out of the bow and shoved through the massed sailors with their bows and spears. Raryn, Will, and Pavel scrambled to join him, the priest pausing to grab the captain and haul him along as well. As they hurried aft, the shadow of the silver that had remained in dragon form swept across the deck, a reminder it was still hanging above the galley like a hawk floating over a hare. Dorn and his companions took up a position between Kara and Azhaq.

When the bard realized what they were doing, she said, "Wait."

"It's what you paid for," said Will.

"I wasn't expecting two of them," said Kara.

The halfling grinned a crooked grin and replied, "We weren't even expecting one. Still, a deal's a deal. Mind you, if we survive this, a bonus would be nice."

Dorn glared up at the transformed shield dragon and asked, "What's this all about?"

"Justice, human," said the silver. "The female must answer for her crimes, but Moonwing and I have no quarrel with you. Stay out of the way, and we won't hurt you."

"What crimes?" Raryn asked.

"That's none of your concern. Suffice it to say, my comrade and I serve in the Talons of Justice. Do you know the name?"

Dorn did. He'd run across it in his studies of dragon lore. The Talons were supposedly a fellowship of silvers who'd banded together to combat evil, rather like an order of paladins. The claim didn't impress him. Even if it was true, who was to say that a dragon's notions of right and wrong were the same as a man's?

"You have no authority over me," Kara said, "nor does the lord to whom you've chosen to bow your heads."

"Someone must lead," Azhaq said. "Otherwise, all will suffer, drakes and these small folk, too."

"If he led to some purpose," Kara said, "I'd agree. But as it stands—"

"Enough!" Azhaq snapped, his patched, faded robe flapping in the frigid breeze. "I didn't come to argue, but to arrest you as the king commands, and a long, hard search it's been. You know what it costs to remain in dragon form for days at a time, so you can imagine that my patience has worn thin. Now, do you surrender, or do you mean to fight a pair of Talons, both older and stronger than you?"

"The lass doesn't stand alone," Pavel said.

The silver regarded the priest as if surprised that any of the other "small folk" would presume to speak again.

"I seek to protect you and all your kind," Azhaq said, "as my race has always done. If you're truly entitled to wear Lathander's amulet, then you should aspire to aid, not hinder me."

"If you truly deserve to proclaim yourself a champion of good," Pavel answered, "then you should understand why decent folk wouldn't surrender a companion to any stranger simply because he demands it—especially a drake, whatever its hue. We've seen proof that a good many of you are running mad." He turned to the captain and asked, "Your passengers are under your protection, aren't they, sir?"

The mariner scowled. Plainly, he was uncertain and didn't like having his hand forced. But he was tough, as any captain had to be to sail the perilous waters of the Sea of Fallen Stars, and perhaps it helped that the shield dragon currently wore the guise of a man. It made the creature somewhat less intimidating.

At any rate, the captain said, "It's true. The bard paid for her passage. I can't just toss her to the sharks. Maybe if you were the Sembian or Impilturan navy, I'd obey your orders, but what do your Talons of Justice mean to the likes of us?"

Azhaq's wrinkled features twisted as if he'd suffered a pang of headache.

"You have no idea what a dangerous game you're playing," he said. "You think that because I'm a silver, I'll coax and coddle you . . . never mind. Just listen to me. Karasendrieth is a dragon in human form, like me."

Dorn turned to Kara.

"Tell me the wyrm is mad," he said, "just like the others."

Kara sighed and said, "I wish I could."

"You see," Azhaq said, "her fate is a matter for dragons, not men."

"That . . . might make a difference," the captain said.

Did it? Were the hunters and sailors under any obligation to protect one cursed wyrm from others, especially when she'd deceived them concerning her true nature? Will, Raryn, and Pavel all glanced uncertainly in Dorn's direction, waiting for their leader to supply the answer. Unfortunately, he didn't know.

"Give the rogue up," Azhaq continued, "and go your way in peace. Moonwing and I are friends to men—and dwarves, and halflings—and have no wish to hurt you. But if you're fools enough to stand with her, we'll do what we must. You'll be throwing away your lives for nothing, for surely you realize you can't stop us."

Maybe it was the memory of Kara risking her life to fight the wyrms of the Flooded Forest. Or maybe Azhaq's arrogance, his certainty that humans could do nothing to balk him. Either way, Dorn knew he meant to side with the female.

But how was he to help her? Even though she was a dragon herself, he questioned their ability to fight off two silvers. It would surely be impossible if the sailors declined to help, and he could tell the captain was wavering. It was impossible to guess which way he'd ultimately jump.

Unless somebody pushed him.

"We need a couple minutes to palaver," the half-golem said.

Azhaq's mouth tightened in vexation.

"Do it quickly," he said, shifting his gaze to Kara. "However they choose, don't make these little ones perish in a quarrel that's none of their making. Llimark isn't dead. Surrender now, and—"

In one smooth, sudden motion, Dorn lifted his longbow and pulled the arrow back to his ear.

For a split second, he had the shaft pointed straight at Azhaq's heart, and to his own surprise, shifted his aim. The arrow plunged into the Talon's belly. That could be a mortal wound, too, but not immediately, and probably not if Pavel or some other healer tended it.

Dorn dropped his bow and rushed the quarterdeck. If he wasn't going to kill the silver outright, then he needed to incapacitate the creature quickly, before Azhaq could revert to reptilian form or start casting spells. As he scrambled up the companionway, sailors started screaming, giving voice to the fear an attacking drake inspired. Evidently Moonwing had seen Dorn shoot his comrade and was diving at the ship.

The captain and crew would have to fight. They no longer had a choice.

As Dorn scrambled up into the stern, Azhaq was still doubled over with the shock of his unexpected wound. Good. The hunter charged the silver, and the galley listed violently to starboard, sending him reeling off course. He slammed into the rail, it cracked, and for an instant he feared he'd crash right on through to drop into the sea. But the barrier held.

Thinking Moonwing must have landed on the ship, he glanced around. In fact, the silver was still in the air, but another drake was swelling into existence on the deck, her burgeoning mass tipping the galley off balance. Kara's reptilian form, though huge compared to a human body, was smaller and slimmer than that of the shield dragons. Her scales were a shimmering silver-blue, and her eyes the same lustrous violet as before, though the pupils were feline slits instead of circles. Dorn had never seen such a wyrm before, but the knowledge he'd collected enabled him to identify the breed. Kara was a song dragon, a rare species allegedly as benign as the metal wyrms.

She had a half-healed wound at the base on one wing, evidently left over from the injuries she'd received prior to stumbling into the wererats' den. Pavel's prayers apparently hadn't mended the gash because he hadn't been able to see it while she was in human guise.

The galley rocked again as she leaped clear. Dorn threw himself at Azhaq.

Unfortunately, the rolling of the ship had given the Talon time to shake off the shock of his stomach wound. He rattled off an incantation and swept his hand through a mystic pass. Dorn felt a sudden, sickening vertigo.

Thanks to his studies, he knew what it meant. Some shield dragons mastered the ability to make a victim fall away from the earth. He had only a moment to anchor himself, or he'd hurtle scores of feet skyward, hang there until the magic ran out of power, and come plummeting down.

He flung himself to the deck, drove his iron claws through the planks, and clutched at the splintered oak. The heavens pulled at him, but his grip anchored him.

It wasn't, however, enough simply to cling there. He had to deal with Azhaq. He kicked the deck with his metal foot, smashing through, then hooked the extremity in the hole. It wasn't as secure a hold as the one he'd established with his talons, but it would have to do. He needed his hands.

He grabbed, caught Azhaq by the legs, and heaved him into a grapple, which entailed pulling him into the zone where things fell upward. Unafraid of such an occurrence, the Talon kicked at Dorn's iron leg, trying to knock it out of the hole. The hunter struggled to shift his hands into a position from which they could batter Azhaq into submission. It was harder than he could have imagined. Despite his scrawny, old-man appearance and the arrow in his gut, the silver was astonishingly strong, and a cunning wrestler as well.

Then the situation became more desperate still as Azhaq started to transform. His limbs thickened. In another second, Dorn wouldn't be able to wrap his fingers around them. The silver's neck stretched, his face extended into a pair of jaws, and his teeth lengthened into ivory daggers capable of shattering a human skull with one nip.

At last Dorn managed to twist his iron wrist free of his adversary's grip. He slammed his knuckle spikes into Azhaq's temple. The silver went limp.

The violent action nearly jerked Dorn's foot out of its mooring. It did make him fumble his grip on Azhaq, who immediately tumbled upward. In a second, the Talon was high above his attacker's head. Dorn couldn't tell if Azhaq was alive or dead, nor at the moment did he care. He had other things to think about.

It was possible that by distancing herself from the galley, Kara had intended to keep Moonwing's attacks directed solely at her, thus sparing her allies. If so, it had worked so far. Pavel, Raryn, Will, and the sailors were still alive. The shield dragon decided it wouldn't endure the steady harassment of arrows, sling stones, and priestly attack spells any longer, even if they didn't seem to be doing him any great harm. He conjured a blast of fire that sent Kara reeling, then, confident she wouldn't trouble him for the next few seconds, swooped at the galley.

Despite Pavel's blessing, some of the sailors couldn't bear the terror of the onslaught and leaped overboard. Other folk managed a final missile. It looked to Dorn as if Will's rock hit Moonwing squarely in the left eye. Alas, the pain wasn't enough to keep the onrushing dragon from breathing out a jet of pearly vapor, a blast that would sweep the galley from prow to stern.

Grimly aware that that one attack might well kill everyone onboard, Dorn held his breath and pressed himself flat against the deck. It was only when the white fumes washed over him, and he discovered they weren't cold that he knew Moonwing had been merciful. Silvers could expel either a breath weapon capable of freezing a man solid or one that merely induced a temporary paralysis, and the Talon had opted for the latter.

Still, that was all Moonwing needed to neutralize most of his adversaries onboard. When the mist dissipated, Dorn saw that the majority of the sailors either stood or lay motionless. Even Will was in the same condition, petrified in the act of plucking another rock from his belt pouch.

But because Dorn hadn't inhaled the fumes and had avoided their touch as much as possible, or perhaps simply by dint of his natural hardiness or luck, he could still move. If he could make his way off the quarterdeck, out of the lingering effect of Azhaq's magic, maybe he could make Moonwing regret it. He dragged himself forward, clawing and kicking new holds in the planks as he went, and heaved himself down the companionway.

He landed heavily, surely bruising himself. He didn't care. It felt too good just to escape the relentless, dizzying pull of the sky. He snatched up his bow and dashed forward, seeking a spot that would afford him a clear shot, past the sail and rigging, at Moonwing wheeling in the sky.

In so doing, he came into proximity with Raryn, who was loosing one arrow after another, seemingly without pausing to aim, though Dorn knew the appearance was deceptive. The tracker's quiver was nearly empty.

"Sorry to leave you to handle the other one all by yourself," said Raryn, without glancing away from his target.

"You needed to focus on the one that was already in drake form and on the wing," Dorn said, drawing his own bow. "I understand. How are we doing?"

"Moonwing doesn't act hurt," said the dwarf. "I cast a charm to help my arrows pierce the scales, but still, I don't feel like I'm accomplishing much more than I would jabbing him with a pin. I fear this is primarily Kara's fight."

"If we let that be true, we're finished," said Dorn, snatching another shaft from his supply.

He would have given anything for an arrow specially enchanted to slay dragons, but alas, he'd only had the one he'd wasted back in Ylraphon.

The two wyrms soared, each evidently trying to gain the

advantage of higher altitude. Then the pounding of Kara's wings became uneven, as if the wounded one had started to fail her. Wobbling in the air, she leveled off.

Moonwing dived at her and spread his jaws wide to breathe. But no more vapor burst from the silver's maw. Evidently Kara had used the same spell she'd employed against the black wyrm, stealing his ability to attack in that way without him even realizing it.

It must have surprised the Talon, but it didn't make him falter. His foe was still floundering beneath him, and he kept on plummeting, talons poised to catch and rend.

Kara waited until he was almost on top of her, so close and hurtling so fast that it was impossible for him to dodge, before unleashing her own breath weapon. The fumes crackled like the tame lightning bolts wizards sometimes conjured, but flared even brighter. Maybe the female dragon had heightened the glare with a spell. In any case, the blaze made Dorn flinch and surely blinded Moonwing, who took the blast right in the eyes.

Still, the shield dragon drove on toward his mark. At the last possible instant, Kara dodged out of his way. It was only then that Dorn realized she could still fly perfectly well. She'd only pretended otherwise to trick Moonwing into doing what she wanted.

As the larger wyrm plunged past her, she clawed at his wing, caught hold, and yanked herself onto his back, where, to Dorn's surprise, she started singing. The words were in Draconic, so he couldn't understand them, but the tune had a fierce, defiant sound.

Kara kept on tearing at Moonwing, shredding his wings, as they plummeted together. When they slammed down into the gray water, the prodigious splash threw cold spray over the side of the galley floating just a few yards away. An instant later, a wave rocked the ship, and Dorn had to fight to keep his balance.

Once he managed that, he saw that Kara had managed to land on top of her adversary. Moonwing, who seemed to have recovered his sight, twisted his head around to bite her, but he was an instant too slow. She used his body as a platform to kick off and take flight once more.

If he was to pursue her, Moonwing would have to get back into the air without the same advantage. As at home in water as on land or in the sky, a black or bronze dragon could have done it easily, but silvers lacked the same facility. Moonwing's damaged wings pounded, straining to lift him from the waves.

Until he succeeded, he'd be close to the galley and relatively stationary, not streaking about high overhead, and Dorn intended to exploit that vulnerability. He and Raryn drove one arrow after another into those spots where a dragon's hide was thinnest. Will dashed forward, leaped atop a bundle of cargo, and balancing as easily as if he stood on solid earth, whirled his sling. Pavel had evidently used a prayer to free the halfling from his paralysis.

Moonwing roared and jerked as the missiles pierced and battered him. At last the barrage was wearing him down.

Wheeling over his head, Kara stopped singing to cry, "You've lost, Talon. Yield, and we'll let you live."

Bugger that, thought Dorn. He reached for one of his last few arrows, and someone gripped his wrist, restraining him. He turned. The meddler was Pavel.

"Moonwing still has his teeth, his claws, and a skull full of spells," said the priest. "Kara's right. If we can end this now, we should."

Dorn glared at him, but when his friend didn't flinch, he left the arrow in the quiver.

Moonwing left off beating his wings to tread water.

"What of Azhaq?" the Talon asked.

Kara peered at the other silver, floating motionless, caught midway between human and wyrm form, high above the sea.

"He's alive," she said, and Dorn could only marvel at the keenness of the senses that enabled her to verify that fact at such a distance.

"I'm a healer," Pavel shouted. "I can help both of you, if you promise that afterward, you'll leave this vessel and everyone aboard in peace."

Moonwing bared his fangs and said, "If Azhaq hadn't taken human form—to avoid terrorizing you, to deal gently with you—you never could have bested us."

"I guess you'll know better next time," said Will. "Meanwhile, what's it to be? I'm running low on skiprocks, but the nice thing about a sling is, you can always find something to throw."

"I yield," Moonwing growled.

"Thank you," Kara said. Her wings hammered, carrying her higher. "I'll fetch Azhaq down."

* * * * *

The aftermath of the fight proved a lengthy business. The ship's company had to recover those sailors who'd jumped overboard—to Raryn's relief, they found all but two—steer their vessel back on course, and get the shield dragons within reach of Pavel's healing touch. The last was harder than it needed to be because, his surrender notwithstanding, Moonwing adamantly refused to assume human form to facilitate his coming aboard. He evidently feared making himself any more vulnerable than necessary.

Raryn was as careful of the silvers as they were of their vanquishers. The Talons seemed honest, which meant that, having given their surrender, they were likely to behave themselves. Still, one never knew. Harpoon and ice-axe at the ready, the dwarf made it a point to watch the shield dragons closely until they took flight, and to peer after them in case they doubled back. Eventually they vanished among the first stars of evening, and still he remained vigilant, grateful that, though his folk didn't spend their lives underground like the other branches of their race, they possessed the same ability to see in the dark.

Fortunately, he could stand guard and attend to his companions' conversations at the same time. Once he had the galley ordered to his satisfaction, the captain, predictably, came to complain.

"It's possible," the scowling seaman said to Dorn, "that if you hadn't loosed that first arrow, we could have avoided a fight."

"Only by giving up Kara," Pavel said. "Were you really willing to do that?"

The captain hesitated then said, "Well, I didn't certainly want to lose two hands or have my quarterdeck ripped to pieces."

In human form once more, Kara stepped forward, a diamond brooch in her slender hand. Finally understanding what she truly was, Raryn assumed the jewelry she carried with her came from her own personal dragon hoard.

"This should pay to repair the ship," she said, "with coin leftover for the kin of those who drowned. I realize treasure alone doesn't make up for lost lives, but I hope it helps a little."

"If the brooch doesn't," said Will, "the glory should. Skipper, if you've got any sense, you'll spread the story far and wide of how you and your men fought off two dragons with only a couple casualties and not a bit of cargo lost or spoiled. Every merchant in the North will be eager to trade with such a hero, and no pirate will dare molest you."

The mariner grunted and took the jewelry.

"What's done is done, I suppose," he said, then tramped away.

Kara surveyed her bodyguards, sighed, and said, "I suppose it will take more than extra gems to regain your friendship."

"It's worth a try," Will said with a grin.

"Silence, insect," Pavel said. "Yes, Karasendrieth, it will take more. From the start, we knew you had secrets, but we didn't require you to give them up. We respected you for helping the folk in Ylraphon, and in any case, guarding you didn't seem any shadier than other jobs we've done. But now we've raised our hands to silver dragons. Dorn started the violence with a foul blow, some would say. This despite the fact that, during my novitiate my teachers taught me that shield drakes are wise and noble beings, not divine, of course, but agents of good and beloved of Lathander. So now I need to understand whether, somehow, my friends and I have acted justly or if I must atone for a heinous sin."

Dorn sneered and said, "What makes you think she'll tell us the truth this time?"

Kara looked as if the gibe had cut her but declined to answer in kind.

She merely said, "Judge for yourself."

And as the frigid night wind moaned through the rigging, and Raryn surveyed the black, starry dome of the sky, she told her story.

SEVEN

14 Marpenoth, the Year of Wild Magic
(1372 DR)

Kara was weary by the time she soared over Blood-stone Pass, for she'd flown hundreds of leagues through air crisp with the promise of winter. Other wyrms of her acquaintance had deemed the journey a fool's errand and declined to accompany her, but she thought she knew what the golds wanted to discuss, therefore she couldn't stay away. Her nightmares wouldn't let her.

She pressed on for another hour, farther north into the jagged, perpetually snow-capped mountains called the Galenas, until she spotted the meeting ground, a rocky natural bowl nestled among the peaks. Despite her anxieties, the sight thrilled her, for she doubted any living creature had ever beheld such a spectacle. The depression blazed with the sunlight reflecting from the scales of dozens of wyrms—golds, silvers, brasses, coppers, bronzes, and even a couple of other song dragons—either crawling around the floor or perched on ledges along the steeply sloping walls. Together, they made a dazzling brightness, like a cauldron of molten metals all swirled together. A few other points of light shot across the sky like falling stars, all converging on the gleaming confusion below. They were latecomers like Kara, hurrying to keep the rendezvous.

As she furled her wings and dived lower, she caught the voices of her kind conversing in their own tongue. The coppers traded jests and japes, even at the start of such a solemn occasion. The bronzes and brasses were equally vocal, speculating about what was to come or complaining that it hadn't begun already. The golds and silvers were more reserved but responded courteously to any who addressed them. To a human, it might have seemed a cacophony of bestial rumbles, hisses, and roars, but to someone capable of understanding, it was music, a symphony expressive of the wisdom and nobility of a great people.

Next, circling lower still, looking for a clear spot to land Kara caught the leathery scent of her kind. Then, to her surprise, she felt the heat. A dragon's blood was cooler than that of men, yet even so, so many wyrms had congregated there that their bodies warmed the hollow.

Finally, after seeking in vain for a more convenient place, she lit on the rim of the bowl, then climbed cautiously down the side. It was even steeper than it had looked from the air, but her strength, combined with her keen senses of touch and balance, allowed her to negotiate it safely. Until the granite turned slippery beneath her talons.

Scrabbling for purchase, she looked down to see that a layer of translucent slime coated the stone. Fortunately, not all of it. She snatched for an outcropping outside the mess and heaved herself to safety. She doubted she looked graceful doing it, but it was better than rolling down the escarpment to smack into the dragons massed on the ground below.

A few yards underneath her and just off to the left, a copper dragon with sky-blue eyes perched on a ledge. He grinned up at her, exposing a gap in the upper fangs at the front of his mouth. She crawled toward him.

"You conjured the grease," she accused.

If he was afraid of retribution, he didn't let it show.

"A little spill wouldn't have hurt you," said the copper. "It would just have broken up the monotony. I've been here for hours, and nothing's happened."

Her anger cooling, Kara realized she wasn't going to attack him. A brawl under those circumstances would disgrace her more thoroughly than any awkward tumble ever could. Besides, coppers couldn't help playing jokes any more than song dragons could refrain from making music.

"If you create any more mischief," she said, "I'll make you wish you hadn't. Understood?"

"Of course, dread lady." He lowered his head to the ground in a parody of submission. "I'm Chatulio."

Kara gave her own name, and the gathering fell silent, save for the rustle of a wing, and the slap of a tail twitching on the ground. She turned to see that Chatulio's boredom was presumably at an end. The conclave was beginning.

Along one wall, just below the rim, were two shelves of rock, with the arched mouth of a cave at the back of the upper one. As she flew in, Kara had observed that, despite the crowding in the hollow, the ledges were entirely vacant, and inferring that those who'd called the gathering had reserved them for their own use, hadn't presumed to light there herself. One at a time, in stately procession, eight huge, ancient golds emerged from the opening in the rock. The scales on their sinuous bodies shined as if a legion of servants had polished them, while their amber eyes burned brighter still. "Beards" of tendrils dangled from their lower jaws.

Seven of the golds perched along the lower shelf. The eighth, the largest and last to emerge, remained atop the higher one, a position that also placed him above every other dragon in the bowl. Plainly, he must be Lareth, King of Justice, the sovereign the golds had chosen for themselves.

The other seven were the lords, his honor guard and the dignitaries of his court.

Golds—and to a lesser extent, silvers—were peculiar in that regard. Few other wyrms ever felt an inclination to acknowledge any authority above themselves. Certainly, song dragons didn't. Nonetheless, anyone beholding Lareth in all his manifest might and majesty would surely feel a shiver of awe, and Kara discovered she was no exception.

Lareth gazed out over the assembly, and said, "Noble friends, I thank you for your presence here today. I know that most of you have traveled a long way."

"So would it have killed you to set out a few casks of wine and some freshly killed game?" Chatulio whispered.

Kara shot him a glare to hush him.

"Under other circumstances," Lareth continued, "I'd open this conclave with all the pomp and ceremony that is your due. But time presses. Many of you know whereof I speak. The Rage is nearly upon us."

On the other side of the bowl, a lithe silver with several vivid battle scars perched on a high ledge among her own entourage. She was Havarlan, Barb—or commander—of the Talons of Justice.

"Can we be certain of this, Your Resplendence?" she asked.

"Yes," Lareth said. "All the portents say so. Those of us with the proper gifts can see it in the shape of the clouds or hear it in the murmur of the rivers. Every divination points to it. Many of you can feel it in your restlessness and ill temper, in the vile pictures that rise unbidden in your mind. I witness it in my dreams, whenever I can bear to sleep.

"A Rage is surely coming, the greatest ever, a madness that will overwhelm every one of us as completely as it will our evil kindred. We must protect the small folk from our fury."

"Well," said the largest of the lords, "at least our ancestors taught us how. For those of us who can shapeshift, the form of a human or some other little, inoffensive creature armors the mind. Others can bury themselves in their lairs so deeply that no matter how they struggle, they won't dig themselves out before sanity returns."

Lareth shook his head and warned, "No, Tamarand. This time is different. What worked before is insufficient now."

"Then what do we do?" asked an old brass, his wings and frills green at the edges.

"We sleep," said Lareth, "more profoundly than nature allows. Otherwise, the frenzy will goad us awake." He extended a wing to indicate a gold perched on another outcropping and continued, "Most of you know Nexus, at least by reputation. He's the greatest mage among us." Nexus acknowledged the praise by inclining his head. "He's crafted an enchantment to bind us in a slumber nothing can breach."

"Teach us," said a bronze, his membranous wings riddled with tiny holes and the rims of his scales blue-black with age, "and we'll spread the knowledge among our kin."

"Unfortunately, Ulreel," Lareth said, "that's not the answer, either. Only the most powerful enchanters can cast this spell. Moreover, it lasts until such a mage sees fit to dissolve it, so even if every drake could ensorcell himself in the solitude of his own den, he would then sleep forever. Thus, each of us needs assistance to avail himself of the protection."

"How will we proceed then?" Tamarand asked.

"You and I," the King of Justice answered, "will establish a sanctuary here in the Galenas. Your fellow lords will create six similar refuges across Faerûn. As it becomes necessary, all our kind will repair to the enclaves and submit to the enchantment. Veils of illusion will keep them safe from molestation, and those of us who can alter our forms will keep watch and wake our kindred when the Rage subsides. Each such warder will perform his duties for a few hours at a time, then rouse the next and return to unconsciousness himself. That will keep the madness from overwhelming him."

The assembled dragons gazed up at the elder gold in astonishment. Rather to Kara's surprise, it was Tamarand who spoke next.

"Your Resplendence, nothing in my life affords me so much honor and joy as to serve you as my sovereign. But as you understand better than anyone, to golds, the King of Justice has always been a source of wisdom, an advisor and adjudicator of disputes, rather than a master who commands his vassals' absolute obedience. While wyrms of other hues have never pledged you any fealty whatsoever."

Lareth's eyes flared, and whiffs of smoke rose from his nostrils and mouth.

"What are you implying?" the king demanded. "That my scheme is some sort of ploy to set myself up as a tyrant over half of dragonkind?"

"I know that isn't true . . ." Tamarand said.

"That makes one of us," Chatulio muttered.

". . . but I worry that some of these others do not. Ours is a proud and independent race. To ask that they meekly permit us to chain them with magic is to ask for more than they have ever given anyone. If we could think of another way to use Nexus's discovery. . . ."

"I've already tried," Lareth said, turning his gaze outward on the assembly. "Noble dragons, I harbor no ill intentions toward any of you, nor ambitions to a higher estate than the one I already enjoy. When disaster threatens, someone must strive to avert it, and that is my sole intent. I beg you to trust me until we weather this crisis. Afterward, I promise, we'll go our separate ways, each as free and hale as before. If you require it, I'll even vow to abdicate my throne on that day, and let the golds elect a new King of Justice in my place."

"No one wants you to step down," said Ulreel, "but Tamarand is right. This scheme troubles us. We have countless foes, the evil branches of our race and lesser creatures too, who would like nothing better than to exterminate us. If they should find us lying helpless, gathered all together. . . ."

"I told you," Lareth roared, blue and yellow flames playing around his immense fangs and on the surface of his forked tongue, "we'll protect the sanctuaries. Is that so hard to comprehend?"

Bronzes were the most warlike of the metallic dragons, sometimes serving in human armies if the cause was just and the pay generous, and Ulreel plainly resented being interrupted as well as the implication he was a dullard. His wings spread, his legs flexed, preparing to leap, and his long neck swelled with the threat of a blast of lightning or noxious gas.

Then, however, he caught control of his temper, and simply growled, "I understand all you have said, just as I know your reputation for wisdom. Still, no one is infallible."

"Indeed not," Lareth said. "Fortunately, in this bleak hour, I have something better than my own poor wits to guide me. I have the dreams the gods vouchsafed me. Visions that show Nexus's enchantment is the only way to avert calamity. Otherwise, we'll lay waste to the cities of men and hammer the small folk down into savagery. We'll slaughter them until the land is red and muddy with their blood. It may be we'll wipe them out entirely. Is that what you want? Is that what any of you want?"

Toward the end, the king's voice rose in a howl of lamentation, as if the massacre he described had already occurred. He was famous for his calmness and dignity no less than his wisdom, and it was possible that his loss of composure impressed the assembled dragons as nothing else could. For the mistrust and resentment seemed to bleed out of them, while a mingled dread and resolve rose to take their place.

"My friend," Havarlan said, "we've known each other for centuries, and I've never seen you commit an ignoble act or set a foolish course. If you say this is the only way, the Talons of Justice will help you as best we can."

"Thank you." Lareth twisted his neck to peer down at the golds below him. "I hope I can depend on the lords as well."

If Tamarand hesitated, it was only for an instant then he said, "Of course, Your Resplendence. We await your orders."

Chatulio snorted and whispered, "That's it, then. If the golds and silvers are united, they can stuff it down everybody else's throat."

Perhaps he was right. The wyrms found it necessary to palaver on for another two hours, but in time, almost everyone, however grudgingly, agreed to Lareth's plan.

Kara thought, I should do the same. Many of these drakes are my elders, some by a thousand years. Surely any wisdom I possess is as nothing compared to theirs. Besides, my scales don't shine like metal. I'm an oddity here. The golds and the rest accept me as a distant cousin, but how likely is it that any of them truly cares what I think?

Yet she had to speak. Her nightmares demanded that of her, as well.

"Your Resplendence!" she called.

Perhaps suspecting what was afoot, Chatulio edged away from her.

Lareth turned in her direction and said, "Yes . . . forgive me, daughter of song. I know most of those gathered here, but you and I have never met before."

"My name is Karasendrieth, and I wish to ask, what causes the frenzy? Can you tell me? Or can Nexus, who knows so many secrets?"

Lareth nodded to the dragon wizard, inviting him to answer.

"I fear," Nexus said, "that no one has ever solved that particular riddle."

"If we know so little about it," Kara said, "then how can we be so confident of sleeping till it passes? What if it never does, and we slumber until we waste away of thirst and starvation?"

"That's ridiculous," Lareth said. "The Rage always subsides. The madness is already tainting your thoughts, prompting you to fear things that can never come to be."

"You said yourself, this Rage promises to be different. The worst ever. Perhaps it will be the one that seizes us in its claws and never lets go."

"My dreams assure me that won't happen."

"I have my own nightmares," Kara said, "and my own premonitions of disaster, but they, coupled with my reason, point to a different path than the one you recommend. Why not attack this affliction as we would any other enemy who sought to cripple or corrupt us? Why not identify the cause, determine the cure, and rid ourselves of the frenzy once and for all?"

As she finished, she hoped someone would call out in support of her idea, but nobody did. Instead, the wyrms just stared at her.

Then Lareth said, "It's not a disease, but simply a part of being a dragon. For as far back as anyone remembers, we've always suffered from the frenzy, our wicked kindred the most susceptible, but even metal and gem wyrms succumbing from time to time."

"I've conjectured," Nexus said, "that the Rage is an inevitable consequence of our link to the primal forces of the cosmos, to which we are bound more intimately than other forms of life."

"But you don't *know*," Kara said. "What if you're wrong? What if we could find a remedy?"

"Even if such a thing is possible," said the mage, "it's preposterous to imagine we could accomplish it in the brief period of lucidity that remains to us."

"Accordingly," said Lareth, "we won't try. Not now. It will be difficult enough already, persuading all our kin to submit to the binding. Some will be suspicious of our true motives or in their pride imagine they have the strength to withstand the Rage. Give them the false hope that if they hold out just a little longer, Nexus will produce a cure, and it will make them even more reluctant."

"What of the reds, blacks, blues, whites, and greens?" Kara said. "They won't submit to you and the lords, and they're going to frenzy, too, unless somebody stops it. What about the mayhem they'll commit?"

"The small folk must withstand them as best they can," said the king. "At least we won't heighten the threat by running amok alongside them."

"The humans have weathered the storm before," Havarlan said.

"This will be the worst storm," Kara said, "and it finds them depleted and divided. Some regions have yet to recover from the conflict with the sahuagin. Cormyr just concluded a civil war. Around the Moonsea, where I make my home, the city-states squabble—"

"Enough!" Lareth thundered, so much flame spewing from his jaws that for a second, Kara believed he was actually attacking her. "I've listened patiently to your fancies and exposed the fallacies they contain. Now it's time for you to heed the wisdom of those older, wiser, and stronger than yourself."

Kara lowered her head in submission and for the rest of the parley said no more.

When the conclave broke up, Chatulio flew southeast, following the Galenas as the mountain range bent itself around the Moonsea. Winging in pursuit, Kara called out to him several times, but he didn't stop. Perhaps the copper was uncommonly hard of hearing for a dragon, but even so it was discouraging, almost enough to make a bard lose faith in the power of her voice.

Well, if he couldn't hear her, she'd simply have to overtake him. She flattened her body to split the air more easily, pounded her wings as fast and as powerfully as she was able, and streaked forward.

Before long, she was close enough to make out individual ruddy-brown scales on his back. She called out once more, and still he didn't so much as glance around. It was inconceivable that he didn't hear her, so he must have been ignoring her.

If he'd decided he wanted nothing to do with her, it was pointless to pursue him any farther. But his rudeness rankled, particularly after the way Lareth had put her in her place, and anger surged inside her. Her throat tingled, offering to discharge its lightning. Resolved to force Chatulio to acknowledge her existence at the very least, she flew even faster. She could only manage such a sprint for a brief time, but that was all she needed.

She caught up with the copper and reached out to grab him by the tail. The instant she touched him, his body popped with a sort of juicy rasp. A burst of the appropriate rotten-egg stink accompanied the flatulent sound, and she snatched her snout back from the foulness.

Behind her, someone laughed. She wheeled to see the real Chatulio flashing his gap-toothed leer and sitting atop one of the peaks. How he'd successfully substituted the phantasm for himself, she couldn't imagine.

She glided back, furled her wings, and lit before him, the snow cold against her feet and tail.

"Do you ever run out of pranks?" she asked.

"I hope not," Chatulio said. "Hello again, Karasendrieth. What's on your mind?"

"I want to discuss the council with you."

"As if we didn't all drone on long enough."

"You didn't," she said, "but from the things you whispered, I thought you might share my views. If so, you didn't declare it to the gathering at large."

He tossed his V-shaped head, the jaws tapered and dainty by dragon standards, a pair of long, segmented horns sweeping back behind.

"When have gold and silver ever heeded copper?" he asked.

"Then you do agree with me."

"I suppose. I don't much fancy the idea of letting a gold put me to sleep for as long as it suits him. What if it's all just a trick to plunder our hoards, and commit obscene violations upon our insensible persons?" He grinned and added, "All right, I admit, I don't really believe that, but I'm still not convinced. Maybe if His Redundancy had come across as serene and godlike as his legend makes him out to be, but he wasn't quite what I expected."

"I suppose," Kara said, "he seemed agitated because of his worry over what's to come. Perhaps if we were wise, that would have made him more persuasive, not less. Most of the others seemed to take it that way. Still, you and I are in agreement."

"Which means little, unless you've concocted a better scheme. I may not want to submit to Nexus's enchantments, but I want to kill and devour innocent small folk even less. They give me indigestion."

She eyed him askance for a moment before deciding the comment was just another joke.

"As the parley unfolded," she said, "I took note of those few who appeared the most disgruntled and those who looked as though they might speak out in support of me if, like you, they hadn't deemed it futile."

"I marked them, too."

"We could contact them and organize a cabal to study and ultimately cure the Rage."

"A chore even Nexus considers impossible."

"Has he ever really tried?" Kara asked. "Has anyone bothered, when we generally go for hundreds of years without an outbreak, and up until now we've had other ways to keep the fury from forcing us into evil?"

"Maybe not. Still, do you even have an idea of where to begin?"

"Not yet," she admitted, "but we're wyrms. Each of us has a clever mind and his own store of esoteric knowledge. Surely, if we ponder together, we can come up with a notion or two, in which case, what harm can it do to explore them? If our efforts come to nothing, then when the Rage threatens to overtake us, we'll simply retreat to the refuges as Lareth bade us."

"While if we actually solve the problem, we'll make the haughty golds and silver look like dunces," Chatulio laughed. "I like the way you think, bluebird. Let's do it."

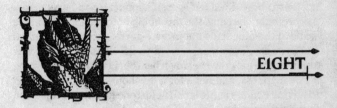

EIGHT

14 Hammer, the Year of Rogue Dragons

The last leaves dropped from the branches, and snowstorms whistled out of the north. One year died, another commenced, and through it all, foul hungers and violent urges nibbled at Kara's mind. It occasionally happened even when she wore human form, which she did except when circumstances demanded otherwise.

Resisting the onset of lunacy as best they could, she and Chatulio recruited wyrms sympathetic to their cause, who then conceived various avenues of investigation. To Kara, some of their hypotheses seemed implausible if not preposterous, symptomatic of the corruption of the originators' reason. Others had their basis in such obscure lore that she couldn't even understand them. Yet even had her fellows ceded her the authority, she would have forbidden none of the inquiries that sent them flying to the far corners of Faerûn. In truth, they knew nothing of the doom that menaced them. What, then, could they do, except grope frantically in the dark?

Frantically and futilely it seemed, for one by one the drakes reported failure. Until late one night, in Melvaunt, a walled settlement of smiths and traders on the Moonsea's northern shore, Kara felt herself slipping into a bleak mood. Accordingly, she sang, the throbbing notes echoing from the walls of the miniscule but private garret room she'd rented. But for once, even music failed to lift her spirits. She was about to give up, crawl between her thin blankets and sagging straw mattress, and hope for a few hours of oblivion, when the dying embers in the small fieldstone hearth crackled and flared a fiercer red.

Alarmed, she jumped out of her rickety chair, recoiled a step toward the shuttered window, and prepared to recite a defensive spell if necessary. A cloud of gray smoke billowed forth from the fireplace as if it had a wind behind it, even though that couldn't be. The fumes massed themselves into the vague shape of a dragon's head, while the sparks inside gathered to form a pair of slanted, luminous eyes. The apparition pivoted to stare at Kara but made no effort to harm her.

"Enough, Chatulio," she sighed.

Evidently the copper had returned from the steppeland of the Ride sooner than expected, and no matter how frustrating their mission became, his relish for juvenile pranks never flagged.

But the image in the smoke laughed an ugly little laugh and said, "No, Karasendrieth, not this time. Chatulio's still far away, and in fact, so am I. I conjured this sending to give you something on which to rest your gaze. It's been my experience that people prefer that to a voice that simply speaks from the air."

"Who are you?"

"An ally. Call me Brimstone."

She frowned, for it seemed an ill-omened name, suggestive of devils and the tortures of the damned. Though conceivably a gold or brass, with his ability to breathe flame, might bear it.

"An ally in what battle?" she replied.

Despite the vague inconstancy of his smoky features, Brimstone managed a sneer and said, "Scrying, I watched Lareth's conclave. I listened to you and Chatulio hatch your plot as well, so it's no use playing ignorant. I know you and your comrades are trying to stop the Rage, and fortunately for you, I mean to help."

"Then why haven't you come forward before now?"

"As you understand nothing, and your studies lead nowhere, I saw no advantage. Now, however, I require a service of you."

Kara neither trusted Brimstone nor appreciated his condescension, but her self-imposed task was too important for her to refuse to hear him out.

"What service?" she asked.

"Do you know of the Cult of the Dragon?"

"Of course," she said.

It was a secret society of lunatics who imagined evil wyrms were destined to become undead entities and ascend to mastery of the world. To hasten the fulfillment of their prophecies, they ingratiated themselves with the chromatic drakes by providing various forms of aid and support and furnished the means of transformation when the objects of their worship opted to avail themselves of them. Apparently they imagined that when the wyrms achieved dominion over Faerûn, they'd reward their longtime helpers with authority over their fellow men.

"I think they have something to do with the Rage," said the apparition.

"How could that be? The cult has only existed for a few hundred years. The frenzy has afflicted dragonkind since the beginning of time."

"Still, it's possible they at least know something about it," Brimstone replied. "I've watched the cult for a long time, seeking to foil their schemes whenever practical. Of late, I became aware that they have a chapter in Lyrabar. Unfortunately, as you probably know, scrying doesn't always work, especially if you're trying to view the activities of wizards and priests who've warded themselves against it. I gleaned something of their activities, but not enough. For that reason, I resolved to hire a spy to infiltrate the cabal."

"A human spy," Kara guessed.

"Yes. The problem was, where and how to find him? I'm not like the bronzes who serve Queen Sambryl and live openly in the heart of her city. The small folk know nothing of my presence, and I wish it to remain so. Happily, not far from my lair, a crew of laborers from Lyrabar was digging a drainage canal. I spied on them and found a young man called Gorstag Helder.

"He seemed as if he might be brave and quick-witted enough to do the job," Brimstone continued. "Just as importantly, he thought himself better than he was. He imagined that somehow, it was only cruel injustice that barred him from the life of ease so many in Lyrabar enjoy. He hated manual labor, and never would have stooped to it had starvation not forced his hand. He intended to earn just enough to keep him alive for a few more tendays, then rush back to the city, where, you may be certain, shame would keep him from admitting to anyone that he'd ever in his life laid hands on a shovel."

"Except that you approached him first."

"Yes," said the phantasm. A bit of the wood smoke was diffusing away from the conjured image to fill the garret with haze. It smelled pleasant enough but stung Kara's eyes. "I did so cloaked in a semblance of human form. I'd seen in the fool's mind that he harbored romantic notions about the Harpers, so I led him to believe I was one. Once I accomplished that, he was eager to serve me."

Kara disliked Brimstone's obvious contempt for his human pawn but supposed that, too, was beside the point.

"Did Helder manage to worm his way into the cult?" she asked.

"Yes, and he told me they were jubilant because some new scheme was underway. I ordered him to find out what it was, but then he stopped sneaking out into the countryside to report, and no matter what magic I employ, I can't locate him. Nor can I go into Lyrabar to seek him. I can veil myself in illusion to fool others for a time, but I can't actually assume human shape."

"But a song dragon can," she said.

"Exactly. You could find Gorstag and fetch him to me. Or bring me his report."

"It's likely the actual cultists realized he was a spy and murdered him."

"But it isn't certain. Perhaps, for some reason, he simply can't get away. Even if he is dead, he may conceivably have left notes or some other indication of what he learned."

Kara frowned, deliberating.

Finally she said, "You still haven't given me any solid reason to believe the cult's plans and the Rage are connected."

Brimstone sneered and said, "Do you think it mere coincidence that both are occurring at the same time?"

"You haven't told me who you are, either. An unfamiliar name means nothing."

"It's all I'm willing to give," he replied, "so long as we're talking through the ether. Some other adept might overhear. I'll reveal myself when you come to me in Impiltur."

"How would I find you?"

"Travel northeast from Lyrabar after night has fallen. Five miles beyond the city, you'll find a ring of menhirs on a hill. Nine of the stones are still standing, but the tenth has fallen down. Go to the center of the circle and speak my name. I'll guide you from there."

The image in the smoke melted into shapelessness.

Kara gathered her few possessions, threw her cloak over her shoulders, and departed the inn. Outside, the air carried the hot-metal tang of foundries and forges, even on such a bitterly cold night.

The streets were mostly deserted, and it didn't take her long to find a square that afforded both the room and the privacy to shapeshift without alarming any of the inhabitants of the town. She swelled into reptilian form, spread her wings, and sprang into the air. The north wind bore her onward. In time, it carried her across the Moonsea, along the marshy river Lis, and on down the eastern shore of the Dragon Reach.

Until Llimark intercepted her.

NINE

16 Hammer, the Year of Rogue Dragons

Even in the dark, Kara recognized the gold by the way he carried himself in flight, his long neck bent in a distinctive S curve. The two of them had been comrades at one time, fighting to turn back a horde of orcs and ogres from a human village—which didn't mean she wanted to deal with Llimark just then.

She thought of diving to hide in the Flooded Forest but realized it would be pointless. He'd spotted her before she'd noticed him, as evidenced by the fact that he was winging straight toward her. If she tried to evade him, it would only arouse his suspicions.

Instead, she maneuvered toward him, and they circled one another as dragons often did when they wished to converse on the wing.

"Hello, old friend," she called.

"Karasendrieth," Llimark replied. "King Lareth commands that you accompany me into his presence."

"I don't understand" she lied.

She flicked her wings, trying to gain a little altitude without him realizing she was shifting into a more advantageous position for combat.

It was a mistake, for he noticed and compensated, and must have known she contemplated resistance.

"You do understand" he said. "Did you think you and your fellow rogues could conduct all these bizarre experiments and stick your noses into strange corners of the world without the lords or the Talons noticing? Azhaq caught Cejor in the act of brewing some useless potion, and she gave up your name, not that Lareth needed it to guess you were involved. You'll tell him the names of the rest of the rebels, then submit to Nexus's spell immediately."

"We're not 'rebels,'" she replied. "And Lareth has no authority over anyone but his fellow golds."

"He does for the time being, while it's necessary. Why can't you accept that?"

"Why can't you see that my plans don't conflict with his? If my comrades and I can't find a cure in time to avert the frenzy, I give you my word we'll sleep with the rest of you."

"Lareth told you, your efforts will produce disunity and dissension, and that could be disastrous."

"I disagree."

She pondered whispering the spell to steal his breath weapon but decided against it. He'd probably hear, and it might provoke him into attacking.

"Curse it," he said, "it doesn't matter whether you agree or not. You simply have to obey. Otherwise, my orders are to compel you, or if necessary, kill you outright. I beg you not to let it come to that."

Kara sighed and said, "You volunteered to hunt me, didn't you, so no one would have to hurt me? You thought I'd defy a stranger but give in to a friend."

"Was I correct?"

"Can't you understand how wrong this is? Never before have golds attempted to dictate how their kin must behave, let alone threatened to slaughter them over a simple difference of opinion. Lareth claimed the Rage is already rotting my judgment, but I think he's the one whose mind is failing, he and all those who follow where he leads."

"That's absurd. The king is the eldest, wisest, and noblest of us all, thus surely the best able to stave off frenzy."

"We don't know that," Kara replied. "We don't know anything. That's the problem I'm trying to correct."

"Not anymore. Will you relent?"

"No," she answered. "Will you, for the sake of the battles we fought together? You can tell Lareth you couldn't find me."

"No, I can't," Llimark replied. "Forgive me, my friend."

He spread his jaws wide and blasted out a plume of vapor, obviously hoping to subdue her without injury. That was why he hadn't used his flame. But the breath weapon he had employed was devastating enough. If it struck her, it would wash away a significant portion of her strength, after which, she would likely be no match for him.

She snapped one wing low, the other high, and veered off in a steep descent. It worked. She dodged his breath, but the maneuver had brought her below him, exactly the vulnerable position she'd hoped to avoid.

He followed up at once, roaring words of power. She twisted, seeking to blast him with her own breath and so disrupt his conjuring, but it took her a second too long to orient on her target. Llimark finished the spell and a cloud of filthy fog boiled into existence around her. It reeked of decay, and the mere touch of it on her scales made her stomach twist with nausea. Unable to abide it, retching, she floundered clear. By that time, the gold was swooping at her.

She folded her wings and fell like a stone, avoiding him. Unfortunately, by the time she managed to level off, she was gliding only a few yards above the surface of the black water, which was to say, nearly out of space to maneuver. Zigzagging back and forth, she sang a spell.

Four exact images of herself, each moving precisely as she did, shimmered into being around her. Since Llimark's ears and nose were as keen as his eyes, it probably wouldn't take him long to pick out the real Kara from the false. But he faltered for an instant, and she finally managed to spit, her lightning crackling upward.

To be precise, her exhalation wasn't a thunderbolt in the purest sense but a burst of sparkling vapor charged with the essence of lightning. Wings pounding, Llimark veered to avoid it. He was a shade too slow, and it caught him in the chest. He flailed spastically, and for a moment, she thought he might fall.

He didn't, though. He regained control and swooped at his foe. Like Kara, he was relatively young for a dragon, yet still resilient enough to survive one such attack.

She couldn't hurl another, not right away. After each expenditure, a wyrm's breath required time to renew itself. She climbed, her illusory counterparts mirroring her actions. She also started to sing a spell.

As he plunged at her, Llimark breathed flame, and it was Kara's turn to try to dodge the expanding burst. The blaze washed over her flank, and the fierce heat made her cry out in pain. It spoiled her incantation and the magic died unborn.

The fire's touch also burned Kara's phantasms from existence. Llimark drove on at what had become his only possible target. Still stuck at a lower altitude, the song dragon tried to fling herself out of the way. Unfortunately, the brush of his searing breath had left her slow and clumsy, and he scored on her anyway. His talons ripped her shoulder and the base of her wing, and he flashed on past.

For a second, she only felt a kind of shock, and the pain flared. The stroke of her wings uneven, the wounded one scarcely able to beat at all, she floundered, struggling to stay aloft. Llimark wheeled, orienting on her.

"Yield!" he roared. "You can't win now."

"I can't surrender," she replied. "Not when it's possible my friends and I are our people's only hope."

"Then I'm sorry," he said.

He climbed, evidently preparing to dive at her. It gave her a moment to prepare for the next attack. Her lightning still hadn't returned to her, and she could feel that it wouldn't, not in time, so she started singing another incantation.

He evidently heard, and as he commenced his dive, responded with his own bellowed cabalistic rhyme. Somehow he finished first, and for an instant, the world blazed as bright as the sun.

Squinting her eyes shut, Kara flinched from the glare, but managed to sing the last few notes of her spell with the proper rhythm and intonation. Power seethed inside her claws. The problem was, she could no longer see where to direct it. For the moment, she was blind, her field of vision a meaningless chaos of sickly yellow afterimage.

She listened for the rustle of his wings, then cast the magic at the sound. A heartbeat later, he slammed into her and grappled, his talons digging into her hide, his tail twining around her. Evidently he meant to cling to her and rip until she capitulated or died.

Twisting her neck, she struck at him. By sheer good luck, her jaws snapped shut on solid flesh, and her fangs plunged through his scales deep into the muscle beneath. Her final spell had found its target to soften Llimark's natural armor.

The unexpected pain made him fumble his grip on her. She thrashed, broke free, and at last felt hot tingling power poised in her throat. Still guided solely by sound, scent, and touch, she spat sizzling lightning.

Llimark screamed. She braced herself for his next attack, but it didn't come. After a few seconds, she heard something big splash down in the Reach.

When her sight returned, she peered down at the water but couldn't see the gold. Had he sunk beneath the waves? Had she killed him? She prayed it wasn't so.

Still, she couldn't search for long. She had to attend to her own survival. She could feel that her torn, throbbing wing wouldn't bear her up much longer. Indeed, a wave of faintness warned that she might not even cling to consciousness, or life itself, for any length of time.

Kara glided to the road that ran along the shore, landed, and shifted to human form. In that guise, she wouldn't frighten the humans on whose kindness she must now depend, and with luck, it would hide her from any other dragons hunting her at Lareth's behest. She stumbled on toward Ylraphon.

TEN

11 Alturiak, the Year of Rogue Dragons

It was late by the time Kara finished her story. Selûne and her glittering haze of Tears had reached the precincts of the western sky. Most of the crew lay snoring about the deck, with only a couple still wakeful to guide the galley safely through the night. The song dragon bard, Dorn, Pavel, and Will had bundled themselves in their cloaks but shivered anyway. Their manifest discomfort made Raryn glad arctic dwarves were impervious to the cold.

Still, tired and chilly though they were, none of the hunters showed any inclination to crawl beneath his blankets. Kara had given them too much to chew on.

"Now I understand why you stared at my bloody hands when I was cleaning the tuna," Raryn said.

Kara looked ashamed and said, "Yes. At that moment, the frenzy was gnawing at me, and I couldn't help imagining your blood. How it would spurt, the warmth of it, the taste. But I swear, I'd never hurt you."

"Until you go mad," growled Dorn.

His friends had gathered in close to Kara to hear her tale, but he hung farther back.

"Yes," she replied. "Until then."

"A Rage of Dragons," said Pavel, sitting cross-legged on the deck, his mantle puddled around him. "Now, in our lifetime. In the abstract, everyone knew another would come eventually, and when we realized two flights were happening at once, naturally, the possibility occurred to me. Still, it's a hard idea to wrap your mind around."

"Maybe if you're stupid," said Will, perched on a crate, short legs dangling. He shifted his gaze back to the willowy, silver-haired song dragon. "Do you really think this . . . Gorstag, was it, and Brimstone can help you cure the frenzy?"

Kara sighed and said, "All I know is that I have to explore every possibility. Because so far, we rogues, as Lareth considers us, have gotten nowhere."

"Well, don't worry about it," the halfling said. "Though our band specializes in tracking down savage beasts in the wild, it just so happens I also know how to find shady characters in the city. I'll flush out Gorstag for you. The only hitch is, you didn't hire us for that particular job, but I'm sure we can work something out. A couple more baubles should cover our time and expenses."

"No," said Dorn.

"I'm willing to give you all the jewels I carry," Kara said, "with a pledge of more besides."

"No," the half-golem repeated. "You wanted protection while you were wounded and hiding in human form, and you tricked us into providing it. Very well, we'll keep our bargain. But once we reach Lyrabar, my partners and I want nothing more to do with you."

"Let's not be hasty," Pavel said. "I don't blame Kara for concealing her true nature from everybody, new friends included, when other wyrms were trying to hunt her down."

"Forgive or condemn as you like, it makes no difference," Dorn said with a scowl. "When we dock, we're cutting her loose."

"Why?" asked Will. "I don't see anyone else lining up to shower us with gems."

"We already have enough to live comfortably until spring, and something else will come along. It always does."

Pavel laughed a humorless laugh then said, "You're right about that. We'll have more offers than we can handle, with all the drakes in Faerûn on the rampage at once. And that's the point. We've wandered into something bigger than we could ever have imagined. Perhaps it was chance, or maybe the Morninglord guided our steps. Either way, he'd want us to see it through."

"If a Rage is actually coming," said Dorn, "we will see it through, by plying our trade as usual. Across the world, other people who know how to draw a bow or cast a spell will fight the wyrms as well, and in the end, we 'small folk' will withstand them as we always have before."

"What if it's worse this time?" Pavel asked. "What if the drakes never regain their senses? What if they just keep coming, month after month and year after year?"

"You only imagine that happening because Kara claims it will, and she admits she's already going crazy. According to her own story, Lareth, Nexus, and a bunch of older, wiser dragons disagree with her."

"Yet Lareth does believe this Rage will be the most terrible ever," Kara said.

"Really, I'm no more interested in his opinion than I am in yours."

"Curse it," said Pavel, "you're letting your hatred of dragons addle you. You want a full-scale Rage to happen, because it'll give you the chance to fight wyrms by the dozen, and never mind that you won't live through it."

"Nonsense," spat Dorn. "You and Will are the ones who are daft. You go soft in the head any time you see a pretty face, even after you know it's just a mask, and he drools whenever he catches a glimpse of gold. But think: Kara has no real reason to think the key to stopping a Rage is in Lyrabar, or that such a thing is possible at all. All she's offered you are wild guesses and wishful thinking. You want to save lives, priest? Fine. Then let's hurry back to Thentia and get the wizards busy outfitting us for the fight to come."

"We can do that afterward," said Will. "Better. Because the mages will want coin, and thanks to the heedless blather of somebody I could name, we didn't collect any pay in Ylraphon."

"Helping Kara is the right thing to do," said Pavel. "Truly. I feel it."

"Well, I feel differently," said Dorn. "So you can follow my lead or go your own way."

Raryn cleared his throat, and they all looked around at him. "Dorn has a point," he said.

Pavel frowned. "How can you say that?"

"Because it's true," the ranger said. He stretched, and his spine popped. "We can handle further outbreaks of the Rage the way we dealt with the drakes in Ylraphon, only better, because next time, with luck, we'll have more time to prepare. We'll arm ourselves with the proper gear, recruit and train helpers, make plans, and build traps and fortifications. If we do our job well enough, and there aren't too many dragons, we'll beat the creatures when they come. We'll save Thentia, or wherever it is we choose to make our stand.

"The catch," Raryn continued, "is that we'll have protected one place—one town out of all the habitations in Faerûn. As you said, Dorn, other men-at-arms, sorcerers, and clerics will defend their own homelands. Still, the dragons will descend on countless folk who have no one to fight for them, no one who stands a chance, anyway. The nice thing about Kara's scheme is that it offers us at least a slim hope of saving those lives as well."

Dorn glared down at him and asked, "So you're against me, too?"

"No," Raryn said. "It isn't like that with Will, Pavel, or me. After all we've been through, you ought to know it isn't. We're friends, so let's stick together. If the dragons Rage, we'll need each other more than ever."

The big man took a deep breath and let it out slowly.

"All right," he said. "We'll help the wyrm finish her errand. We'll look for this Helder person and take Kara to Brimstone, who- or whatever he is. But that's the end of it."

Dorn turned and stalked away, the deck groaning and bouncing beneath the stamp of his iron foot. It woke a sailor, who muttered a drowsy curse.

ELEVEN

2 Ches, the Year of Rogue Dragons

Taegan circulated through the soiree, gossiping, joking, paying compliments, flirting, drinking in moderation, dancing the occasional dance, and in general, playing to perfection the part of a sophisticated Impilturan blade. That was what he wanted to be, what he'd worked tirelessly to become, and he thoroughly enjoyed the performance. That night, though, he couldn't quite shake the feeling that it was a performance, an impersonation, and that if he slipped for even a moment, everyone would see him as the interloper he truly was, a barbarian with no proper place in the life of a splendid city.

Well, he wouldn't slip. However he looked on the outside, and whatever esoteric elven disciplines he'd mastered, he was human in his heart. So he told himself, and as if in affirmation of his conviction, a lackey approached, murmured his name, and discreetly proffered a folded pink slip of paper scented with rosewater.

Written with extravagant flourishes in a feminine hand the brief note invited Taegan to meet its author in the gazebo in the east garden. It was unsigned, perhaps for fear it would fall into the hands of a disapproving father, husband fiancée, or chaperone, or maybe simply to lend a piquant air of mystery.

Taegan decided that whoever had written it, a dalliance might be just the thing to fend off the sour mood that was creeping up on him. He took his leave of his current companions, who, having spotted the missive, offered ribald, good-natured gibes, and exited the gleaming marble ballroom with its orchestra and buffet.

Outside the mansion, the night was cold enough to make him reconsider his amorous inclinations. But perhaps the lady didn't intend to conduct their entire tryst outdoors, or conceivably she possessed some petty magic to warm her immediate vicinity. He strolled on down a paved walk with banks of shoveled snow heaped to either side, past bare trees, inactive fountains, and statuary. Above the wall encircling the grounds, stars burned in the black sky.

The gazebo proved to be an octagonal structure with a conical roof, its facade shrouded in dead-looking vines that would presumably resurrect themselves in the spring. It had benches inside, but no one was sitting on them, or loitering anywhere in sight, for that matter.

Taegan smiled wryly. Either his correspondent was having difficulty getting away, or else she was one of those females who believed it enhanced her allure to make a male wait. Whatever the reason for the delay, he hoped he wouldn't freeze to death before she deigned to appear and decided to saunter about in an effort to keep warm. Really, more vigorous exercise would serve him better, but a rake should never look uncomfortable, put out, or inconvenienced.

At first, he was merely impatient, but as the minutes passed, gradually he became uneasy. In the days following the battle in the street, he'd walked warily, but when nothing happened and other matters demanded his attention, he abandoned his precautions. Taegan had come to wonder if he'd lowered his guard too soon. What if Gorstag's cultists had finally made their move? What if they'd lured him out in the dark to attack him?

Ridiculous. He had no reason to suspect such a thing. Yet the idea nagged at him until he had to do something to appease it. He drew his rapier, murmured an incantation, and dusted the sword with powdered lime and carbon. Power groaned through the air, a line of icicles hanging from the gazebo's eaves shattered, and for a moment, rainbows rippled along the blade. Satisfied that, until morning, it would be about as deadly a weapon as he could make it, he slid it back into the scabbard.

"Interesting," said a husky feminine voice.

Taegan turned. A woman sat inside the shadowy gazebo. He couldn't tell much about her. She'd bundled up in a voluminous cloak, pulled up the cowl, and covered her face with a layer of black veil.

He did know one thing. He'd been waiting right in front of the doorway. She couldn't simply have sneaked past him to appear in her present position. Somehow, magic was involved.

"I can cast that spell, too," the stranger continued, "but my master taught me to make the passes differently. Evidently avariels have a cruder style of conjuring. But then, everyone's magic is crude compared to his."

Taegan wondered if she was talking about Sammaster, or at any rate, the person Gorstag had believed to be the legendary madman, but instinct warned him not to let on he'd ever heard the name.

Instead, he bowed and said, "It's a delight to make your acquaintance, my lady. May your servant request the privilege of knowing your name?"

"I'm sorry," she said, "you may not. Not yet, anyway. I will tell you I'm Lyrabar's Wearer of Purple." She paused as if to judge his reaction, but Taegan didn't have to feign ignorance. The peculiar title meant nothing to him. "You may address me as High Lady."

As one would address a duchess, he thought. She thinks well of herself.

"High Lady it is, then," he said. "I assume I needn't introduce myself, since you asked me here."

"Indeed not, Maestro. Come and sit."

Why not? If she tried to cast a spell on him, it would be helpful to have her within arm's reach.

"Nothing could give me greater pleasure," Taegan said.

He entered the gazebo, bowed again, and seated himself on the bench across from her.

Up close, she smelled of the same floral perfume as the note, but that and her voice were the only details to suggest she was a relatively young, well-educated woman or even alive. Otherwise, her shapeless mantle, hood, and mask of dark lace made her look like a specter lurking in the gloom.

"Did it alarm you," she asked, "when I appeared out of nowhere?"

"To the contrary," he said. "It was the fulfillment of my fondest yearnings."

"I did it to show you how easily we can take you unawares. In which case, your skill with a sword won't save you."

"It almost sounds as if you're threatening me, High Lady, and that truly does surprise me. Ordinarily, I enjoy amiable relations with the fairer sex. It's specimens of my own gender who more often conceive a desire to poke holes in me. How, pray tell, have I offended?"

"Surely you see such evasions are a waste of time," the woman said. "A couple of my brothers survived their encounter with you to report your meddling, and you're the only avariel in Lyrabar. You can't possibly hope to convince me it was some other winged elf who flew to Gorstag's aid."

If the zombies' living allies were her "brothers," then that ended any faint hope Taegan had entertained that she might represent the Harpers. Rather, she must belong to the Cult of the Dragon.

He gave her a grin and said, "Fair enough, High Lady, it was I. In my defense, I can only say that if I'd realized that Helder had trespassed against a maiden as captivating as you, I would have left him to his fate. But I didn't, and he owed me coin—coin I'd never collect in the event of his demise."

"I've thought a good deal about you," the veiled woman said. "You defended a traitor to the brotherhood and slew our wyvern. The creature wasn't a true Sacred One, but spilling its blood was a heinous sin nonetheless, and you deserve to die for it."

"That seems harsh for a first offense."

"I wouldn't be flippant if I were you," the woman threatened. "Your life balances on the edge of a knife. We would have killed you already, except that we want the answers to some questions. What did Gorstag tell you before he died?"

"Nothing," the avariel lied. "When I returned to him after the fight, he was already dead."

"What about when you first made contact with him?"

"I had to confront his pursuers," Taegan replied. "We didn't have time for conversation."

"And in the tendays prior to that?"

"Nothing. I had no idea he was in trouble until I chanced to spot him staggering along with your minions on his tail."

"I ordered him to try to recruit you to our cause," said the woman. "He claimed he had."

"But he didn't. Truly, I know nothing about your necromancers' coven or whatever it is, except that it seems to take a lot of you just to kill one undernourished novice fencer, and that you yourself are far too charming to squander your nights on such gauche companions."

"Who did Gorstag work for?" she asked, ignoring his flattery.

"You should have asked him."

"I would have, if the fool who first suspected him of being

a spy had communicated his suspicions instead of trying to deal with the matter by himself."

"It's hard to find good help."

"I already warned you to spare me your japes," the woman hissed. "Where is the tome?"

That would be the purple book. Didn't she realize Gorstag had stolen the folio as well? If not, Taegan had no intention of alerting her.

"I don't know what you mean," he lied.

"Yes, you do. Gorstag gave you a book written in cipher, or else you found it on his body."

"No," he replied. "Either he never took it in the first place, or he disposed of it somewhere before I found him."

"You're lying."

"A gentleman never lies to a lady about anything except his marital status or the depth of his devotion."

"We want the tome back, and your silence. We're even willing to buy them."

It was tempting. Gold always was. But even if he decided he was willing to betray Gorstag, he doubted the cultists would leave him alone once they recovered their text. Still, he might as well play along and see where it led.

"Alas, as I said, I don't have the volume in question. But just for curiosity's sake, suppose I could lay my hands on it. How much are you offering?"

"Ten thousand in gold," she said.

The sum was almost enough to blind him to loyalty and caution alike. Almost.

"Make it twenty," Taegan said, "and I'll see what I can do."

She sat quietly for a moment, then said, "You're lying."

He wondered how she knew. More magic, conceivably, or maybe she simply had good instincts.

"That's the second time you've accused me of that," Taegan retorted. "Let us thank Lady Firehair you're a woman. Otherwise, a gentleman might feel obliged to call you out."

"If I can't appeal to your greed, Maestro, what of your desire to go on breathing? I told you, my comrades and I are quite prepared to kill you."

"I beg you to forgive me if I don't blubber in terror, but have you any idea how often I fought when I first came to Lyrabar, simply to build a reputation?"

"I guarantee, you can't defend yourself against us."

"Oh, I trust I can make do. I slew your overgrown lizard, your walking dead men, and your live cutthroats, and I know how to suddenly pop up out of nowhere myself. It really isn't all that awesome a tri—"

Clutching a curve-bladed dagger, a black-gloved hand shot from a vent in the cultist's mantle. She leaped up and slashed at his throat.

Taegan hadn't seen her tense, lean forward, or make any other preparatory movement that would have given away her intention to attack. Still, he was on his guard and reacted instantly. He swayed backward, the cut fell short, and he punched her in the stomach. She floundered backward, banging the backs of her calves against the seat she'd just vacated, giving him space to spring to his feet.

They were still so close together that it would be awkward to use a rapier. He snatched out his poniard, poised it to thrust, then decided it might be better to take her alive. He grabbed the wrist of her knife arm, immobilizing it, reversed his own blade, and hammered her shrouded head with the pommel.

For a moment, the gilded knob seemed to meet resistance, and just a yielding softness. At the same time, his grip crushed her wrist into something he couldn't even feel inside his clenched fingers. With a rustle of fabric, she crumpled into an odd shallow heap like a tangle of dirty laundry. It didn't look as if anyone was inside.

Taegan crouched over it, tore the veil aside, and discovered that was in fact the case. The cloak and other garments had evidently constituted a sort of puppet, a contrivance that had allowed the Wearer of Purple to quiz him without coming within reach of his weapons.

The real cult mistress was presumably lurking nearby and might not be alone. While Taegan had wasted precious seconds wrestling with the decoy, she and her minions could already have advanced on the gazebo. He drew his rapier, sprang to the doorway, and came face to face with the thing that was hopping in.

It walked on two legs, had dirty white scales, and was half a head shorter than Taegan, though its torso was thicker, and it had to pull its wings in close to fit them through the doorway. Its snarling features, though somewhat manlike, reminded him of the wyvern. Was it a demon with dragon blood or something comparable? It made sense that the Wearer of Purple might conjure such beings to serve her.

It glared into Taegan's eyes. He felt strange for an instant, but that was all. Evidently it had tried and failed to cripple his mind. He thrust the rapier deep into its chest, and it collapsed, pawing weakly at its wound. It seemed astonished the blade had done it so much harm. Perhaps if he hadn't thought to enchant the weapon, it would have only have scratched the demon's hide or glanced off entirely.

Another such creature came scuttling forward, claws poised, its prehensile tail, possessed of a sting like the wyvern's, arching over its shoulder. Taegan decided to take the battle to the air, where, he suspected, he could outmaneuver the ash-colored spirit as he had its gigantic cousin. He ran right over the demon sprawled on the gazebo's little ring of porch, spread his wings, then heard the genuine Wearer of Purple chanting words of power.

Taegan's wing muscles cramped. He gasped at the unexpected stab of pain, then tried to beat his pinions anyway. That was even more excruciating and useless, too. The limbs were essentially paralyzed.

The onrushing demon pounced at him, clawing and biting, pointed tail striking like an adder. Its sting radiated a cold so intense that he could feel it even on such a frigid night. The chill would surely sear whatever the member pierced.

The creature attacked so furiously that it was challenging to find an opportunity to riposte. He pierced its membranous wing and its snout, but neither wound sufficed to put it down. The sting leaped at his chest, and he only just managed to twist out of the way.

The demon simultaneously raked at his head and whirled its sting in a low, cunning jab at his lead foot. He thrust the rapier through one of its misshapen hands, snatched his leg up, and stamped down, pinning the spirit's tail beneath it. Blessed Sune, the stinger was cold. Despite his boot, the chill nearly made him flinch away.

The two hurts, coming so close together, made the demon falter. He jerked the rapier from its extremity and drove it through its torso. The creature collapsed, and two more came shambling to take its place. The Wearer of Purple's voice commenced the sibilant rhymes of another spell.

Taegan realized he needed more of his own magic. Otherwise, the chances were good that his foes would overwhelm him. Even as he met the demons' advance with a sudden leap that he hoped would startle them, he whispered his own incantation.

Meanwhile, he pondered how best to use it. The same spell that had flung him into the wyvern's path could carry him back inside his host's mansion or beyond the wall enclosing the grounds to lose himself in the night. That might be the prudent course. But while he no longer found it worthwhile to initiate fights, he wasn't inclined to run from them, either. Moreover, it occurred to him that if he could only dispose of the Wearer of Purple, her followers might leave him alone thereafter. So he risked taking his eyes off the demons long enough to glance quickly around, whereupon he spotted another cloaked figure, veiled and hooded like the puppet, lurking in the shadow of a chestnut tree.

The world seemed to shatter and recreate itself all in an instant, and he was standing behind her. He drove his rapier at her back.

It should have been a killing stroke, but somehow she sensed him, left off conjuring, and spun around. The sword plunged through her arm and pinned it to her torso. It was a nasty wound. Perhaps he'd even pricked a lung. But not the heart as he'd intended.

Well, a second thrust would finish her. He yanked the rapier from her flesh, and she surprised him. He'd expected the shock of her injury to stun her for at least a moment or two. But she pounced at him, and as she scratched at his face, he realized she didn't look precisely like the puppet after all. Her white hands with their long, dark-lacquered nails were bare.

He tried to sidestep, and she snagged his cheek anyway. No matter, he thought, she'd missed the eye. As he shoved her away, however, making room for his sword to continue its work, his strength deserted him all at once, his knees buckling and the rapier nearly slipping from his grasp. It was happening more rapidly than even a potent poison could act. Once again, she'd crippled him with magic. Since he'd interrupted her casting, the power had likely come either from a talisman or some strange innate capability, not that it mattered at the moment.

She laughed, snatched out a claw-shaped dagger identical to the one the decoy had carried, and sprang. He gasped a battle cry and strained to raise his rapier. For a split second, he thought he wouldn't be able to manage it, and his strength surged back. Her own momentum served to drive his point deep into her abdomen. She gasped, and he pulled the sword back for the death stroke. At which point, the demons caught up with him.

Cursing, he had no choice but to wheel and defend himself from their assault. One was still on the ground, and the other was flapping through the air, at the moment higher than his rapier could reach. Taegan had guessed right, the wretched brutes did fly less nimbly than an avariel, for all the good that did him.

He lunged at the demon in front of him. His point drove into its chest, and it fell to its knees. But it wasn't finished.

Snarling, slavering blood, it clutched his blade with both fists while its tail stabbed repeatedly at his forearm.

Taegan understood what it was trying to do: immobilize the rapier, or disarm him altogether, while its comrade dived at him. He could have abandoned the sword and relied on his poniard, but he hadn't prepared a second enchantment to enhance a blade's capabilities, and thus he doubted the dagger could do his opponents any significant harm. No, he needed the longer weapon. Frantically parrying the sting with his off hand he hauled on the rapier with all his might, only to discover the creature was about as strong as he was. He carried a charm in his head to augment his natural strength but knew he had no time to cast it.

Fortunately, though a rapier was primarily a thrusting weapon, the edges were sharp, and at last the blade jerked free by slicing so deeply into the demon's fingers than it could no longer maintain its hold. Succumbing to its wounds at last, the creature collapsed facedown in the snow. Taegan looked up and thrust at the pallid thing plummeting at his head.

The rapier rammed deep into the demon's body a split second before it slammed down on him and smashed him to the ground. He floundered out from underneath it, distancing himself from its talons, fangs, and sting, only then discerning it was dead.

Good, but what about the Wearer of Purple? He pivoted, surveying the battlefield, and was disappointed to find her gone. The wounds he'd given her would have incapacitated most people, but evidently she had a strong constitution and a will to match. Or perhaps she'd drunk some restorative elixir.

He recovered the rapier and cloaked himself in magic that would make it more difficult for a foe to aim an attack at him, another spell he'd never found a chance to cast while the demons were pressing him hard. Then he followed the Wearer of Purple's footprints through the snow until they ended at one of the shoveled walks.

He picked a direction at random and continued the chase. But as the seconds passed, no cloaked figure appeared in the darkness ahead, and the path intersected with others, so he had to admit his quarry had eluded him.

Nor was that the end of his frustrations. When he returned to the vicinity of the gazebo, he discovered the demons had disappeared as well. Either their corpses had faded back into the infernal realm from which they'd originated, or—disquieting thought—the creatures had gradually recovered from their seemingly mortal wounds, risen, and limped away.

In any case, even if Taegan decided he wanted to ignore Gorstag's dying plea for secrecy, he had no proof of what had happened and doubted the authorities would credit his story without it. Other maestros had spun wild tales to enhance their reputations and drum up trade. Moreover, even if the paladins did, in some measure believe, they might find a way to turn the affair around on him somehow. To make it a pretext to denounce him as a threat to the peace, close his school, perhaps even banish or imprison him.

All things considered, he thought he was still on his own. And in considerable danger of catching a cold. His exertions had warmed him, but having stopped to catch his breath, the chill was settling into his bones.

Accordingly, he wiped the gore from his rapier, sheathed it, combed his hair, adjusted his attire, rearranged his features into the proper insouciant expression, and rejoined the ball. In time, his knotted, aching wing muscles relaxed.

TWELVE

12 & 13 Ches, the Year of Rogue Dragons

Will and Pavel found "Winking Murene" drinking raw spirit in a tiny excuse for a tavern, really just a brick alcove open to the wintry air blowing in from the street. The place did possess a door, but salvaged from somewhere and resting atop a pair of beer barrels, its tarnished brass handle and hinges still attached, the matchboarded panel was doing service as the bar. A couple of other kegs reposed on trestles behind it, while corked clay jugs and dented pewter cups sat along the shelves on the back wall.

When she realized the hunters were interested in her, Winking Murene gave them a scowl.

"What?" she demanded.

All in all, Will considered his present life preferable to the one he'd fled years before with his guild master crying for his blood, a falling out occasioned by his decision to restore a kidnapped child to its parents despite their failure to raise the ransom. Still, Lyrabar had given him a pang of nostalgia, for with its imposing architecture, manifest prosperity, and air of optimism and stability, its bountiful comforts and amusements, the place was a far cry from the rough Moonsea towns to which he'd become accustomed. Rather, it reminded him of the Sembian cities in which he'd spent his formative years.

Which meant the queen's men should have kicked out Winking Murene to keep up the tone, for like the grimy little pocket of poverty in which she dwelled and the ordinary surroundings in which she chose to swill her liquor, she seemed out of place. As her epithet suggested, one eyelid sagged so low it was hard to imagine she could see past it, but she was notably homely in other respects as well, obese, with red, scrofulous patches on her pasty skin. In a city so full of temples and shrines, it was hard to believe she couldn't find a healer to cure such a condition. Evidently she was simply too lazy to seek one out.

Still, despite her ugliness, sour body odor, and lack of manners, Pavel addressed her with flawless courtesy.

"Good afternoon, Maid, or is it Goodwife?" he said. "My name is Pavel Shemov. I'm a servant of Lathander. The halfling is Wilimac Turnstone. We understand you rent a room to a young man named Gorstag Helder."

"Then you understand wrong."

The cleric blinked, seemingly uncertain how to respond. Will thought he knew. He extracted a gold piece from his belt pouch and tossed it clinking onto the bar.

Her reaction surprised him. She stared at it and swallowed, as if she wanted to pick it up but didn't dare. That was when he realized she was afraid.

Pavel discerned the same thing and said, "Whatever you tell us, we won't let anyone know where we heard it."

"You're a priest of the dawn?" she asked, peering at him in the suspicious, truculent manner of the half-drunk. "Where are your robes?"

"Worn out," he said. "I've been traveling and had to replace them with what I could get."

"What do you care about Gorstag?"

"It's a long story, but I promise, we came to Lyrabar to help him."

She laughed and said, "You're too late for that."

Will's mouth tightened in vexation. He'd figured the spy was probably dead, but had hoped he was wrong.

"What happened to him?" asked the halfling.

She hesitated once more, then said, "I can't quite remember. If I had a little something more to jog my memory. . . ."

Will sent two more coins ringing after the first.

"It happened last month . . ." she said. "Everybody was talking about it. Late one night, the watch found a dead wyvern and dead people lying in the street. A number of the men were rotten, but apparently they'd been up walking around with the others until somebody cut them to pieces."

"What does that have to do with Gorstag?" asked Will.

He assumed a wyvern tied in with the Cult of the Dragon, but nothing else was clear.

"He was one of the corpses. A fresh one." She pulled back her sleeve and scratched one of her blemishes. Flakes of epidermis drifted to the floor. "The worst part is, the worthless fool was behind on his rent as usual."

"Did the guards seem to have any notions about what happened?" Pavel asked.

"How would I know?"

"Did they search his room?" asked Will.

"Yes."

"Did they take anything away?"

"How could they? He liked to put on airs and pretend he was better than the rest of us, but the truth was, he didn't have a rag to wipe his nose. It was pathetic."

Pavel said, "Thank you," then motioned for Will to step away from the woman. He stooped down and spoke in a lower voice. "I'm afraid your coin didn't buy much. We could try talking to the watch, I suppose, but—"

Will said, "We're not done here, you dunce. She was afraid to talk, remember? What has she told us so far that would account for that?" He turned back toward Winking Murene and said, "Give us the rest of it."

"I've told you all I know. Go away and leave me alone."

"You heard her," the burly man behind the makeshift bar warned.

His matted hair and beard were visibly astir with wriggling lice. He reached for the heavy club he kept leaning in the corner.

Pavel started to speak. Most likely he meant to neutralize the threat with a spell, but Will reacted at the same time, and his response was even faster. He spun the warsling and hurled a skiprock at the jugs on the top shelf. Even by his exacting standards, it was a good cast. The stone rebounded three times before running out of momentum, shattering four containers in all. Shards of pottery and torrents of spirit rained down on the tavernkeeper's lousy head, filling the air with the pungent smell of the drink. Evidently deciding that, on further consideration, Winking Murene's problems were none of his affair, he froze.

The landlady herself looked equally rattled.

"Don't hurt me." She turned to Pavel and said, "You're a priest. You can't let him stone me."

"Nobody wants to hurt you," Pavel said. "We simply need to know what you can tell us. It's important, and I already gave you my word we'll never reveal where the information came from."

"Swear by your god."

"I swear by Lathander, Lord of the Morning."

"As I swear," said Will, "to thrash you bloody and take back my gold if you don't stop wasting our time."

"All right," she said. "I knew something had happened to Gorstag even before the watch came to the house."

"Because someone else came first," Pavel said.

"Yes. They got inside somehow and broke into his room, just down the hall from mine. They were trying to be quiet, but I heard them anyway. I sneaked to his door to see what was happening. I saw all right, more than I wanted."

"Who were they?"

She shrugged and said, "A couple of men I'd never seen before and a walking corpse. I guess they brought it along for protection. I heard the live ones say their 'brothers' had taken care of Gorstag, but they had to find out if he'd made any notes or held onto any written orders from his master."

"Since you're still alive," said Will, "you plainly had better sense than to let them know you were eavesdropping. You probably tiptoed back to your own room. But do you have any idea whether they found what they were looking for?"

"They didn't. I overheard them say as much when they slunk back down the stairs."

"Then, once you were sure they were gone, you entered Gorstag's room and ransacked his belongings yourself."

She glowered in false indignation.

"It's all right," said Pavel. "We won't tell anyone you saw what you weren't meant to or that you tried to rob a lodger, either. We just need to know if you found something the intruders missed."

"No. I didn't find any notes nor anything worth taking."

"I need to search the place myself," said Will, "and to save time, yes, my dear, we'll pay for the inconvenience." He fished out two more gold pieces, one for her and one to placate the barman for the breakage and the affront to his dignity, such as it was. "Drink up and we'll go."

The boardinghouse was as squalid as Will had anticipated, and Gorstag's room, with its crumbling plaster and damp-spotted ceiling, as depressing. It took the former burglar about half an hour to toss it. It was nice to find that, despite a lack of practice in recent years, he still remembered how to look for loose floorboards, caches concealed inside furniture, and the like.

Unfortunately, no matter how cleverly he searched, it was to no avail. Finally he turned to Pavel and Winking Murene.

"Nothing," he sighed.

The obese woman sneered and said, "I told you."

"This place," said Pavel, "is remarkably bare."

"I told you that, too," said Winking Murene. "He didn't have anything."

"He must have owned something," the priest persisted. "You said he wanted to pass for a man of means. Well, he couldn't play such a part without at least a couple changes of decent clothing. It isn't here. You did pilfer after all."

"No, I—"

"Enough!" Pavel snapped. Up until now, he'd taken a soothing, kindly tone with her, but apparently he'd finally run out of patience with her habit of obscuring the truth even when, by any sensible calculation, it was pointless. "What did you steal?"

"It wasn't secret papers," Winking Murene said sullenly. "It was just things."

"I need to see them," said Will.

"You can't. I sold them already."

"Then tell us what they were," Pavel said.

She gave them the inventory, mostly a sad listing of tawdry finery passing for real silk and velvet, and paste rings and brooches masquerading as jewels. Will had just about decided it would reveal nothing useful when she reached the significant items:

"A couple of those blunt swords duelists use to practice, a set of the padded tunics and gloves they wear, and two little books full of woodcuts showing how to stick a man or whack his head off."

Will and Pavel exchanged glances.

"He must have loved fencing," said the halfling, "if, poor as he was, he invested in more than one foil and training manuals, too."

"Obviously," said the cleric, "and that means he took instruction someplace. Perhaps it's where we'll find his friends and confidants."

Winking Murene snorted and said, "Do you know how many maestros there are in Lyrabar?"

"We're about to find out," Pavel said with a smile.

------ ∞ ------

In his vision, Taegan had returned to adolescence. Once again, he wore a deerskin tunic and leggings and carried an ancient cut-and-thrust sword with a broken cross guard sheathed on his hip. The latter was a treasure, because lacking fresh iron and forges to work it, a small, isolated community of hunters had no way of replacing such a weapon. Most of their tools were made of flint. Still, despite his youth, he'd earned the right to bear the heirloom by learning to wield it better than any of his fellows, then mastering bladesong as well.

He and his companions were slinking along the arboreal pathways of the Earthwood, moving from tree limb to tree limb. For an avariel, it was safe to travel at such a height. A beat or two of his wings sufficed to carry him across empty spaces or catch him if he fell. Yet the forest was so thick, the branches so dense and interwoven, that true, sustained flight was difficult. Taegan frequently wished his people lived in clearer terrain, where they could soar freely whenever the mood took them, but he knew the others didn't share his yearnings. The foliage was their shield against hostile eyes.

Taegan heard voices. He skulked forward, peered down into a glade, and beheld his first humans. He recognized them from the descriptions of his elders. A man in a brown robe was harvesting mistletoe with a sickle, mixing the cuts with ritual passes. Two maidens crowned with wreathes of oak leaves sang a hymn. The one with the freckled nose quavered a little off key on the high notes.

To Taegan's eyes, everything about them was wonderful. Their bodies, bulkier than those of elves, but possessed of their own kind of grace. Their clothing, woven of fiber, not cut from hide. The abundance of metal they carried about their persons. . . .

He desperately wanted to reveal himself to them. Perhaps sensing the tenor of his thoughts, his father touched him on the arm, then beckoned him away.

Taegan might have protested that the druid and his acolytes appeared entirely harmless. Unfortunately, he was certain such an argument wouldn't sway the older elf in the slightest. Avariels kept themselves hidden whenever possible. Supposedly it was the only way a people so few in number could survive. Hating his sire at that moment, he took a last long look at the humans, then turned and followed him back the way they'd come.

Meanwhile, the adult Taegan felt a pang of exasperation. One of the nice things about Reverie was that he could choose which of his memories to relive. Why, then, was he dwelling on the shame and frustration of his early years instead of the pleasures he'd won by forsaking the tribe to join the world of men? He could only assume the anxieties that had overtaken him since he'd rashly chosen to intervene in Gorstag's troubles were interfering with his repose.

He groped for some happy experience to revisit, but for some reason, he could think only of flame and smoke. After a moment, he realized he actually did feel unpleasantly warm. His eyes stung, and a cough was building in his aching lungs.

He forced himself entirely awake to find the school was burning. No flames were licking at the walls of his own apartments, not yet, but he could hear them crackling elsewhere, even as he could already feel the heat rising through the floor.

The strange thing was that no one was crying the alarm. True, it was late. Even the most sociable students had either stumbled home or passed out in a drunken stupor, just as even the most industrious of the bawds had suspended trade till the morrow. Still, somebody should have noticed.

But that was a mystery to ponder later on. First he had to make sure everyone evacuated the building, determine the location and size of the conflagration, and extinguish it if possible. He threw off his blankets, sprang from his bed, pulled on breeches, boots, and one of his special shirts with holes for his wings, took a stride toward the door, then hesitated.

Much as he begrudged the moment it required, he grabbed a rapier, dagger, and pouch of spell foci, imbued the longer blade with magic, and only then exited his quarters.

His rooms weren't the only ones occupying the top story, but no doorways or halls connected his private accommodations with the rest of the area. He resolved to work his way down to the ground floor then back up. Once he checked the entire building, he could fly out one of the casements if need be.

He ran down the stairs into denser smoke that really did set him coughing, into murk and flickering red-yellow light that somehow illuminated little but itself. He threw open the door to the room where one of his provosts made his home. Taegan had four assistant instructors, but as he was suddenly glad, only two who chose to reside on the premises.

Stedd lay snoring beneath tangled covers, oblivious to the leaping, rustling flames already gnawing at the foot of his bed. Taegan hauled the wiry young human with the premature bald spot clear, and still he didn't wake. He was just flopping dead weight in his employer's arms.

Evidently the Wearer of Purple's minions had set the fire, for surely it was magic keeping Stedd insensible. Perhaps they'd cast a spell to sink everyone in the school into a slumber so deep that even the blaze wouldn't wake them until it was too late to escape. Presumably the trap had failed to hold Taegan, because unlike his human associates, he never truly slept.

He shouted Stedd's name, shook him, and finally backhanded him across the face. The human's eyes fluttered open. Taegan had never felt more glad of anything in his life, for plainly, had it proved impossible to rouse any of the sleepers, a single would-be rescuer could never have carried each and every one of them out in time.

"What?" Stedd asked drowsily.

"The school is on fire, and everyone's—" Taegan had to break off talking to cough. "Everyone's asleep. We have to wake them, or if we can't, haul them out. Do you understand?"

"Yes," the provost said.

"Then put on your shoes and get moving. Clear this area, and the ground level. I'll handle the second floor then work my way up the other side of the house."

Stedd nodded. He looked frightened, but not panicky, and not groggy anymore, either. Taegan clapped him on the shoulder, turned, and ran back to the stairs.

On the second floor, the smoke and heat were even worse. At every turn, the avariel found sheets of roaring flame devouring sections of wall. He was no expert, but to him, the scattered pockets of fire seemed additional proof that someone had set the blaze deliberately, for wouldn't an accidental conflagration spread continuously outward from a single point of origin? Whereas in this case, it looked as if an arsonist had broken into the building and run about setting multiple blazes.

Taegan felt fast, heavy footsteps bouncing the floorboards. He turned, and a bizarre figure, a huge man with pieces of astonishingly bulky iron plate armor affixed only to the left side of his body, emerged from the swirling gray smoke. Ripples of firelight ran along the metal. He wore a scarf tied around the lower half of his face, a simple means of delaying death by smoke inhalation that Taegan wished he'd thought of for himself. Possibly it was also intended to mask the cultist's identity.

A cramped hallway inside a burning building was about as undesirable a dueling ground as Taegan could imagine, but he assumed he had no choice. If the arsonist had remained on the premises after completing his task, it was likely to kill anyone who somehow woke and tried to flee. Fortunately, the intruder nonetheless seemed startled to see the avariel. It gave Taegan the second he needed to draw his rapier.

A split second later, the cultist rushed him. It was a reckless action, and for that very reason it took Taegan by surprise. He extended his arm, and the stop thrust bit into the cultist's torso. Reflex saw to that much. But he wasn't sure he'd made the kill, and didn't quite manage to sidestep out of the arsonist's path afterward.

The big man plowed into him, threw an arm around him, and bulled him through a doorway. Together, they reeled off balance and fell. The cultist landed on top, half-crushing the avariel. Taegan scrambled clear, and since his sword was still underneath his enemy, drew his dagger to finish off the arsonist if he wasn't dead already.

Then, squinting, he spied something that stayed his hand. The section of floor outside the doorway was all roaring brightness. Somehow, flame had engulfed it in an instant. The human had realized it was going to happen and hauled Taegan aside to save him from being caught inside the eruption, which suggested that the stranger, grotesque appearance and unexplained presence notwithstanding, wasn't the arsonist after all.

Aghast, Taegan started to check and see if the poor fellow was still alive, but at that instant, another strange figure appeared in the doorway. It looked like the leathery-winged, half-man/half-reptile demons the Wearer of Purple had produced to attack him before. But it was bigger, taller even than the human Taegan had just stabbed, and its scales were red. It crouched unharmed in the midst of the blaze, its own long, pointed stinger burning like a torch. Plainly, the brute was admirably suited to the task of arson.

Yet even so, it evidently didn't mind using tools to speed the process along, for it wore a harness with loops for carrying objects. Though most were empty, one still held a flask. The demon freed it, pulled the stopper out, and poured the contents over its head. The oil called "alchemist's fire" ignited on contact with the air.

Its entire body haloed in flame, talons and sting poised to rip and stab, the spirit pounced at Taegan.

He grabbed the hilt of his rapier, rolled aside, and scrambled to his feet, his back to the cot where one of the cook's helpers lay slumbering. As the demon wheeled to face him, he brandished a scrap of licorice root and rattled off a charm. He grunted and jerked as the magic shrieked through his body, and the wyvern-faced brute's movements seemed to slow. Even its corona of flame appeared to jump and writhe more sluggishly.

He knew that wasn't actually the case. The reality was that the magic had accelerated his own reactions. He thought it might be enough to save him, until a second demon scuttled through the door.

Taegan believed himself to be one of the four or five best duelists in Lyrabar, yet even so, he doubted whether, fighting in such tight quarters, he could kill the two demons before either they or the heat and smoke incapacitated him. Then, however, the human reared up and punched the second brute in the knee. The knuckle spikes on his gauntlet must have borne an enchantment, for they nearly tore the creature's limb in two. As it staggered, Taegan saw the puncture in the big man's right shoulder. His rapier had driven all the way through but had evidently missed any major arteries. For the moment at least, the stranger could still fight.

Encouraged, Taegan resolved to slaughter his own opponent quickly, so he could help his newfound ally if need be. Still, it took an effort of will to press the attack against an opponent shrouded in flame. The heat blistered his exposed skin, seared his lungs with every inhalation, and infused the rapier until it pained him to grip the hilt. The real problem, however, was the glare. Even with heightened speed, it was difficult to parry the demon's assaults when he could barely see them coming.

He hit the demon twice without disabling it, and it slipped an attack past his guard. The back of his calf burned. His foe had whipped its tail around to stab him in the leg.

The searing agony intensified. It was digging the bony point in deeper, while the flame cooked his flesh. He wanted—no, needed—to grab the tail and jerk it out of the wound, yet he forced himself to let it be, because fumbling at the pain was surely what the demon wanted him to do. As soon as he diverted his attention to it, the spirit would rip him apart.

So he launched himself at his assailant instead, and his relentless aggression seemed to catch it by surprise. Its talons raked, and he twisted out of the way. It jerked on its stinger, striving to trip him but not quite succeeding. He feinted low and thrust high. The blade pierced the demon's slit-pupiled eye and slid deep into its head, grating on bone as it penetrated. The brute collapsed, and Taegan used the sword to yank the fiery tail out of his calf.

Starved for clean air as he was, Taegan felt as if his strength was failing fast but also knew he had to keep moving. He pivoted to help kill the other demon, only to find that the big man had the situation well in hand. The dragon-faced thing was squirming on the floor and he was crouching on top of it, pulping its upper body with his iron fist.

It was in that moment that Taegan finally discerned something else. The stranger wasn't actually wearing plate on the left side of his body. Though they moved and flexed like ordinary limbs, the iron arm and leg weren't mere metal sheaths. They were prostheses, replacements for extremities their owner had evidently lost in battle or as a result of some terrible mishap. Even though Lyrabar had its share of wizards, and Taegan had some limited knowledge of magic himself, he'd never seen anything like it.

Still, it was no time to pause and marvel. When the demon stopped squirming, Taegan limped to the human and hoisted him to his feet. The stranger had bloody claw marks to go with his sword wound.

"I'm sorry I attacked you," the avariel wheezed. "It was a misunderstanding. How badly are you hurt?"

The big man shook his head as if to indicate it was a stupid question, that they had to press on no matter how injured or exhausted either of them was.

"Wake the girl," he said.

"Right, but the doorway's impassable. Can you—?"

"If the fire hasn't spread too far, I can make a way around. Go."

Taegan hurried to the cook's assistant and slapped her to consciousness. Meanwhile, his ally smashed down sections of wall to circumvent the blaze raging just outside.

They sent the girl running toward safety, did the same for everyone else in that portion of the building, then descended to the first floor themselves. There the fire ruled absolutely.

Taegan found a narrow, rapidly shrinking path through the patches of flame and started toward the other end of the house. His companion grabbed him by the arm and turned him toward the nearest exit.

"There's another stairway." Taegan had to shout to make himself heard over the endless bellow of the conflagration. "With more people living at the top."

The big man tried to answer, doubled over coughing, then managed to force out: "My partners already went that way to help whomever they found. We have to get out. We're out of time."

"If they met more of those demons . . ."

"Then the demons are dead. Come on!"

"Very well." Taegan hesitated. "No. You go. I have something to do."

"I'm telling you, the whole place—"

"I'll be all right. Save yourself."

The human eyed him dubiously, then gave a brusque nod and turned away.

Taegan hobbled past the pantry to the cellar steps, or rather, to the shaft they'd occupied earlier that night. The shaft was empty except for a pile of red-hot embers at the bottom.

He jumped and beat his wings. For a creature larger than a bird, genuine flight was impossible in such a confined space, but he managed to touch down on the far side of the burning rubble.

Unable stop coughing even for a moment, he dashed on past forgotten crates and battered old fencing dummies. The far end of the cellar held wrought-iron wine racks loaded with costly vintages that were boiling into worthless swill. He jammed the rapier into the crack between two of the stones in the floor then pried. His first effort failed, and shouting—well, croaking, really—he threw all his weight against the weapon. One of the blocks hitched up to expose the leather bag beneath.

Inside was a grimoire, vital if he was to renew his spells each day; his savings, though they didn't amount to much; and lastly, the cult's book and folio.

He felt a sudden vicious impulse to leave the secret writings, the cause of so much calamity, to burn, but he disregarded it. He snatched up the bag as blazing chunks of the ceiling rained down. He could tell it would all come down in a second to smash, burn, and bury him. He had no hope of escaping back the way he'd come.

He began the incantation that would fling him instantaneously from one point to another, no matter what barriers stood in the way. The need to cough burned in his throat and chest, doing its utmost to spoil the recitation, and he strained against it.

The avariel wheezed out the final word of power, and with a great roaring crash, the entire ceiling plummeted. Uncertain whether he'd succeeded in working the magic or not, he threw himself to the floor and covered his head.

He landed in a snowdrift. For an instant, it was strange to feel cold air, as if he'd never experienced it before. Then he realized the outside world wasn't all cold. His sleeve was on fire. He slapped it out.

Taegan turned and looked at the blazing shell of his school some thirty feet away. The sight engendered a numb, sick fascination. He might have lain on his stomach and stared at it for quite a while, if not for his duty to those who'd shared the ruin with him. He dragged himself to his feet, coughing still, his burns and torn leg throbbing, and limped to see if everyone else had made it out alive.

Ches, the third month, was commonly called the Claw of the Sunsets in honor of the vivid reds and golds that bloomed in the west at dusk. Actually, though, the dawns were often equally gorgeous, and Lathander had served up just such a spectacle that morning. Taegan found himself incapable of appreciating it. Rather, it felt as if the god was mocking him.

For certainly, the splendor in the sky made a cruel contrast to the misery on the ground. Miraculously, only three people had perished in the fire, but many of the survivors were burned, shaken, filthy with soot and ash, and coughing and shivering in the cold. Silver-robed priestesses of Selûne from the temple down the street ministered to them, dispensing healing spells, medicinal salves, blankets, water, and mugs of hot vegetable soup. Though he looked in need of tending himself, the stranger with the sun medallion, evidently a priest of the Morninglord, assisted, forgoing his customary early-morning celebration of the deity to ease the suffering of mortals.

Taegan still felt dazed and kept wanting to stare stupidly at the black husk of the school and the column of smoke dirtying the sky. Eventually, though, he noticed the clerics weren't the only folk moving among his associates. Buxom Halonya Clayhill, owner of the largest brothel on the waterfront, her plump face a mask of paint and black paper beauty spots, whispered in the ears of the younger and prettier whores and slipped them coins depending on what they whispered back. Even worse, Maestro Zalan, resplendent in green velvet despite having gotten up hours earlier than usual, stood chatting with Stedd. The two of them passed a silver flask back and forth.

A surge of anger stabbed through Taegan's befuddlement. He hadn't issued a challenge in years, but by sweet Lady Firehair, he thought Zalan had earned one. He arranged his features into the sneer appropriate to the occasion, then sauntered forward, avoiding any appearance of haste or agitation.

"Don't," Corkaury said.

Taegan turned. The wizened halfling had come up behind him and stood half-hidden by the folded wool garment in his arms.

"A crier passed under my window, bawling the news of the fire," Corkaury continued. "I came as quickly as I could. Now take this thing. I'm afraid it's not your usual style—I was lucky to lay hands on any elf-sized tabard at this hour, and had to cut it up myself to make room for your wings—but it's still more stylish than what you're wearing now."

Taegan dropped the blanket in which he'd awkwardly wrapped himself and replaced it with Corkaury's gift.

"Thank you. Now I have business."

"Don't," the bookkeeper repeated. "It's pointless. You'll see that when you've had a chance to rest."

"The ashes of the school aren't even cold, these vultures come circling to loot the wreckage, and my staff, folk I just saved from a horrible death, are eager to listen to their blandishments. It's disgusting."

"What would you have them do? They still have to eat. Can you continue paying their wages?"

"Don't you see? If Zalan hires Stedd to be his provost, he'll require him to disclose all my secrets."

"You once told me swordsmanship doesn't actually have any secrets. I ask you again, can you go on supporting Stedd and the others?"

Taegan felt his wrath turn into something heavy and impotent, like a chunk of lead inside his belly.

"Of course not. As you must know better than anyone, I'm ruined."

"You had nothing when you first came to Lyrabar."

"Whereas now at least I have my debts."

Corkaury scowled and said, "What I'm saying is you climbed the ladder once. You can do it again."

"Perhaps."

But perhaps not. The first time around, he'd managed to become fashionable. He had some notion as to how he'd accomplished it, but he knew luck had played a part as well. Only Tymora knew whether it would favor him once more.

"I suppose I have no choice but to try." He gave Corkaury a wry smile. "I daresay you need to seek new employment yourself."

"Until you find your feet, you won't need a clerk. When you establish a new academy, I'll be glad to return if you'll have me."

Taegan extracted most of the gold from his leather sack and said, "Do one last chore for me. Take this and pay everybody off to the extent you're able. Don't neglect yourself."

"I may not work for you at the moment, but I'm still your friend," said the halfling. "You can live in my house for as long as you like."

"Until I bash my brains out bumping my head on those low ceilings. Still, you're a staunch friend to offer, and perhaps you'll see me later on. For now, though, I'd like to be alone. Maybe it will clear my mind."

"As you wish."

Though he looked reluctant, Corkaury turned away.

Taegan spread his wings to escape into the sky, whereupon the man with the iron limbs spotted the motion and waved for him to stay put. The avariel saw no choice but to comply. He owed the stranger and his companions too much to flout their wishes.

The big man approached with his friends trailing along behind. He carried a hand-and-a-half sword, a longbow, and a quiver of arrows. Apparently he'd discarded them before entering the burning school for fear they'd get in his way. With the exception of the slender woman with the long moon-blond hair, his partners were equally well armed. That, their rugged clothing, and the confident yet watchful manner in which they carried themselves gave them the air of folk accustomed to peril and hardship.

Taegan bowed and said, "I'll never forgive myself for attacking you. I'll do anything in my power to make amends."

"I'm used to being mistaken for some kind of ogre," the huge man said with a shrug. "I'm Dorn Graybrook. These others are Pavel Shemov, Will Turnstone, Raryn Snowstealer, and Kara."

The avariel said, "My name is Taegan Nightwind, former maestro of the Nightwind Academy, and I'm grateful to you all. If you hadn't passed by. . . ."

"We didn't just pass by," said Will, the halfling. "We were looking for you. Well, your school. We've been going from one salle to the next, trying to find out where Gorstag Helder studied. I kept thinking we should stop, get some sleep, and take up the search again come morning. But we were too keyed up, and I guess it was just as well."

"Gorstag was my student," Taegan admitted.

Pavel glanced around, making sure no one was close enough to eavesdrop, then said, "We're trying to learn more about the trouble that led to his death, and we know fencing meant a great deal to him. Did he confide in you? Or was he particularly close to any of his fellow pupils?"

"Unless I'm very much mistaken, you're outlanders," Taegan said. "Why do you care what happened to Gorstag?"

"Because he ran afoul of the Cult of the Dragon," Kara said. "Do you know of it?"

"Of course he does," Dorn snapped, as if it had galled him just to hear her speak. "That's why the demons—"

"Abishai," Pavel murmured.

Apparently his store of esoteric knowledge had enabled him to identify the creatures.

"That's why the *abishai* attacked the school," Dorn went on, "and why he immediately assumed I was an enemy. Isn't that right, elf?"

Taegan disliked being called "elf," but thought he had more important issues to address.

"I ask again," said Taegan "How does this concern you?"

"If Gorstag told you anything," said Kara, "he probably said he was working for the Harpers."

"That's you?"

"No," she said. "He was mistaken. But what matters is that we know what he believed. We wouldn't, had his employer not sent us to investigate his murder."

"So," said Will, "can you help us?"

Taegan wondered if the outlanders would buy the book and folio, and if so, how much they'd pay. It could be the remedy to the disaster than had overtaken him, yet he found he couldn't quite bring himself to ask. Somehow honor precluded it, though he wasn't sure if it was an irrational feeling of obligation to Gorstag, his genuine indebtedness to Dorn and his companions, or the lust for a pure revenge on the cultists, unsullied by considerations of profit, that balked him.

Whatever it was, he simply said, "We have stories to trade, and I suspect it will take a while. Let's not do it standing in the street. I know a tavern nearby where they'll rent us a private room, fetch water, soap, and towels so we can clean up, and cook us breakfast, too."

The kippers, eggs, and scones were only a memory by the time Taegan had heard their tale and related the greater part of his own.

"I suppose," he said, "that after two failed attempts to kill me eye to eye and blade to blade, they decided to try arson instead. Even if the fire didn't eliminate me, it would probably destroy the purple book, and that was preferable to leaving it in the hands on an unbeliever."

"I hope," said Dorn, "that when you separated from me at the end, you went to retrieve it and the loose papers, too."

"Actually," said Taegan, "yes."

He made a stack of dirty plates to clear a space on the ring-scarred tabletop, then fetched out the articles in question.

"May I?" Pavel asked. He picked up the book, frowned

at the sigil embossed on the spine, and riffled through the pages. "It's the *Tome of the Dragon*. The unholy screed of the sect."

"Can you read it?" Raryn asked.

"No. It's written in cipher. But I'm sure that over the centuries, somebody succeeded in translating a captured copy. My hunch is that if . . . well, call him Sammaster for the time being, even though we pray he's an impostor . . . if Sammaster recorded any information about the Rage just now commencing, it's in the notes."

He traded the book for the folio, examined the first few pages, and his mouth tightened in vexation.

"I take it," Taegan said, "you can't make sense of those, either."

"Worse," said the cleric. "At least the tome uses Thorass. The characters in the notes don't come from any alphabet I've ever seen."

Perched atop the long-legged stool that raised him high enough to use the table comfortably, Will snorted. "As if that means anything. You pretend to be a scholar, but we all know you can barely write your name."

Pavel bristled and said, "You slandering maggot. I'm literate in eight languages and can recognize a good many more."

"Well, I doubt you know all the tricks thieves use to keep their business secret. Give me those." He took possession of the documents, made his own inspection, and eventually said, "Bugger."

"We don't need to read them," growled Dorn. "We just have to hand them over to Brimstone, whoever he is, and we're done, remember?"

"Do you mind if I tag along?" Taegan asked.

The gods knew, he no longer had anything else of pressing importance to do.

The night was warmer than Dorn had expected. Balmy air had blown up from the south to provide a first teasing promise of spring. Still, though he'd done plenty of it in his time, he disliked traveling cross-country in the dark, even when the territory seemed as clear, settled, and peaceful as the farmland surrounding Lyrabar. Something could still creep up on you.

Accordingly, he supposed he should be glad Kara retained something of a dragon's keen senses even in human guise. She seemed to see in the dark as well as Taegan, maybe even as well as Raryn, which meant the band had another able lookout watching for trouble. Yet it irked him somehow.

His mood soured still further when she dropped back from the head of the column to tramp at his side along the slushy, rutted road.

"If we truly are about to part," she murmured, "I want to thank you and apologize for deceiving you."

"Just pay what you owe."

She sighed. "I understand why you hate dragons. But we aren't all alike."

He didn't bother to answer.

"If you think about it," she persisted, "you'll realize I only lied that first night and only about how I received my wounds. Everything else I told you was the truth. I just didn't give you all the details."

"You did lie afterward. You pretended to like me."

"I did. I do."

"Like me . . ." It was hard to say. The mere thought seemed to trigger a chorus of derisive laughter inside his head. "Like me as a woman likes a man. A trick to make sure I'd fight to protect you even against Lareth's agents."

"You're wrong."

"Curse you, can't you talk straight even now, or does your tongue always fork whatever form you wear? We're two completely different kinds of creature."

"It doesn't matter," she said. "Through the ages, drakes who can shapeshift have often loved humans or elves."

I doubt they picked cripples and freaks to be their partners, Dorn thought, but that retort was too bitter to utter.

Instead, he said, "Maybe every species has its perverts."

"It isn't perverse. It's natural, particularly for song dragons. We differ from the rest of our kind in a number of ways, and one is that we're particularly at home in human guise. We spend the majority of our time that way. We have a legend that our earliest ancestors were entirely human, until a god blessed them with the power to transform."

"I don't care," he said. "I'm just your hired bodyguard doing a job that's nearly over."

"Very well, if that's the way you want it."

She lifted her hand as if to touch him, evidently thought better of it, and returned to the front of the procession.

A few minutes later, Raryn called, "I think I see it."

He led them off the road and up a hill. Deep snow lay there, untrodden by anyone before them, and they slipped and floundered as, their steps crunching, they made their ascent. Taegan spread his raven-feathered wings as though he meant to fly to the summit, then opted to remain on the ground. Maybe it was a gesture of camaraderie, or maybe he wanted to make sure he didn't blunder into a trap all by himself. For after all, what they did know about Brimstone, except that a damned lying wyrm wanted them to bring him the tome and folio.

As it turned out, they weren't advancing into any sort of ambuscade. Nothing waited on the hilltop but the ten weathered menhirs, nine standing, one toppled. Will paced about, peering down the slopes.

"Say his name and Brimstone will hear and come running, but from where?" he asked. "It's just open fields for a mile all around."

"He'll hear by magic, you dunce," Pavel replied.

His own powers were largely depleted. He'd cast a good many healing spells to help the victims of the fire and wouldn't have a chance to replenish them until dawn. Still, he managed to set the head of his mace shining like a lamp, then used the golden light to examine the nearly illegible glyphs incised on the menhirs. He scowled.

"What's wrong?" Raryn asked.

"This is a bad place," the priest replied. "Servants of Bane raised this circle."

Dorn understood why that concerned him. They'd had dealings with Zhents and other adherents of the Black Lord of Hatred and Fear—unfortunately, the god's worship flourished in the lands surrounding the Moonsea—and found them to be a despicable pack of reavers and necromancers. Still. . . .

"It looks like the Impilturans exterminated this particular coven a long time ago," he said. "Or else it died out on its own."

"True. Yet I have to wonder what sort of person would choose to associate himself with this site for any purpose whatsoever."

Will said, "We know how to find out."

"Yes," said Dorn, "and let's get it over with. Everyone, look sharp. Brimstone!"

The response came instantly. For a split second, he had the dizzying sensation of plummeting—or hurtling, he couldn't really tell—through a void seething with light. Then, once again, he had a solid surface beneath his feet. He peered about, felt a jolt of terror, and reflexively snatched for the hilt of his sword.

Transported by magic, he and his companions had materialized in the very place Will had always dreamed of: a dragon's cavern lair, where the flickering greenish light of two huge, ever-burning torches glinted on the coins and gems that overflowed their coffers to carpet the limestone floor. Unfortunately for the halfling thief, or anyone else inclined to pilfer, the owner of all this wealth crouched in the midst of it, regarding his visitors with crimson eyes luminous as coals.

Like most people, Dorn generally used the terms "dragon" and "drake" interchangeably, but from his studies, he knew that sages, when speaking precisely, employed them to designate two different genera of wyrm. Drakes were generally smaller than their cousins, but not always. The ooze drake he'd hunted in the Flooded Forest had been one exception, and the smoke drake who even then loomed before him was another.

His scales charcoal gray with dark red dabs and streaks, a jet-black ridge of stiff cartilage jutting from his spine, stinking of combustion, Brimstone was almost as huge as Azhaq.

The half-golem had his sword halfway out of the scabbard before recalling he'd expected Brimstone to be a wyrm and that they'd come to deliver Sammaster's papers to him, not fight. True, it was startling to find himself face to face with the creature so suddenly and equally disquieting to see that Brimstone belonged to a notoriously vicious species instead of one of the ostensibly kindly ones, but maybe that in and of itself was insufficient reason to deviate from the plan. With a pang of regret, he shoved his weapon back into its sheath, then glanced around to make sure his companions had no immediate intention of attacking the reptile, either.

Most of them were all right. Pavel, however, his normally calm, pleasant expression supplanted by a snarl of righteous fury, recited the opening words of an exorcism and brandished his sun medallion. The sacred amulet shone with a dazzling brightness. For a second, Brimstone flinched from the glare. Then he lunged, huge jaws spreading wide.

Dorn, Kara, and Will scrambled into the smoke drake's path. Brimstone could easily have smashed right through them, possibly trampling them in the process, but lurched to a halt instead. Meanwhile Taegan grabbed Pavel's upraised arm and struggled to wrestle it, and the luminous medallion, down.

"Stop this!" Raryn shouted.

"It's not just a dragon," Pavel replied, "it's undead! Can't you feel it?"

Actually, Dorn couldn't, but he didn't doubt that his friend could. Priests had special powers against the restless dead and accordingly, a special duty to suppress them. Servants of the Morninglord, with their bond to the purifying sun, waged the eternal war with particular zeal.

"It doesn't matter," Raryn said. "We promised to help Kara. We need to, if we're going to deal with the Rage. That means a parley, not a hunt, so put out the glow!"

Pavel stopped struggling against Taegan, and the bright white light faded away. He glared at Brimstone.

"You and I aren't finished," he said.

The smoke drake ignored him to glower at Kara.

"I didn't tell you to bring anyone else," he hissed. His voice was startlingly soft for such a vast creature, virtually a whisper. "Certainly not a fool like this."

"What are you?" she said.

"Drake," he said, "and vampire, as the little sun priest perceived."

"Then you can only mean us ill," Pavel said. "The charter of the Cult of the Dragon is to help undead wyrms conquer the world."

Brimstone sneered and said, "But not undead wyrms like me." He returned his attention to Kara. "Must you have your lackeys here?"

"We're not leaving," said Raryn. "At least not until we're sure we aren't delivering the information we carry into exactly the wrong set of claws."

"I want them with me," Kara said. "They've earned the right, and it's my hope they'll agree to aid me further in the days to come."

Not a chance, Dorn thought. Still, somewhat to his annoyance, he discovered he agreed with Pavel and Raryn. It wasn't time to leave, not yet, not if they could stay and learn more about the frenzy.

"So be it, then," Brimstone said. His scarlet gaze swept over Taegan and the hunters, and though his eyes resembled huge embers, their regard was chilling. "They can stay if you keep them on their tethers. I'll even tell you all something about myself, so you'll understand how it is that you can trust me."

Pavel made a scornful face at the very suggestion.

"How much do you know about Sammaster?" Brimstone continued, settling onto a heap of gold and silver; the coins clinked and rustled beneath his weight.

Taegan said, "With your kind permission?" He closed the lid of a treasure chest and seated himself on top, right in front of the huge reptile's demonic eyes and immense teeth and claws, with an insouciance that was either admirable or daft. "All I know is that he was a mad mage persuasive enough to found a conspiracy based on his delusions."

"He was a great wizard," Brimstone replied, "so gifted that while he was still a young man, Mystra, goddess of magic, appointed him one of her Chosen, a champion of the arcane."

"That," said Kara, "suggests he was a good man, not a wicked one."

Brimstone sneered, and Dorn picked out the two slightly elongated upper fangs that betrayed the creature's vampirism. They'd lengthen considerably more when the drake wanted to draw blood from his prey.

"If you believe those terms mean anything, then perhaps he was," the dragon said. "But it didn't matter. He had too much pride, and his election to the ranks of the Chosen swelled it further. He came to imagine he himself was almost a god, and the Lady of Mysteries had selected him to be not merely her agent but her consort."

"So he was mad even then," said Will, pushing back his cowl to bare his head.

Brimstone flicked his wings in the draconic equivalent of a shrug and replied, "Perhaps. It could be that underneath the surface, a covert madness simmered from the start, though why a deity with all her supposed wisdom would select such a deputy is an enigma. At any rate, as you'd expect, his amorous ambitions came to nothing, and he was accordingly disappointed. He continued to serve Mystra, but he began to resent her as well. Shrewd as he considered himself to be, he found it difficult to believe he'd simply misconstrued the goddess's attitude toward him. Rather, he decided she'd led him on to guarantee his loyalty."

Dorn scowled. He never would have expected to feel sympathy for any legendary dastard, particularly one who'd conceived a fondness for wyrms, yet in this one respect at least, he knew exactly how Sammaster had felt. The difference was that Kara really had tried to manipulate him. Hadn't she?

"I don't know exactly what happened next," Brimstone continued, "but I've heard several stories that all arrive at the same point. Sammaster undertook to help some humble folk in need. Things went awry, and he accidentally slaughtered them himself with an ill-considered spell. As sensible people realize, such mishaps occur all the time in war. But despite his learning, Sammaster was a fool and fell prey to a guilt that dogged him thereafter. It first made him question his fitness to be one of the Chosen and eventually whether his service was the worthy endeavor he'd imagined it to be.

"After the debacle, he studied necromancy, perhaps in hope of restoring his innocent victims to life, and in time, he sought out Alustriel, another Chosen. He hoped that, delving together, they could uncover secrets that had eluded his solitary investigations.

"Alustriel was beautiful, gracious, and at first happy to join forces with a colleague as accomplished as herself. Since Sammaster was lonely and unhappy, the result was predictable."

"He fell in love with her," said Kara, pity in her voice.

"Yes," said Brimstone, "and he wanted to make sure the new object of his affection wouldn't refuse him as Mystra had. He tried to spend every moment with her, make every decision for her, and shape her every opinion, all with the aim, conscious or not, of turning her into his adoring chattel."

"You're right," said Taegan, shaking his head, "he was an ass. No doubt the poor woman sent him packing to save her sanity."

"Indeed," said the drake, "and so, apparently, cost him what remained of his own. He slunk away to brood and in time decided that every frustration and heartache he'd ever endured was the result of treachery on the part of Mystra and his fellow Chosen. They wanted him to fail and suffer because they feared his potential for magical supremacy.

"Eventually, he returned to confront Alustriel. I'm not sure what he intended, murder, rape, or her abject submission. Perhaps even he didn't know. At any rate, raving, he attacked her with such puissance, cunning, and savagery that he would have overwhelmed her, except that she was able to call two of the other Chosen to her aid. Their magic transported them across Faerûn in an instant, and together the three of them killed Sammaster."

Will grinned and said, "I like a tale with a happy ending, but I take it this doesn't qualify."

"No," Brimstone said. "Sammaster had made unsavory friends as he studied the darker aspects of his Art. One was the powerful priest of a malevolent god, and he managed to raise his comrade from the dead. When Sammaster woke, he found he was still one of the most formidable wizards in the world but no longer possessed the unique powers of the Chosen. Evidently the Mother of All Magic had taken them back.

"Perhaps his defeat taught him a measure of humility, for he no longer imagined that he alone could ever cast down Mystra and the Chosen and enthrone himself in their place. Yet still he yearned for the day when all those who'd 'wronged' and 'betrayed' him would meet their dooms, and he would achieve a kind of mastery. He returned to his studies and found an answer in *Chronicle of Years to Come*, a volume of prophecy by an oracle named Maglas. One passage therein foretold a world ruled by undead dragons, or at least that was Sammaster's interpretation, and he decided he himself was the force that would make it happen. It was the high destiny for which Fate had always intended him. He elaborated on the lines from Maglas to pen the first version of the *Tome of the Dragon* and set about recruiting followers. Shortly thereafter, I met him."

"You actually knew him?" Kara asked.

"To my misfortune, yes. At that time, Faerûn didn't have any undead wyrms fit to rule it. For his vision to come to pass, he needed to invent new magic to create them, and like all such efforts, it would require experimentation. He had to seek out drakes willing to submit themselves to the rituals and potions he concocted."

"And you volunteered," said Taegan. "Weren't you running quite a risk?"

"As you observed," Brimstone said, "Sammaster was persuasive. Or perhaps he cast a charm to cloud my judgment. Either way, I was willing to wager my life against the opportunity to be one of the overlords of all the world, and luck was with me. Unlike the others who first offered themselves, I didn't perish. I changed into the being you see before you, possessed of new strengths and capacities."

"Yet I gather," said Will, "things didn't work out."

Brimstone bared his fangs as if he resented the halfling's bantering tone, but held his temper in check.

"No. Sammaster eventually decided vampiric dragons weren't the creatures of the prophecies after all. In his view, we had too many limitations to offset our advantages. He needed to make something more powerful still."

"Dracoliches," Kara sighed.

"Yes, but I couldn't become one. He had no way of changing me a second time, and it soon became clear he no longer foresaw any lofty station for me. He simply intended me to serve him, to fight for a prize in which I would have no share. The ingratitude and sheer presumption of it enraged me. I escaped his custody and swore revenge. From that day to this, I've watched the Cult of the Dragon and hindered them in any way I could."

"I find that hard to believe," Pavel said. "Even if Sammaster did injure your pride, he also made you stronger."

Brimstone glared, his red eyes flaring brighter, and said, "You consider undeath a vile condition, don't you, son of Lathander? That's why my very existence disgusts you. Well, rest assured, I don't share your prejudice. Still, vampirism isn't a state of being I would willing have embraced with centuries of vigorous life remaining before me had not Sammaster promised me a commensurate reward. As it stands, he cheated me out of countless pleasures I can never experience again, and I'll do anything—even make common cause with posturing, sanctimonious vermin like you—to pay him back."

"Perhaps," Pavel said, "but you have yet to convince me we have anything to gain by cooperating with an evil, unnatural thing like you."

"Whatever I am," Brimstone said, "I know Sammaster's mind. Moreover, as an undead, I'm immune to frenzy. I'll retain my reason when Karasendrieth and the rest of her feckless circle are slipping into dementia. You need me."

"Don't—" Pavel began.

Dorn raised his human hand signaling him to be silent. The gods knew, he shared the priest's instinctive revulsion, though in his case, it was more because Brimstone was a dragon. Vampirism was just the pepper in the stew. Still, verbally antagonizing the huge gray horror was pointless and possibly dangerous as well.

"You say you're out for vengeance on Sammaster," the half-golem said, "and Gorstag—who's dead, murdered by the cult—claimed he met the man. But is it possible? Didn't the Harpers or somebody kill him about a hundred years back?"

"In a sense," Brimstone said, "but by that time, Sammaster himself had become a lich, the better to pursue his goals. His spirit wears a body as does yours, but flesh and bone aren't the anchor that holds him on the mortal plane. He has a talisman called a phylactery hidden somewhere for that purpose. As long it exists, it doesn't really matter if his corporeal form perishes. Eventually his soul will find or make another and walk abroad once more."

"So it's possible," said Will, "Gorstag really did meet him and not just some faker."

"Considering that a great Rage is coming," said Brimstone, "and the cult is more active than it's been in decades, I think it's almost certain."

"We still don't know," said Kara, "what the one thing has to do with the other."

"No," said Brimstone, "we don't. It's what we must determine. So it's your turn to spin a story, singer. Tell me what my spy discovered and exactly how he came to grief."

"I'll let Maestro Nightwind tell it," the slender bard replied, her long, pale hair tinged green by the torchlight. "He's the one who was with Gorstag at the end and who's crossed swords with the cultists since."

Taegan related his experiences with a panache that would have done credit to Kara or any other bard. Under the circumstances, the polished phrases, flashes of wit and irony, and expressive hand gestures set Dorn's teeth on edge. He wished the avariel would just tell it as tersely as possible.

But Taegan reached the end eventually, whereupon Brimstone said, "You're correct about one thing. I've read the tome, and nothing in it explains what's happening now. Show me the folio."

"With pleasure," Taegan said.

Pavel still didn't look happy, nor had Dorn's own mistrust of the smoke drake subsided. But no one objected as the winged elf lifted out the stolen notes. Brimstone jerked his snout toward the floor, directing Taegan to set the scuffed brown leather bundle down in front of him.

Dorn wondered how the reptile would manipulate the sheets of parchment with his enormous claws. It turned out he didn't have to. He murmured a charm in his hushed, sibilant tones, and afterward, the pages floated up one at a time to hang before his eyes, as if supported by an invisible hand.

After a time, Brimstone bared his fangs in a show of pique. Dorn felt a surge of frustration, and Will said what everyone had no doubt realized: "You can't read the wretched things, either."

"I've never even seen these symbols before," the dragon growled, "and it's likely their meaning shifts from one page, line, or even word to the next. It may be that some of them are mere place holders, intended solely to confuse. That makes it difficult even to determine the alphabet to which they correspond, or the language Sammaster is speaking, let alone the actual content of the text."

"I thought we guildsmen used some complicated codes back in Saerloon," Will said, "but it sounds like this beats anything a thief ever cooked up."

"Sammaster's insane," Brimstone said, "but also more brilliant than any man or even dragon I ever met. Still, I can offer one morsel of encouragement. Even for a genius, it takes considerable time and effort to devise or employ a cipher as intricate as this. If he went to this much trouble to hide his thoughts from prying eyes, they must be important."

"Knowing that is no help," Pavel said, "if you can't read them."

"Patience," Brimstone said. "Where simple cunning fails, magic may yet succeed."

His phantom servant, if that was the proper description, replaced the very first page before his smoldering gaze, whereupon he muttered another incantation. A momentary distortion rippled through the air, warping and blurring everything in view.

Brimstone stared intently at the paper hanging in front of his snout. His eyes widened, glowed brighter, and he hitched forward.

By the moon and stars, Dorn thought, it's working. He's reading it.

The drake shuddered, threw back his head, and screeched. Foul-smelling smoke jetted from his jaws to splash against the stalactites dangling from the ceiling.

Dorn didn't understand what was happening, but it didn't look good. As a precaution, he drew his sword. Taegan jumped up off the chest, whipped out his rapier, and backed away from the gigantic creature. Raryn, Will, and Pavel readied their own weapons.

Brimstone snarled words in a language Dorn had never heard before. His voice was louder, the hiss less pronounced, the timbre altered. Eyes flaring, he pounced at Taegan, who was still the closest person to him.

Once again, Pavel shouted the opening words of a prayer and made his medallion shine like the sun. Brimstone froze for a split second, and Taegan's agility notwithstanding, perhaps that was the only reason the drake failed to spear him with the first snap of his long, curved vampiric fangs. The fencing teacher sidestepped the attack, drove his rapier into the creature's lower jaw, and evaded a swipe of its talons by leaping backward, increasing the length of the jump with a beat of his wings.

While Brimstone was attacking Taegan, the hunters took the opportunity to flank the undead reptile. It seemed they had no choice but to do their utmost to kill him after all, and in his heart, Dorn was glad.

But just as he was about to close, Kara shouted, "No! Give me a chance to help him!"

Though he didn't like it, Dorn held back, and so did his comrades. Kara started singing a spell, her high, vibrant voice resounding through the limestone chamber. Brimstone pivoted toward her and charged, his feet throwing up coins and jewels.

Dorn sprang forward and hacked at the dragon's neck. The bastard sword inflicted only a shallow gash, but Brimstone broke stride and swung his head toward his attacker. It gave Kara the moment she needed to finish the musical incantation.

Brimstone fell down thrashing, and Dorn scrambled back to keep the immense drake from rolling on him. For a time, he wondered if the fit itself would kill Brimstone, but then the vampire stopped convulsing and clambered, shaking, to his feet. From his manner, it was plain Kara's magic had restored him to his right mind, for whatever that was worth. His wounds bled more sluggishly than those of a living creature, dark fluid seeping like sap from a tree.

"Well," panted Will, lowering his short sword but keeping it in his hand "so much for the idea that you're immune to frenzy."

"That wasn't the Rage," Brimstone whispered. "Sammaster laid a trap for anyone who could actually read his musings. It poured . . . well, call it a semblance of his own personality into me. It overwhelmed my own identity and possessed me. All I cared about was protecting his secrets. Fortunately, Karasendrieth dispelled the influence."

"Does that mean you can read the notes now?" Taegan asked.

He wiped the gore from his rapier, flourished it with a showmanship so well practiced it had seemingly become unconscious, and returned it to its scabbard.

"No," Brimstone said. His long, forked tongue twisted down to examine his wounded jaw by feel. "The trap is still waiting."

"And I wouldn't want to have to try to break its grip a second time," Kara said. "The magic is powerful, and I was lucky."

"If you turned into Sammaster," Raryn said, "maybe now you already know what the notes say."

Brimstone paused, evidently examining the contents of his memory. "Alas, no."

"That's it, then," said Will. "For the time being, anyway. Maybe it we take the notes back to our wizard partners in Thentia."

"Perhaps they can help," Brimstone said, "but first, we have more work in Lyrabar. I planted a spy in the Cult of the Dragon, and as a result, we learned a bit. Perhaps if we assault their stronghold, take prisoners, and interrogate them, we can discover more."

"When you say 'we,' " said Pavel, I assume you mean us. You already told Kara you wouldn't enter Lyrabar, and now I know why. Perhaps with your sorcery you could put on human form, but it would still scare, pain, and perhaps even cripple you to enter such a holy city, full of servants and temples of the gods of light."

"You have no concept of my capabilities, priest. For your own safety, don't flatter yourself that you do."

"I must confess," Taegan said, "that whether Sir Brimstone is comfortable assisting or not, I'd welcome another chance to pay my compliments to the Wearer of Purple."

"Good luck," said Dorn. "My friends and I have finished our part of this chore."

To his chagrin, even Pavel responded by showing him a troubled expression.

"You must know," said the handsome priest, "just how reluctant I am to follow any suggestion this foul thing offers. Yet I still feel the Morninglord has set us a task."

"Think about what you're proposing. It's one thing to play bodyguard. It's something else entirely to enter a city where nobody knows us and try to capture or kill some of the locals. Forget the danger the cultists present. The watch, the paladins, or whoever are likely to string us up themselves."

Will smirked as he sometimes did when called upon to use his wits to solve a problem.

"I can finagle a way around that," the halfling offered.

"Don't bother," said Dorn. "Worry about seeing the folio safely back to Thentia, if you think it's worth doing."

"I agree with Pavel," Raryn said. "We started a hunt, and we need to finish. If we break off now, it's like wounding an animal, then not bothering to track it down, finish it off, and end its pain."

"It's not anything like that," Dorn replied.

The white-bearded dwarf shrugged his massive shoulders and said, "Well, maybe not. But look at it this way. The cult's gotten busy, and one thing we do know is, they're dedicated to turning ordinary wyrms into dracoliches, more powerful and almost impossible to destroy, since I imagine they store their essences in phylacteries, too. Does that strike you as a good thing, either for lads in our trade or the world in general?"

Dorn shook his head in disgust but said, "All right. One last job."

"Naturally," said Will, "it means a modest increase to our fee." He looked around at the wealth glittering on every side, then up at Brimstone. "Perhaps you'd like to donate a trinket or two for the good of the cause."

"Our first problem," Dorn continued, "will be finding the cultists, since Gorstag died before passing along the location of their lair."

"We know more than one way to catch what we're hunting," Raryn said. "If you can't spot it, flush it out of hiding, or track it, you set out bait."

Taegan grinned and said, "I take it that would be me."

THIRTEEN

14 Ches, the Year of Rogue Dragons

Taegan lifted his pewter goblet of brandy, guzzled it down, and waved for another. He wondered vaguely if had he not met Dorn, Kara, and the others, he might have spent the night actually doing what he was pretending to do: drowning his misery at the destruction of his school.

Not that there was anything fraudulent about his intoxication. He'd always enjoyed alcohol as he did all the other luxuries of the civilized human world, but not nearly enough to parade himself before Lyrabar as anything other than a gentleman with impeccable self-control, thus he almost never over-indulged. At first his muddled thoughts and loss of coordination dismayed him, and he began to forget he was even impaired. He found himself craving more and more liquor, even though he was already about as drunk as a person could get and had to struggle to limit his further consumption at least a little. Otherwise he wouldn't be able to walk out of the filthy little tavern when the time came.

Finally Pavel pushed through the door. With his hood pulled up to shadow his features and his sun amulet tucked inside his clothing, he was, in a predominantly human city, the most nondescript of the hunters. Accordingly, he was the best suited to approach Taegan without arousing suspicion. He didn't even glance at the avariel, let alone speak, but it wasn't necessary. Simply by making his appearance, he'd given the signal that the cultists had gathered outside to waylay their intended victim.

The dastards thought they were so clever. It was comical, and Taegan had to stifle a laugh. He rose, the room tilted, and he clutched at the edge of his rickety table until it steadied itself. He tossed some coins down to clink among the empty cups, and some of them rolled off clattering onto the floor. He had a murky sense he was leaving too much coin, but it was easier than counting it. Besides, he was supposed to look drunk and heedless, wasn't he?

It was still work to keep his balance. He took two careful steps, then remembered the *Tome of the Dragon*. The wretched book had sat in front of him all evening in plain view of anyone who passed by, a lure to snag a cultist's attention. Presumably it had already accomplished its purpose, and Pavel, Kara, and Brimstone all agreed it had no light to shed on their current problems. Still, Taegan supposed he might as well take it with him. He returned to the table, tucked the purple-bound volume under his arm, and stumbled onward. The murmur of his fellow topers and the melancholy music of the longhorn, yarting, and hand drum trio followed him out into the dark.

The weather had grown cold again, frigid enough for the chill to bite even through his numbness. It couldn't clear his head, though. He supposed that was bad. Or would be, if he didn't have friends watching over him. In theory, they'd protect him from would-be assassins no matter how incapacitated he was.

He spread his wings, ascended a few feet, then let himself drop to land on one knee. Too tipsy to fly, that was how it was supposed to look, and it wasn't far from the truth. Chuckling to himself, unsure if his amusement was genuine or feigned, he stumbled onward, down a dark, crooked lane that seemed a perfect hunting ground for footpads and their ilk.

Where was everyone? He couldn't spot any of the cultists or his allies, either, and for a few moments wondered why. Then he remembered he was drunk. Evidently it clouded the eyes as much as it deadened the hands and tangled the legs.

Something thrummed through the air above him. It took him a second to recognize the sound of arrows in flight, and another after that to recall that at least some of the missiles might be streaking at him. By then, it was too late to dodge, but nothing hit him.

The cult had stationed archers on the rooftops, killers well positioned to shoot him whether he departed the tavern on foot or on the wing. Fortunately, his allies had neutralized the marksmen before they could accomplish their objective.

A wounded cultist started to scream, but the sound cut off in mid-cry. Evidently Pavel had followed Taegan out of the tavern and used a spell of silence to keep things quiet, as per the plan.

Leathery wings pounding, abishai, their scales either black as ink or the tainted white of dirty, trampled snow, sprang up from nearby rooftops. More arrows flew to pierce their flesh, as did darts of azure light. The latter were Kara's contribution. Apparently she had more potent attack spells at her command but feared they'd make too much of a commotion. No doubt Will was slinging skiprocks as well, though Taegan couldn't see them.

A couple of demons crashed down in the street. Others streaked toward their assailants, and one of the black ones landed to scuttle toward Taegan. Its fangs were bared, its talons poised to rip, and its upraised stinger sweated drops of acid that steamed and sizzled on the cobbles.

Taegan hadn't felt particularly frightened even when battling the gigantic wyvern and its spellcasting rider, but he was growing increasingly alarmed in the street outside the tavern. He wasn't supposed to have to fight and had no idea whether he could manage it in his current condition. He prayed for one of his comrades to shoot the abishai or jump to the ground to engage it, but none of them did. Apparently they were all busy with opponents of their own.

He chucked away the tome to rid himself of the encumbrance, drew his rapier, and came on guard. He started an incantation to create multiple images of himself, illusory decoys to draw the abishai's attacks, but his tongue stumbled over the cabalistic words. It spoiled the magic, and the demon pounced into striking range.

The creature clawed and whipped its tail at him. He retreated and parried. Clanking, the rapier knocked the abishai's hand out of line, but it couldn't simultaneously catch the stinger, and the avariel realized he hadn't stepped back far enough. The long, bony point with its glistening coating of acid was going to plunge into his belly.

At the last possible instant, he beat his wings, and it just sufficed to lengthen his hop backward enough to carry him out of range. Unfortunately, when he landed, he lost his balance and staggered to avoid falling on his rump. The abishai sprang, taking up the distance, renewing the attack.

Fangs, talons, or sting—in that moment of confusion he couldn't even tell which—tore into his wing and lodged there. Gritting his teeth against the resulting stab of pain, he wrenched himself free. No doubt it exacerbated the damage, but it was the only way he could swing around and threaten his opponent anew.

The demon kept pressing the attack, and it was virtually all he could do to parry and evade. When he did manage a riposte, either it came too late to reach the target, or else the abishai slapped the point away.

The demon clawed bloody furrows in his forearm, then nearly succeeded in grabbing his wrist and immobilizing his blade. He realized the foul thing was going to kill him, probably in the next few heartbeats, unless he changed tactics. Alas, fear and the stupidity of intoxication blinded him, and for a moment, he couldn't see what to do.

Finally, though, a notion came to him. It was a lunatic, quite possibly suicidal maneuver for the flailing, awkward clod the brandy had made of him, especially against an adversary capable of making multiple attacks simultaneously. But in theory, it could work, and even if it didn't, perhaps he could at least dispatch the demon as it slew him in its turn.

As every duelist learned, no foe could launch an attack without opening up his guard to a counterattack. Accordingly, the next time the abishai drove in at him, he simply extended and lunged, dropping low and twisting his body to provide as small a target as possible, but otherwise making no concession to defense.

The demon's claws ripped his scalp and its stinger grazed his ribs, but none of its attacks found his vitals. Meanwhile, the rapier drove entirely through its torso. It collapsed against him, helpless for the moment with the shock of its wound.

Refusing to let his own fresh injuries make him any slower than he was already, he shoved the demon away, yanked the rapier out, and thrust again, at which point his foe fell on its face. Having identified the creatures as abishai, Pavel had also known how to fight them. He'd blessed everyone's hand weapon with a virtue that negated the brutes' regenerative powers.

Certainly the one in front of Taegan showed no signs of clambering back to its feet. He congratulated himself that, even drunk, he'd proved a match for it, then glimpsed a pale flicker at the corner of his eye. He pivoted, already knowing he was too slow. Another abishai, one of the whites, would have its teeth and claws in him before he could present his blade.

But Pavel was behind the abishai, and he swung his mace. Bone crunched. Its skull smashed, the demon toppled.

The priest turned, peering, making sure no other foes were advancing on them. Then he made Taegan the beneficiary of his healing prayers and luminous touch. First the Morninglord's golden light mended the maestro's wounds, then purged him of his intoxication with a spell devised to cleanse the blood of any poison.

"Thank you," Taegan panted.

"You're welcome," Pavel answered. "I'm sorry those creatures slipped past the rest of us. It turned out we hadn't spotted quite all of them."

"Remind me, whose job was that?"

"Will's. I'd be happy to hold your cloak while you give him a thrashing."

"What a couple of whiners," the halfling said, grinning down from atop the eaves of a nearby house. "You ingrates should be praising me for concocting a perfect plan. We're all fine, the watch is nowhere to be seen, none of the cultists escaped, and we took a few of them alive. Now all we have to do is drag them somewhere private for questioning."

⟐

The zombie shambled out of the foul-smelling darkness in the abandoned tannery, and Pavel lifted his sun amulet. The medallion blazed. The walking corpse flinched and shielded its eyes, and as it stumbled about in seeming confusion, Dorn sprang at it. One swing of his iron fist nearly sufficed to tear its head from its shoulders. Another buried the knuckle spikes in its chest. The creature fell and lay inert.

When a bladesinger knew he was headed into battle, he could magically enhance his own strength and quickness before the fact, and Taegan had availed himself of the opportunity. Still, his comrades had eliminated the threat with such brisk efficiency that he'd barely had a chance to lift his rapier.

"Nicely done," he said.

"Not really," Pavel said. "Lathander's light should burn a zombie to smoke, but this whole place has been imbued with unholiness, to strengthen the cult's magic and weaken that of their foes."

"Rubbish," said Will. "You're just making excuses for being inept."

"Find the secret door," Dorn growled, stingy with words as usual.

Taegan had noticed Raryn often had even less to say, but that seemed to be simply because he was quiet by nature. The white-haired dwarf ambled through the world with an air of calm affability and often enough, amusement, while the half-golem stamped along seething with sullen anger.

Obeying his leader's order, Will scrutinized a particular section of wall, looking for traps. Their informant, a prisoner who'd proved more interested in earning his release than protecting the secrets of the cult, had sworn there weren't any, and Pavel, who'd cast a spell that supposedly enabled him to tell when someone dissembled, believed he was telling the truth. Still, it seemed best to be certain.

At length the halfling unlatched the hidden panel and swung it outward. On the other side was a flight of steps leading downward. The greenish light of ever-burning torches leaked up from below. So did the echoing drone of a sonorous chant. That, too, was as the intruders had expected. Their captive had told them the cult was performing magic tonight, and they hoped to surprise the conspirators in the act, before the dastards had any inkling their latest attempt to murder Taegan had gone awry.

The winged elf and his comrades skulked down the stairs and on toward the chorus. Will, with his knowledge of snares, and Raryn, with his ability to see even if the torchlight failed, took the lead. Dorn followed, his massive form shielding Kara. When she assumed dragon form, she was unlikely to require such protection, but her reptilian body would jam in the narrow tunnels. Taegan played rearguard. Someone had to. The way the dank, gloomy corridors forked and snaked around, it would be easy for an enemy to come up behind them.

The stink of the derelict tannery faded, which merely made the rotting-flesh stench of a den of zombies and necromancers that much plainer. Taegan was almost surprised it didn't make him sick to his stomach, just as it bemused him that he scarcely felt a flutter of trepidation, invading the cult's stronghold with such a small force. But he was too eager to go on the attack, to confront the Wearer of Purple once more and avenge the outrages her followers had perpetrated at her behest.

A man wrapped in a dark mantle with an amice-trimmed collar stepped through an arch up ahead, glanced casually at the party slinking down the passage, then peered more intently, trying to determine whether he knew them or not. His eyes widened in dismay, and Raryn's arrows took him in the heart. He crumpled with scarcely a thump, let alone an outcry to herald his demise. The dwarf dragged the cultist back into the crypt from which he'd just emerged and stashed him where no casual passerby would see the body. The intruders stalked deeper into the catacombs.

Finally they spied a particularly high and ornately embellished horseshoe arch. The chanting, which had become a kind of catechism, with a single female voice and the rest of the assembly speaking contrapuntally, seemed to issue from just beyond it. A noisome feeling of unholy force accumulating, a nasty prickling on the skin, leaked out as well. Will tiptoed up to the doorway, peeked inside, then turned and gave his comrades a nod, indicating that, yes, they'd found the place they sought. As the rest of them crept forward, Taegan whispered a charm to shroud his body in blur.

On the other side of the arch, three semicircular steps led down to the floor of an expansive crypt with a lofty rib-vaulted ceiling. A score of common cultists stood in a ring around an arrangement of bones laid out to form sigils or runes. The air above the symbols squirmed and curdled, continually on the verge of congealing into translucent shapes which then dissolved before the eye could quite make them out. Zombies and abishai stood along the walls, perhaps comprising a grotesque ceremonial guard. Five more living humans, evidently true spellcasters and the officers of the cabal, presided over the ceremony from a dais at the far end of the chamber. The one in the middle was an attractive, middle-aged woman with an impish face and brown curls frosted with golden highlights. At the moment she wore ornate purple robes, but Taegan had often seen her in more conventional attire.

She was Cylla Morieth, a respected instructor at Lyrabar's school of wizardry and a welcome guest at the banquets, dances, and other social functions hosted by the city's elite.

It was a mystery that such a person would betray the kingdom that had given her such a congenial life, but Taegan would have to puzzle over it later. At the moment, he and his comrades had cultists to kill. If the plan worked, many of the enemy would die without the chance either to surrender or raise a hand in their own defense, but the maestro felt no pity. These were the same despicable folk who'd murdered Gorstag and set fire to the academy while dozens of his associates slumbered helplessly inside.

Dorn glanced at his companions, making sure they were ready, then snapped them a nod. It was time to begin.

They spread out across the archway. The enemy noticed them almost at once, the chanting dissolving into a babble of alarm, but by that time, arrows and skiprocks were flying. Raryn, Dorn, and Will targeted the figures on the dais first, reckoning them the most dangerous among the opposition, and by a pleasant chance, the combination of the sunken floor and elevated pedestal afforded the marksmen clear shots. Two of the spellcasters fell. A third merely staggered when a shaft struck him in the chest but glanced off the armor evidently hidden beneath his robes.

Meanwhile, Pavel recited words of power, and Kara sang them. The effect of the cleric's spell wasn't immediately perceptible from Taegan's vantage point, but when the bard finished conjuring, a point of light streaked from her outstretched hand into the midst of the cultists, where it exploded into a spherical blast of dazzling, crackling lightning. People, zombies, and abishai jerked, burned, and fell. But not all of them, and the survivors howled and rushed the steps.

Dorn cast away his longbow, whipped out his bastard sword, and stepped forward to meet them. Raryn and Will followed suit. Pavel lifted his sun amulet, and singing once more, Kara started to grow, her fair skin taking on a sheen like blue crystal.

Taegan recited a spell, and in an instant it shifted him across the crypt onto the dais, where everything fell so utterly silent it was as if a god had struck him deaf. He knew Pavel's spell was actually responsible. The cleric had sealed that end of the chamber in silence to hamper the enemy spellcasters.

Unfortunately, not all magic required the spoken word, and his square, black-bearded face a mask of fury, the man who'd survived the arrow was even then sweeping his hands through mystic passes. As Pavel sent Lathander's sunlight blazing through the chamber, balking the animate corpses lurching toward the steps, Taegan lunged. The bearded man tried to deflect the rapier with a dirk, but the avariel deceived the parry. His sword, its strength and sharpness augmented by enchantment, pierced the cultist's breastplate where the arrow had failed. The human fell.

Taegan whirled, seeking the Wearer of Purple. Though the bearded man had been too provocative a target to ignore, she was his particular task. She knew the answers Kara needed if anyone did, and for that reason, he was supposed to take her alive.

Cylla Morieth was a few feet away, casting a handful of powder into the air. The motes of dust flashed and disappeared, and sound surged back into the world. The stuff had counteracted Pavel's charm.

That was bad. It would allow her and the other surviving cult spellcaster to use every charm they carried ready for the casting. With a snap of his wings, Taegan sprang, intent on incapacitating her before she could start conjuring.

She pointed at him, and some invisible force slammed him backward. As she hadn't had time to weave a spell, she must have had the effect stored in a ring, talisman, or some other piece of her regalia. He crashed down hard on the stone platform, shook off the shock of the impact, and scrambled to his feet.

It took him too long, and Cylla had time to conjure. She swept two daggers through mystic passes then tossed them into the air. They lengthened into weapons the size of broadswords then sprang at Taegan, assailing him and blocking the path to the wizard who'd animated them.

He could parry their attacks, but when he riposted to the seemingly empty spaces behind them he found nothing to hit, no invisible but tangible wielders into whom he could drive his point, which meant he could see no way to eliminate the threat. He tried to fly over the weapons, but they simply ascended with him. Safe behind her magical protectors, the Wearer of Purple rattled off another incantation and snapped a handful of black ribbons like a whip.

Jagged lengths of darkness exploded outward from a central point in the air, so sudden and thick that Taegan couldn't dodge. Their icy touch froze him with sudden nausea and terror. As if sensing his incapacity, the living swords sprang in hacking.

Somehow he broke free of the crippling effect an instant before the blade in the lead would have split his skull. He parried that one and dodged a chest cut from the other, which only preserved his life for a few more seconds.

Soon enough, his luck would run out, and Cylla would kill or cripple him with her wizardry. He had to reach her. He spun the rapier, captured one broadsword in a bind, and flung it away. By that time, the other was slashing, but he twisted aside, then beat it out of his way. Wings hammering, he streaked at the Wearer of Purple. He had no doubt the animated blades were hurtling right behind him, and he prayed he could stay ahead of them.

Taegan lashed the flat of his weapon against Cylla's temple. He wouldn't have been surprised if some defensive enchantment had deflected the blow, but it slammed home, and she reeled. Touching down on the dais once more, he whirled.

He'd hoped that if he broke the mage's concentration, it would stop the living blades, but it hadn't. They were still chasing him and already leaping in for the kill. If not for the charm that had quickened his reflexes, even Taegan, with all his skill, could never have parried both attacks in the split second he had left.

The fencing master glimpsed motion from the corner of his eye. Her forehead bloody, Cylla had fallen and looked as if she'd stay down for a while, but the other surviving spell-caster, a scrawny little man armed with a skull-topped staff like the wyvern rider, had oriented on the avariel and was using the rod to sketch a glowing pattern on the air. Taegan wanted to turn and attack the cultist, but it was impossible. Cylla's blades were still pressing him too hard.

As he wondered if he could withstand another curse, the strains of a savage yet beautiful battle anthem swelled above the muddled roar of the battle at large. Kara, fully transformed into draconic form, snapped up the man with the staff, bit him in two, then wheeled to face the trio of abishai flying in to assault her from behind. She puffed out a plume of vaporous lightning, or something akin to it, suffusing the air with the smell of ozone and burning the demons from the air. Then she lunged after other foes, leaving Taegan to manage the floating swords that still doggedly labored to spill his blood.

Fortunately, without Cylla to worry about, it wasn't too difficult. Like most duelists of flesh and blood, the blades had a few attacks they repeated over and over, and once he identified them, it was even possible to defend and watch the rest of the battle at the same time. It was a relief to see that his comrades were faring at least as well as he had. By the time Cylla's spell ran out of power, and the broadswords shrank back into daggers and dropped clanking to the floor, the fight was essentially over.

Raryn swung his ice-axe and gutted a final white abishai. Pavel shattered a zombie's bones with his mace. Those cultists still capable of flight bolted through other, smaller openings in the wall, and exchanging his short sword for his warsling, Will started to give chase.

"Let them go," said Dorn. "It's a bad idea to chase them through a maze they know and we don't. Besides, we have what we came for. Who's hurt?"

"I've got nicks on my arm and knee," said Raryn.

"I took a bang on the back," panted Will. "I don't think it's bad."

At which point, Taegan noticed something that gave him a pang of alarm. Her jaws and talons crimson, the song dragon stood trembling, seemingly sick or dazed.

"Kara?" he called. No answer. "Kara! Are you all right?"

"Yes," she sighed. "Yes. The blood is stirring the frenzy, but I can control it."

Her lithe, serpentine body dwindled, the long neck shortening, the wings and tail retracting, until she was a human woman once again. She seized a corner of her cloak and wiped her mouth and hands as if she meant to scrub them raw.

Taegan and the hunters turned their backs on her, giving her the privacy they sensed she needed while Pavel inspected everybody's cuts and bruises. All the wounds proved to be superficial.

"We were lucky," said Raryn, and even though they were able fighters all, and had enjoyed the advantages of a sound strategy, a surprise attack, and a dragon battling on their side, Taegan agreed.

"We'll find out just how lucky," the maestro said. He hauled the still-groggy Cylla to her feet. "Let's find someplace cozy and see what this charming lady has to say."

Under ideal circumstances, Kara would have preferred to depart the catacombs as quickly as possible, and not just because it was remotely conceivable a second group of cultists would turn up to rescue their leader. The very atmosphere of the cellars, tainted as it was with the residue of necromancy, was oppressive to those with the sensitivity to detect it, especially if their souls were troubled. But it seemed more practical to interrogate the Wearer of Purple on site than to march her through the streets and risk attracting the attention of the watch. So the intruders located a crypt their foes had evidently furnished for conversation and relaxation and pushed Cylla into the least comfortable-looking chair. Serving as lookout, Raryn stationed himself by the doorway, while Will and the humans glowered down at the mage.

Kara tried to share in the general mood of righteous satisfaction. It would be better than dwelling on the sickening, enticing taste of human blood that still lingered in her mouth and the shameful, seductive urges it stirred in her head. Better than recalling that, once again, Dorn had seen her teetering on the brink of madness. Even though she doubted his opinion of her could sink any lower, somehow that was the most painful aspect of the whole repulsive incident.

Taegan smiled at Cylla and said, "As I anticipated, you look even more beguiling without your veil."

Though her brow was split and bloody, and her captors had divested her of her outer robe with its countless hidden pockets for talismans and spell foci, the cultist sneered back with commendable composure.

"You should have returned the tome when I asked for it, Maestro. You may think you've won a victory, but it's an illusion. You and your peculiar assortment of friends are all going to die for your transgressions."

"But not tonight," said Will, "which likely means you'll see the Nine Hells before us. Save me a seat near the ale."

"If you wanted to murder me," the cult leader said, "you could have done it back in the conjuration chamber."

The halfling leered at her and said, "What if Taegan's idea of a proper revenge is to pull out your fingernails, stick your feet in hot coals, and slit your throat later on?"

Cylla looked at Pavel and replied, "I see a priest of the Morninglord." Her eyes shifted to Kara. "And a song dragon. You two won't tolerate torture, even if these ruffians will."

"You could be right," the brown-eyed cleric said, wiping his mace with an oily rag. Blood still glued abishai scales and strands of human or zombie hair to the steel head. "But Lathander wouldn't mind us turning you over to the queen's men for hanging, burning, or however they execute traitors and diabolists in these parts."

"Which brings us to an interesting question," Taegan drawled. "Which kind of cultist are you, my turtledove? We identified two varieties while quizzing your followers earlier this evening. One was made up of lunatics fanatical enough to die for Sammaster's creed, but the others were opportunists who served the cult simply in the hope of garnering wealth and power and were pragmatic enough to betray it to save their skins."

Cylla studied him then said, "Somehow I doubt that even if I answer your questions, you'll actually feel inclined to set me free."

"Because it would cheat me of my vengeance?" asked the avariel, arching an eyebrow. "You have a point. I would prefer to thrust my sword through your alabaster bosom and watch your exquisite but lifeless body crumple to the floor. But happily for you, I owe my companions a great deal, and your information is important to them. Besides, I'm not offering to forfeit every iota of satisfaction. We don't promise immunity, merely a head start. The paladins will hear of your treachery in due course, and by then, you'd better have made yourself scarce. You'd better keep running and looking over your shoulder all the days of your life. Never again will you see your friends and family. Nor enjoy the comforts and honors of the life you enjoyed in Lyrabar, an existence that would have contented any person possessed of decency or sense."

"What do you know about it?" she spat back. "Evidently you've picked up a few tricks, but I assure you, you comprehend nothing of genuine magic. I'm a true wizard. The powers we master through intellect and hard study overshadow all others accessible to men. Yet in Impiltur, I must curtsey to those who are lords merely by an accident of birth, or because they babble prayers with the proper servility. I—" She caught herself, and smiled bitterly. "Pardon me, Maestro. You touched on a subject close to my heart, but I suppose we should stick to the matter at hand. Give me a moment to consider your offer."

"While you're pondering," said Will, "think about this. You may imagine you can lie to us, but Pavel, stupid as he looks and generally is, will babble a prayer that enables him to tell. You may think we don't really want to snitch to the authorities. After all, we didn't bring them along tonight. But before, they might not have believed what a notorious fencing teacher and a band of outlanders had to say. Now we can show them the catacombs to back up our story. You may believe that if the paladins questioned you, you could bluff your way through. But I'm guessing they can sense lies, too, and even if they can't, I promise you, you've left proof of your involvement lying around down here somewhere. Finally, remember that, now that you've let us ruin your operation here in the city and are going to tattle to us, the Cult of the Dragon will hunt you, too. So you really do have to tell, and you truly do need to disappear."

"Enough persuasion," growled Dorn. He lifted his iron fist—like Pavel's mace, it was still filthy with gore—and shoved it in Cylla's face. "Some of my partners may be squeamish about torturing and killing helpless prisoners, but I'm not. So talk. Otherwise I smash your skull and splash your brains on the wall."

"All right," Cylla sighed. "What do you want to know?"

Pavel murmured an invocation and swept his medallion through a complex figure, leaving a trail of golden luminescence. The floating sigil glowed for a moment, then faded.

"Explain all of it," Kara said. She no longer felt sick or ashamed. She was too eager to find some answers at last. "What's Sammaster's grand strategy? Why did he have your cabal procuring gems and precious metals in such quantities? What do you know about the Rage?"

"I'll tell you everything I know." Cylla smiled a malicious little smile and continued, "It won't allow you to stop what's coming. Most likely it will only break your hearts."

FOURTEEN

9 Uktar, the Year of Wild Magic

Even in autumn, with their leaves fallen to make a dry, rustling carpet on the ground, the branches of the ancient trees of the Gray Forest tangled so thickly they blocked the sun and shrouded the spaces below in cool shadow. As a result, brush had a hard time growing, and hiking was easy. Sammaster liked the enormous wood as he tended to like all wild places. They were the uncorrupted corners of the world and would endure in their present form even when so much else was scoured away.

His companions, however, failed to share his appreciation. Sweating, eyes wide, they jumped at every little noise and peered nervously about. They had some inkling what the resounding hisses and bellows of the Sacred Ones portended, and even though they worshiped the creatures, the danger still frightened them. But at least they were doing better than the pack mules. The animals had refused to enter the forest at all. Their masters had had no choice but to leave them tied up and carry the sacks full of coin, ivory, amber, wine, and other gifts themselves.

Cylla Morieth quickened her step to reach the head of the column and walk alongside her master.

"Are the dragons already in frenzy?" she asked.

Sammaster smiled at her with the visage he'd worn in life, the comforting illusory mask he used to conceal the shriveled skull-face of a lich, and said, "Essentially, but they're still congregating to form a proper flight. That's why they need to call out to one another. Are you frightened?"

"I suppose I shouldn't be," she replied with a wry smile, "since I'm with you."

"Indeed you are. Though ultimately you'll have to get used to dealing with wyrms by yourself. In the world to come, you, as their trusted lieutenant, will find yourself consulting with them all the time. You may even—" An ear-splitting screech sounded off to their right—"Ah. Somebody caught our scent or heard us coming." Sammaster peered back at the column of followers straggling out behind him and said, "Stay close, as I instructed you. Your Wearer of Purple and I can't protect you otherwise."

Three wyrms, two greens and a black, burst into view, snarled at their intended prey, and charged. Despite Sammaster's orders, some of Cylla's people couldn't bear the terror of the onslaught, shrieked, and bolted. One of the greens veered off to run them down.

Sammaster gritted his teeth, annoyed. The fools would die, and he couldn't do anything more to prevent it. He had to direct all his efforts at the two dragons still racing directly at him. Otherwise, their vast strengths might overwhelm even the one wizard so formidable his arcane might had roused the jealousy and fear of Mystra herself.

The green with her proud spiky crest sucked in a deep breath, preparing to puff out a jet of corrosive vapor. The black just kept charging, apparently consumed by a bloodlust that only rending flesh with fang and claw could satisfy. Sammaster recited words of power and made the proper pass, tossing glittering powder into the air.

Before he'd perceived the discontent eating at Cylla's soul and offered her a place in his cabal, she'd been merely a teacher of minor magic devised to aid and safeguard ships at sea. Under his tutelage, she'd learned a good deal since but still lacked the innate power to cast the enchantment he'd just created. Fortunately, he'd procured her a scroll containing the same spell, and containing her dread of the huge, onrushing wyrms, she read the trigger phrase with scarcely a quaver in her voice. Together, the twin wards encompassed enough area to protect everyone who still huddled close to the wizards.

Yellow-green fumes poured from the jade-colored dragon's maw, fanning outward to engulf all the humans gathered so temptingly before her. The exhalation would have rotted their lungs, had it not failed to penetrate the domes of invisible force the mages had created. An instant later, the black drake smashed into Sammaster's effort, rebounded, then launched himself forward once more, clawing furiously but futilely at the obstruction.

Some of the cultists were unable to bear the proximity of the immense, savage creatures ripping and snapping mere inches away—the deafening roars were terrifying in and of themselves—and tried to flee. Luckily for them, they couldn't get out of the invisible shields any more than the Sacred Ones could get in. They'd be all right if they didn't crush, trample, or otherwise mangle one another in their efforts to escape.

Perhaps Sammaster could have calmed them, but he deemed it wiser to keep an eye on the wyrms, because they were warlocks in their own right. Certain spells existed that would breach or bypass the domes, and he had to be ready to react if the Sacred Ones tried to cast them.

Though confident of his ability to defend himself, he didn't want to hurt the drakes, so he was glad it didn't come to that. Either they didn't know the appropriate countermeasures or were unable to call them to mind in their current addled state. The green merely conjured a barrage of jagged ice and followed it up with a blast of shadow. The black attempted the most elementary dismissal. When sorcery failed them, they went back to assaulting the barriers with brute force. The ebony-scaled skull wyrm took to flapping up into the air then dropping on top of Sammaster's shelter, trying to smash through with his weight and momentum and no doubt risking bruises and perhaps even broken bones in the process.

The First-Speaker of the Cult of the Dragon let the gigantic reptiles continue for a while, demonstrating the futility of their aggression as a father might permit a toddler in the throes of a tantrum to rage helplessly in his grip, just to make a point about who was actually in control. It was a paradox, he supposed. He truly did revere drakes. Yet he'd also found that their pride, justifiable as it was, could make them perversely willful and short-sighted. For all their wisdom and cunning, they could be like children, and he often had to guide and even discipline them as would a loving parent if they were to mature into the omnipotent overlords of Maglas's prophecy.

When he thought he'd balked them long enough, he reached out with his mind and took hold of the Rage festering inside them. Whispering words of power in Draconic, he commanded it to disappear.

The two wyrms froze, then scuttled back a little ways, crouched down, and glared at the cultists. They were sane but still in a foul, aggressive humor. They didn't fully comprehend what had just happened to them, but rightly suspected that one of the "small folk" had tampered with them somehow.

Sammaster thought a show of confidence was the likeliest way to avert further hostilities. First, he dissolved his semblance of life. Some of his disciples moaned and cowered, but they were just going to have to cope. Next he waved his hand and wiped away the domes. It was a risk. With their keen senses, the wyrms surely felt the barriers fall and might have opted to attack immediately. Still, he needed to move the encounter along, and the simple truth was that his followers, much as he valued them, were expendable if their deaths would further the cause.

He looked up at the green and said, "Good afternoon, Needle." He shifted his gaze to the black with his withered, rotten-looking rings of flesh around the eyes and nostrils. "Dransagalor. Do you remember me?"

"Yes, Sammaster," Needle hissed.

The lich recalled that her nickname referred to the delicacy with which she could employ her prodigious talons to torture a smaller creature. Some of her unfortunate victims lingered for hours.

"Well," said the wizard, "at the risk of sounding presumptuous, I thought you would. I've visited you on several occasions over the course of the past couple centuries. From time to time, my fellow believers have called as well, always bringing tribute, useful information, and whatever aid they had to offer. We have additional gifts today."

He waved his skeletal hand at the sacks of treasure. Some had burst open when their panicked bearers cast them away, the better to run, and their scattered contents glittered on the ground.

"Good," Dransagalor grunted.

"Of course," Sammaster said, "our greatest gift is no mere bauble, but the power and immortality you've spurned since the day I met you."

Needle snorted, and a leftover trace of poison gas set the lich's disciples coughing.

"Spare us yet another regurgitation of your pleas and prophecies," said the green. "Perhaps one day, when we near the ends of our natural spans, we'll choose to perpetuate our existences by becoming dracoliches, but for now, we have no reason to divorce ourselves from the pleasures of the living."

How often had Sammaster received that same rebuff. Since its inception, the Cult of the Dragon had struggled against the implacable opposition of Mystra, the Chosen,

Harpers, and pretty much every monarch, noble, and miscellaneous busybody across the length and breadth of Faerûn. Yet even so, in the wizard's view, the greatest reason his schemes had foundered time and again was the reluctance of the wyrms themselves to embrace their destiny. For that reason, Needle and Dransagalor's lack of interest might once have elicited a spasm of frustration, but no longer. He knew how to open the creatures' eyes.

"A few minutes ago," he said, "you attacked recklessly. Stupidly."

Needle bared her fangs and hissed, "What of it? Why bother working out tactics and such when we have nothing to fear from puny creatures like men?"

"Had I wished," said Sammaster, "I could have hurt you. Certain other spellcasters and even warriors could do the same."

"It was the frenzy," Dransagalor said, flicking his black wings in a shrug.

"Yes," said the lich, "I know."

"It's taking hold of every dragon in the forest," said Needle, an eager note entering her sibilant voice, "and I think in the Earthfast Mountains, too. Soon we'll gather into flights and take to the skies to slaughter, devour, and destroy."

"You sound as if you're looking forward to it," Sammaster said, "and I understand why. Humans like to go mad, too. We drink alcohol or inhale dreammist. Some of us deliberately stoke our anger until it explodes into violence. We hold festivals where, for a day or so, people are given tacit license to indulge their carnality or any other wildness they've kept pent up inside. But few among my folk would ever aspire to go insane and stay that way forever after, and I doubt many dragons would, either. Yet that's the doom that threatens you."

"What are you talking about?" Needle growled.

"As you know," Sammaster said, "I make a study of all matters pertaining to you Sacred Ones. I've investigated this fury that periodically overwhelms you, only to discover something alarming. Another Rage is coming, and this one will differ from all that preceded it in that it will never end. It will reduce you to the level of rabid beasts."

"Why?" asked Dransagalor. "Why should this episode be any more severe than the others?"

"That I don't know," said the lich. He disliked lying to the wyrms, but it was for their own good.

"I don't think you know anything," Needle sneered. "I think this is a load of dung."

"I've already proved I've acquired some understanding of the frenzy," Sammaster said. "How else could I calm you? Do you need another demonstration? If necessary, I can make lunacy pop in and out of your head like a pendulum swinging back and forth, but you won't find it pleasant."

"I think," Dransagalor rumbled, his great voice troubled, "that the dead man's warning may actually be true. I've seen it in my dreams that this frenzy will be different—a sickness and a calamity. I hoped it was just a morbid fancy, but if Sammaster himself, a dragon friend whatever else is said of him, comes bearing the same tidings. . . ."

"Then we have nothing to fear," said Needle, "for the wizard has already given us the cure."

"I wish that was true," Sammaster said. "But in truth, I've only granted you a temporary reprieve. As the Rage intensifies, it will eventually wax strong enough to smash through any protection I can raise against it. Well, any protection except one."

The green eyed him suspiciously and replied, "Now you'll tell us dracoliches are immune to frenzy."

"As a matter of fact, yes. Surely you, with all your wisdom, already know the undead are famously resistant to any magic or force that influences the mind. This is the moment, Sacred One, the crisis—no, say rather, the *opportunity*—that will raise your exalted race to its greatest glory. So give yourself over to growth without fear or regret. Yes, it will cost you a few base pleasures of the flesh. Who knows better than I? But it would be a small price to pay even if the only effect was to preserve your profound and subtle minds, and in fact, you'll achieve far more. Undeath will increase your might tenfold and make you the unchallenged masters of the world. I know. I see it as clearly as I see your august and holy selves standing before me."

The dragons regarded him in silence for a few seconds.

Finally Needle said, "How, exactly, would we undertake this transformation?"

"Well," said Sammaster, "that's the tricky part. You'll need phylacteries fashioned with the finest gems, an elixir brewed of other rare and costly ingredients. . . . If your worshipers had prospered in recent years—perhaps, if you drakes had made as much of an effort to support us as we have to aid and nurture you—we'd already have an abundance of the requisite talismans and potions stockpiled. As it is, we'll have to create them quickly, in sufficient quantity to succor every green, black, blue, white, and red in the world."

"How can you possibly do that?" Dransagalor asked.

"By establishing secret havens," Sammaster said, "where spellcasters can perform the necessary rituals safe from interference, and your kin will come to undergo the change. I'd like to locate one such stronghold hereabouts. Your servants in Lyrabar will provide the skilled workers and supplies required." He smiled and added, "I suppose it goes without saying that the wyrms who help build and defend such a bastion will earn the gratitude of their fellows. No doubt they'll enjoy particularly high status in the world to come."

Needle said, "We might find it amusing to rule such an enclave."

"Then we have our work cut out for us," Sammaster said. "I need to find and calm as many other local drakes as I can, before they go tearing off beyond our reach. Certain lesser creatures inhabit the wood and we'll want to press them into service. We must likewise find a suitable site, consecrate the ground, build shelters and fortifications, and fetch in our mages, priests, artisans, and supplies, preferably, all before the snows begin to fall."

15 & 16 Ches, the Year of Rogue Dragons

"**I** assume," said Brimstone, his snide, insinuating whisper of a voice setting Pavel's teeth on edge, "that after the Wearer of Purple told you this, you killed her."

"No," said the priest. "We set her free as promised."

"Idiots!" the gray drake snarled, his red eyes flaring.

"She'll run," said Will, sprawled on a heap of gold in what was surely the realization of a private fantasy, "and stay well away from other cultists hereafter. She's too smart to do anything else."

"You don't know that," Brimstone replied.

"It's done," growled Dorn. He was leaning against a limestone wall at the back of the chamber, as distant as possible from both Brimstone and Kara. "So let's figure out how Cylla's information helps us. If it does."

"A pity she couldn't read Sammaster's notes, either," Taegan drawled.

The avariel had returned to his seat atop the treasure chest, once again lounging without a hint of trepidation within easy reach of Brimstone's fangs and talons.

"Well, she couldn't," said Dorn. "She'd never even seen the cipher before. So let's work with what we have."

"It seems plain," said Kara, standing beneath one of the ever-burning torches in its tall wrought-iron stand "that Sammaster understands the frenzy even better than he's admitting to the chromatic dragons. Actually, he's both inducing the coming Rage and heightening it to unprecedented levels."

"I think so, too," said Raryn, seated cross-legged on the floor and scraping at the edge of his ice-axe with a hone. The whetstone rasped rhythmically against the steel. "It's the goad he's always needed to force all the evil wyrms to change as he wants them to. If we understood exactly what it is he's discovered, maybe we could spoil his plans."

"Or maybe not," said Will. "Remember, we're talking about one of the most powerful mages the world has ever seen."

The dwarf shrugged.

"You're right," said Kara, "the idea's worth exploring. We can infer Sammaster didn't always have the power to spur and quell frenzy. Otherwise, he would have used it before this. He must have discovered it at some point during the past century, after his last great defeat."

"What if," Taegan said, "the pages in the folio are the journal of his investigations?"

"They could be anything," said Will. "A five-hundred page letter to Muffin, the puppy he doted on as a child. He is crazy, right?"

Evidently annoyed by the halfling, Brimstone showed his fangs and said, "I agree the pages may be important, but they're useless to us if we can't read them."

"Maybe not," Pavel said. "Maybe we just need to look at them in a different way."

"What do you mean?" Kara asked.

"I studied for the priesthood in Lathander's house in Heliogabalus and worked there for some years afterward. It's not the largest temple in Damara—Ilmater and Silvanus are the most popular gods thereabouts—but it's a notable seat of learning nonetheless. Reading in the scriptorium, I noticed that papers and inks manufactured in one place differ from those of another, and I picked up the knack of distinguishing between them."

"Without so much as a glance at the content of the writing?" Dorn asked.

"Yes. The most basic distinctions are obvious. Some papers are made of wood pulp. Others are goat-, sheep-, lamb-, kid-, or calfskin. Some are even woven of reeds, and some have watermarks. Beyond that, parchments vary as to hue, thickness, coarseness of grain, and the manner in which the maker separated the sheets. It's the same with inks. Pay attention to the precise color, and the degree to which they fade or flake away, and you can tell what they were made from, and where."

"So what?" Brimstone hissed.

"I see it," said Dorn. "As Sammaster wandered about trying to puzzle out the Rage, he resupplied himself with writing materials at various stops along the way, which is to say, he left tracks."

"And if we hunters follow them," said Raryn, holding his axe up to the light to inspect the edge, "go where he went, then maybe we can learn what he learned."

"Preposterous," the smoke drake said. "How does it help us to know that he spent time in, oh, say, Tantras, for example? We still won't know what he did there."

"Perhaps someone will remember him," Kara said, "or he'll have left some other indication. Or maybe we can simply guess. Suppose he's rediscovered a secret the wise once knew and subsequently lost. He may well have found it in the same kind of place where you or I would look for ancient lore."

Brimstone's luminous eyes narrowed.

"Give me the notes," Pavel said. "Let's see if I can glean anything from them."

Dorn pulled the scuffed leather folio out of a rucksack. Pavel took it into the circle of wavering glow shed by one of the torches, sat down on a rounded hump of stalagmite, and rested the bundle of papers in his lap. After what had befallen Brimstone, he felt a twinge of trepidation opening the cover, even though he himself had already looked at the notes without harm.

Mainly, though, he was worried not that Sammaster's shadow would possess him, but rather that his idea would come to nothing.

Please, Lathander, he silently prayed, let me be right. We've fought dragons and demons to accomplish the task you set us, but none of it will mean anything if we can't figure out what to do next.

He examined a number of sheets, peering, fingering the edges and texture, and holding them up to his nose to smell them. After a time, he nodded.

"What?" asked Will.

"By and large, I recognize what I'm looking at. These could have been papers and pigments from some faraway land we know nothing of, but they aren't. Sammaster penned the notes here in our part of the North. They're jumbled, though. I have vellum from Phlan intermingled with folded leaves of foolscap from Trailsend. I think somebody—Gorstag, perhaps—dropped the folio, the pages scattered, and in his haste, he stuck them back together any old way. The sheets aren't numbered, but I'm going to try to group like with like."

The chore took a while, and during the course of it, he noticed something else.

"Some of the sections are plainly older than others," he said. "They smell mustier and have seen more wear. I'll try to use that to arrange the sections in some semblance of chronological order."

As he finished up, Will said, "Sammaster's supposed to be a mastermind, but apparently it still took him years to suss out the secret of the Rage. Maybe that's because he followed some leads that didn't pan out. So let's say we figure out all the different places he went. If we visit every one, we could waste a lot of time, and unlike him, we haven't got it to spare."

"I imagine," Kara said, "the lengthy sections of the journal are the significant ones. Where he failed to discover anything, he wouldn't have much to write."

Pavel separated a thick sheaf of pages from the rest. "He wrote a lot here, and it's one of the older sections. It's possible this is where he recorded his first breakthrough."

"Then what does it tell you?" Brimstone demanded. "Anything?"

"What we have," the priest said, "are kidskin pages from Elmwood and inks from Melvaunt, both towns on the shores of the central portion of the Moonsea."

"Towns built on the ruins of older settlements," said Dorn, the firelight glinting on the iron portions of his body, "in a country thick with forgotten tombs and abandoned, tumble-down towers. Where would you start?"

"Maybe," Pavel thought aloud, "with the oldest thing of all."

But it was only a guess and could easily be wrong. He flipped through the notes, looking for some additional bit of information to support his hunch. Even though he couldn't read the wretched things, surely something—

Perhaps the Morninglord aided him, for the figure popped out at him, even though it was only a crude little doodle virtually lost among countless lines of tiny script.

"Look at this," said the priest.

The others gathered around. Proximity to Brimstone made Pavel feel the usual pang of outrage and loathing, but he was so intent on his discovery that for once, it seemed more a simple distraction than a call to arms.

"What's it supposed to be?" asked Will. "A misshapen, one-eyed head?"

"It's a map," Pavel said, "rendered in a style we Northerners rarely see anymore. But the elves sometimes put west at the top. Isn't that right, Maestro Nightwind?"

Taegan's mouth tightened almost imperceptibly for an instant, as if he found the question annoying, though he answered with his customary courtesy and poise.

"I really have no idea. But if you maintain it, prince of scholars, I'm sure it must be so."

Will cocked his head to look at the doodle sideways, then let out a whistle.

"Exactly," Pavel said. He looked around at the rest of the company. "I assume that if even a dullard like Will comprehends, the rest of you do, also."

"I comprehend that the place has an evil reputation," growled Dorn, "and that even if it didn't, it would be hard to explore."

"Please," Kara said, with an urgency in her comely face and sweet voice that would surely have swayed Pavel even if he wasn't already disposed to help her. "You're going home to the Moonsea anyway, aren't you?"

Dorn made a spitting sound and turned away. His show of ill temper didn't surprise Pavel, but something else did. From long experience, he knew that if the big man actually meant to refuse Kara, he would have said no in a manner so blunt and clear as to be unmistakable.

"Before you all grow too excited," Brimstone whispered, "realize that everything the sun priest has said is pure speculation. It's possible he's misinterpreted the significance of the folio entirely. Still, I agree it's worth following where the clues seems to lead. But we have other work as well."

Will said, "If somebody doesn't stop the cult's mischief in the Gray Forest, we'll soon be up to our arses in indestructible dracoliches. That could be even worse than ordinary dragons running around in a Rage."

"Kindly allow me to attend to that," Taegan said. "Impiltur is my home, so it seems sensible for me to expedite matters here."

"Thank you," Kara said. "You have a noble heart."

"You're far too kind," Taegan replied. "I don't generally fight for anything but my own well-being and satisfaction, and I've achieved the latter. For after all, Sammaster didn't kill my student and burn my school. Cylla and her underlings did, and with your help, I've avenged myself on them. Unfortunately, however, I remain impoverished, and it hasn't escaped my attention that the cultists have imported gems and precious metals into the wood. Exactly the plunder I need to recoup my fortunes."

"You give yourself too little credit," said Kara, shaking her head.

"I've endured my share of criticism," said the avariel, "but never before that particular opinion."

"You can't storm the cult stronghold by yourself," snapped Dorn. "You need soldiers."

"Well, we told Cylla we were going to confer with the authorities," Taegan replied. "Apparently, I actually am."

"Just give the rest of us time to disappear," Kara said. "Queen Sambryl employs a troupe of bronze dragons. It's likely some of them have offered their allegiance to Lareth as well. I don't need any more of his agents accosting me."

"Perhaps the time has come for you to plead with him again," Pavel said.

"It's as Brimstone said," Kara replied. "So far, all we really have is speculation. Much as I'd like to, I can't believe it would change his mind, especially now that I've fought Llimark, Moonwing, and Azhaq."

"It appears we have our strategy," Brimstone said.

Raryn said, "Not quite. What will you be doing while the rest of us are running about risking our necks?"

"For now, I'm the weapon we hold in reserve. Rest assured, I'll take the field when the time is right."

"Don't count on it," said Pavel to the dwarf. "You know how a common vampire must linger close to his coffin. Most likely this dead thing before us has some similar limitation that makes him fear to stray too far from home."

"You know nothing!" the gray wyrm snarled. "Our business is done, so go. Or stay. All this talk has made me thirsty."

* * *

When Dorn stepped onto the balcony outside the room he and his comrades had rented, he found Raryn taking the night air. Clad only in his breeches, indifferent to the cold night wind that stirred his long white hair, the arctic dwarf stood gazing out across Lyrabar. The moon had set, and to human eyes, the countless temples and mansions were little more than streaks of pale blur, but of course, Raryn could see considerably more.

"You couldn't sleep either?" the tracker asked.

Dorn grunted.

"I wanted another look at this place," Raryn said. "As we worked our way south, the galley put in at a whole series of interesting towns, but this is the grandest of the lot. It's a pity we have to leave before we've had a chance to explore it."

"I just hope," Dorn said, "we can go away quicker than we came. We need to book passage on a faster ship, one that doesn't stop at every dilapidated hut and rotting dock along the shore or go by way of Sembia. We're lucky spring is at hand. More skippers will be putting out to sea."

"So we can probably find one who's looking to make a fast run up the Dragon Reach back to our usual hunting grounds. That should make you happy, but you don't look it. Does it still rankle that Taegan flirted with Kara, and she smiled back at him?"

"What in the name of Baator are you talking about?"

Raryn shrugged and said, "You glowered at them like you're glaring at me now."

"If I did, it was just because the avariel's manner gets on my nerves. It's all pose and affectation. But he's proved he's solid enough where it counts, and I have no reason to care what passes between him and the wyrm. He's seen what she is. If he still hankers after her, it's his lookout."

"I don't think he does, really. As you said, he's just decided to wear a certain mask."

"They should get along well, then, since she's a fraud, too."

"I knew you hadn't forgiven her her deceptions. You make it plain whenever we're all together. That's why I was surprised when you didn't argue against helping her any further."

Dorn snorted and said, "We've already played that game, and I know how it ends. I say no, the rest of you say yes, and I wind up giving in to avoid breaking up the partnership. Why go through the same stupidity another time? But I don't like this, and it's not just because I hate working for a dragon."

"What is it, then?"

"This affair is just too huge. Have you really thought about it, even to the extent of just putting it all together into words? We're supposed to spoil the schemes of an infamous undead archmage and his cult of followers. That's how we preserve the sanity of the entire race of wyrms and keep them from either laying waste to all Faerûn or becoming invincible dracoliches and ruling humans and dwarves forever after. It's like something out of those old, long-winded sagas that take all night for a bard to chant. It's a task for these Chosen and Harpers we keep hearing about or whole armies of knights and wizards, not a handful of ruffians like us."

"Well, Taegan is supposed to scare up some men-at-arms. As for the rest of it, it wasn't the Chosen who ran into Kara or wound up in possession of the folio. It was us, and wishing won't make it otherwise."

Dorn felt chilly and pulled his cloak tighter around him. "It's all right for Pavel. He decided early on that the Morninglord wants us to carry out this task, and even Brimstone's involvement failed to shake his conviction."

"Maybe he's right."

"Maybe, but since I'm not able to feel what he feels, it doesn't help me. Will sees all life as a game and himself as the cleverest player of all. So even matters as weighty as these can't overawe him, especially if greed is undermining his judgment."

"Will's good at his trade. As are you."

Dorn, scowling, replied, "I'm a big, mean freak with a knack for slaughtering big, mean animals. Maybe I help a few people that way, folk who would otherwise get eaten. But the notion that thousands of men and women I've never even met will live or die depending on not just my ability to hunt but to unravel arcane mysteries and the gods only know what else . . . it's laughable and terrifying at the same time. You're sensible. Doesn't it bother you?"

"When I was a boy," Raryn said, "living with my tribe on the Great Glacier, we went forth every day and hunted. If we found enough game, everyone could eat, and everyone would live. If we failed, some or even all of us would die. It was very simple. Then I developed a yen to see what lay beyond the ice, and drifted south to the lands of men."

"Where you found everything was much more complicated."

"No," Raryn said, grinning. "That's what I expected to find, but truly, I discovered life was just the same in its essence. The only complicated thing is the way 'civilized' folk fret about their problems. You twist and pick at them until they look bewildering, but really, they're not."

"I don't understand."

"You said it yourself. Ever since you ran away from Hillsfar, you've fought to protect others, and you still are. The fact that more people are in jeopardy this time around doesn't change anything. Just do your work as usual."

Dorn smiled slightly. He felt a little better, though he wasn't quite sure why. The dwarf's stark perspective on duty, struggle, and survival didn't actually seem all that comforting.

"This way of thinking heartens you, does it?" Dorn asked.

"Well, when it fails, I tell myself that none of this foolishness with indecipherable papers and conspiracies of rogue dragons matters a hair on a mole's rump. Surely Mystra and the Chosen know all about Sammaster's scheme and are even now hurrying to foil it. We just can't tell it from our vantage point."

"If we really believed that, we could cut Kara loose and forget all about the cursed Rage."

"But where would be the sport or profit in that?"

"Nowhere, I suppose." He used his hand of flesh and blood to clap Raryn on the shoulder. "I guess I'll see if I can get at least an hour or two of sleep. We want to be down at the harbor well before the morning tide."

SIXTEEN

1 Tarsakh, the Year of Rogue Dragons

Before his academy burned, Taegan had possessed a number of outfits so fine they were even suitable for a formal appearance before the Council of Lords. Now he was down to one, purchased with coin he'd obtained by selling the pearl ring Kara had pressed on him at their parting. She tried to give him other jewels, but he'd refused her. Foolish of him, perhaps, but she was a comrade, not a patron, and it just hadn't felt right.

In point of fact, the new suit was only barely good enough. Cognizant of his misfortunes, all the best tailors had refused to create anything new for him until he paid the considerable sums he already owed. He'd had to make do with a journeyman's efforts. He straightened his scarlet caffa doublet, checked the hang of his newly oiled leather scabbard, and tugged his billowing black cambric sleeves down, making sure he looked as elegant as possible.

The liveried servants, evidently responding to a signal he'd failed to notice, swung open the tall, arched double doors. A herald thumped a staff on the floor and announced him. Taegan strode over the threshold.

The white marble hall with its high, barrel-vaulted ceiling was a place of blank surfaces and simple lines, considerably more austere than Taegan would have expected of an important chamber within the royal palace. That, however, was not the biggest surprise awaiting him. Everyone said Impiltur's queen was more devoted to her pleasures than the cares of government and generally content to leave the latter to her ministers. Yet Sambryl, a thin, sharp-featured, but comely middle-aged woman with dyed brassy hair piled high in an elaborate coiffure, attended their deliberations that afternoon, enthroned alone on the higher tier of the semicircular dais. She had a sour look about her. Perhaps she wished she was elsewhere, or maybe she was simply cold. In keeping with its severe appearance, the hall lacked a fireplace or any other means of warding off a chill.

Nine of the twelve lords sat along the step below their sovereign. The other three were evidently otherwise engaged or absent from the citadel entirely. Paladins all, not merely barons but mystic warriors sworn to one or another of the gods of light, they wore—as protocol required, evidently— plate armor and white surcoats emblazoned with their arms, which incorporated emblems of Ilmater, Lathander, Helm, or Sune. They'd left off the helmets, though. No doubt it made it easier to hear one another's pronouncements.

A halberdier stood at attention on the floor at either end of the curved platform. Most monarchs would have demanded more bodyguards. But Impiltur had been peaceful and prosperous for a number of years, and perhaps Sambryl had no fear of assassins. Or maybe she believed the martial prowess and supernatural powers of the lords rendered additional protection superfluous.

After what felt like a long hike under the cold regard of the aristocrats, Taegan reached the section of floor between the curved arms of the dais, bowed low, and straightened up again. Even the greatest folk in Impiltur didn't require the extreme deference that would have required a commoner to remain in a servile posture until granted leave to rise.

An old man with a hooked blade of a nose and a lipless slash of a mouth sat up even straighter, if that was possible. His coat-of-arms was an elaboration of the eye-and-gauntlet symbol of Helm, god of vigilance.

"Maestro Nightwind," he growled.

"Lord Oriseus," Taegan replied.

Of all the council, Oriseus was the most vehement opponent of the fencing academies and had tried to shut them down on a number of occasions. Which ought not to matter in relation to the current situation, but the elf already had an inkling it was a shame the old buzzard wasn't one of the paladins busy elsewhere.

"You escorted several yeomen of the watch through the cellars of an old tannery," Oriseus said as he lifted a piece of parchment. "I have the commander's deposition here."

"I'm gratified to hear it," Taegan said. "It took me a while to persuade the officers of the law to accompany me, and a considerably longer time to gain admittance here. It's good to know we won't waste any more time trying to lay hands on the captain or his report."

Oriseus frowned. "You're insolent."

"So people tell me, but truly, I don't mean to show disrespect to Her Gracious Majesty or her deputies, either. If I seem out of sorts, I beg you to attribute it to the fact that I have serious matters to present for your consideration, and I fail to understand why you've chosen to keep me waiting."

"Did it occur to you it might have something to do with your trade and reputation?"

"My trade is teaching people to defend themselves, a right that Her Majesty's law justly and compassionately recognizes. My reputation, if it speaks the truth, is that of a master who gives sound instruction and exhorts his students to use their skills prudently. But even if I was the vilest blackguard ever to set foot in Lyrabar, the tidings I bring would still be vitally important."

"Perhaps so," said a beefy, relatively young man with a pink complexion and curly, sandy goatee. The device on his surcoat featured the bound-hands sigil of Ilmater. If Taegan wasn't mistaken, he was Lord Rangrim, a dragon rider celebrated for his campaigns against the raiders of the Pirate Isles. "Would you give us your story from the beginning? We know what you told the watch, but it's evident you have a good deal more to say."

"It will be my pleasure," Taegan replied, and he spun the tale as he'd rehearsed it, omitting any mention of Kara, her circle of rogues, Brimstone, or the folio lest word of them reach either wyrms devoted to Lareth or surviving members of Sammaster's conspiracy. Dorn's hunters became a fellowship of wandering adventurers with an old score to settle against the Cult of the Dragon, who'd helped Taegan smash the Lyrabar chapter before heading out to parts unknown. Similarly, the avariel maintained he never had succeeded in learning the true identity of Gorstag's employer, and would have told the same lie even if Kara hadn't urged him to keep certain aspects of the affair a secret. He was reasonably certain the paladins wouldn't like the thought of cooperating with a vampiric smoke drake any more than Pavel had.

By the time he finished, his throat was dry. Unfortunately, the only beverage in evidence was in a golden cup sitting on a little table by the queen, and even he wasn't impudent enough to request a sip from that.

Lord Idriane, another of Ilmater's warriors, a petite woman who would have been rather pretty if not for her broken nose and the close-cropped hair that exposed a pair of protruding ears, said, "This is . . . unfortunate."

"That's one word for it," Oriseus said. "Private feuds and vendettas . . . slaughter in the street and in hidden warrens underground. . . . At the start of this interview, Maestro,

I alluded to your reputation. Whatever you may imagine, you're infamous as a promoter of brawls, duels, and licentiousness in all its aspects, a common whoremonger, in fact, and your conduct in this matter proves you fully deserve your notoriety."

"Because I didn't report my troubles to the authorities as soon as they began?" Taegan asked. "I promised a dying friend I wouldn't and only recently realized it's a pledge I must disregard for the kingdom's sake. Anyway, considering the scorn with which you knights regard me, would you have credited my story?"

"What makes you assume," Oriseus said, "that anyone credits it now?"

Taegan felt a surge of anger but made sure the emotion didn't show in his face.

"Milord," said Taegan, "I perceive that you and I, however dissimilar we may be in many respects, are alike in one. We both love to spar, be it with blades or words. But is this the time? Your priests and wizards have examined the lair of the cult. They saw the remains of the zombies and abishai as well as the glyphs, pentacles, and grimoires, instruments all for invoking Velsharoon, Shar, and the rest of the deities and lesser powers of evil. I gave them the *Tome of the Dragon* to authenticate. I explained why Cylla Morieth absconded in the night. Surely it's obvious I truly have been brawling and dueling with necromancers and traitors to the Crown."

"He has a point," Rangrim said, "so much as we may regret the way he handled this business, let's concentrate on matters of greater import. Maestro, would you like to know why it took us so long to grant you an audience? It's true, your reputation, fairly earned or not, was partly to blame. But it was mainly that we have other urgent matters to concern us."

"He doesn't need to know about that," Oriseus snapped.

"The news will reach the city at large soon enough," Rangrim said, "and perhaps, given his recent experiences, he can contribute something to our discussion."

"If I can," Taegan said, "I certainly will."

"Until you came to us," Rangrim said, "we had no inkling the Cult of the Dragon was currently active in Impiltur. But we had heard tidings of dragon flights. Wyrms are attacking out of the Earthspur Mountains and from across the Easting Reach, threatening Sarshel, Dilpur, and the whole northern part of the kingdom. Three lords have already ridden forth to direct the defense. The rest of us will follow soon enough. Perhaps you understand the implications."

The elf hesitated, then said, "I see it lends additional credence to my story, but I take it you refer to something more."

"We don't have any drakes attacking out of the west," said Idriane. "If you were a war captain, in which direction would you march your forces?"

"It's possible," Taegan replied, "Sammaster himself set the wyrms on their rampage as a feint to keep your attention off the Gray Forest. Or maybe the frenzy is to blame. Either way, you can't let the problem, grave as it is, prevent you from addressing an even greater threat. As I understand it, dracoliches are even more formidable than living dragons, indeed, virtually unstoppable and indestructible."

"Yet no one has seen any dracoliches," Rangrim said. "Perhaps things aren't going according to plan in the Gray Forest. Perhaps, for whatever reason, nothing is happening there at all."

"Whereas things are definitely happening to the east and north," Oriseus said. "Thousands of people are in danger, and the farmers flee their lands. If they can't manage the spring planting, the entire realm will starve in a few months' time."

"I understand" Taegan said. "But you must confront both menaces."

"Why?" Oriseus said. "Because of hearsay? For that's really all you've given us. You tell us what Cylla Morieth and Gorstag Helder allegedly said, but the one vanished and the other is dead. We can't interrogate either for ourselves."

"I give you my word," Taegan said, "that I've accurately repeated what they said. If you doubt me, cast a spell to test my veracity. I know you can."

"As far as I'm concerned," Rangrim said, "that isn't necessary. I suspect you haven't told us everything, Maestro, nor are you a person of saintly character. But I certainly don't sense the wickedness required to send the royal army chasing off on a fool's errand while countless innocent lives hang in the balance. I'm satisfied you believe you're giving good advice.

"But that," the curly-bearded human continued, "doesn't mean it really is. Perhaps your informants misled you, either intentionally or because they themselves misunderstood the situation. In any case, it's my opinion we should first devote all our efforts to suppressing the dragons who are even now devastating the settled parts of our country. Afterward will be time enough to take a look at a wood where no one lives. What do the rest of you think?"

Without exception, though some looked more certain than others, the other lords declared their agreement.

Oriseus gave Taegan a smug, unpleasant smile. Had it not come from a knight of unimpeachable holiness, the avariel might even have deemed it spiteful.

Taegan looked up at the woman seated on the uppermost portion of the dais.

"You see . . ." the noble began.

"Your Majesty," the avariel cut in, "it appears the lords have formed their opinion. But surely it's the queen's decision that counts."

Oriseus glared at him as he said, "Her Majesty trusts her knights' judgment in military matters."

Taegan kept gazing up at Sambryl as he said, "Your Majesty, I love Impiltur, this splendid land that has accepted me as one of its own even though I'm not human, nor even a dwarf or halfling. Terrible as this current crisis is, I thought I discerned one glimmer of light amid the darkness. I believed it had put me in a position to repay the kindness and opportunity I've found here. If that isn't true, if I'm simply a fool wasting a great monarch's precious time, I beg you to tell me so directly. I at least want to go away knowing that my wise sovereign herself has weighed my words and found them wanting."

Oriseus twisted his head to look up at Sambryl.

"Yes," he said, "please do tell him, Your Majesty, if that's what it takes to shut him up."

Perhaps it was his manifest certainty that the queen would do as he said that irked her. At any rate, she gave him a frigid stare.

"Without even a thank you, Lord Oriseus? Whatever you think of him and whatever the worth of his suggestions, he was instrumental in rooting out a nest of traitors none of my paladins or Warswords even suspected."

Oriseus hesitated a beat then said, "So it seems, Your Majesty, and a reward is probably in order. I'll see to it."

Taegan's pulse quickened at the mention of payment, but not enough to permit the paladin to buy him off and so vanquish him in their duel of words.

"I don't want coin," the maestro said, reflecting that he seemed to be saying that constantly anymore, even though nothing could be farther from his actual sentiments. "I want you to act on the information I risked my life to obtain."

"We told you," Oriseus said, "that would be reckless and generally inadvisable."

"And I told you," Taegan said, "I'm still waiting to hear the queen's opinion. Please, Your Majesty."

Sambryl sat and chewed at her lower lip for a few heartbeats, her little white incisors marring the scarlet paint. Evidently it was her habit when pondering.

"We've been at peace for a long while," she finally said. "Our soldiers have repelled the occasional band of marauders but have had no occasion to fight an actual war or endure the losses such a conflict brings. Which means that barring gross mismanagement, we should have plenty of men, horses, and supplies. Enough, perhaps, to send one force northeast and another west."

"Your Majesty," Oriseus said, "we don't know precisely how many enemies we have to fight in the country along the Easting Reach, but we do know they're all dragons."

"And our men-at-arms," she replied, "constitute the assembled might of a powerful kingdom."

"It's still my opinion we may need every bit of our strength. I hope you trust my advice, and the judgment of my peers, over the fancies of a troublemaker, an outlander from who knows where."

"I may look peculiar in your eyes," Taegan said, "but I reiterate, I consider myself a son of Impiltur no less than you. A loyal subject who reveres his noble queen and looks to her, not her deputies, to decide the most vital questions facing our homeland."

Sambryl laughed. It startled Taegan, and by the looks of it, the lords as well.

"What a paragon of virtue I must be," she said. "So far, Maestro, I believe you've praised me as gracious, just, compassionate, noble, wise, and great. Is this relentless parade of compliments the technique you use to lure rich merchants and their sons to your school and their wives and daughters to your bed?"

"I'd like to think I generally display a lighter touch," Taegan replied with a grin, "but in some measure, I suppose the answer is yes. It's been my experience that the wealthy are susceptible to flattery."

"Perhaps queens hear so much, they become immune."

"I thank the Watcher," Oriseus said, "that Your Majesty sees through this clown and refuses to let him drive a wedge between yourself and your faithful lieutenants. Will you send him away?"

"No, Milord, I will not."

Oriseus's trap of a mouth tightened as he said, "As you command."

"Yes," Sambryl continued, "as *I* command. Because, his blandishments aside, Maestro Nightwind has alluded to an important truth. I do rule here."

Rangrim frowned and said, "No one disputes that, Your Majesty."

"You may not even realize it," the queen replied, "but you do. Possibly it's my own fault. I've generally been content to enjoy life and let the council run the kingdom. Why not? The land prospered, the people were happy, and I trusted that a council of paladins was about as wise and incorruptible as any governing body could be."

"We've done our best to—" Oriseus began.

"Yet I always remembered," Sambryl interrupted, "that I'm the sovereign, and like my ancestors, have the duty to lead the realm in times of crisis."

"Your Majesty," Oriseus said, "if I may speak bluntly, your predecessors were paladins. You aren't even a warrior. It only makes sense for you to delegate these decisions to those who are."

"No," she said. "Whatever you may have assumed, I didn't come to these chambers today simply to smile and nod at whatever you proposed. Rest assured, I value the council's advice, but I believe that with regard to the Gray Forest, you're underestimating the danger. Perhaps your disdain for the maestro's profession, your nostalgia for the days when burghers knew their place, and no one but a chevalier schooled in the old traditions would dare call himself a master swordsman has blinded you."

Idriane said, "Your Majesty, we will of course obey you in this as in all things. That understood, may I at least recommend that we send the greater part of our troops northeast, where battle already rages, and a smaller force west to assess the situation there?"

"Yes," Sambryl said. She sipped from her golden goblet then continued, "But a number of the Queen's Bronzes will accompany the lesser force to make sure it's strong enough to do whatever needs doing. Afterward, dragons on the wing can cross the realm swiftly enough to join the campaign on the other side."

"In that case," Rangrim said, "I volunteer to lead the

scouts. I suppose one of us lords ought to do it."

"Thank you, Your Majesty," Taegan said. "When do we depart?"

Oriseus made a spitting sound then said, "Don't be absurd. Evidently you know how to conduct yourself in a tavern brawl, but you'd best leave real fighting to the Warswords."

Taegan could all but feel the gems the cultists had amassed slipping through his fingers, and perhaps that wasn't even the worst of it. The patronizing dismissal stung his pride.

"You continue to underestimate me, Milord."

"Perhaps he does," said Rangrim unexpectedly. "At any rate, I think you've earned the right to tag along, and since it's my command I suppose that settles it."

Taegan bowed.

"Just promise me," Rangrim added, "we'll have something more interesting than chiggers and mosquitoes to fight."

"You can count on it," replied Taegan. "As I said, according to the fair Cylla, even if the cult hasn't succeeded in making any dracoliches yet, they have live wyrms defending their stronghold."

"It's a good thing, then, that we'll have our own dragons, powerful, fearless, and true," said the paladin. "Wait until you meet my friend Quelsandas. I'll match him against any black or green ever hatched."

SEVENTEEN

11 Tarsakh, the Year of Rogue Dragons

"**O**h, blood and dung," the sailor cursed.

Dorn had been standing in the bow taking in the unique purple hue of the Moonsea. Unlike normal people, he had no actual home, but except for the past couple months, he had spent his entire life near that body of water, a deep freshwater lake despite its name, and somehow it pleased him to see it once again. Jarred from his contemplation, he turned and saw that the ferryman had genuine cause for dismay.

Earlier that afternoon, the bargelike ferry with its wide deck and shallow draft had finished its transit of the marshy River Lis and turned west toward Elmwood, the first settlement of any size whatsoever along the southern coast. The town was a smallish place that made its living fishing, farming, and facilitating the passage of travelers and goods back and forth between the Moonsea and the Dragon Reach. Over the years, Dorn had exterminated several dangerous beasts on the settlement's behalf and found it to be something of an oddity. Some inexplicable chance had by and large exempted it from the bloody strife and full-scale disasters so often afflicting the rest of the region, and perhaps as a result, the inhabitants tended to lack the dour, grasping, suspicious mindset exhibited by so many of their neighbors.

But maybe they were on their way to learning; it looked as if trouble had found Elmwood at last. Three war galleys and a couple of smaller patrol boats floated at anchor in her harbor. Each flew the device of Zhentil Keep, a dark scepter ablaze with green fire, set against a golden disk clutched in the claws of a black wyrm. A single such vessel might have stopped at the village to conduct some innocuous bit of business, but the presence of so many at once seemed a sure sign the agents of the Black Network, the Zhentish hegemony's ruling cartel, were up to something sinister.

"Everybody!" Dorn bellowed. "Come here, now!"

His comrades hurried forward. So did a number of the other passengers, ferrymen, and the captain himself, all wanting to see what was the matter. Nobody looked happy when he found out.

Will rounded on the skipper, a weather-beaten fellow who went about with a stubby, straight-stemmed pipe constantly clenched between his yellow teeth whether he'd bothered to fill and light the bowl or not.

"Why didn't you warn us?" the halfling said.

"They weren't there when we headed down river," the captain said.

"Can you land elsewhere?" Pavel asked.

"If we turn tail, I reckon the Zhents'll chase us, and we can't outrun a war galley in this tub. It's less risky just to go where we meant to and see what happens. I hate the thieving bastards too, but at least I don't see anybody fighting."

"Likely because the Zhents don't need to," Raryn said, and Dorn could only agree. Whatever the reavers from the great citadels at the western end of the Moonsea wanted, little Elmwood with its lack of men-at-arms and fortifications would have had little choice but to accede to their demands. "Still, you're probably right. We should dock as planned."

The captain started giving orders to his crew. Kara approached Dorn and murmured, "In my other form, I could fly us all to shore."

He sneered and said, "Good idea. The Zhents would never notice, and even if they did, they wouldn't think it worth investigating."

"I was just pointing out an option," she said with a sigh.

To his surprise, Dorn felt a pang of shame.

"I know," he said, "and it wasn't a completely stupid idea. But we agreed that to protect your sanity and keep Lareth's agents off our track, you'll only change when you absolutely have to, and this isn't an emergency yet. Just be ready with your spells."

It took another hour of gnawing apprehension before the ferry tied up at its berth. In many respects, it looked to Dorn as if the docks were operating normally, but things were different in at least one unfortunate respect. Like a murder of oversized crows, a dozen black-clad warriors swaggered down the pier to meet the arriving vessel. In the lead slouched a barrel-chested priest of Bane, who with his greasy, uncombed hair and stained clothing, looked more brutish ruffian than scholar of divine mysteries. He wore the Lord of Darkness's clenched-fist emblem and carried a morningstar, the god's sacred weapon, in his gauntleted hand. The harbormaster crept along at the tail end of the procession, silent and ignored. The priest climbed aboard the ferry without waiting for an invitation.

As the first of his minions followed, he announced, "I'm Pharaxes Zora, servant of the Black Hand captain of the warship *Dagger* out of Yulash, and now customs agent of the alliance."

"Well, aren't you special," murmured Will.

"What alliance?" Pavel asked, without any overt show of hostility.

Having known him for years, Dorn could tell his friend didn't like Pharaxes much better than he had Brimstone, but he wasn't yet making an issue of it. He'd even tucked his sun amulet inside his brigandine to avoid revealing to which god he'd vowed his own service.

"Why, the alliance against the wyrms," Pharaxes said. "Haven't you heard? They've started attacking all across the North . . . and the South too, for all we know. We folk of the Moonsea must forget our differences and band together to stave off the threat. Otherwise, the drakes will eat us all, and since we Zhentarim have the biggest army and most powerful spellcasters in the region, it only makes sense for us to lead the defense."

He spoke with a cynical leer that suggested he was enjoying the knowledge that his audience mistrusted his words but it didn't matter anyway.

"Did the defense," Kara asked, "require you to occupy Elmwood? Coming in, I didn't see any signs of marauding dragons along the southern shore."

Pharaxes said, "You mistake me, lass. Naturally, we haven't seized control here. Much as this wretched little pest-hole would benefit from our guidance, that could be misconstrued as an act of war. But I'm sure you understand it takes resources to fend off wave upon wave of dragon flights, which is exactly what we're facing. Therefore, since we're fighting for the benefit of all, we're asking everyone to contribute to the effort."

"In other words," Pavel said, "trying to extort fees and duties from every ship that sails these waters."

The ferry captain's jaw clenched as if he was in danger

of biting his pipe in two, but he was too cautious to say anything.

"As well as requisitioning vital materials from their cargoes," said the priest of Bane, "and likewise taxing those who travel overland. Our plan is that henceforth no vessel or caravan will embark without purchasing a license. Not only will that provide for our warriors' needs, it will help the wayfarers as well, because when we know who's traveling where, it will be easier to watch over them."

"What happens to folk caught wandering without permission?" asked Will. "Something nasty, I suspect."

"As I said," Pharaxes replied, "we've established this scheme to protect everyone. Those who seek to undermine it are traitors to the common weal and must expect stern treatment."

"I doubt," Pavel said, "that Hillsfar, Thentia, Melvaunt, or Phlan have agreed to this scheme, which means your grand alliance has some major holes in it."

Pharaxes scowled.

"Everyone will come around in time," he said. "Meanwhile, we're in Elmwood, not Hillsfar, and I've spent enough time explaining the realities of life." He smirked at the ferry captain. "You owe ten gold. In addition, my men will inspect your cargo. You understand you're forbidden to set sail again without the proper document." He rounded on the passengers. "You folk must contribute also, each according to his ability to pay. To determine your proper share, we'll examine the contents of your purses, pouches, and baggage."

Dorn scowled. It was robbery, pure and simple, and he resented it. Still, he and his comrades had a job to finish, and it would probably be easier if they didn't have to contend with the enmity of the Zhentarim in the process. Much as the prospect rankled, it might be preferable simply to surrender a portion of their coin.

Kara's treasure, however, was a different matter. He was reasonably certain that if the reavers caught a glimpse of the fortune in jewels she carried, they'd greedily conceive a pretext for seizing it all, and that would be too great a loss to accept. Trying to be stealthy about it, he reached for the hilt of his knife.

"Wait," Kara whispered. "Just stand in front of me. Block their view."

Dorn did as she asked. She sang a spell under her breath, then gave him a little pat on his human arm to signal she was done. When he glanced down at her, she no longer appeared to have a pouch hanging on her braided blue leather belt. He inferred that she'd turned it invisible.

It was a good trick, but as it turned out, the wrong move. Pharaxes wore a silver ring set with a milky oval stone. Strands of red twisted through the whiteness like blood billowing in water. When he noticed the transformation, he extended his arm and turned, aiming his hand at all the ferrymen and passengers in turn.

When he came to Kara, the gem, if such it was, turned entirely scarlet. Evidently it was a device for detecting spellcasting.

Pharaxes gave her a malevolent grin. "What was the magic, bitch? What did you do?"

"She's a bard," said Dorn. "She uses petty charms to make people like her. She probably hoped it would move you to treat her kindly."

"I didn't ask you, tinface," the Zhentish captain said. "What did you do, whore?"

"What my friend told you," Kara said.

Pharaxes glanced around at some of his men and said, "Search her. If she resists, beat her senseless. If you find some indication she's misbehaved, we'll take her aboard *Dagger* and punish her properly. We'll have some fun and make an example of her."

Two warriors advanced on Kara, and Dorn sprang to intercept them. Even as he lunged, he was conscious of the irony implicit in his response. He was scrambling to protect a dragon. True, in human form, Kara was in many respects as vulnerable as an ordinary woman, but even so, what did it matter? He hated dragons.

Pavel, Will, and Raryn attacked at the same instant he did, and they all caught the Zhents by surprise. Apparently the soldiers, though they'd seemed reasonably alert, hadn't truly imagined that any of the motley assortment of ferrymen and travelers, even rough-looking types like the hunters, would dare assault well-armed agents of the Black Network in broad daylight with still more Zhents close at hand.

Dorn swiped with his iron claws, and his target fell with half his neck torn away. Pivoting, the half-golem punched. Kara's other assailant caught the blow on his buckler, hopped backward, and snatched to draw his blade. That was all right. At least he no longer posed an immediate threat to Kara, who, singing, brought a floating blue translucent shield glimmering into existence in front of her body.

Dorn jerked his knife from its sheath. The deck was too crowded with milling, babbling bystanders for him to use a blade as long as the bastard sword to best effect. He turned, looking for Pharaxes, who surely represented the gravest threat. He was too late. The sudden assault had startled the Zhents, but someone had trained them well. A pair of them had positioned themselves in front of their leader to keep him safe while he cast his spells.

Pharaxes started shouting an incantation, but Pavel rapped, "Stop."

That single word carried its own palpable charge of magic, and the cleric of Bane faltered and botched his prayer. He spun around toward the wayfarer in his nondescript travel-stained clothing and acid-scorched leather armor, who was wearing his sun amulet in plain view. Pavel gave the Zhent a malevolent smile, and a duel of priestly magic began.

A warrior advanced on Dorn. The hunter blocked a sword cut with his metal hand and instantly hit back. The Zhent knew his business and parried in his turn. Dorn's knuckle spikes ripped the small, round wood-and-leather shield to useless scraps, but at least it had saved its user once.

The iron half of his body forward, Dorn advanced. The Zhent fell back, and such was the press and confusion he bumped into one of the boatmen despite the latter's attempt to scramble out of the way. It cost the warrior his balance, and that was all the opening Dorn needed. He lunged and killed the man with a punch to the torso, the spikes on his artificial hand piercing the Zhent's mail as if it was made of paper.

When the soldier dropped, he dragged Dorn's fist down with him. The knuckle blades had somehow tangled in the corpse's ribs.

Dorn was still trying to pull free when orbs of ice exploded from the empty air immediately above him. He attempted to shield himself with his iron arm, but because of the dead weight hanging from it, he was a moment too slow. One of the missiles smashed down on the top of his head. The shock made him collapse to one knee. Blood flowed down from his torn scalp into his eye.

Around him, other folk similarly afflicted screamed in pain. Dazed, half blinded by gore, he cast about, seeking the wizard who'd been ruthless enough to conjure the attack without caring that it would likewise injure many of those who'd offered no resistance. After a moment, he spotted the bearded, whippet-thin Zhent in question. The reaver was one of the couple who'd stayed on the dock, and because he'd worn a broadsword, helmet, tunic, and buckler like the common men-at-arms, Dorn hadn't recognized him for what he was. No doubt that was as the mage had intended it. The shield lay at his feet, discarded so he could make his cabalistic passes more deftly.

Brandishing some sort of talisman, he commenced another spell. Dorn shook the corpse loose, lurched upright, and flung his knife, realizing even as he did so that it probably wouldn't help. He was a good marksman with a bow, arbalest, or spear, but had never spent much time practicing to throw a dagger.

As expected, the blade tumbled off course. He charged the pier, bulling people out of his way, taking too long. It was sickening to know he wouldn't reach the wizard in time to avert the next spell, whatever painful, potentially lethal effect it would produce.

Fortunately, something else stopped it. A mote of light streaked through the air, hit the magician's chest, and exploded into a dazzling, booming blast of yellow fire large enough to engulf both him and the warrior poised to protect him. Squinting against the glare, Dorn realized Kara must have seen his plight and conjured the attack. The magical blaze winked out of existence within a heartbeat, but not before setting the Zhents' somber uniforms and the top of the wooden walkway aflame. Howling, the burning men leaped into the water. The warrior weighted down with mail was almost certain to sink to the bottom and drown. The magician might make it ashore, but even if he did, it seemed unlikely he'd be willing and able to rejoin the fight.

Grinning, Dorn turned to find another foe. In so doing, he startled the small man who'd been creeping up to stab him in the back. Eyes wide with alarm, the fellow recoiled. He wasn't one of the black-clad warriors, but rather, another passenger. Maybe he was a loyal subject of the Zhentish lords, stupid or wicked as that would make him, or perhaps he simply thought that in any conflict, the side that included creatures as monstrous as half-golems was the side any decent person ought to oppose.

Whatever the fool was thinking, Dorn, whose head was still throbbing and bleeding copiously, was in no mood to let him live, and he rushed in. The little man slashed frantically, but Dorn could see the attacks wouldn't penetrate deeply enough to reach the vulnerable flesh behind his iron parts. He simply ignored the would-be back-stabber's assault and raked him open from lungs to guts.

Dorn turned, looking for someone else to kill, but no one was in reach. Across the deck, a chop from Raryn's ice-axe slew the Zhentish priest's remaining defender even as one of the flying luminous maces Pavel liked to conjure bashed in the skull of the Banite cleric himself, and that appeared to be that. The fight was over, Dorn and his comrades had won, and the others appeared essentially unscathed.

They'd overcome long odds and bested representatives of a predatory fraternity less clandestine but as generally despised as the Cult of the Dragon itself. That, however, failed to elicit any cheers from the other folk on the boat, who were looking on aghast.

"By Umberlee's fork" a sailor whined, "now the bastards will murder us all."

He might be right. Aboard the Zhentish vessels, crossbowmen and spellcasters were scurrying into position to attack at range. Other men-at-arms aboard the full-size warships were lowering longboats into the water.

"We're leaving," said Dorn. "Explain you took no part in the fight, and the Zhentarim will understand they have no reason to harm you."

He was by no means certain of that, but it was the best he could offer.

"We need to run now," Raryn said, spatters of someone else's blood caught in his white goatee and the polar bear fur covering his massive chest, "before the quarrels and thunderbolts start flying."

"Wait one moment," Kara said.

She sang the ascending arpeggio of another incantation. The magic whipped up gusts of wind that somehow only buffeted her, lashing her skirt and long, moon-blond hair this way and that.

The ambient temperature plummeted, the first feeble warmth of the northern spring lapsing back into the chill of the winter just concluded, and the air between the docks and the Zhentish vessels curdled. A pearly fog bank oozed into existence above the purple water, depriving the reavers of visible targets.

"We still must hurry," Kara said. "I don't know how long the obscurement will last before one of their mages succeeds in dispelling it."

"Right," said Dorn. "Everybody who wants to be elsewhere when the mist disappears, grab your belongings and go."

Luckily, the whole dock wasn't burning yet. They could still use it to scramble from the ferry onto the shore. As soon as they reached dry land the other travelers scuttled off in various directions, distancing themselves from the madmen who'd openly killed Zhents. Dorn didn't blame them and in fact was glad to see them go their own way. He and his partners didn't need any useless new companions slowing them down.

The half-golem led his friends south, away from the docks and on through the village. Even running flat-out, it was impossible to miss the signs of trouble. No children were in view. Indeed, even adults seemed to be staying off the streets as much as possible, and the houses were closed up tight, though normally, the occupants would have flung open all the doors and windows to air out the winter staleness. Zhents had painted obscenities and crude symbols of Bane and the Black Network on various walls, taking special care to deface the Grange and the Temple of the Half-Moon, a house of worship devoted to Selûne, and to a lesser degree, the other deities of light. Plainly, even if the invaders didn't choose to formally proclaim themselves the conquerors of Elmwood, that was the ugly truth of it.

"Where are we going?" panted Will, warsling dangling ready in his hand.

He was hearty, but any halfling had difficulty covering ground as quickly as long-legged humans.

"Out of town," Dorn said, well aware that it wasn't a particularly satisfactory response.

"They'll hunt us," Raryn said. "We either need to lose them or set a trap."

Something small swooped past Dorn's head. Edgy as he was, he nearly grabbed and crushed it in his iron fingers before realizing it was simply a robin.

Or maybe not, for it didn't behave like any songbird he'd ever seen before. The little creature with its brown back and yellow-red breast landed on the muddy ground in front of the fugitives, twittered, flew off down a side street, wheeled, returned, chirped some more, and flapped away in the same direction a second time.

"It wants us to follow it," Kara said.

Will shrugged and said, "Well, it doesn't look Zhentish."

"If you had a brain," said Pavel, "you'd know what's going on. Dorn?"

"Yes." Feeling somewhat foolish about it, the half-golem looked down at the robin, which, its head cocked, was peering back with a beady black eye, and said, "Lead on."

The bird seemed to understand for it took off immediately. The fugitives followed it past the last houses, across a boggy field, and toward a wood. If that in fact was their destination, Dorn wondered grimly how folk without wings were supposed to make their way in, for tangles of brush and briars choked the spaces around the old oaks and pines.

The answer came a moment later. Rustling and rattling, a mass of brambles divided to expose the start of a trail. Once everyone had passed, the brush wove itself back together, sealing the entrance once more.

The path led to a shadowy glade containing a low, shapeless, sod-roofed hut that looked more like a bump on the ground than anything manmade. A gray-haired female dwarf armed with a cudgel and short sword, a slender woman of mixed human and elf blood dressed in the silvery robes of a priestess of Selûne, and a bald, middle-aged man attired in rough brown homespun stood in front of the humble shelter waiting to greet the arrivals. The robin swooped to perch on the hairless fellow's hand where it warbled with excitement.

"Yes," the man said, stroking the bird's head with his fingertip. "You did well, and I thank you." He gave the newcomers a mournful smile. "Welcome, friends."

"Are you all right?" Thoyanna Jorgadaul asked.

The dwarf was Elmwood's constable and de facto mayor.

"You mean, aside from having my head split open?" the half-golem growled.

"Sit down," said Pavel. "Let me check that."

"You know," said Will, doing his best to speak in the earnest tone of someone who only wanted to help, "Alamarayne Moonray's a real healer. Maybe she—"

"Silence, worm," Pavel said. He peered down at the gash in Dorn's scalp. "You'll be all right." He murmured a prayer to the Morninglord, set his hand glowing with red-gold light, and laid it on the wound, closing the cut and stanching the flow of blood. "Does anyone else need care?"

Apparently, no one did.

"You should be safe here for the moment," said Ezril Treewarder, Elmwood's resident druid, tossing his hand to send the robin fluttering off. "Though I fear it's only a matter of time before the Zhents discover the sacred grove."

"At which point," said Alamarayne, "they'll come for the lot of us." Will remembered the pretty half-elf as merry and even coquettish, but just then she seemed about as cheery as a mass grave. "Thoyanna and I earned their ill will by defying them when they first sailed into port."

"We thank you," said Dorn, "for taking us in. But how did you even know we were here, let alone that we needed to disappear?"

"The birds and animals watch the town for me," the druid replied.

As if to make the point, a huge gray wolf padded out of the gloom beneath one of the holy oaks and nuzzled at his hand. He scratched the beast under one of its ears, then waved toward the low wooden benches arranged around a fire pit, where, by the looks of it, no one had kindled a blaze in a number of days, probably for fear the invaders would see the smoke.

"Shall we sit and refresh ourselves?" Ezril asked. "The cusp of winter and spring is the hungriest time of the year, especially for folk in hiding, but I still have some acorn crackers, jerky, and beer."

The hunters brought out some of the emergency rations they habitually carried in their packs. Combined with Ezril's provisions, they made for a meal that was stale, tasteless, and hard enough to break a beaver's teeth, but at least it stretched farther than it would have otherwise.

After everyone had pretty much eaten his portion, though the tall, terra-cotta communal beer stein was still making its way around the circle, Dorn said, "We have to reach Thentia fast and do some more traveling around the Moonsea."

Thoyanna snorted and said, "Good luck. Now that you've killed some of the Zhents, they'll be watching out for you, and you're about as distinctive a band of travelers as I can imagine. They won't let you sail anywhere."

"Maybe not from Elmwood," said Will, "but you can't tell me they control the whole southern shore—every inlet, rowboat, and fishing shack. Shadows of Mask, the region's famous for its pirates and smugglers. Somewhere we can hire a knave to sneak us north."

"You'd think so," said Ezril, still petting the wolf, which lay at his feet, "but travelers report the Black Network has some way of finding and attacking folk who sail without permission."

"Well, naturally the Zhents would put that story about," said Will. "If they said anything else, it would only encourage people to flout their rules."

"The rumor may be true," Alamarayne said. "I've performed divinations to find out, and the results, though inconclusive, are alarming. I think folk are right to be afraid."

"So what are we talking about?" asked Dorn. "They locate ships by peering in magic mirrors then raise storms to sink them?" If so, Will reflected, the time of year was probably conducive to it. The month of Tarsakh generally brought heavy rain. "Or send unnaturally fast enchanted war galleys or trained water monsters to catch them? Whatever the problem is, surely the cities that always stand against the Zhents will do their best to wreck their plan."

"That's our hope," Thoyanna said, crunching a final mouthful of cracker, "but no one's turned up to free Elmwood yet. Maybe these dragon flights, if they're real—"

"They are," Kara interjected.

"Then maybe the forces of Hillsfar, Phlan, and whomever are pinned down fighting wyrms on their own lands, and the Zhents are taking advantage of it, making a bold play to take control of all trade across the Moonsea. For the time being, at least, they've already gone a long way toward asserting authority over traffic to and from the realms in the south."

"Because Elmwood is the choke point," Raryn said, nodding. "If the situation drags on indefinitely, Zhentil Keep will grow steadily richer and stronger, and her rivals poorer and weaker, until ultimately a time will arrive when they can resist the Black Network no longer."

"But it won't drag on," Pavel said. "The other city-states won't stand for it. Eventually they'll drive the Zhents back to their castles in the west."

Alamarayne gave him a wan little smile and said, "Every night, I pray to Our Lady of Silver that you're right."

"What I don't understand" Kara said, "is how any of your people can behave this way."

Ezril peered at her quizzically and asked, "Our people?"

"She's from Impiltur," said Dorn.

Evidently he saw no reason to trust anyone, even folk who'd treated him fairly in the past, with Kara's secret unless it was absolutely necessary.

"What I mean," the slender bard continued, "is that a Rage of Dragons is upon you."

Thoyanna's eyes opened wide.

"Truly?" she asked. "You're certain it's a full-blown Rage?"

"Yes, and humanity's best hope of weathering it is to unite and fight the rampaging drakes together. If you scheme and struggle against each other, it will be much harder for you. Your entire world could collapse. The wyrms could harry you to the brink of extinction."

Dorn sneered, though at precisely what, Will wasn't certain.

"But that's who we are," said the half-golem. "We take advantage. The greedy do it because they covet riches and slaves. The rest of us do it when it seems the only way to survive. As the dragons wreak havoc, the devastation will leave some folk weak and helpless, ripe for exploitation, and others hungry and desperate enough for any betrayal or atrocity. Rest assured, a good many of us will strive to wrest all we can from our neighbors."

"I don't believe that," Kara said. "Oh, I know some corrupt or terrified folk will seek to prey on others, but not the majority. They'll bear up bravely and try to help their fellows, because that's the authentic human spirit, and the essential nature of dwarves and halflings as well. I know. I hear it in your music."

Dorn shook his head and replied, "They're just songs."

"They're your soul," the bard insisted. "You don't recognize it, Dorn Graybrook, because you don't know yourself. You think anger and bitterness define you, but they aren't what prompted you to risk your life to help the folk of Ylraphon."

"We're prattling about nonsense when we have practical problems to solve," the half-golem said with a scowl. "We could march overland to Thentia and sail from there with whatever protections the wizards can provide."

"The Zhents have patrols on the roads, too," Thoyanna said, "and the way leads through Mulmaster, a part of their dominions, or near enough."

Raryn took a drink from the stein, belched, and passed it on.

"We don't need to use the roads," said the dwarf tracker, "or tramp through the heart of the High Blade's lands. But to do anything else will take a while. Truly, if we're in a hurry, sailing's the fast way to get anywhere around the Moonsea."

"However the Zhentarim are finding the unlicensed ships," Dorn said slowly, the fleshy half of his forehead furrowed, "it seems likely the spotter merely glances at what are plainly their own vessels. Our band is too small to handle a war galley, and we're no expert sailors in any case. Still, with luck, I'll bet we could steer one of those patrol boats north to Thentia."

"We could certainly seize one," said Will. "As with many thefts, the biggest difficulty would be making our getaway. Once the Zhents noticed the boat was gone, they could overhaul us in the galleys or failing that, pass word of the robbery to their fellows." He grinned and added, "Still, I admit I like the audacity of it."

Dorn turned to the village elders and said, "Striking by surprise, in the night, we might be able to wipe out the Zhents occupying your town."

"You truly have that sort of power?" Ezril asked.

"Maybe, but here's the thing. We owe you for sheltering us here, and we won't wipe out the intruders without your leave. Because even if we succeed, liberation comes with a risk. Another bunch of Zhents could show up after we're gone and hold you accountable for the slaughter."

"We'll chance it," Thoyanna said. "Maybe the other cities will strike against Zhentil Keep, foiling the Black Network's strategy, and no more reavers will come here. If they do, we'll claim that ships from Hillsfar came and killed their comrades. Why shouldn't they believe it? Elmwood itself obviously lacks the strength to destroy such a force."

"Better yet," Kara said, "blame dragons, for that's what the evidence will indicate."

EIGHTEEN

12 Tarsakh, the Year of Rogue Dragons

It rained steadily through the night. Taegan, whose turn it was to stand a predawn watch, tried to maintain a good vantage point and stay dry at the same time by perching fifteen feet above the ground in the fork of a sycamore. It didn't work all that well. Logic indicated that the canopy of branches overhead must be catching some of the raindrops, but plenty more spilled right on through. By the time a first hint of Lathander's light gleamed in the east, and the downpour subsided to a drizzle, his clothes were soaked, and he was cold and in a foul mood generally.

Nor did it help when Rangrim tramped forth from camp and called a jovial, "Good morning! I brought you some hot soup."

Taegan flicked his wings, shaking rainwater out of the black feathers, spread them, and leaped from the sycamore. His pinions trapped air to slow his descent, and he floated down gently.

"My dear but seemingly demented friend," the maestro said. "How can you bed down in cold mud, rise with the sun on such a dreary morning, and be cheerful? It must have something to do with your being a paladin."

The chunky, curly-bearded human grinned and proffered a steaming tin mug of lentil broth. The warmth of the cup felt good in Taegan's chilled fingers, and so did the heat of the first sip going down.

Rangrim glanced around at the towering, mossy trees dripping glistening water from every branch and twig. Spring had found the Gray Forest, and new green leaves and buds were sprouting despite the occasional patch of snow still spotting the ground. Birds, some newly returned from the south, chirped to greet the morning.

"I like the woods," said the paladin, "even on a cold, damp morning. I'm amazed you don't."

"I don't see why my indifference constitutes such a marvel. I like soft beds, blazing hearths, well-made roofs, comfortable chairs, fine wine, gourmet cooking, and luscious, affectionate women. Everything Lyrabar affords, and the wild doesn't."

"But you're an elf."

"An accident of birth," Taegan replied, "that I strive to transcend."

They turned and headed toward the camp, where other paladins and Warswords could be heard muttering and rattling around. One of the Queen's Bronzes lifted the tapered head at the end of its long, sinuous neck and peered around. Its forked tongue darted forth to taste the morning air.

"You shouldn't be ashamed of your heritage," Rangrim said.

"What heritage would that be?" replied the avariel. "In case you haven't noticed, all the cities of Impiltur and the surrounding lands are the work of men, with a degree of assistance from dwarves and halflings."

"Still. . . ."

"Please," Taegan said, "let's speak of something else, for I assure you, I'm delighted to be what I've become, a loyal subject of Impiltur and our wise and gracious queen. Surely you, her sworn champion, don't mean to imply it was an unworthy aspiration."

The paladin snorted and said, "You're twisting my meaning, and you know it. But have it your way. How much longer do you think it will take to find the cult's stronghold?"

"We should be drawing close, but who knows? We simply have to follow the directions dear Cylla gave me and keep looking. If you like, I can do some more scouting above the treetops while everyone else is breaking camp."

"Don't you want more breakfast?"

Taegan realized he didn't. For some reason, even though he'd endured such comments many times before, Rangrim's witless albeit well-intentioned observations about his race had left him feeling restless.

"I believe I can forgo it."

"Well, in that case," said the paladin, "Quelsandas and I will tag along."

Taegan hoped he could prevent that. He didn't fancy any more of Rangrim's hearty, virtuous company just at present, and in fact, never particularly enjoyed being around the bronze. The paladin doted on Quelsandas, his faithful comrade in countless exploits, but though Taegan had made an honest effort to like the dragon for his new friend's sake, he couldn't quite manage it. The gigantic reptile had a sullen, guarded quality that bothered him.

Or perhaps, given that Rangrim seemed oblivious to his mount's glumness, the problem was simply that Taegan didn't understand drakes and their ways. He certainly hadn't spent enough time with Kara and Brimstone to make him an expert. But he did know he'd prefer solitude for the next little while.

Accordingly, he said, "If we are nearing the enemy, perhaps I should scout alone. I'm considerably smaller and harder to spot than a dragon wheeling against the sky. Besides, you're the war captain. Your faithful followers need you here to put them in order for the new day."

"Suit yourself. Good hunting."

Taegan sprang into the air and flew upward. He looked for vertical pathways wide enough to accommodate an avariel's beating wings, but the branches grew thickly, and at certain moments, it was easier simply to seize hold of them and clamber like a squirrel, as he had in the Earthwood years before. The memory made him frown.

Fortunately, he reached the treetops soon enough. He took a wary glance around, making sure no wyvern, abishai, or whatever was hovering close at hand, was in position to attack as soon as he broke cover. Then he launched himself higher, where he soon found a friendly updraft to hold him at that altitude with minimal effort on his part.

Gliding between the gray overcast above and the dark green foliage below, Taegan's mood brightened despite his sopping clothes and the persistent drizzle. He could see for miles, from the ranks of mountains in the north to the blacker clouds, their bellies full of flickering lightning, massed far to the south above the Sea of Fallen Stars. If he'd needed to forsake his timorous, reclusive people to experience such vistas, that alone had been sufficient reason to turn his back on them.

But he knew he mustn't simply float and enjoy the spectacle for long. He had work to do. He flew west, looking for the fortress Sammaster and Cylla had established. It was possible that, shielded by layers of overhanging branches or even veils of illusion, the place was invisible from the air. But if he could spot it from on high, it might well save the expedition days of tedious groping about on the ground, days during which the cultists could strengthen their defenses, make more dracoliches, or Sune only knew what. At least avariels had sharp eyes. Taegan thought he had about as good a chance of sighting the secret fortress as—

What was that? For a moment, he glimpsed something big moving along far below on the ground. Then it disappeared, concealed by the canopy.

Plainly, it hadn't been a stationary manmade structure of the sort he was seeking. But it could certainly have been one of the wyrms Sammaster had recruited to guard the stronghold and eventually undergo the transformation into undead, in which case, it could annihilate a lone avariel with one snap of its jaws or a single puff of dragon breath. Accordingly, he made his way back down through the branches as warily and silently as he could, until he finally saw more.

He wasn't sure if one of the creatures he observed stalking eastward was the same immense being he'd glimpsed before, but it made no difference. The only important thing was to reach his comrades in time.

Though he wouldn't reach them at all unless he continued to go unnoticed. He whispered a spell, and bladesong instantly transported him a couple hundred yards eastward, onto the limb of a different tree.

Peering down, he saw it wasn't far enough. He was still above a portion of the advancing force, its leading edge, composed of scouts and skirmishers. Nor could he use the same magic to shift himself a second time. At his level of skill, he could only hold a single spell of such power in his memory, and having expended it, it was gone until he had a chance to study his grimoire once again.

So he crept along the branches with all the stealth his father and the rest of the tribe had taught him, crouched, wings folded tight to make himself smaller, spreading only when he needed the exquisite balance they afforded him, or to spring across a gap his legs couldn't manage by themselves.

It was a race of sorts, one he could never have won if the creatures on the ground hadn't been trying to prowl along unobtrusively themselves, an effort that slowed them significantly. As it was, he gradually outdistanced them, and when reasonably confident he was far enough ahead that they wouldn't spot him, he unfurled his wings and flew the rest of the way to camp at top speed. It felt bizarre that his comrades were chatting, folding tents, tying bedrolls, inspecting the horses' hooves, and in general, calmly preparing to march, but of course they had no inkling of what he'd rushed to tell them.

"Lord Rangrim!" he shouted.

"Here!"

The paladin was busy saddling Quelsandas, a task he insisted on performing himself. His caution was understandable considering that if the job was done incorrectly, he might conceivably lose his seat and plummet hundreds of feet to the ground.

"Did you see something?" asked Rangrim.

"To say the least," Taegan replied as he landed in front of the knight and dragon. "A band comprised of men, wyrms, hobgoblins, and what I take to be werewolves is stealing up on us. In a few minutes, our pickets will spot them, but by then it will be too late."

"Did you see a dracolich?"

"No, but that doesn't mean it isn't there. With all the trees obstructing my view, I couldn't see everything."

"How did they know we were coming?"

We have a traitor, Taegan thought. He didn't know why his instincts instantly suggested that answer, but it felt right. Somehow, someone in the expedition had made contact with the cultists during the night.

Rangrim waved his hand impatiently dismissing his own question. He turned and found his trumpeter, who'd obviously overheard the conversation, already standing close at hand awaiting orders.

"No, Jal," Rangrim said. "You can't sound the call to arms, or the enemy will hear, and come running before we're ready. We need to get ourselves into a battle formation quickly but quietly. Help me round up the officers and sergeants."

Once apprised of the danger, the Warswords prepared to meet the foe with a brisk efficiency that attested to their quality. The trees made it difficult for them to arrange themselves in the straight unbroken lines their commanders might have preferred, but they managed to mass a goodly portion of their strength in a central position, with other warriors and the six bronze dragons stationed in two wings that extended diagonally forward from the ends. Taegan was no war captain, but he understood how the formation was supposed to work. Rangrim wanted the cultists to advance into what amounted to a box, so some of his troops could attack their flanks.

Since he wasn't one of the leaders, responsible for readying the men-at-arms, Taegan concentrated on preparing himself. He cast spells to heighten his strength and agility and to sharpen the point and edges of the sturdy cut-and-thrust sword he currently carried in preference to his beloved but flimsier rapier. His purely defensive enchantments, like the one that shrouded him in blur, didn't last as long, so he'd put off conjuring them until the foe actually came into view, or simply trust his martial skills and the brigandine one of the queen's armorers had made to protect him. Though he didn't bother wearing such things in the city—few rakes did, either for fear of being thought craven or out of reluctance to cover up any portion of their handsome clothes—he was a deft enough bladesinger that the light leather armor wouldn't hinder him from making cabalistic passes.

When he'd enhanced his natural capabilities as best he could, he went to stand beside Rangrim and Quelsandas. The bronze repeatedly spread his membranous wings, casting the avariel into shadow, then retracted them again. Lance in hand the lord sat gazing intently into the trees, watching for a first glimpse of the foe, but eventually he took note of his mount's restlessness.

"Are you all right?" he asked.

"Yes," Quelsandas rumbled.

"Just eager to strike a blow, I expect. And here we were worried the army in the east would have all the fun."

The huge reptile with his webbed feet, gleaming scales, and catlike emerald eyes stood silent for a moment.

Then he said, "We've been through so much together. If I asked a favor, would you grant it?"

"Of course."

"Then climb down off my back and direct the battle from the rear."

Rangrim smiled a perplexed sort of smile and said, "After all these years, you're developing a very odd sense of humor."

"I have a premonition. This one time, it's better if you're not in the thick of the fray."

"I'm the one with a special bond to the Crying God," the human chuckled. "I'll handle the prophetic dreams and intuitions, if it's all the same to you. Seriously, your nerves are getting the better of you. It happens to all of us occasionally, just before a battle. But there's no need for worry. We may have a relatively small company, but we have discipline and training no rabble of madmen and hobgoblins can ever hope to match, to say nothing of half a dozen of the Queen's Bronzes and the favor of the gods of light. We're going to be fine."

"I knew you'd say that," Quelsandas replied, "but I had to try."

The exchange unsettled Taegan. He sensed the bronze had left something unsaid, even if Rangrim, with his trustful and straightforward manner of thinking, didn't. But before the fencing master could decide what, if anything, to do about it, the first of their foes appeared beneath the trees.

Stalking on two legs in beast-man form, a werewolf snarled when it saw the Warswords drawn up in battle array. An instant later, an arrow plunged into the lycanthrope's gray-furred chest, and it fell backward. The shaft had to have been silver-tipped or enchanted to kill a shapeshifter so expeditiously. The archer's comrades started to cheer until their sergeant's bark cut through the clamor to upbraid the eager bowman for shooting before he gave the order.

Tall as the tallest human, scarcely less hairy than the werewolves, and clad for the most part in animal hides dyed a bloody red, a trio of brutish hobgoblins reached for their own arrows. Then, behind them, appeared the most terrifying thing Taegan had ever seen. He shivered uncontrollably at the sight of it.

Like the bronzes, it had chosen to stay on the ground. For such huge creatures, flight through the dense branches in that portion of the wood was problematical. Once it had evidently been a gigantic living green, but the tissue of its wings hung in tatters, and bone showed through the rents in its decaying, withered flesh. Its sunken yellow eyes shone with a spectral radiance somehow perceptible even in the pale gray morning light. A man wearing the ornate robes of a Wearer of Purple bestrode the base of the creature's neck, a skull-tipped ebony rod in his hand. No doubt he was a formidable combatant in his own right, but compared to the dracolich, he seemed utterly insignificant.

Some of the Warswords moaned.

"Steady!" Rangrim shouted. "Steady! Don't meet its gaze, and you'll be all right." His lieutenants called similar words of reassurance.

Somebody yelled, "Impiltur, Impiltur!" and others echoed the battle cry.

Rangrim recited a prayer that made Taegan, and presumably others, feel somewhat less afraid. Quelsandas took a deep breath, then started whispering a spell of his own. Taegan was about to do likewise when he marked the sound of the bronze's snarling, sibilant incantation. He couldn't understand the arcane words, but even so, they filled him with an instinctive revulsion, as if they'd been devised to invoke the foulest powers of the Nine Hells.

Confused, he turned to Quelsandas, who instantly lashed a wing down to swat him like a fly. Taegan tried to leap out from under it, but the scalloped edge of the limb still caught him and dashed him to the ground.

It knocked the wind out of him, and he could only look on helplessly as the first volleys of arrows and blazes of magic from spellcasters on both sides flew, and Quelsandas finished his conjuration. The other members of the Queen's Bronzes threw back their heads and screamed.

The screeching startled everyone. The arrows stopped arcing back and forth, and the human cultists, werewolves, hobgoblins, and even the dracolich faltered in their advance.

After a few moments, the hideous noise subsided. The bronzes peered about in seeming confusion, as if they didn't remember where they were or what was happening. Taegan heard a dragon rider on the far side of the Warswords' formation ask his mount what was the matter.

The reptile responded by snapping its head toward the ground like a striking serpent and spewing a stroke of dazzling lightning down the line of Impilturan men-at-arms. It all happened so quickly the victims couldn't even scream. They simply jerked and died, the stench of their burning flesh mingling with the smell of stormy skies.

The other bronzes attacked an instant later. Two more chose to unleash their lightning, another pair shredded Impilturan men-at-arms with fang and claw, and a fifth breathed out a plume of sparkling brownish vapor that inflicted no wounds, but set a dozen horsemen galloping away in panic. With their backs turned, they were easy prey as the wyrm raced in pursuit.

The dragons carried the paladins on their backs helplessly along. The knights shouted at their huge and cherished comrades, beat them with the flats of their weapons, or chanted prayers, trying frantically to bring the reptiles to their senses, though most likely they had no idea precisely what had gone so horribly wrong.

Taegan thought he did. The Rage in all its power had taken possession of the bronzes in an instant. Because Quelsandas's magic had made it so.

The Warswords had stood ready to battle the cultists, but

when the bronzes, the very foundation of their might, turned on them, it caught them completely by surprise. It only took a few heartbeats for their formation to start disintegrating, as the humans scrambled desperately to distance themselves from the maddened wyrms.

"Ilmater, help us!" Rangrim said.

He started chanting another invocation, no doubt the mightiest magic at his command though Taegan doubted even that would be enough to avert the catastrophe threatening his command. Then it was Quelsandas's turn to scream and thrash.

"No!" the dragon whimpered, and it was profoundly strange to hear such dread in so enormous and mighty a creature's voice. "Not me! He promised I'd stay sane!"

He howled a second time, and when he stopped, his green eyes burned with demented fury. He sucked in a breath.

Taegan was still dazed, but the threat spurred him into motion, and he flung himself to the side. Even so, the thunderbolt struck his wing. Agony burned through his body, so intense he couldn't even scream, just shudder in its throes. When it subsided, to his surprise he found himself still alive. Others in the path of the blast had been less fortunate and lay black and smoking on the ground.

Taegan's pinion continued to hurt fiercely, but he was too full of anger and fear for it to balk him. He lurched up and threw himself at Quelsandas. If the gods were exceedingly generous, perhaps he could strike the treacherous bronze a mortal blow before the wyrm's ability to spit death returned.

He thrust his sword deep into Quelsandas's breast. The bronze pivoted, nearly tearing the hilt from his grasp, and raked at him with its talons. The attack might well have torn him to pieces if he hadn't leaped backward. As it was, it only missed him by scant inches. When he tried to beat his wings to lengthen his spring, the charred one just twitched and gave him a fresh stab of pain. Until it healed, he wouldn't be able to fly.

Quelsandas pounced after him. The great jaws shot forward, spreading as wide and as high as the gateway into death, which swallows countless souls every day. The elf wrenched himself to the side, and the bronze's enormous fangs clashed shut on empty air, spattering their elusive target with saliva. The droplets bore a trace of lightning within them, and crackled and stung like needles when they hit.

Taegan lunged and cut, striking for the throat. Quelsandas twitched his head back, and the sword merely inflicted a shallow gash on the jagged collar of bony plates behind the jaws and eyes. The drake bit, the avariel dodged, then had to defend again when Quelsandas instantly followed up his with claws. The bronze lifted his right forefoot high, threatening a vertical slash, then lashed out with the left in a horizontal stroke. Momentarily deceived, Taegan ducked the genuine blow with not an instant to spare.

He realized he had to make himself harder to hit, otherwise Quelsandas was going to rip him to pieces, probably with a single attack and most likely within the next few seconds. Dodging and retreating, cutting and thrusting when the wyrm gave him the chance, he started conjuring an enchantment.

Quelsandas was in frenzy, quite possibly not fighting with the cunning he would normally display. Yet he still recognized spellcasting when he saw it, and it prompted him to return to his initial tactic. He hopped backward, out of reach of Taegan's blade, lifted his head, and sucked in a breath. A whiff of ozone betrayed his intention to blast forth another flare of lightning. Taegan had little confidence in his ability to avoid the attack but realized he had no alternative but to try. He held himself ready while continuing his incantation. If he dodged too soon, the bronze would simply compensate.

Then Quelsandas jerked, and with a deafening boom, his breath burned harmlessly into the tangled branches overhead, shattering some, bringing chunks of wood showering down, and setting sections aflame despite the damp. Taegan was so intent on his foe that he'd nearly forgotten Rangrim, and to all appearances, the rogue bronze had too. But the war captain was still in the saddle and had finally abandoned his fruitless efforts to calm his mount by counterspell or exhortation. He'd cast away the long spear that was his weapon of choice for fighting from the back of such a gigantic steed, seized the warhammer he carried as a backup, and his face contorted in mingled anguish and resolve, pounded it into the base of the reptile's neck, spoiling his aim.

Quelsandas twisted his head around to snap at his rider, but the posture was plainly awkward for him, and perhaps that was what gave Rangrim time to block out the attack with his kite shield. When the dragon's teeth slammed against the barrier, they scored and dented the steel, defacing the painted coat-of-arms. The impact jolted the paladin backward and made the segments of his plate armor clash together. But the shield must have carried powerful enchantments, for both it and its wielder survived.

Rangrim riposted with a blow to Quelsandas's snout.

Meanwhile, Taegan finished his spell, creating the same defense he'd used the night Gorstag died. Quelsandas would see him in a slightly different position than the one he actually occupied. It might help protect him, if the drake's keen senses of scent and hearing didn't pinpoint his location even so. It was a start, anyway. He charged Quelsandas, whose long, lashing tail and stamping, earth-shaking feet posed a deadly threat even when the wyrm wasn't actually assaulting him, and he cut at the creature's belly, simultaneously commencing another charm.

He gashed the dragon's torso twice before raking claws drove him backward. He finished the spell, and Quelsandas appeared to slow as his own perceptions and reactions quickened. He attacked furiously when the bronze oriented on Rangrim and fought defensively when the wyrm returned his attention to him, and the paladin adopted the corresponding strategy.

Taegan drove his sword between Quelsandas's ribs. When

he yanked it out again, blood spurted, and kept rhythmically pumping forth.

A moment later, Rangrim bellowed, "Ilmater!" and smashed the warhammer down.

A vertebra audibly cracked, and the bronze thrashed in pain.

It was hard to believe, but Taegan thought that he and Rangrim might actually be on the brink of winning. Quelsandas started to pivot, and the fencing master scrambled to stay on the dragon's flank, away from the jaws and forefeet. The bronze flung himself sideways and down.

If not for the spell of quickness, Taegan would surely have been crushed. As it was, he had just enough time to recognize that his only chance of survival lay in diving toward the dragon, inside the arc of the creature's fall. He darted under Quelsandas, and the bronze's vast, toppling bulk crashed to earth behind him.

The avariel whirled and saw that Rangrim had been less fortunate. The lord was still in the saddle, his feet hooked in the stirrups, and Quelsandas rolled like a gigantic hound smearing itself with some enticing scent discovered on the ground, grinding his longtime human friend beneath him. When the bronze heaved himself to his feet, Rangrim flopped atop him like a rag doll, his suit of plate flattened out of shape.

Quelsandas wheeled toward Taegan, snarled, and pounced, perhaps not quite as nimbly as before. The elf lunged beneath the dragon's snapping jaws and thrust his sword through the scales armoring the throat. The blade drove in deep, and he heaved on the hilt, tearing the wound wider. Quelsandas snatched his head away from the pain, and that too served to enlarge the hurt before he ripped himself free. Blood gushed and splashed on the ground.

Quelsandas poised himself for another attack, then faltered. His sides heaved rapidly, and air whistled in and out of a breach that hadn't existed a moment before. Taegan recognized the signs of a punctured windpipe. The dragon couldn't catch his breath.

The elf sprang in, avoided a relatively clumsy talon strike, and rammed his sword into the wyrm's belly. Sparks sizzled and popped around Quelsandas's wet, glistening fangs, and the bronze crumpled to the ground.

Taegan rushed around the enormous corpse to reach Rangrim. Up close, a look sufficed to dispel any lingering doubt that the paladin was dead. The avariel supposed he'd already known that, but he had hoped he was mistaken.

Nor was that the worst of it. When he surveyed the battlefield as a whole, he saw three other dead bronzes, slain in self-defense by their human comrades as he and Rangrim had needed to kill Quelsandas. The other two had evidently run off, possibly chasing fleeing prey. So that particular threat was over, but it had done all the damage necessary to turn the day into a disaster.

The Warswords had sustained heavy casualties and were in general disarray, whereas, since they'd had the good sense to keep their distance from the frenzied bronzes, contenting themselves with shooting arrows and casting spells at the queen's men as targets of opportunity presented themselves, the cultists and their minions were still fresh and relatively unscathed. The dracolich and its rider leaped forward, leading a wave of loping werewolves, hooting hobgoblins, human fanatics, and black and green wyrms their foes no longer had any hope of withstanding.

Some of Rangrim's warriors simply threw away their shields, weapons, and any other object whose weight might slow them down, turned tail, and bolted. Others tried to retreat in good order. A knight with a crimson scarf—a lady's favor, evidently—knotted to his helmet bellowed for his retainers to keep together as they galloped into the trees. A wizard cast a spell that made a band of archers fade from view, threw blasts of fire and frost to hold back the advancing foe, then blinked from sight himself an instant before a skull dragon's acidic spew splashed over the patch of ground where he'd been standing.

But it was hard to believe that the cool-headed bravery of such folk actually mattered. The expedition was still routing.

In a few minutes, the survivors, assuming there were any, would be scattered far and wide.

A javelin plunged into the earth beside Taegan's foot, reminding him that he needed to rout just as much as the next fellow. His wounded, useless wing throbbing, he ran.

The charm of haste wouldn't last much longer, but for the moment, it enabled him to stay ahead of the charging foes. Well, most of them. Coarse, gray-black fur bristling, slaver foaming from its jaws, a female werewolf leaped in on his flank and clawed at him. He pivoted, blocked the stroke with a cut that half severed the beast-woman's misshapen hand finished her with a thrust to the heart and dashed on.

Dorn and his companions had rowed most of the way toward the war galley that was their destination before the yellow flame flowered back on shore. The blaze constituted a fairly desperate diversion, the folk of Elmwood sacrificing one of their own houses to draw the Zhents' attention. But at least it was a decrepit, ramshackle structure, unoccupied, Thoyanna said, since the spinster who'd dwelled therein died of old age and influenza two months before. Assuming the fire didn't spread, the loss would be relatively insignificant.

Those Zhents who were still awake gathered in the bow of their vessel to gawk at the flickering light in the darkness. They didn't seem particularly alarmed, and that was as Dorn had expected. A fire on land didn't look like an attack against a ship floating at anchor in the harbor.

Still, with several of the invaders peering out across the black, rippling surface of the inlet, Dorn had to resist an impulse to duck down, even though they weren't actually looking in his direction and probably couldn't make him out in the murk even if they did. Just as importantly, even he couldn't hear his sweeps creaking in the oarlocks or swishing through the water. Pavel's magic muffled any noise that might otherwise have sounded from the rowboat. In theory, the launch should be virtually detectable, but the Zhentarim had spellcasters, too, and it was impossible to be sure.

He and his companions guided their craft into proximity with the galley's elevated stern. While the hulls bumped together, Will took a sturdy hemp line tied to a fisherman's heavy lead sinker and tossed the weight upward. It was a deft throw. The sinker looped the rope up over the rail and dropped back down into the halfling's outstretched hand.

Will climbed the rope as agilely as a spider ascending a strand of webbing, peeked over the gunwale, then scrambled onto the galley's stern, out of his comrades' view. After a moment, he peered back down at the rowboat and beckoned for the others to ascend.

Dorn hauled himself up next. As he clambered aboard the warship, he exited the bubble of silence Pavel had created around the launch. He could hear the faint groan of stressed timber that attended any large, floating vessel, even one at rest, the snoring of the Zhents still wrapped in their blankets on deck, and the conversation of the men at the far end of the craft. One of them expressed the hope that the entire village and all its inhabitants would burn. Then the Black Network could bring in its own folk and build the kind of outpost it truly needed from the ground up.

Dorn glanced over the side. Alamarayne appeared to be having trouble scaling the rope, so he pulled it in hand over hand and dragged her up. He hoped the moon priestess fought better than she climbed. He was by no means certain of it. Not every cleric possessed Pavel's courage and combat skills. But she, like the other village elders, had insisted on taking part in the raid. Ezril and Thoyanna had accompanied Pavel and Raryn to the next galley over.

Once he helped Alamarayne over the rail, the two of them hunkered down. In their dark cloaks, they hoped to go unnoticed in the gloom or failing that be mistaken for black-clad Zhents bundled up against the chill night air. Muffled in his own inky garments, dagger in hand but hidden inside his cape, Will crept forward through the shadows to peer closely at the sleepers.

The Zhents were all human, with nary a halfling among them. If any of them so much as caught a glimpse of Will, he'd surely cry out a warning to his fellows. But the former guild thief maintained no one would spot him, and Dorn shared his confidence. His partner had a talent for stealth that bordered on the uncanny.

Will was looking for mages and Banite priests. All three war galleys likely carried spellcasters, and such folk posed the greatest threat to the success of the raid. Accordingly, the hunters hoped to neutralize them before the Zhents even realized anything was amiss.

They might have managed it, too, except that they ran out of time. With their small force divided into three contingents, none able to communicate with the others, it was impossible to coordinate their actions precisely, and from Dorn's perspective, anyway, Kara attacked too soon. He couldn't yet see her—she'd presumably flown in low from the north while the Zhents looked at the burning house to the south, as per the plan—but her song throbbed through the night to cast a spell. A crashing, clattering noise drummed from the war galley at the far end of the line as conjured chunks of ice pounded the vessel and the folk thereon. Men cried out. A moment later, a plume of Kara's bright, crackling, lightning-laden breath swept across the deck.

If she'd caught the crew by surprise, she'd quite possibly wiped them out already, but the Zhents aboard the other ships realized they were in danger. Such being the case, their archers or crossbowmen might be lucky enough to shoot the dragon down, but considering that they'd be loosing their shafts at a target possessed of natural armor hurtling through the dark, it seemed unlikely. Left to their own devices, however, wizards and priests were likely to fare much better.

Accordingly, as one of the reavers cried for everyone to wake up, and slumbering men threw off their covers and reared up from the deck, Dorn squinted against the gloom, looking for some sign to tell him which of his enemies was a spellcaster. After a moment, he spotted a long-legged man bearing a morningstar. The Zhent had been wearing a steel gauntlet, too, even as he slept. He was almost certainly a cleric of the Black Hand. Unfortunately, he was most of the way forward. Maybe Will was maneuvering close to the priest, working his way into position to strike him down, but if so, Dorn couldn't tell it. He'd lost sight of his small comrade when everyone started jumping up and scurrying about.

Dorn thought he had to try for the Banite himself. Keeping his head down and his cloak wrapped around the iron half of his body, he shoved his way toward the bow. The confusion aided him. The Zhents were too intent on arming themselves and peering at the war galley already under attack to pay much attention to one more dark figure pushing his way through the press.

Then, however, one of the reavers stooped to retrieve his conical helmet from the deck, chanced to glance up, and evidently discerned Dorn's metal half-mask despite the obscurement provided by his hood. The Zhent cried out in surprise. Dorn sprang and smashed the fellow's head in with a sweep of his iron fist.

At least he'd made it almost within reach of the priest before being spotted. He took another stride, and a warrior rushed at him, swinging an axe at his head. Dorn caught the blow on his artificial arm, riposted with a punch that drove his knuckle spikes into his foe's chest, and charged on.

Two more Zhents came at him with broadswords. He shifted so they couldn't both cut at him at once, parried a slash from the one that still could, hitched forward, caught hold of the reaver's extended arm, jerked it out its socket, and flung him aside.

The other swordsman lifted his blade, then froze. Thanks to his years with Pavel, Dorn recognized the effect of that particular sort of clerical magic when he saw it. Evidently Alamarayne was useful in a fight, for wherever she was at the moment, she'd paralyzed the Zhent. Hoping she was taking care to protect herself as well, Dorn smashed the warrior out of his way before his mobility could return. That brought the half-golem face to face with the Banite.

Unfortunately, the soldiers had delayed him long enough for the priest, a thin man with a sly, foxy face, to use his magic. He swept a talisman shaped like a clenched fist through a mystic pass, and Dorn's guts twisted in pain and nausea even as his muscles cramped. At once the Banite lashed out with his morningstar, which had blue-white sparks jumping and crackling along the chain and massive spiked bulb of a head.

Dorn tried to block it, but his sudden illness hampered him. The morningstar slammed into the ribs on the human side of his body. His brigandine cushioned the blow, but it could do little to stop the essence of lightning contained in the weapon from burning into his body. He jerked with the pain of it, and the priest whirled the morningstar back for another swing.

Dorn made a desperate grab, and despite his sickness and dizziness, caught hold of the chain before the end of the morningstar could strike him. Unfortunately, that contact alone sufficed to send more lightning blazing down his metal arm and into the vulnerable flesh beyond. Still, much as he needed to, he didn't let go, lest the cleric continue bashing him. Instead, forcing his twitching, spasming muscles to obey him, he jerked the Banite close and drove his knife into his heart.

Only then did Dorn drop the morningstar. That ended the shocks jolting along his nerves, but not the weakness and queasiness with which the Banite had cursed him. That would simply have to run its course, and he'd just have to go on fighting in spite of it.

To his relief, he didn't have another foe poised to attack him that very instant. In the darkness and chaos, some of the Zhents probably had yet to realize foes had boarded their vessel, and thus he had a second to brace himself for the next fight, as well as glance about and try to assess how the raid as a whole was going.

Back toward the stern, Will faked a step to the right, then darted left, rolled, and somersaulted to his feet. The maneuver carried him safely past the fangs and fiery breath of a huge, houndlike thing with glowing red eyes and into striking distance of the plump, bearded man who had evidently conjured it. Will drove his short sword into the wizard's groin, and the Zhent went down.

That didn't end the threat of the hell hound, which, still following its summoner's orders, lunged after the halfling. But before it could quite close the distance, Alamarayne called out to Selûne. The mace she brandished in the air, its head studded with four crescent-shaped flanges, blazed with silvery radiance, pinpointing her location. The demonic canine simply faded away, dismissed, evidently, back to the layer of the Abyss from which the magician had called it.

Across the harbor, Kara, her outstretched wings a slash of deeper black against the night sky, dived at the galley in the center position. No flares of magic rose to meet her. Evidently Raryn, Pavel, and the others had succeeded in eliminating the spellcasters onboard. She scoured the deck with a burst of her dazzling breath.

When she finished killing the Zhents on that ship, she'd move on to the last one. Dorn and his companions had to hold out until she did. Will and Alamarayne had the advantage of being in proximity to one another. They could protect each other's flanks. It was Dorn's bad luck that he'd wound up too far away to make it practical for him to rejoin them. Sick or not, he would have to fight alone.

He put his back to the water, so the Zhents couldn't come at him from behind, and his iron half forward to weather their blows. Judging he had ample room to swing it, he drew his bastard sword. He just had time to cock it into a proper guard before more reavers assaulted him.

He clawed one Zhent's face to shreds and hacked another's leg out from under him. By sheer luck, his iron arm deflected a sword thrust from an opponent he hadn't even noticed slinking up on his side. He caught the blade in his metal fingers, squeezed, twisted, and broke it.

The Zhents screamed. Dorn didn't have to look up to know what had terrified them. Kara was swooping at the galley, and her approach was as much a threat to her allies as the enemy, because the kinds of attack she was using blasted an area and everybody caught inside it. It was the only way to slaughter the Zhents as fast as the raiders needed to kill them.

Dorn and his companions were supposed to protect themselves by diving for cover. A glance around his immediate vicinity convinced the half-golem that for him, the best option was to swing himself over the side. He dropped his sword and did precisely that, digging his talons into the gunwale to anchor himself. But the wood was rotten and crumbled. He plummeted.

He couldn't swim. The weight of his iron limbs would drag him to the bottom. When he splashed down in the cold water, he raked frantically at the side of the galley. His claws snagged in the hull, and gasping, he heaved his head above the surface. Over the deck, the air flickered yellow, and an explosion roared. Zhents shrieked, and their bodies burning, tumbled overboard.

Then some force or weight shoved the galley downward, dunking Dorn's head in the process. For a second, he was terrified that the vessel would continue to float that low and that he wouldn't be able to clamber back into the air before he drowned, but then it bobbed upward once more. As he coughed and spat, a great sheet of something flopped down over the side to hang beside him. At first, with his eyes full of water, he mistook it for a fallen sail, then realized what it really was.

He hesitated briefly, then, making sure his talons didn't cut, caught hold of one of the bony vanes running through the leathery membrane. Kara pulled up her wing and heaved him out of the water.

From the looks of the deck, the Zhents were all unconscious, crippled, or dead. Will and Alamarayne, however, were alive. The latter had nasty gashes on her forearm and calf, but presumably her prayers or failing that, Pavel's, would stanch the bleeding, prevent infection, and accelerate the healing process.

That was all Dorn had time to observe before Kara flipped her wing in some cunning way that broke his grip and sent him rolling and bouncing down the inclined surface to fetch up on her back.

"Hang on!" she cried, and Dorn barely had time to obey before she leaped off the deck and took flight once more.

Her wings slashed up and down as she rapidly gained altitude. Her voice soared, too, in another fierce yet lovely song of battle.

Dorn felt stupid with surprise. It hadn't specifically been part of the plan that he'd help with this particular part of the raid, and the gods knew, he'd never in his life wanted to ride a foul, cursed dragon.

Yet once he collected himself, he had to admit, however grudgingly, that it wasn't entirely unpleasant. Maybe it was even exhilarating, to streak along high above the water, his wet garments flapping in the wind. Or maybe it was Kara's singing that lifted his spirits. Bardic music could do that, he knew, tamper with a man's emotions and make him feel things foreign to his nature.

When she reached the end of a stanza, he shouted, "Raryn, Pavel, and the others!"

"Everyone's all right," she replied. "Look, we've found a patrol boat."

It was true. The vessel floated below them. Witnessing the fate of the war galleys, the crew of the relatively small, single-masted sailboat had decided to make a run for it, but to no avail. They couldn't outdistance a dragon on the wing, nor could the night hide them from Kara's senses.

They were watching for her, and when she swooped out of the southern sky, some cowered blubbering or sprang overboard, but others prepared to fight. If they possessed any genuinely powerful spellcasters, they might have a chance, but Dorn was gambling they didn't. He'd based his strategy on the notion that all such folk would be based aboard the larger, more formidable and imposing galleys.

Arrows streaked upward from the boat, and so did a couple of shafts of crimson light. Kara jerked, and Dorn was sure that the sorcerous missiles, at least, had struck her. Still, it had been a relatively weak spell effect, potent enough to kill many a human being but not enough to balk her. She proved it by blasting a sizzling flare of breath across the deck, slaughtering the crew and setting sails, lines, and even timber ablaze. Kara climbed and rushed onward, leaving the fiery hulk in her wake.

"If we want a serviceable craft," she cried, "we have to take the last one without burning it or smashing it to pieces."

"I understand" Dorn answered.

It only took another couple of minutes to find the second boat. Singing, Kara plummeted through a hail of arrows. A dart pierced her dorsal surface just in front of the place where Dorn was riding then instantly liquefied, becoming a steaming, bubbling acid that ate away flesh around the initial puncture. The pain must have been intense, and Dorn felt a pang of pity for her, as well as the angry desire to make her attacker pay. For the moment, sympathy was all he could give. He was no healer or priest and thus had no means of neutralizing the corrosive agent.

Fortunately, like the bolts of magical force, the acid wasn't strong enough to stop Kara. Nearly on top of the boat, she spread and hammered her wings to slow her precipitous descent just a little. She still slammed down on the bow so hard it nearly shoved the whole front of the boat underwater.

The slanted deck would make for treacherous footing, but Dorn figured he'd just have to cope. Lacking his bow or even his long hand-and-a-half sword, lost when he'd lowered himself over the side of the galley, he had no way of reaching the enemy if he stayed perched on Kara's back. He scrambled down and aft.

Zhents advanced to meet him. He parried a spear thrust with his iron arm, then snapped his opponent's neck with a backhand blow to the jaw. By that time, a second soldier was cutting at his kidney. He pivoted, blocked that stroke, shifted in close, and drove his knife between the Zhent's ribs. The warrior collapsed, and Dorn stooped and appropriated his broadsword.

At which point, the deck jerked, nearly tossing the half-golem off his feet. The boat had leveled off. He didn't have to glance around to guess why. Kara had returned to human form, probably because she feared that otherwise, her immensity would damage or even sink the craft.

She could still fight with her sorcery, assuming she had any spells left. Yet even so, she was far more vulnerable, and it gave new hope to those Zhents who hadn't perished or jumped into the sea in dread. Howling battle cries, they charged the bow, and Dorn scurried into their path.

He beheaded one with a rake of his talons and spitted another on the point of his sword. Kara's vibrant song became a melody that reminded him somehow of a lullaby, and two more Zhents fell unconscious.

Then Dorn found himself face to face with a shaven-headed man in voluminous, sigil-bedizened robes who was surely the magician who'd conjured the arrow of acid. He'd cast at least one more enchantment to prepare for fighting at close quarters. A yard-long length of crimson fire wavered from each of his hands. Though he'd never encountered that particular magic before, Dorn was certain the flames would do at least as much damage as ordinary blades should they strike their target.

He advanced as usual, leading with his metal side. The wizard took a retreat, then instantly sprang forward again with a suddenness that would have done any warrior credit. Perhaps he'd used magic to heighten his agility. The fire-sword in his left hand slashed at Dorn's eyes.

The hunter jerked up his iron arm just in time to block. Fortunately, the solid metal stopped the seemingly insubstantial flare, even though he didn't feel the usual shock of impact. He riposted with a sword thrust at the Zhent's guts.

It should have been a mortal blow, but Dorn's point glanced aside as if it had struck plate armor. Some protective spell, one that didn't generate any telltale glimmer of light or swirl of shadow, was evidently to blame. The wizard hacked with the fire-blade in his left hand.

Pain seared Dorn's ribs, and he leaped backward. His own speed, together with the protection of his brigandine, were all that kept the flame from burning into his vitals. He let his guard drop, trying to look as if the wound had crippled him, and the Zhent took the bait. He rushed in, and the half-golem pounced to meet him. He knocked both fire-swords aside with a sweep of his iron arm, then struck hard with the broadsword.

Dorn penetrated the magician's invisible armor. The blade bit deep into the Zhent's neck, and he dropped. The half-golem pivoted in time to see Kara kill another reaver with her own azure darts of light. That appeared to be the last of the Zhents.

"Are you all right?" the song dragon panted.

Dorn was relieved to see that she showed no signs of frenzy.

Teeth gritted against the smoldering pain of his burn, he said, "Near enough. You?"

"The same."

She bore the ugly mark of the acid at the juncture of her neck and shoulder, and tiny cuts dotted the rest of her body. A number of arrows and quarrels littered the deck around her dainty feet. He realized they must be shafts that had stuck in her while she was in dragon shape. Fortunately, they hadn't driven all the way through her scaly hide, and had fallen out when she'd shifted to human form.

"Some of the Zhents aren't dead," she continued. "A couple aren't even hurt, just sleeping."

"They can't go free to tell what happened."

"I know. It's just . . . I'm used to slaying creatures that pose a threat to men, not men themselves. I realize what the Zhents are, what god they worship, what atrocities they commit, but . . ."

She shrugged.

"I've had to kill a lot of people in my time, some when they were already helpless," said Dorn, seeing no point in mentioning that he didn't particularly relish it, either. "I'll do it, and we'll get the boat turned around."

He started chucking bodies overboard. One of the sleepers woke in his grip, and he had to stick his claws into the wretch's heart.

NINETEEN

13 Tarsakh, the Year of Rogue Dragons

The black sky blazed white, and thunder boomed, loud enough to rattle Taegan's teeth in his jaw, or so it seemed. The rain hammered down. It had been storming since early afternoon, and he couldn't decide if that was bad or good. The downpour blinded and generally hindered him, but presumably it was doing the same thing to the creatures who were hunting him and the other survivors of Rangrim's company, trying to make certain that no one would escape to confirm that, yes, the Cult of the Dragon had indeed established an enclave in the heart of the Gray Forest.

Perhaps the rain didn't matter one way or the other, any more than Taegan's efforts to remain alert, stay low, and keep moving. Except for the hot, pulsing pain in his charred wing, his entire body was numb with cold and fatigue. He'd long since expended all his spells. He was hungry, alone, and unable to see the moon or stars behind their veil of clouds, blundering in circles as like as not. It was virtually impossible to doubt that the enemy was going to catch him, and he wondered why he didn't just sit down and wait for the inevitable. At least it would be less work.

Damn you, Gorstag, he thought, did you know Quelsandas had turned traitor? Why didn't you warn me?

Why didn't you do a better job of saving me? If I hadn't bled out, I could have told you all kinds of things.

Taegan knew he was only imagining his student's retort, but it was as if he was actually hearing it, which meant that in his exhaustion, and perhaps, fever-induced delirium, he was hallucinating. It was another bad sign, another indication that his inglorious end was close at hand. He hated the thought of dying like that, stalked and slain by brutes in the wilderness. It was a demise fit for the primitive elf he'd once been, not the cultured quasi-human he'd worked so diligently to become.

A wolf, or something akin to one, howled on his right. It sounded close, but though he turned and peered, he failed to spot it. Elsewhere in the wood, the creature's packmates answered its call. So did hobgoblins, yelling or blatting away on bugles.

Taegan couldn't even tell which way to run. It sounded as if his foes were all around him. He picked a direction at random, took a stride, then glimpsed motion from the corner of his eye. He pivoted and raised his sword just as the beast sprang.

His stop thrust took the attacker in the center of its furry chest, whereupon it fell to the ground, dragging the deeply embedded blade down with it. In the dark and the rain, its looks were indistinguishable from those of a natural wolf, but when it scrambled backward, dragging itself off the sword, Taegan realized it must be a lycanthrope going on four legs. No ordinary lupine could sustain such a hurt and continue fighting.

He wondered if he had any hope whatsoever of killing it before it ripped him apart in its slavering jaws. The enchantment had long since faded from his sword, and for the present, he had no way of casting another. The weapon was just a piece of steel, and at best of limited utility against phantoms, shapeshifters, and their ilk. But it was all he had.

Taegan yanked the weapon all the way free and cut at the werewolf's head before it could recover its balance. The blade split skin and grated on bone, but that didn't stop his foe. The creature snarled and lunged at him.

The fencing master jumped backward and extended. If the werewolf kept rushing in, it would impale itself once more, so it stopped short. Taegan feinted a thrust at its eyes then slashed at a foreleg.

He had to believe he was hurting the werewolf at least a little. The gory wounds Taegan inflicted remained after he pulled back his sword. The creature's paw was half-severed. Yet it was still game. Holding its maimed foot off the ground but scarcely less quick than before, it started to circle right, and he turned to keep it in front of him. Instantly it spun back to the left and pounced in on his flank. He slashed but only gave it a shallow gash he knew wouldn't stop it.

The werewolf grabbed Taegan's leg in its teeth. The pressure was agonizing, but the avariel couldn't tell if the fangs had penetrated the sturdy leather of his boot to pierce his flesh. The beast-thing wrenched the limb out from under the winged elf, and he fell hard on his back. The werewolf scuttled forward over the top of him, intent, perhaps, on biting out his throat.

Taegan thrust his sword into the lycanthrope's chest, gripped the hilt with both hands, and shoved with all his rapidly dwindling strength. The action served not merely to arrest the werewolf's advance but to lift its jaws out of striking range. Taegan's arms trembled with the strain of holding the creature aloft.

The werewolf thrashed furiously, trying to shake itself loose, and scrabbled at him with its nails. It started to melt into its beast-man shape. Evidently it realized clawed hands would be useful in its current situation. Most likely they'd enable it to slaughter Taegan in short order—but it never completed its transformation.

Taegan's point slid out of the creature's back. Its gradual passage entirely through the torso must have done so much damage than even a lycanthrope couldn't endure it, because the werewolf shuddered, coughed blood, and went limp.

Gasping, Taegan dumped the corpse to the side, relieving himself of its weight, then he sat up to check his leg. The werewolf's fangs had shredded his boot and the layers of cloth inside but hadn't broken his skin, which meant he wouldn't become a shapechanger himself.

For a moment, Taegan felt relieved, then grinned bitterly, as he realized what a ridiculous concern that really was. Even if the werewolf had infected him, it would take time for the disease to develop, and time was one thing he most assuredly lacked. His foe had called to his comrades before trying for the kill, and he could hear them approaching despite the ceaseless sizzling sound of the rain. They were drawing in all around him, and in his current condition, he had no hope of fighting so many at once. He clambered to his feet and dragged his sword out of the werewolf. It was conceivable that he might slay one or two more adversaries before the rest overwhelmed him. It was worth a try.

Off to his left, lights appeared among the trees. Taegan assumed they were lanterns, since the rain would quickly douse an open flame. A hobgoblin saw them, too, and shouted to its fellows, whereupon the points of light rapidly receded.

Behind Taegan, human voices jabbered, then likewise drew away. On his right, several soaked, bedraggled knights walked their destriers into view, then, evidently realizing they'd blundered into another encounter with the foes who'd routed them that morning, wheeled the war-horses around. They shouted and dug in their spurs, demanding speed of the exhausted mounts for a perilous gallop in the dark, through low-hanging branches and over uneven ground. No doubt anticipating an easy chase, werewolves bayed and raced after them.

In the aftermath, Taegan stood alone beneath rattling, storm-tossed branches and flaring thunderbolts. As the seconds crawled by, and no enemies slunk or charged into view, he gradually realized they weren't going to. They'd all dashed off in pursuit of more conspicuous prey.

He then waited for his benefactor to appear. He was certain he had one. It hadn't been mere coincidence that three separate diversions had occurred simultaneously, just when he needed them most. Tymora didn't send anyone that much luck.

Yet even so, the creature startled him, for it popped into view immediately in front of him, as if it had been invisible until that instant. His nerves were so frazzled that he nearly stabbed at it before he caught himself.

It was a dragon, or something resembling one, no longer than his arm from its toothy leer to the tip of its serpentine tail. He couldn't make out its color in the gloom, but its scales had a sparkle to them that reminded him of Kara's iridescent sheen. As it hovered before him, its wings were a glimmering blur. As best he could determine, they were shaped more like a butterfly's than a bat's.

"All hail Jivex," the diminutive dragon piped, "king of the forest." He laughed. "All right, not really. But I did save you, so you should at least thank me."

"I do thank—"

"You're an elf, aren't you? Who are you? What are you doing here?"

"I was born an avariel, and my name is Taegan Nightwind. I came here with Queen Sambryl's troops to destroy the hostile creatures in the wood."

Jivex grinned even wider and said, "It doesn't seem like it's going very well. Why'd you bother? Humans and elves don't live in the Gray Forest anymore."

Though it seemed entirely good-natured, a product of simple curiosity, the relentless interrogation made Taegan feel even edgier, if that was possible.

"The dastards are plotting harm to the entire kingdom," he said. "Now shouldn't we move away from here, before the goblins and wolves return?"

Jivex blinked and replied, "If they did come back, I'd just fool them with more illusions. That's how faerie dragons stay safe. But pitiful as you look, maybe I should take you someplace. Come on." He flitted a few feet forward. "What kind of dastardly plot is it?"

Jumping from topic to topic as unpredictably as Jivex darted about through the air, the questions kept flying as the small wyrm led his new companion through the trees. Speaking softly lest some foe overhear, Taegan gradually unfolded the tale of Gorstag's murder and the subsequent struggle against the cult much as he'd related it to Sambryl and the paladins, albeit in a more disjointed fashion.

Once he'd seemingly absorbed the substance of it, Jivex made an angry spitting sound.

"I don't want to Rage!"

Taegan shifted his burned wing in a futile attempt to ease the pain and asked, "Does the frenzy affect your kind as well?"

"We're dragons, aren't we, and I've had my own grumpiness and bad dreams."

Spent, feverish, and half-delirious as he was, Taegan had to stifle a hysterical laugh at the thought of faerie dragons trying to rampage like their gigantic kindred, but really, it wasn't funny. No matter how tricky they were, the small creatures would surely die by the score, by the hundred, should they seek to wage war on humanity. If Jivex was any indication, they were a harmless and even benevolent race, undeserving of such a fate.

"Well," said the avariel, "some wise folk are trying to figure out how to avert the Rage." Without going into specifics about Sammaster's folio, it was as much comfort as he had to offer.

"Meanwhile, we who serve Her Majesty must find a way to keep the cultists hereabouts from birthing one dracolich after another, until the land is overrun with them. I doubt your phantasms would keep you safe from them."

"You might be surprised," Jivex said. He lit on a tree trunk, clawed the bark, pulled something from the gouge with his teeth, gulped it down, and flew on. "But it doesn't matter."

"It doesn't?"

"Some folk might say that since the hobgoblins and were-wolves came, the Gray Forest is already tainted, but such creatures are a part of nature. We faerie dragons don't mind sharing the woodlands with them unless they make themselves particularly obnoxious. But the undead are unnatural. Just by existing, they poison the earth and air. Corrupt a being as powerful and magical as a wyrm with undeath, and it will become an especially nasty blight."

Taegan thought of Pavel and Brimstone and said, "I have a friend who agrees with you, and an acquaintance who wouldn't."

Jivex continued with his own chain of thought: "So it's a good thing you're an elf."

"How so?"

"Since the battle this morning, I've watched a lot of human warriors fleeing for their lives, but I didn't help them. My folk are leery of men. Some are all right, but some try to kill or cage us, whereas the old stories say the elves were our friends, until they went west."

"Which is why you decided to save me."

"Right, and because I did, perhaps we still have a chance to stop these cultists and wicked wyrms and such."

"If I can make my way to Lyrabar."

"Wouldn't it take a lot of time for you to reach there and fetch another army back, assuming your queen and lords will even consent to it? Mightn't the cult be even stronger by then? Maybe we can still quash it now, if the other elves will help us."

Taegan shook his head. Perhaps his weariness, sickness, and the clattering downpour were interfering with his hearing.

"I thought you said the elves had departed," the avariel said.

He'd certainly never heard of any settlement in the Gray Forest.

"They did, and they didn't," Jivex replied. "You'll see. I just hope they'll talk to one of their own. Usually they ignore me."

It was such an opaque pronouncement that Taegan wondered if the faerie dragon was not merely eccentric but genuinely mad. But perhaps it didn't matter. Demented or not, Jivex had rescued him, and he had no better plan than to follow the reptile. At least it seemed that their path had taken them far away from any pursuers.

Though that would be scant consolation if he dropped dead of exhaustion. Jivex kept him trudging until the storm finally stopped, and the first pale light of dawn filtered down through the canopy, revealing that the faerie dragon's wings were a silvery color, while his scales rippled with all the colors of the rainbow. Shortly thereafter, the two companions reached a circle of towering deciduous trees with gray bark and a grayish cast to their foliage. Taegan wondered if they were the plants that had given the forest its name. One thing was certain. Despite a youth spent in the heart of the Earthwood, he'd never seen their like.

❧ ⟡❧

"Elves," Jivex cried, "look! Here's one of your relatives."

Taegan peered about, perplexed.

"Whom are you addressing?" he asked. "We're the only ones here."

"No. They're all around us."

"Hiding? Invisible?"

Hovering, his butterfly wings a smear of gleaming whitish blur, the faerie dragon shook his head and replied, "They're the trees."

The fencing master sighed. That settled it. Jivex was crazy, and Taegan himself should have known better than to believe he had any chance of receiving aid from his vanished and inconsequential race.

Evidently affronted by his skepticism, Jivex said, "They are. When it was time to leave, some couldn't bear to go. They turned themselves into the gray trees instead."

"How ingenious."

"It just takes them a while to wake. Or notice visitors. Or stop thinking big, slow tree thoughts and remember how to talk to quick little creatures like us."

"If you say so," Taegan said. "While they collect themselves, I'd very much like to rest. Are we relatively safe here?"

"Yes. No wicked creature can find these glades."

"I am a wicked creature. Just ask Lord Oriseus."

Jivex cocked his head and asked, "What are you saying?"

"I'm too weary to know myself. Please, if you're able, stand the first watch."

Taegan unbuckled his sword belt then lay down on the wet ground with the weapon ready to hand. Jivex spotted an insect in flight and flitted off in pursuit.

At first Taegan's wing throbbed so badly that, exhausted as he was, he couldn't fall asleep, a circumstance that nearly made him cry. Eventually, though, when he'd all but abandoned hope of it ever happening, he slipped into slumber.

At first his dreams were a jumbled recapitulation of the ordeals and calamities of the previous day. Then he found himself standing in the center of the ring of gray trees once more. His thoughts were more lucid, clear enough to recognize he was dreaming.

Jivex flew up, perched on a low-hanging branch, and grinned.

"I told you," said the dragon.

"Told me what, precisely?"

"This makes it easier for the old elves to talk to you. I'm glad they pulled me in, too."

"I'm sorry, my gallant friend," Taegan said, "but none of this is actually happening. Even you are a figment. The real Jivex is off chasing bugs for his breakfast."

Hail, avariel, someone said. The voice seemed slow, soft, and deep, even though Taegan perceived that it wasn't sound so much as pure thought somehow resonating from one mind to another. *Once, we were moon elves, and thus we claim you as our kin. Jivex, we greet you as well, much as you've often wearied us with your chatter and inexhaustible store of questions.*

Taegan belatedly realized that it was all indeed more than a simple dream, though whether the gray tress were able and willing to help him remained to be seen. He gave them an elegant bow, though doing so hurt his wing considerably.

"I'm pleased to meet you," he said. "My name is Taegan Nightwind."

We rarely use our names.

For a moment, a pale face wavered inside one of the tree trunks, like a flame shining though thick, pebbled glass.

It no longer seems necessary. Our essences have blended over the centuries, even as our spreading roots and limbs have tangled.

"I see."

He didn't, really, but didn't think it would do any harm to pretend otherwise.

It gives us joy to behold a winged elf. We feared the Aril-tel-quessir extinct, another voice sounded, and another visage, female, gleamed briefly behind a translucent shell of bark.

"Not quite," Taegan said. "A handful still survive."

By hiding from the rest of the world. Though contemptible as that existence was, he supposed it had proved more successful than the way of the moon elves. Except for magical trees, the latter really were gone, from this part of Faerûn, anyway.

For a time, the ghosts, if that was the right term for them, just peered at him. Taegan could feel the pressure of their scrutiny.

Then they said, *You speak of your people without pride.*

"If that gives offense, you have my abject apologies. I certainly don't mean to imply disrespect for you or anyone with whom you share a bond of blood. But truly, we have more important matters to discuss than my manners. Are you aware of what's happening in the forest?"

To some degree. Sometimes it takes us time to perceive. We live at a different pace than you. Yet we're vigilant, after our fashion. That's why we remained behind, to protect the wood.

Even in the dream, Taegan was tired and miserable with pain, and perhaps that was what made it difficult to curb his tongue: "Well, so far you're doing a splendid job of it."

The hobgoblins were a scourge to moon elves, but neither they nor werewolves nor black and green drakes pose a threat to the forest itself. More white faces glimmered inside the tree trunks. *We stayed here to shepherd our homeland through times of fire, blight, and drought, to balance forces you cannot comprehend.*

"Well," Jivex said, "these Cult of the Dragon humans are making undeath in the forest. They've already killed one green wyrm, then filled it with shadow to walk and fly again. You care about that, I hope."

Once again, the trees remained mute for a time, perhaps conferring with one another.

Finally they said, *Tell us more.*

Taegan managed to relate his experiences despite frequent interruptions from Jivex, who evidently regarded himself as the central figure in the tale.

At the end, the maestro said, "I still intend to oppose the cult if I can, but I'm in urgent need of assistance. If I don't receive it, I don't know that I'll even survive this wound in my wing."

We have power, said the trees, *but since our transformation, we've never tried to direct it to heal a single small creature of flesh and bone. It isn't well-suited to that, not anymore. It could do harm instead. But we're willing to try.*

"Then please do," Taegan said.

Faces glowed from the boles of the trees, the early-morning sunlight brightened until he had to squint, and Jivex's scales fairly blazed with a hundred vivid colors. Abruptly, agony stabbed through the avariel's pinion. He clenched his jaw to keep from crying out, and all his discomforts disappeared.

So did Jivex and the circle of gray trees. Taegan found himself standing in the center of a habitation the like of which he'd never seen.

That was because it was a city and a forest at the same time. Instead of clearing the enormous trees to erect houses in their place, the builders of the enclave had by power of enchantment coaxed them to grow into forms suitable for their needs, with hollows in the heartwood for rooms, apertures for doors and windows, sculpted ridges for staircases and balconies, and broad, flat, fused limbs to provide walkways from one spire to the next. Perhaps the city planners had even persuaded certain trees to pull up their roots and shift themselves a little, for broad avenues ran between them to facilitate traffic at ground level.

"Welcome," said a pleasant soprano voice.

Startled, Taegan pivoted. Beside him stood a female moon elf, or the semblance of one. A head shorter than himself, with impish features that contrasted oddly with a palpable air of dignity, she had azure tresses and slanted turquoise eyes flecked with gold. Her garments were predominantly blue as well.

"This is our home as we remember it. Here, I'm still Amra, discrete in some measure from the others."

Taegan bowed and said, "It's a delight to make your acquaintance, Lady, but I fear I don't understand the point of this."

"We said we'd try to heal you," Amra replied. "You carry a wound of the spirit, too, a scar of ignorance and shame."

"Are you certain? I'm told that if anything, I'm prone to conceit."

"Yet you regret your blood, and that diminishes you. We'll try to relieve you of the burden."

"That's kind, but I assure you, unnecessary. I'm quite content with the person I am. Or I will be, if you simply mend my wing."

"We're trying. Meanwhile, walk with me. Come see what your kin once accomplished. It's our gift to you."

He supposed he might as well humor her, particularly since he'd begged her and the other trees for succor.

"Very well, then, Lady," he said as he offered her his arm. "I'm at your service."

It soon became clear they weren't really strolling, or anyway, not merely sauntering from place to place. Rather, the magic engendering the dream within a dream whisked them from one vista to the next, compressing space and time to impart a sense of the life of the city as rapidly as possible.

Laughing children played tag around a gigantic oak. A craftsman crooned charms, and an emerald grew and branched on the table before him, forming itself into an exquisite tiara. Ladies and gentlemen danced in a high-ceilinged hall lit by floating spheres of soft white light. Farmers hiked through the forest to gather a harvest as bountiful as any yielded by human fields, provided one knew where to look. A priest recited an invocation, and a lammasu, a divine emissary with the body of a winged lion and the face of a bearded saint, swooped down from the sky to counsel him. A chorus sang a lament so beautiful and poignantly sad that every listener wept. Lancers in silvery mail paraded on steeds slimmer and more delicate-looking than any horses bred by men, while warrior maidens cantered on unicorns. It all really was rather marvelous. Taegan had never dreamed elves could create such grandeur.

"If your people possessed all this," he asked, "why would they abandon it?"

"The hobgoblins came," Amra replied. "For more than a hundred years, we repelled them, slaughtering horde after horde. But over time they wore us down until we were too few to resist. The survivors had to forsake their homeland or perish."

"It's a great pity," Taegan said, and he meant it.

Yet it also occurred to him that it was additional proof that elves, even ones as blessed with learning and grace as the folk of the Gray Forest had evidently been, lacked some fundamental resiliency or essential worthiness the human race possessed.

Perhaps Amra sensed the tenor of his thoughts, for she said, "Everything has its season, Taegan, and every season passes. One day, this Impiltur you so admire will fade and die as well."

"You may be right, but it won't be anytime soon if I can help it. That's why I'm fighting." Well, he thought, that and plunder, and a second helping of revenge. "Are you and your fellows healing my wing?" Or are you crippling it permanently, Taegan asked himself, or killing me outright?

She cocked her head and stood silently for a moment, evidently communing with the other trees.

"We've done what we can," she said finally. "You can judge the results for yourself when we leave the realm of memory."

"I implore you, don't keep me in suspense. Return me now."

"As you wish."

A moment later, he was lying on the ground. Somehow he could tell that the trees had whisked him back to wakefulness and not just another level of dream. Jivex crouched on top of him, peering at his face. Obviously the spirits had roused him as well.

"Avariels are big babies," the faerie dragon sneered. "You were screaming and thrashing around all the time they worked on you."

"Since my mind was elsewhere, I can honestly disclaim any responsibility for my deportment. Get off me, please."

Jivex sprang into the air. Taegan clambered to his feet and took stock of himself, angling his wing forward to inspect the burn. He was still tired, hungry, stiff, and sore, but the excruciating pain that had flared every time he shifted the pinion was gone. The wound looked as if it had been healing for tendays and doing so cleanly. He spread both wings, beat them experimentally, and found them strong enough to carry him aloft. Probably he couldn't yet fly as fast, far, or nimbly as before, but at least he was no longer earthbound.

Grinning, Jivex spiraled around him.

"I told you they'd help," the reptile said.

"Indeed you did, and I thank all of you."

You're welcome, said the trees. Even awake, Taegan could still hear them, though their silent communal voice seemed much fainter, like a mild breeze sighing through leaves. *Did you likewise profit from your tour of our city?*

Landing, Taegan said, "It was very interesting."

The spirits contemplated him for a time then replied, *So be it. Everyone must decide for himself what to prize and what to cast away. We merely hoped to plant a seed.*

"When I have the leisure, I'll certainly reflect on what fair Amra showed me. Meanwhile, I have a military disaster to reverse. You and Jivex have already saved my life. It's presumptuous of me to expect any further aid. Yet if you won't tender it, the necromancers will continue polluting your forest."

What do you want us to do? Jivex asked the trees.

It was a good question, one that brought home to Taegan the difference between a teacher of individual combat and a war captain. He struggled to assess the current dismal situation as Rangrim would have.

"As I can't do anything alone," he said, "I have to assume a reasonable number of the Warswords yet survive. If I could reassemble them into an army, perhaps we could still strike a telling blow. The problem being that they're scattered through miles of woodland hiding from pursuit, and no doubt intent on fleeing east as expeditiously as possible."

"The other faerie dragons and I could try to find them," Jivex said, grinning, "and shield them with our illusions as we herd them together."

"How many of you are there?" Taegan asked.

The small reptile hesitated before saying, "Some."

The avariel arched an eyebrow and asked, "Could you be more specific?"

"No," the little dragon replied. "I can't count that high. I'm just as smart as you, but my mind works differently."

"I understand."

"If you're so great, let's see you make some illusions."

"I said, I understand and I assure you, I regard you as an altogether sagacious and wondrous creature." Taegan turned to one of the gray trees, selecting it at random. It was difficult to know where to look when the former elves were all around him. "Can you offer further help as well?"

A little, the spirits replied. *Several circles of elven trees stand in the wood. Each can shelter some of your comrades until you're ready to march against the foe. Perhaps we can even call to them to lead them to safety, if they'll heed our whispers.*

"That could be a problem," Taegan said, "getting them to trust you or the faerie dragons, for that matter, but we'll simply have to do our best. Perhaps if you invoke my name, it will allay their misgivings."

"Or," said Jivex, leering, "we'll just trick them into heading where we want them to go." He exuberantly flew through a vertical loop, as if he thought the desperate venture they contemplated would prove a merry lark. "Is that the plan, then?"

"Evidently," Taegan replied, and the absurdity of the statement hit home. "What am I saying? That can't be all. Because otherwise, even if we succeed in reassembling the expedition, with the casualties we endured, and the bronzes slain or lost to frenzy, we don't have a prayer of defeating the cult."

Perhaps, said the spirits, *we can help a bit more. Long before any of us was even born, another chose to remain in the forest when by rights she should have departed, to protect the Teu-tel-quessir who were her friends. Alas, as the centuries passed, her slumber deepened, and it became increasingly difficult to rouse her. In the end, when the city fell, she didn't hear our pleas. But she's enjoyed a long rest since, and maybe if another elf calls her, she'll wake one final time.*

TWENTY

Jivex and another of his kind—it had turned out the Gray Forest was home to six faerie dragons, each with its own extensive territory—led Taegan and a dozen of the queen's men skulking through the wood. Finally the reptiles wheeled and flew back to their bipedal companions.

"Here we are," Jivex said.

Taegan surveyed the patch of ground ahead of him. If it had ever been a carefully shaped and tended burial mound, that time had long since passed. It had no discrete edges or discernible form and had seemingly fallen in on itself until it was scarcely higher than the surrounding earth. It even had old maple trees growing out of it.

"Are you sure?" the maestro asked.

Jivex snorted and said, "Who lives hereabouts, you or I? Of course I'm sure."

Sir Corlas moved up beside Taegan. The cavalier's surcoat was torn and grimy, his plate and shield battered, his destrier slain, but he still had his lady's crimson scarf knotted to his helmet.

"I'll post sentries," he said, "while you begin the ceremony."

Though by no means servile, Corlas's manner was respectful. It had been disconcerting to discover that, with Rangrim and his senior lieutenants either dead or at best still missing, the Warswords regarded the duelist responsible for their reunification as a de facto officer. Accordingly, Taegan tried to behave as if he merited their confidence, and to ignore the inner voice whispering that a war-leader of his meager qualifications was bound to fall well short of expectations.

"It isn't a ceremony as such," he replied. "Apparently I simply talk to her, but I have no idea how long it will take, so pickets are a sound idea."

With Jivex flitting along beside him, Taegan advanced until he was standing at the foot of the dilapidated mound. He drew his sword and saluted the entity who theoretically lay sleeping before him.

"Vorasaegha," he said. "My name is Taegan Nightwind. Your friends the moon elves sent me to ask you to come forth."

Nothing answered except for a jay chattering in the meshed branches overhead. Well, he hadn't expected it to be that easy.

"The city is gone now," he continued, "and the elves themselves, much changed. But they still revere your memory and pray you'll help them as you did before, to cleanse the forest of corruption. Since your time, a new evil has come into the world. An insane wizard named Sammaster invented a way of infusing dragons with the most virulent kind of undeath . . ."

He pressed on, spinning the tale of the Cult of the Dragon and of his own protracted duel with it, looking for any subtle sign that something under the moist earth with its coating of slippery rotten leaves could hear him. He couldn't discern one.

He concluded by once again imploring Vorasaegha to reveal herself. Still, nothing happened. He felt a crushing disappointment.

"Louder," Jivex said.

"I beg your pardon?"

"She has dirt in her ears, and more of it piled between you and her. Maybe you need to yell."

Taegan smiled wryly and said, "An interesting conjecture, but I doubt that's truly the problem."

He turned. Corlas was standing with Uthred, the wizard who'd protected the archers' retreat when the Warswords routed. Like the knight, the latter was a relatively young man, but affected long, wheat-colored, grandfatherly whiskers that he probably felt made him look more the learned and formidable battle mage. It was plain from their glum expressions that both humans understood what had just occurred. Or failed to. Still, Taegan supposed he ought to say it anyway, for form's sake.

"I'm sorry. The creature has apparently slipped too far from this world and its cares for us to summon her back. The gray trees warned it might be so."

Corlas unconsciously squared his shoulders, bucking himself up.

"Well," said the knight, "at least we're one army again. Maybe we can retreat in good order, muster reinforcements in Lyrabar, and march back."

"If everyone else isn't already off fighting to the east," Uthred said somberly. "Still, you're right, it's the only way. Jivex, will you and your folk continue helping us conceal ourselves from the enemy?"

"That's it?" the faerie dragon shrilled. "You're just giving up? My kin and I have been wasting our time on you."

"We truly will return if we can," Taegan said.

"And maybe we'll have a dozen dracoliches running around by then. Won't that be fun?"

Taegan looked at his human companions and said, "Sune knows, I wouldn't choose to flee, not if I could see any hope of avenging our fallen comrades and smashing the cult now."

"In our present circumstances," Corlas said, "every minute we can use to distance ourselves from the enemy is precious. But I suppose we can spare a few more."

Uthred made a sour face, but said, "Why not?"

Taegan faced the mound, then on impulse went down on his knees and set his sword on the ground as he might lay it at the feet of the queen. Who knew, it might help. He recited the same string of pleas and explanations he'd offered before. By the end, his mouth was dry, and to all unaltered appearances, that was the only thing he'd accomplished.

"That's it, then," Uthred said.

Jivex flitted up to the wizard, hovered at the right height to glower at him eye to eye, and said, "You humans are a bunch of quitters."

"I cast some divinations," Uthred said. "Once something powerful lay in this ground, but now, only faint traces of its magic remain." He looked at Taegan. "Maestro? Are you ready to go?"

"Yes," Taegan said. "No. I concede it makes little sense, but give me one last chance."

"I realize," Corlas said, "that Jivex saved your life. We all owe him and the other faerie dragons a huge debt. But we can't repay it by persisting in an effort that's manifestly futile."

"I know," Taegan said. "I won't deliver my entire oration a third time. I just need another minute."

The knight shrugged. "Do what you must."

Which was what, exactly? At first, Taegan had no idea what to try that he hadn't attempted twice already. Then intuition, or perhaps mere desperation, prompted him.

"I myself am an elf," he said, and it felt strange to proclaim it with such fervor. "I, who summon you. This is my elf blood. Feel it. Smell it. Taste it. Recognize it, damn you."

Taegan drew his dagger, sliced the heel of his palm, and squeezed red droplets onto the ground.

They simply made a stain, without glowing, catching fire, or doing anything else overtly supernatural. They didn't even soak into the soil with unusual quickness. Nothing stirred.

"We'll see you out of the wood safely," the faerie dragon said, an unaccustomed dullness in his voice.

"Thank you," Taegan replied. He rose and inspected the gash in his hand. He'd sliced it fairly deeply. "We brought along a priest or paladin, didn't we? If he has any healing left after tending the wounded, perhaps he could look at this."

"Mystra's stars!" Uthred swore, his eyes widening.

"What is it?" Taegan asked.

"Come away," the wizard said. Taegan realized that the divinatory spells Uthred had mentioned must still have been altering his perceptions, revealing phenomena other people couldn't see. "Come away from the mound."

Taegan beat his wings and leaped clear. Jivex whizzed after him. The slight hump in the ground began to shake as if experiencing its own private little earthquake. The maples lashed back and forth.

In time, the trees toppled, crashing against each other. An archer had to scramble to keep one from falling on him. Fissures snaked through the mound, splitting it into pieces. The fallen maples jolted upward and tumbled aside as the entity beneath them heaved herself into the light of day.

It occurred to Taegan that the process was a bit like a hatchling struggling forth from an egg, but everything else about Vorasaegha bespoke might and majesty. She was at least as huge as any of the other drakes he'd encountered. Her gleaming bronze scales, from which the dust slid as if it had no power to sully her, were blue-black along the edges, while her eyes shone like luminous green pearls, without visible pupils. Such details were marks of the extreme age that only made a dragon stronger.

Still, the awe she inspired in every trembling observer lay in more than her physical appearance. While plainly as solid as metal, Vorasaegha nonetheless had an elusive but unmistakable uncanniness about her. Though her existence predated theirs by centuries, she might almost have recreated herself specifically to battle dracoliches, for she was their counterpart, a wyrm who'd cheated death for benevolent reasons instead of selfish ones.

She turned her gigantic serpentine head toward Taegan. Her radiant gaze was terrifying even though nothing about it conveyed hostility.

"You called me," she rumbled.

"Yes, Milady."

"I didn't believe I'd walk this world again. These are surely the final hours."

Taegan took a deep breath to steady himself and said, "Then we'd better make them count."

"Come here."

Taegan walked to her. She lowered her head, and her forked tongue, longer and thicker than his arm, flicked forth to swipe across his hand. Its touch was rough and wet, and afterward, his cut was gone.

"Now," said the dragon, "tell me what you need of me."

TWENTY-ONE

16 Tarsakh, the Year of Rogue Dragons

It made Dorn edgy simply to float at anchor with the sail lowered. He glowered out across the purplish expanse of the Moonsea and saw the same nothing as before.

"To Baator with this," he growled.

"He promised he'd join us," Kara said with a sigh. "Please, give him a little longer."

"Just because we've fooled the Zhentarim up to now, that doesn't mean they won't eventually figure out we stole one of their patrol boats. Besides, we're wasting daylight, and we'd have to be even stupider than we evidently are to do this after dark."

"On the other hand" said Raryn, "if we're going, we might as well go as strong as possible."

His long hair and goatee shining particularly white in the sunlight, the arctic dwarf sat on a coil of rope sharpening the point of his new harpoon with a hone.

Upon reaching Thentia, the hunters had discovered that, wonder of wonders, their partners among the city's motley collection of wizards had been doing their jobs for a change. Instead of squandering all their time on bizarre experiments, they'd actually enchanted some items to replace the gear the travelers tended to lose or damage in the course of fulfilling their commissions. The mages had, for example, produced a new bastard sword and quiver of arrows for Dorn, and a new curved hornblade and pouch of skiprocks for Will.

Most of those weapons and pieces of armor were packed away. They wouldn't help the hunters where they were headed. Fortunately, by rummaging through the wizards' storerooms and scouring the marketplace, they'd managed to lay hands on a few implements that would.

"I'm tired of waiting, too," said Will from the top of the mast. "We could at least toss Pavel overboard and see what happens. Then the rest of us will know what to expect."

"I had a similar thought," the priest replied, wrapped in a garment that, out of the water, appeared to be nothing more than a leather cloak. "The gods know, you've never been good for anything else, but perhaps you could finally play a useful role as chum."

The patrol boat jolted as if it had run aground on a reef or sandbar, though that was plainly impossible. Dorn and his companions staggered, fighting for balance.

All around the sailboat, beautiful mermaids leaped into view and somehow pirouetted along the surface of the lake, with only the tips of their green, piscine tails touching the waves. Then their comely faces warped into grotesque ugliness. They puffed out their cheeks and spat prodigious jets of water. Though Dorn tried to dodge, the frigid spray soaked him anyway.

Or at least it seemed to, but the next instant, he was dry, and the mermaids vanished like popping soap bubbles. Kara sighed like a mother enduring the antics of a mischievous child and peered over the side.

"We know it's you, Chatulio," she said. "Show yourself."

A dragon with scales the metallic orange of newly minted coppers swam out from under the boat, and treading water with his feet and wings, lifted his head to peer over the side. His blue eyes shining, he gave the bard a gap-toothed leer.

"I just thought I'd show the small folk what I can do."

Kara replied, "Thus wasting magic we may soon need to save our lives."

"If you can't have a laugh, what's the use of living anyway? Introduce me to your friends."

That took a few moments then, with Chatulio looking on curiously, it was time to make the final preparations. Essentially it was a matter of casting spells and drinking potions. Pavel prayed for Lathander's blessing, bolstering the party's vigor, courage, and luck. Kara sang a charm that would enable her to breathe underwater. Dorn gulped a lukewarm, sour-tasting elixir that was supposed to confer the same benefit, and a sweeter one generally employed to give a person the power to float up into the air. Under water, it would keep the weight of his iron limbs from dragging him helplessly to the bottom.

Still, when he picked up his long spear and joined his companions at the side, he felt a pang of trepidation. As a child, he'd loved to swim, but that was long ago. Evidently sensing his anxiety, Kara touched him on the arm. He didn't know how that made him feel or how to respond.

"Last one in's a three-legged tortoise," said Will.

He sprang high and somersaulted into the water, and his comrades jumped after him.

Dorn had to force himself to stop holding his breath. The first inhalation of water was cool in his lungs, more substantial than air, but not unpleasantly so. He experimentally willed his weight away, then brought it back a bit at a time until he achieved the neutral buoyancy that served a swimmer best. Meanwhile, Kara swelled into dragon shape, while Pavel's cloak spread itself into the winged, rippling shape of a manta ray. Dorn had to peer closely to make out the human form within. The hunters hoped that if they had to fight, the disguise would give the cleric a chance to weave his magic unnoticed by those who might otherwise do their utmost to disrupt the casting.

Dorn pointed at the bottom, and they all swam downward around the anchor line, toward the spires of Northkeep.

A thousand years ago, it had been the first human city on the Moonsea, until a "Dark Alliance" of giants, chromatic dragons, orcs, and other hostile creatures sacked it, then performed a magical rite to sink the very isle on which it sat. As best as Pavel, Kara, and Brimstone could guess, it was the first location Sammaster had visited and written about extensively, and it certainly seemed a plausible site to harbor ancient and forgotten lore, about the madness of wyrms or anything else.

Yet as Dorn contemplated the devastation spread out below him, he wondered if such a secret could possibly have survived the conflict that had broken the ramparts, the upheaval that thrust them beneath the currents, or all the centuries that had passed since, wrapping the feet of the towers in weed and miring them in silt. Even if it had, could seekers who lacked Sammaster's level of arcane power and knowledge find it in a sprawling, ruinous underwater warren or recognize it if they did?

For that matter, could they even survive the attempt? Because Northkeep, though devoid of life, was still inhabited. Dozens of grisly tavern tales agreed that the ghosts of those who'd perished in the fortress-city's defense abided there still and had a brutal way with trespassers. On moonless nights, they rang the bells in the tallest towers, perhaps to warn mortals away. The sound was audible for miles across the water. Growing up in Hillsfar, Dorn had heard it himself, and wrapped his pillow around his ears to muffle the eerie tolling.

Keeping a wary eye out for wraiths and other dangers, Dorn and his companions dived lower, toward the imposing castle-like complex at the center of the ravaged city. There stood the palace of the lord of Northkeep, the residences of the dignitaries of his court, and temples consecrated to the gods they'd worshiped. If seemed the most likely place to hold the secret of the Rage.

Battle, or the plunge to the bottom of the lake, had opened breaches and fissures in many a wall, and caved in sections of roof. Descending swimmers could enter the damaged buildings in a hundred different ways. Dorn chose to lead his allies down into the central courtyard and view the mansions, fortifications, and shrines somewhat as the living inhabitants of Northkeep must have experienced them. He hoped it would give him a sense of the place, and that in turn would help him guess precisely where to start the search.

It seemed worth a try, anyway. But when they'd swum so low they could almost have planted their feet in the muck on the bottom, and the high arched entryways to stone bastions and graceful spires yawned all around, the world turned black in a single instant, as if the water had changed to ink, or the sun in the sky overhead had winked out.

Fighting panic, Dorn thought he knew what was actually happening. The phantoms of Northkeep had conjured the darkness to help them dispose of the intruders.

Dorn's spear was enchanted, and his iron arm was a magical weapon in its own right. He had at least a slim chance of defending himself against the dead, but only if he could see them. Floating blindly in the cold murk, he prayed that one of his spellcasting comrades possessed a magic sufficiently potent to wipe the darkness away.

Time crawled by, measured out by his racing heartbeats, punctuated by uninterpretable little noises that jabbed at his nerves. Were Kara, Pavel, and Chatulio trying but failing to make light, or were they dead already? Had the spirits possessed the wit to strike at them first?

Finally brightness glowed through the water. Spear leveled, Dorn turned, seeking the spectral men-at-arms of legend. They weren't there, but something else was. Malevolent dragons had given their lives to cast down Northkeep, and their gigantic skeletons burst forth from their hiding places in the silt, stirring dirt into the water in the process. Points of red light burning deep in the eye sockets of their naked skulls, the entities oriented on the intruders.

Dorn was reasonably certain it wasn't a haunting in the truest sense of the term. Necromancy had animated the wyrm skeletons as it had the human corpses serving the Cult of the Dragon in Lyrabar. Conceivably Sammaster himself had laid the trap to insure that no one else would carry secrets out of Northkeep.

Thanks to their own magic, Dorn and his companions were no longer sightless and helpless, but they were in serious trouble nonetheless. Lacking vital organs, the undead were notoriously difficult to destroy in the best of circumstances. It was going to be even harder employing only such weapons and spells as were efficacious underwater.

Wheeling in the cloak that, among its other virtue, let him swim as fast and as nimbly as a manta ray, Pavel dodged the raking talons of a rearing skeleton, then brandished his sacred amulet. A red-gold beam of Lathander's light blazed forth and burned the creature to powder.

Another skeleton flung itself onto a copper dragon. The metallic drake's body exploded into leering clown faces, which then blinked out of existence. Wings stroking to propel him through the water, the real Chatulio appeared out of nowhere above the undead construct and seized hold of the length of vertebrae between the bony armature of its wings. He tore at the creature with his jaws.

Ducking and twisting, avoiding gnashing fangs and scrabbling claws by inches, Raryn thrust his harpoon at a skeletal wyrm's head. The point only chipped and scratched the bone, but while the dead thing was intent on the dwarf, Will squirmed between two of its ribs, and safely ensconced inside its torso, attacked the withered ligaments binding it together with his knife.

With her song, eerily distorted by the water but still somehow as beautiful as ever, Kara conjured a block of ice into being within the rib cage of another skeletal drake. The white expanding mass shattered the unnatural thing into fragments.

That was as much as Dorn could take in before he found it necessary to focus on his own onrushing opponent. The bony thing snapped at him and caught his iron arm in its jaws. He simultaneously wrenched himself free, breaking a couple of its fangs, and drove his lance into an eye socket. He hoped that if he could hit one of the points of crimson phosphorescence, maybe that would kill it.

But when he pulled the spear back, the light was still smoldering at the back of the cavity, and the skeleton was as active as ever. It reared and slashed at him with its talons. He caught the stroke on his metal arm and so prevented it from ripping him apart, but the sheer force slammed him down into the muck on the floor of the lake. Blindness swallowed him once more as the silt covered his face. The undead wyrm clutched and squeezed him in its claws. The left side of his body with its shell of iron could take the pressure. It was obvious from the pain that the right side couldn't.

He tore frantically at the bony phalanges with his own claws until the members came apart then floundered upward out of the mud. The undead drake bit at him through the murky water, and he punched with his knuckle spikes. The impact jolted him backward but likewise unhinged one side of the creature's jaw. He assumed that, mindless and lifeless, the construct didn't feel pain any more than he felt it in his metal limbs, but some reflex made it snatch its head back anyway.

That gave Dorn an opening. He flung himself in close and clawed at the base of its long, fleshless neck. The spinal column broke apart, scattering loose vertebrae wide as dinner plates, and the skeletal drake's head tumbled away from the rest of it. The body collapsed, more bones separating or twisting into awkward relationships to reduce it to an inert and meaningless jumble.

Dorn turned, seeking the next threat. His first chaotic impression was that while they had more skeletons to dispatch, he and his comrades were holding their own. Then Kara's song swelled. Even if, perchance, she wasn't using some esoteric or occult language, he had no hope of comprehending the words. The water robbed them of sense. But somehow they conveyed an urgency that made him cast frantically about.

The warning didn't help as much as Kara must have hoped. When Dorn turned himself into the right attitude, the creature was already striking at him.

The thing was huge as a wyrm and resembled the dragons he'd encountered in certain respects, yet it was nothing he'd ever seen or even heard reports of hitherto. In its essence, it was a colossal serpent with dark, slimy scales, yet possessed of stunted wings and legs, far too small to enable it to walk or fly, but useful, perhaps, when it swam. Its long tail split into two writhing, whiplike appendages, which it lashed at its target. A man couldn't effectively swing a flail or even a sword at the bottom of a lake. The water offered too much resistance. But the drake was so prodigiously strong that it suffered no such limitation.

Dorn tried to dodge and shield flesh with iron, but surprise and the water cost him a critical moment, and he knew with a sickening certainty that the beast was going to strike him a solid, perhaps lethal blow. Then Kara lunged between the human and the aquatic wyrm. Its tail struck her instead.

Evidently the tips of the appendage were as sharp as blades, for they split her shimmering hide, then sliced deeper as it pulled them along in a wicked, drawing cut. Twin clouds of blood billowed forth, mixing with the muddy water to make it even more difficult to see.

Kara snapped at the water dragon. It twisted clear of the attack, then instantly lashed her again. She convulsed at the shock. The aquatic wyrm coiled around her like a python, then proceeded to constrict, bite, and slash at her at the same time. She kept trying to fight back, but her foe clasped her so tightly that it was impossible for her to strike a telling blow.

Enraged, Dorn kicked forward, but the wyrm was cunning. It had, after all, waited for the newcomers to focus their attention on the skeletons before attempting a surprise attack. Perhaps it had even manufactured the initial darkness. At any rate, it saw no reason to allow a second foe to jab and claw at it before it finished with the first. A flick of the forked tail sufficed to shoot it several yards out of reach.

Wishing that he'd claimed the manta ray garment for himself, Dorn labored after the creature through water that tasted of dirt and Kara's blood. Perhaps amused by his pursuit, the dark-scaled wyrm let him close almost into spear range before widening the distance once again. As far as the human could tell, the trivial exertion in no way slackened the serpent's grip or otherwise hindered its efforts to kill the song dragon. Kara's struggles grew weaker by the second. A wing and hind leg protruded from her adversary's slimy coils at odd ankles, manifestly dislocated or broken.

Dorn realized he couldn't swim fast enough to overtake the huge, yellow-eyed snake thing until the latter decided to permit it, not without help, anyway. He peered through the cloudy, filthy water. His friends were still battling skeletons, fighting so hard they might not even have noticed the water drake and surely couldn't break away to confront it even if they had.

Or so it seemed. But then Chatulio, hard-pressed though he was by a pair of enormous undead wyrms, spun away from their gnashing fangs and raking talons to peer across the battlefield at Kara's captor. A mass of scuttling crabs abruptly appeared on the aquatic drake's head and the uppermost section of its body, where they started pinching and picking away with their claws.

Mad as a hound covered in stinging ants, the dark drake convulsed and bent its body in a circle, swatting at its own throat and skull to dislodge the crustaceans. It maintained its death grip on its feebly squirming captive, but evidently forgot about Dorn, for it finally let him swim close enough to strike.

The half-golem drove his spear twice into the coils of scaly muscle gripping Kara. The dark wyrm's body twisted, whipping its head into position to bite. Though raw little pockmarks freckled its mask, it didn't have crabs worrying it anymore. Either the skeletons had shaken Chatulio's concentration and so put an end to his magic, or the aquatic dragon had rid itself of the harassment in some other way.

It struck. Dorn ducked under the attack, then sank his talons into a patch of the slimy, scaly hide behind its jaws. Whatever else happened, the filthy thing wasn't going to retreat beyond his reach. Dorn drove his spear into the underside of its throat.

Its neck swelled, and its jaws opened wide. Evidently it truly was some sort of dragon, for it was unleashing a breath weapon. In air, the exhalation might have leaped forth in the usual cone or streak. Underwater, a dirty stain billowed in all directions.

Its touch made Dorn's mind turn slack and dull, so that all its contents—rage, fear, his very awareness of what was happening—threatened to slip away. He clamped down on them, resisting the stupefying effect with all his will, and at that same instant, the wyrm snapped its head in an arc.

The sudden jerk nearly shook Dorn loose. It did make him fumble his grip on the spear, which slipped from his grasp. His iron hand was the best weapon remaining to him, which meant he needed to hang on with the other one to free it up. He prayed his human fingers were strong enough to keep him anchored.

Dorn ripped at the serpent's scales and the meat beneath. It breathed, and the murk diffusing through the water burned the half-golem's skin.

Acid, he thought, clenching himself against the pain, squinting in the hope that the stuff wouldn't sear his eyes out.

He found a spot that, when attacked, made the water wyrm convulse—a vulnerable place, maybe a particularly sensitive cluster of nerves. Dorn clawed it furiously, and the huge creature slashed at him with its tail blades. He twisted and caught the stroke on his iron half. The impact jolted him but couldn't cut through the armor.

The dragon swung its tail back for another blow, and though he couldn't have explained how, Dorn understood what could happen next if he was strong, quick, and skillful enough to make it happen. It was a sort of fighter's intuition that sometimes spoke when he needed it most, an instinct he'd first discovered in the arena.

He clawed some more. The creature's pain needed to be constant and unbearable. It whipped its tail at him, and he flung himself clear of its body. If his timing was off, or he failed to push off with sufficient agility, the blow would hit him, and almost certainly cleave flesh. Even if he survived that by releasing his grip, he'd given up the only advantage he possessed. If his trick failed, it was unlikely the wyrm would give him the chance to hurt it any further.

But the ploy worked. Frantic, maybe spastic with pain, the serpent slashed the tail blades deep into its own throat, half-severing the amber-eyed head. Its blood streaming upward like smoke from some great fire, it drifted toward the bottom.

Dorn pulled at its coils but couldn't loosen them. Then something cut off the sunlight shining down from the surface, casting him into shadow. Certain some new horror had arrived to menace him, he looked up. Bearing several bite and claw wounds along his flanks, Chatulio swam above him. The copper used his talons to pry the motionless Kara from her bonds.

By the time Chatulio finished, the rest of their comrades had gathered around. Each was wounded, even Pavel, who, in the manta cloak, had seemed to have the best chance of escaping injury. Heedless of the blood leaking from his own gashed leg, his handsome face grave and intent, he set about the business of trying to save Kara's life. The water garbled his words in a way that, in other circumstances, might have seemed comical. Dorn could only hope Lathander still understood the prayers.

The priest's hands shone with rich golden light. Then, at the tops of the ravaged towers rising throughout the city, bells began to toll. Strangely, the water didn't muffle or warp that sound in the slightest.

No, Dorn thought. It isn't fair that this should happen when we've just finished a fight, when we're hurt and exhausted and have already expended a goodly portion of our magic. It doesn't even make sense. Why is it the wraiths never attacked the skeletal dragons or that gigantic serpent?

Maybe Sammaster has a way of suppressing the phantoms, he continued to muse, a forbiddance that lost its power with the demise of his agents. Maybe the spirits had no objection to letting other entities defend their domain for them, or perhaps those dead things reserve their spite for the living.

Dorn supposed that ultimately, the reason didn't matter. The only thing that did was that, at the worst possible moment, the ghosts of Northkeep were coming forth.

Taegan crept through the canopy, stalking from one branch to the next, peering. Jivex flew close at hand. The faerie dragon was invisible, but at certain moments, Taegan could hear the flutter of his wings or catch the leathery tang of his reptilian scent.

They were hunting pickets. While the queen's men regrouped, Taegan had managed to locate the cultists' stronghold, and he and his comrades hoped to take the enemy unaware. As best they could judge, Sammaster's minions didn't expect an assault. They imagined that any surviving Warswords had fled the Gray Forest in disarray. Moreover, the expedition's spellcasters, working in concert with the faerie dragons, could mask the entire company in illusion. Thus, a surprise attack seemed feasible.

But only if someone first eliminated the sentries the cult had posted around their citadel. Otherwise, one of the guards was bound to discern something amiss. Taegan and Jivex's ability to move stealthily through the foliage, above the eye line of the average picket, made them good choices for the task.

Taegan spotted a pair of hobgoblin warriors on the ground ahead. Evidently their kind kept watch by day, while the werewolves took over the duty after dark. The goblinkin with the thick russet hair on its hide stood idly fingering its bulbous blue nose. The slate-colored one squatted staring at the ground. After a moment, Taegan perceived that the creature had stirred an anthill with the dirty dagger still in his hand and was watching the insects scurry around.

"I'll take the red one," Taegan whispered. "You take the gray."

"There are just the pair," Jivex replied. His hushed, reedy voice and tickling breath came right into the avariel's ear. Taegan was so startled, he nearly jumped and revealed his presence to the hobgoblins. "If you're going to deal with the red, then of course I have the gray."

"It's gratifying to discover you can at least count as high as two."

Jivex gave an affronted sniff and Taegan skulked forward. Presumably Jivex was doing the same. The fencing teacher maneuvered around behind the hobgoblins then sprang to the ground, spreading his wings just enough to insure a safe landing.

He was still trying to be quiet, but the hulking goblinkin with the rust-colored hair sensed him anyway. As it pivoted, it poised its round wooden shield in a middle guard and lifted its spear for a thrust.

Its defensive posture wasn't enough to save it. Taegan had used bladesong to heighten his strength and agility and sharpen his sword to a supernatural keenness, and it was simplicity itself to stab over the top of the targe and drive his blade completely through the creature's skull. The hobgoblin collapsed.

As he jerked his weapon free, Taegan looked around to see if Jivex needed help. Evidently not. His invisibility forfeited in the act of attacking, scales rippling with rainbows, the faerie dragon clung between the gray hobgoblin's shoulder blades, biting and tearing. Blood spurted from the torn arteries in the warrior's neck. The goblinkin tried to scream, yet only managed a soft gurgling before it fell.

Taegan smiled wryly. Jivex's small size and impish, almost childlike demeanor had initially led him to assume that faerie dragons were peaceful creatures dependent solely on trickery for self-protection. It had been mildly disconcerting to find out they could fight as savagely as panthers when necessary.

Jivex spat out a mouthful of gore and said, "That tastes disgusting. I ought to get a sword. Should we look for more guards?"

"No. We're only a stone's throw away from the stronghold itself. I doubt they have pickets posted any closer in."

Taegan dragged the corpses into a patch of brush and kicked old rotten leaves over the blood they'd shed. With luck, it would keep any casual passerby from discovering them. Then he and Jivex skulked back to the place where many of their comrades waited. Once they reported their success, they had nothing to do but wait for the others performing the same chore to do likewise.

Taegan drifted over to Vorasaegha, who was turning her huge bronze head this way and that like a traveler in an exotic land.

"The world seems so strange," she rumbled, "like a dream. I dwelled here for more than a thousand years, but still, I've been gone so long. . . ."

Taegan mistrusted the fey, abstracted note in the bronze's voice.

"Are you all right?" he asked.

Her emerald eyes blinked and she said, "What? Yes, fine."

"I'm relieved to hear it, because Sune knows, we need you."

"Perhaps," Vorasaegha said. "But in the old days, the elves were mighty fighters in their own ri—"

Uthred scurried up to them. The mage's long, yellow-brown beard was matted and tangled after his days of living rough, bereft, apparently, of a comb.

"Everyone's back," he reported, "and we killed all the sentries. Are you ready, Lady?"

"Yes," Vorasaegha said.

She, Jivex, Uthred, and the others who commanded the proper magic assembled to collaborate on the ritual that would conceal the entire company.

Meanwhile, the men-at-arms gave their weapons and armor a final check, and priests prayed for the blessing of Ilmater, Selûne, and the rest of Impiltur's beneficent gods. A subtle shimmer spread through the air. When it passed, Taegan could still see his comrades perfectly well, as was necessary if they were to advance in an orderly fashion. But supposedly no hostile eye could glimpse them.

Their officers formed them up then led them forward through the trees. Their progress made a certain amount of noise. The wizards and clerics had deemed it best not to wrap the company in magical silence, lest it hamper further spellcasting once combat began, and Taegan winced at every creak of leather, clink of mail, or rattling branch. Still, he felt they were advancing about as quietly as a sizable force could, and they reached their destination without incident, spreading out to assault it on three sides.

The stronghold stood in a bare wound in the midst of the wood, where either wizardry or the strength of dragons had torn the trees from the earth to make a space for it. Some of the uprooted giants still littered the ground, perhaps to hinder the advance of an attacking force. Others had likely gone to feed the cultists' fires, or make them furniture.

At the center of the clearing rose a citadel so rough and irregular in form that one could almost mistake it for a natural rock formation. Sammaster had evidently conjured masses of ruddy sandstone up out of the ground then crudely sculpted them into walls and keeps. The result lacked any semblance of grace but looked dauntingly defensible.

Taegan and his companions halted at the edge of the trees that were still standing. Archers nocked arrows. Uthred and another magician floated up into the air, achieving the height necessary to hurl attack spells over the top of the ramparts at targets inside. Vorasaegha stared at the stronghold and whispered under her breath, while Taegan shrouded his body in blur.

A paladin raised his sword then swept it toward the ground. The arrows flew, and hobgoblins on the battlements fell. An instant later, shafts hurtled from the east and west as well. Thunder cracked, and streaks of lightning burned through the air. Blasts of fire exploded inside the citadel, tongues of yellow flame leaping so high they showed above the top of the wall.

It seemed a promising beginning. Taegan reflected that in its essentials, war truly did have a fair amount in common with a duel between single opponents. If one army surprised the other, the former enjoyed a considerable advantage.

Still, not everything was proceeding as the queen's men had hoped. Responding to Vorasaegha's incantation, a section of castle wall wavered and became semitransparent, revealing the murky shape of a wyrm on the other side. A hobgoblin on the battlements sank into the stone walkway beneath his feet as if it was quicksand. Then, however, the wall became opaque and solid again, trapping and crushing the shrieking creature's legs. Sammaster's magic was evidently stronger than the guardian bronze's, and she couldn't unmake an object he'd conjured into being.

Vorasaegha roared and charged into the open, toward the high gates that were likewise slabs of sandstone, apparently intent on battering them down by brute force. Knights and men-at-arms charged in her wake, some carrying crudely fashioned siege ladders. Taegan and Jivex raced along with them. The avariel wasn't yet willing to fly. He feared it would make him too conspicuous a target. But by beating his wings, he covered the ground in long leaps that kept him at the forefront of the charge. Meanwhile, arcanists and archers shot over the heads of their comrades at their foes within the fortress.

Roaring, batlike wings rattling and eclipsing broad swaths of sky, black and green dragons soared up from within the castle, and even paladins faltered at the terror of it. Vorasaegha reared, spat lightning, and engulfed in the dazzling flare, a skull wyrm burned and crashed to the ground. A wizard—Taegan didn't see who—attacked a green with cold, encrusting its flank in frost. It wasn't enough to kill the reptile, but it hissed in pain and wobbled crazily in flight. Heartened, the Warswords drove on.

Into the Abyss, or a fair approximation of it. In the mad confusion of the moment, Taegan couldn't even tell how many dragons the cult had left—at least half a dozen, he thought—but several opted to defend the approach to the gate, clawing, biting, squashing men with their sheer bulk, spewing poison and casting spells. Individually, none of the chromatic drakes was a match for Vorasaegha, but no matter how furiously she fought, she couldn't aid all her allies at the same time. Some of them simply had to fend for themselves.

A green wyrm swooped and spat corrosive fumes. Taegan dived out of the way, and the gas only stung his eyes and skin and made him cough. Jivex also made it clear. Several men were less fortunate. They collapsed, skins blistered, lungs rotting in their chests.

With a ground-shaking thump, the dragon set down to finish off anyone who still lived. A paladin of Ilmater lurched up from the earth and the charred, dead horse he'd been riding, rasped out the name of his god, and hacked at the green's mask with his greatsword.

The blade bit deep. Though still coughing painfully and uncontrollably, clumsy with it, Taegan rushed forward to help the knight. The dragon clawed, tore away part of the paladin's plate armor, and ripped bloody furrows in the flesh beneath. The knight riposted with another stroke that cut deeply and split the wyrm's left eye. The dragon roared and spewed greenish-yellow vapor. Unable to weather a second such assault, the human collapsed.

Hating the green, and himself for reaching it a heartbeat too late to aid the paladin, Taegan thrust his sword into its chest. It started to whirl in his direction, and he took a chance and stabbed again before leaping back.

The gamble paid off. The paladin had already sorely wounded the wyrm, and Taegan's second thrust either killed it or at least stole the strength from its limbs. It fell on its side, and he gave it three more stabs, trying to make sure it was really was out of action. Jivex lit on its snout and clawed away its remaining eye.

Taegan cast about, trying to determine what to do next. It was hard to tell. Dragons and humans were still fighting almost within sword's reach. But maybe, just maybe, Vorasaegha and his other comrades were holding their own, and their struggle was only one part of the battle. To win, the Warswords needed to penetrate the castle, and so far, it didn't look as if that was happening. Though the queen's men had hit hard at the start of the fight, the cult had plenty of minions and had succeeded in positioning many of them atop the walls. There, with the advantage of the high ground and the crudely shaped battlements to shield them, they'd thus far succeeded in keeping any of Sambryl's troops from climbing up to their level and surviving for any length of time.

Scrambling back from a black drake's lashing tail that might otherwise have broken his legs, Taegan wheezed—his lungs were still sore, curse it—"Conjure more protection if you can!"

He used bladesong to sheathe his limbs in invisible armor—weightless, imperceptible to a casual touch, yet resistant to cuts and blows—and to make himself so unnaturally fast that the rest of the world seemed to slow to a crawl.

Jivex faded from view.

Taegan made sure no drake was hovering directly overhead, ready to rip him to bits of bloody meat and loose feathers, then he spread his pinions and flew at the top of the battlements. Presumably Jivex was speeding at his side. Arrows and javelins hurtled at the avariel, but they either missed or glanced off his shell of enchantment.

Two hobgoblins and a werewolf in beast-man form poised themselves to repel him. He knocked a pair of stabbing spear points aside with a sweeping parry, then dispatched one of the goblinoids with a chest cut. Snarling, the shapechanger lunged and raked at him with its claws. Dodging the stroke, he grabbed the lycanthrope by the wrist, flew backward with a beat of his wings, dragged it forward over the ramparts, and let go. The plummet to the ground might not kill a werewolf, but at least it got the brute out of Taegan's way.

The remaining hobgoblin aimed his lance for a second thrust, and Jivex appeared right in front of him and puffed sparkling vapor into his face. The brutish warrior smiled blissfully, stupidly, and was still smiling when Taegan shoved him off the wall walk to crash down in the castle courtyard.

The fencing master lit on the elevated path and pivoted to confront the foes already driving in from the right. Jivex hovered at his back to meet the ones on the left.

Taegan's adversaries pressed him hard. Still, occasionally, after he killed one, it took the next a fraction of a second to scramble forward to engage him. With his accelerated reactions, that gave him enough time to glance over his shoulder and see how Jivex was faring. Thus, he glimpsed the second plume of euphoria-inducing breath that neutralized several foes at once, the mind-altering charm that persuaded a werewolf to change sides until its own packmates ripped it apart, and the gigantic eagle that flew down from the sky to harry the cultists.

Both Taegan and the faerie dragon were staying alive and holding their position. The avariel doubted they could do it for long, but luckily that wasn't necessary. Some of the Warswords had spotted them. The humans planted their scaling ladders below the length of wall walk their allies had cleared of the enemy, then scrambled upward.

Once he thought that enough men had reached the battlements, Taegan shouted, "The gates!"

Without even glancing to see who besides Jivex was ready to follow, or if folk without wings yet had a clear path on which to descend, he leaped down into the courtyard. Perhaps it was mad to charge on in advance of his comrades yet again, but his blood was up, and it felt right.

When he reached ground level, a werewolf in its four-legged guise pounced at him, and he spitted it on his sword. His blade was still stuck in it when a tawny-haired hobgoblin bellowed and charged him with a spear. He sidestepped the attack and tripped the brutish warrior as it blundered by. It recovered its balance and whirled around just in time to receive a slash to the belly. Clutching the wound to keep its guts from spilling out, it crumpled to its knees. Meanwhile, Jivex dazed a few of its fellows with another puff of sparkling breath.

The attackers scrambled onward toward the massive, asymmetrical stone leaves, the gigantic timber that barred them, and the contrivance of windlasses, chains, pulleys, and counterweights evidently needed to swing them on their hinges. Then, somehow, Taegan abruptly sensed a presence so vile, so overwhelming, that it stopped him in his tracks then dragged him around to face it. Silver-white wings flickering, Jivex also wheeled, prey to the same compulsion.

Trembling, heart pounding, Taegan belatedly recalled how the cultists in Lyrabar had liked their underground crypts. Evidently their counterparts in the forest had dug out their own burrows, where, perhaps, they wove their foulest magic in the perpetual dark. In any case, a ramp leading down into the earth descended into shadow in the middle of the courtyard—maybe it had been there all along, veiled in illusion, or maybe a charm had just then opened it—permitting the dracolich to slither forth into the light of day.

It stank like carrion, and its withered green hide bore patches of black, wet rot. It was plainly a dead thing, like the zombies Taegan had fought in Lyrabar, but infinitely more terrible. Where they had lurched and shambled awkwardly, it, for all its hugeness, prowled like a hunting cat. The zombies' ashen faces had been slack and mindless, but the dracolich's sunken yellow eyes burned with an intelligence as keen as it was cruel.

Taegan had known since the previous battle that the cult had already created a dracolich, but he'd dared to hope that some of his allies had already engaged and destroyed the thing. No such luck. It had sat out the first minutes of the fight, but evidently it meant to purge the fortress of intruders. Some of the humans on the ramparts moaned or wailed at the sight of it. The hobgoblins and werewolves raised a savage cheer and hurled themselves at the queen's men with renewed ferocity.

The undead green took a stride toward Taegan. Shouting, he broke through the dread that had unmanned him, not banishing it utterly—for how could anyone look at the dracolich and not know fear?—but at least compressing it into something that didn't reach into and strangle the part of him that knew how to fight. He came on guard and only then recalled Rangrim's warning: Don't meet its gaze, and you'll be all right.

The memory came back to him too late. He already had looked into its luminous eyes, and he froze once more—but not out of fear. Some supernatural power made his muscles clench and lock. At his side, something thumped on the ground. He couldn't turn his head to see what, but after a moment, realized it must have been Jivex. The faerie dragon was paralyzed too, and unable to beat his wings, he had fallen from the air.

Taking its time, the dracolich stalked closer.

"Did you actually think you were winning?" it asked. "Nothing you and your humans have done means anything. You could kill every one of my slaves, and it wouldn't matter. I'm strong enough to wipe out the lot of you, all by myself. I'll show you just how easily small folk die."

It reared, evidently preparing to breathe. Werewolves and hobgoblins scrambled, distancing themselves from Taegan and Jivex. Then a shadow swept across the courtyard.

The dracolich looked up and spat its acidic fumes into the air. An instant later, a beam of scarlet light spat down and burned through the creature's torso. It roared, and Vorasaegha dived out of the sky and plunged her talons into its body.

The two colossal wyrms grappled, and intertwined, rolled back and forth across the courtyard, tearing at one another with fang and claw. Some of the werewolves, hobgoblins, and cultists failed to scurry out of the way in time, and the dragons crushed them to jelly, perhaps without even noticing they were there. Sometimes the reptiles slammed into one of the walls, and the jolt knocked other folk toppling off the battlements. Taegan wondered how long it would be before the dragons smashed down on top of Jivex and him.

The struggle between the two drakes so pounded at the senses that it took the avariel a few seconds to notice the flying orb, a thing like a disembodied eye, flitting around the periphery of the battle. It seemed to be something Vorasaegha had conjured into existence, for it assaulted the dracolich with one magical effect after another, just as, apparently, it had first discharged the crimson lance of heat. An orange beam spattered the undead green's flesh with steaming, smoking acid. A yellow one became jagged, crackling lightning, which seemed to do it no harm. A blue beam made it falter for a second—which allowed Vorasaegha to score with a couple deep claw slashes—and sent a grayness rippling through its scales. Then its natural color and agility returned.

As the fight proceeded, both wyrms suffered enormous, ghastly wounds, but perhaps Vorasaegha was faring better than her opponent. She was even huger and presumably stronger, and the floating eye gave her another advantage. She broke free of the dracolich's coils, slammed it onto its back, and crouched on its torso. Her forefeet pinned it in place while the hind ones raked away chunks of decaying flesh. She opened her jaws to bite. Then the undead green laughed, and she hesitated, not paralyzed—her wings were still flapping, her hind talons ripping a little—but rattled somehow. Without her will directing it, the hovering orb stopped shooting magic.

"I know you," the dracolich said.

"No," she said.

"But I do, Vorasaegha, and you're even deader than I am. You no longer belong in this world, and you know it. You feel the wrongness of it in every breath you take."

"I return when the elves need me."

"The elves are no more, your pact is ended, and the quarrels of this latter-day world are none of your affair. Return to your rightful place, spirit. Return to your rest."

She won't do it, Taegan thought. She doesn't have to. The dracolich didn't throw a spell on her or anything. It just talked to her.

Certainly he had the feeling that Vorasaegha didn't want to abandon the fight. She shook her head and gripped the undead green's hide as if to anchor herself to the world of the living. Yet she faded, dwindled, and finally shattered into a drift of dust and chips of bone.

The dracolich rolled to its feet and pivoted toward Taegan.

"Now," it said, "where were we?"

TWENTY-TWO

16-22 Tarsakh, the Year of Rogue Dragons

As the bells tolled, the water darkened once more, though the blackness wasn't absolute. Dorn could still see his exhausted, wounded comrades, and in fact, it was easy to spot the ghosts of Northkeep. Stalking from doorways or simply materializing above the layer of silt fouling the courtyard, the spectral men-at-arms glowed with their own pale inner light.

In those first moments, Dorn couldn't tell how many there were. Dozens, certainly. Maybe hundreds. He turned to Pavel, who, wrapped in his manta ray cloak, his hands shining with red-gold light, was still laboring to resuscitate the torn and mangled Kara. The priest shook his head, signaling that, though Lathander granted his vicars special powers versus the undead, he'd already expended his daily ration in the fight against the skeletal dragons. He had nothing left to repel wraiths.

Glimmering, translucent swords and spears leveled, the phantoms encircled the intruders. Chatulio jerked his head, motioning for his comrades to swim upward. The copper drake evidently meant to cover their retreat.

Even if it would work, it meant abandoning both Chatulio and Kara. And Dorn didn't think it would work anyway. The ghosts would cut off those who sought to flee. The explorers in their current depleted condition couldn't hope to stand against so many terrible foes.

Dorn could only think of one thing that seemed worth trying. He gestured for his comrades to stay where they were and do nothing. Then, his hands raised to indicate peaceful intentions, he swam away from his friends and toward the circle of phantoms.

On guard in the manner of living warriors, their figures vague and blurry one moment and more sharply defined the next, several of the wraiths advanced to meet him. They walked as if moving through air instead of water. He wondered how their ghostly blades would feel, shearing into his flesh. His intuition told him they'd be freezing cold.

One of the specters appeared right beside him. Clad in a coat of scale armor and a conical helmet with a nose guard, it lifted its battle-axe for a chop at Dorn's head.

Reflexes honed over decades of fighting demanded that Dorn strike first, or at least assume a defensive posture. Denying them, he forced himself to remain perfectly still.

A second ghost lifted its hand. That one wore a surcoat embroidered with a double-headed eagle, the image spoiled by the bloodstained tear in the center, and he had the look of a knight or captain. Heeding the silent forbiddance, the wraith with the axe didn't swing after all, though it still held the weapon ready. The leader stepped forward and stared into Dorn's eyes. For a moment, the phantom's lean, melancholy face flickered into the fleshless visage of a naked skull, then, wavering, put on something of the appearance of life once more.

That's right, thought Dorn, *look at me. Read my thoughts if you can. I'm not like the others who came before me. I don't want to loot your bodies and homes. I'm only here to learn. Your city holds a secret I need to protect other folk, as you defended your families and neighbors in your time. As you defend them still in their final rest.*

Ghosts glided forward, surrounding him, their weapons poised to strike. The sickly, oozing sheen of them made him feel cold and ill.

He was certain he was a fool. It couldn't possibly work. Even if they heard his silent pleas, they wouldn't believe them, because they wouldn't take him for human. With his ugly, freakish iron limbs and metal profile, he surely resembled one of the ogres or trolls that had helped to destroy Northkeep.

Yet he continued standing as he was, allowing them to draw as close as they wished, affording them every opportunity to strike him down if that was what they wanted. It was too late for anything else.

Look at me, he begged. *Look past the iron. I'm the same as you. I want what you wanted when you were alive.*

The knight gestured, and his men stepped back a pace. The bells stopped their clanging, and the ghosts faded from view. The shadow melted out of the water, permitting sunlight to filter down once more.

Dorn slumped with relief, felt a presence behind him, and turned. Kara had swum after him. Pavel hadn't succeeded in healing all her wounds, but he had saved her life and restored her to consciousness.

Dorn realized he was glad, even if she was a dragon. He gave her an awkward pat on the side of her neck. She pressed gently back as a cat might lean into a caress, and feeling strange, he snatched his hand away.

He waved for the rest of their companions to join them. Apparently the ghosts had decided to let them explore as they would, provided they didn't despoil Northkeep—he prayed Will could resist the temptation to fill his pockets—but that didn't mean it was going to be easy. The place was big and ruinous, sections of it collapsed, buried in muck, or otherwise impassable, and he wondered just how long the search would take.

Taegan lurched off balance as the rigidity left his muscles. Vorasaegha had occupied the dracolich just long enough for the supernatural paralysis to lose its grip on him.

The undead green flapped its wings and pounced. The charm of quickness no longer accelerating his reactions—alas, that too had run its course—Taegan simultaneously scooped up the fallen Jivex and rattled off another spell.

The magic instantly transported him partway across the courtyard. The dracolich slammed down on the spot he'd just vacated with an earth-shaking jolt. Underneath his arm, Jivex squirmed as he too shook off his immobility. Taegan released the faerie dragon, who then took flight.

The avariel assumed Jivex would flee for his life. If Taegan had any sense, he'd do the same. But somebody had to try to slay the dracolich, he was in the proper position to attempt it, and it was conceivable that the undead wyrm was actually vulnerable. Vorasaegha had nearly torn it limb from limb. That didn't appear to have slowed it down any, but still, it seemed remotely possible that a swordsman might be able to finish it off.

Taegan lunged and drove his blade into the dracolich's hind leg. Jivex streaked alongside him, lit on the undead dragon's haunch, and clawed away scales. Meanwhile, the magical eye floated uselessly overhead.

Snarling, the dracolich wheeled, and Taegan sprinted along with it, trying to keep away from the head and forefeet—attempting to stay in close, too, despite the constant threat of being trampled or rolled on—even though his comrades had warned him that the mere fleeting brush of an undead drake's flesh could freeze him in place. He hoped that if he hovered near to his enormous foe, the creature would find it more awkward to strike at him.

Jivex whirled up into the air. The dracolich's serpentine head twisted toward him, and a haze of bright golden sparks appeared around the dead thing's head. Jivex had evidently conjured the glittering mist to blind the behemoth, and perhaps it had. But a wyrm's every sense was keen, and the dracolich nonetheless blasted forth a plume of its roiling yellow-green breath. A chance shift of one of its wings blocked Taegan's view a split second later, and he couldn't see whether his small ally managed to avoid the toxic jet or not.

Taegan sprang in and cut. Gigantic claws raked at him, and he dodged. Encrusted with sparkling flecks of gold, the dracolich's jaws arced down at the end of its long, flexible neck to snap at the avariel, and he evaded those as well. He slashed at the side of its mask, but his blade glanced off a protruding ridge of bone without doing any appreciable harm.

The dracolich tried to bite his legs out from under him. He beat his wings, flew above the threat, and attempted to thrust at its neck. Unfortunately, it was already compensating for his shift in position, already renewing the attack, and he had to abandon his own offensive action to twist frantically in the air. The gigantic fangs clashed shut without catching his flesh, but the dracolich's snout caught him a glancing blow. His muscles spasmed, and he floundered in the air, trying to shake off the crippling effect of the dead reptile's touch. Its jaws gaped, and he realized he'd never evade the next bite.

Then, patches of his rainbow hide raw and blistered, Jivex soared over the dracolich's head, and a loud screech cut through the air. Taegan realized that his ally was attempting to block their foe's senses one at a time. The golden dust was supposed to blind it, and with luck, the ear-splitting wail would deafen it.

At the very least, it made the dracolich falter for an instant. Recovering his coordination, Taegan thrust his sword into its neck. At the same time, arrows and spears rained down on it from the battlements. Apparently the struggle up there was going well enough that some of the queen's men could turn their attention to the undead green. Though the barrage looked ineffectual, maybe it would at least help confuse the creature.

The dracolich flapped its wings and bounded to the flat roof of one of the crudely fashioned sandstone keeps. The screech followed it, and so did Taegan and Jivex. The dracolich snarled words of power, the sound barely audible over the shrill wailing, and magic shimmered through the air. Taegan realized he and Jivex wouldn't reach the undead green in time to interrupt its spellcasting.

Then a blast of fire engulfed the corpse-drake, though to Taegan's disappointment, the explosion seemed to do it no harm. It did, however, prompt the wyrm to orient on Uthred, who at some point in the past couple of minutes had made his way onto the top of the west wall. The dracolich broke off its conjuring to spew poison smoke. The young wizard and three comrades standing nearby charred, withered, and fell.

It was horrible, but Taegan couldn't dwell on it. He had to focus on the fight, on exploiting the opportunity Uthred had bought for him at the cost of his life. Wings hammering, he flew along the dracolich's flank, thrusting and thrusting. He realized he'd lost track of Jivex again and could only hope his comrade was still alive and doing something useful.

Instead of striking back, the dracolich commenced another incantation. That had its positive aspect, but Taegan suspected that it was, on balance, bad. He attacked even more furiously, striking to spoil the cadence or pronunciation of the cabalistic rhymes, but the green rumbled and hissed inexorably onward as if his sword caused it no discomfort whatsoever. Perhaps it didn't. Who knew what dead things truly felt?

Waves of power pulsed outward from the dracolich. The sparkling golden dust on its wedge-shaped head with its crest of horns vanished. The disembodied shrieking died. A shock ran through Taegan's frame as all the enchantments that had bolstered his prowess abruptly ceased to be. His strength and agility dropped to their normal levels, while his shroud of blur and invisible armor winked out of existence. No doubt his sword shed its magical enhancements as well. The dracolich had wiped it all away with a counterspell devised to arrest every ongoing magical effect in its immediate vicinity.

All Taegan had left was his own martial skill and innate capacities. Well, so be it.

The dracolich turned. Dodging the whipping tail and immense, ragged wings that might otherwise have bashed him unconscious, he flew around the creature. Trying to keep away from the head and fore claws, he cut and thrust into the putrid bulk of it. From the corner of his eye, he glimpsed a rainbow flash that told him Jivex was still fighting, too.

Someone threw a javelin that narrowly missed Taegan's pinion before glancing off the dracolich's shoulder. Then, despite all the fencing master's evasions, the wyrm swung into position to bring its gaze, fangs, and breath weapon to bear. Filthy vapor blasted from its jaws. Taegan dodged the worst of it, but it still burned him, set him coughing, and flooded his stinging eyes with tears. Momentarily blind, he couldn't see it when the dracolich followed up by striking at him like an adder. Rather, he knew by pure instinct.

He spun aside, and the huge teeth rasped shut on empty air. Perhaps surprised that, even sightless, its prey had avoided the attack, the wyrm hesitated for a second. Taegan flew down the length of its extended neck with its ridge of spikes along the top, hacking savagely.

The dracolich decided that it too would fight on the wing. It roared, flexed its legs, and leaped from the rooftop. As it wheeled and climbed, seeking to rise above its foe, it snarled the opening words of another spell.

Then one of its wings tore away from its torso. The creature plummeted and hit the top of the wall. The impact broke it into two pieces, which, when they struck the ground—one outside the citadel and one within—smashed into a number of smaller ones.

Hovering, coughing and gasping, feeling the pain of his blisters more acutely than he had in the frenzy of combat, Taegan peered down at the wreckage. He supposed victory shouldn't seem so unbelievable. Vorasaegha had done an amazing amount of damage to the corpse-wyrm, after which he'd slashed and stabbed it dozens of times himself. Yet he still knew in his bones that he and Jivex had been very, very lucky.

The faerie dragon flew up beside him.

"I killed it!" Jivex crowed.

Taegan smiled. He knew the claim was inaccurate in more than one regard. According to those who understood such things, the dracolich's spirit had returned to its phylactery, where it would abide until the talisman came into proximity with a draconic cadaver. Then the ghost would leap into the body and animate it.

Except that it wouldn't get the chance. Once Taegan and his allies took the stronghold, they'd find the phylactery and destroy it.

He had no doubt they would take it. Below him, appalled at the destruction of the creature they'd served as if it was a god, werewolves, hobgoblins, and cultists babbled, shrank from their foes, and cast about for a way to escape their fortress, which suddenly seemed more like a deathtrap. Though still outnumbered, the queen's men attacked them ferociously.

"Can you continue fighting," Taegan asked, "or would you prefer to remove yourself from harm's way? Sune knows, you've done enough."

"I can still fight," Jivex said.

"Then let's open those gates."

As it turned out, the search took days. Days of groping through cold darkness. Days of waiting for Zhents to show up and attack them. They soon ran out of the elixirs that enabled a person to breathe underwater, and from that point forward, were dependent on Kara and Chatulio's spells to accomplish the same effect. That meant not everyone could dive all the time, which made the hunt go even slower.

Finally, though, Dorn and Pavel entered the apartments that had plainly once belonged to a scholar. The golden glow Pavel had conjured onto the head of a spear to light their way shone on the sodden, swollen, surely illegible remains of countless books, shelf upon useless shelf of them. The sight of so much lost knowledge made Dorn feel angry and desperate.

Then, at the edge of the yellow light, he glimpsed a section of wall that the long-dead sage hadn't lined with shelves. Instead, he'd hung slabs of marble there.

Dorn pointed, and he and Pavel waded forward to inspect the display. The irregular sheets of white stone looked as if the scholar had chiseled them from the walls of a palace or temple. They had pictures on them, and viewed in sequence, the carvings seemed to tell a kind of story. Pavel was the first to decipher it, and when he did, he grinned like a madman and threw his arms around his friend.

Once everyone had had a chance to view the marbles, the hunters, clad in their drier clothes—after days of diving, no one had any that were truly dry—gathered in the bow of their stolen sailboat. Wearing human form, Kara sat with them. Chatulio perched on the stern, his weight making it ride low in the purple-blue water, his coppery neck, agleam in the spring sunlight, arcing to bring his head into proximity with his assembled comrades.

Pavel looked at the two dragons and said, "Perhaps one of you can explicate our discovery better than I can."

Sitting her back against the mast, Kara shifted, trying to get comfortable. No doubt her wounds still pained her.

"You're a learned man," she said. Will snorted. "And in fact, the tale touches on . . . well, matters that shame drakes of our kind. Subjects painful to discuss. So, please, you start."

"All right." The days of exploration had left Pavel weary, yet he still succumbed to a restless urge to stand. It was the way he'd instructed novices, before he left his temple to wander. "Long, long ago, before Northkeep, before even the Crown Wars—"

"The which?" Will interrupted.

"A series of catastrophic wars among the early elven peoples, you ignoramus. Anyway, before even those, at the dawn of history, dragons pretty much ruled the world and ruled it harshly. Other races were their slaves, their cattle, or at best, lived in constant fear of them. The first couple marbles show that age in all its horror."

"We metal dragons," Chatulio said, sounding entirely serious for once, "like to think we ruled less brutally than the reds, greens, and their ilk, but maybe that's just a lie to ease our guilt. In any case, we weren't the same creatures we are today. We weren't merciful or gentle. I guess we needed a comeuppance to temper our pride with wisdom."

"Which is what the rest of the carvings show," said Will.

"So it seems," Pavel said. A gust of breeze chilled his lanky frame in its damp garments, and he repressed a shiver. "In the third, we see a circle of elf spellcasters gathered together, collaborating on what surely must have been a prodigious work of high magic. In the fourth, we see what may be the climax of the ritual, and the enchantment they created springing into existence around them."

"The web of lines," said Raryn, dragging a wooden comb through his mane of long, tangled hair.

Sometimes the strokes tore white strands loose, and he had to pause to pick them out of the teeth.

"Yes," Pavel said. "It's hard to know exactly what the

image is supposed to represent in all its aspects, but beginning in the fifth marble, we see the effects."

"Wyrms running mad," said Dorn.

Pavel said, "The elf mages cursed them with the Rage. That's where it came from."

"It seems like a funny way to try and fix the problem," said Will. "We're scared of dragons, dragons kill and eat us, so let's make them meaner."

"I suppose," Kara said, "it was the only way they could devise of striking a blow against my entire race at once. You're right, at first, their fellow elves and the rest of the vassal races must have paid a terrible price. But frenzy makes dragons reckless, hence vulnerable to attack. Sometimes it impels us to smash our own eggs and devour our own wyrmlings, and it probably prompted the tyrants to lash out at their own armies. Eventually, their numbers diminished, their kingdoms toppled, and they lost their absolute dominion over Faerûn. In the final carvings, we see elves and giants founding their own extensive and independent realms.

"Today," the willowy bard continued, "the wise know what happened, but not why. Even the elves no longer recall how they brought about my people's downfall. Yet we can only infer that somewhere the enchantment—the mythal—endures, still afflicting dragonkind with periodic bouts of madness, like the wheel of an abandoned mill turning in the stream even though the miller is long gone."

"My guess," said Dorn, "is that the wizards left the spell in place to make sure wyrms would never take over the world again. It's what I would have done."

"Whether they left it going on purpose," said Will, "didn't know how to stop it, or just forgot about it, the important thing is that our friend Sammaster found the place where the magic lives, the place where a spellcaster can control it, and figured out how to make it even stronger."

"That's how it seems," Pavel said, frowning, "though it's hard to understand. By all accounts, the magic of eld was somehow different than the power wizards command today, and even now, elven high magic is special—unique to the race. How, then, could Sammaster, born human, trained only a few hundred years ago, seize control of a mythal powerful enough to endure since the dawn of history and affect every dragon in the world?"

"That's one of the things we have to figure out," said Will, "as we keep following the trail he left us, which is what we have to do, isn't it, if we want to stop the Rage?"

"Perhaps," said Pavel, "we should ask the whole world to help us look for answers."

"No," said Dorn. "Who knows if we could persuade other folk to take us seriously? Even if we could, it would take months, years, and we don't have the time. Nor do we want to attract more attention from the Cult of the Dragon or King Lareth's flunkies. I reckon that for better or worse, this is still a job for Kara, Chatulio, and their circle; our partners in Thentia; and us."

Pavel sighed and said, "In that case, I pray we're up to the challenge."

"It's a hunt," Raryn said. "It's what we do."

EPILOGUE

Greengrass, the Year of Rogue Dragons

Metal banged and clattered in Olpara Mindle's kitchen. Lounging on a stubby-legged divan in the parlor, Taegan winced. He'd noticed the rotating rack of hanging pots and skillets Corkaury's wife kept on the ceiling, and it was all too easy to imagine a faerie dragon playing on it and somehow knocking the cookware down. When he'd learned of Taegan's intentions, Jivex had insisted on accompanying his new comrade back to Lyrabar, where, never having seen a city or even houses before, he kept poking his inquisitive nose into everything.

Sure enough, Jivex shot out of the kitchen doorway, streaking as fast as he'd flown to avoid the dracolich's jaws. Plump little Olpara scrambled after him, upraised broom in hand. Outdistancing her, the reptile hurtled up the stairs to the second floor. The halfling with her white curls stamped her foot in seeming exasperation, but she had a hint of a smile tugging at the corners of her mouth. She turned to resume the cooking that suffused the air with an enticing, spicy aroma.

Corkaury looked across the low table at his guest and said, "Go on with your story."

"As you wish," Taegan said. "I was just coming to the important part. Naturally, it had occurred to me that once we won the battle, the Warswords might try to confiscate all the cultists' wealth to fill Sambryl's coffers or to return stolen articles to their original owners, so I made a point of finding a treasure chest or two in advance of my human comrades." He shifted a white porcelain vase of scarlet tulips—Olpara had set out flowers in every room in observance of the spring festival—to clear the center of the table. He picked up a saddlebag from the rug beneath his boots and dumped out the sparkling, clattering contents.

Corkaury stared at the plenitude of star sapphires, emeralds, clear king's tears, red pieces of tomb jade, and other gems.

"It seems you've solved your financial troubles," said the halfling.

"One would hope."

"And are you more comfortable in your own skin now?"

Taegan cocked his head and replied, "What a curious question."

"I suppose. I don't even know why it occurred to me. I just thought . . . I mean, you said that the city the gray trees showed you was grand."

"So it was, but it died a long time ago, and in any case, avariels didn't build it. Or anything else, ever, as best I can determine. So I believe I'll continue thinking of myself simply as a loyal subject of Impiltur. I assure you, I'm blissfully happy that way."

"That's good. I didn't mean to suggest you shouldn't be. With this wealth, we can start tomorrow, settling your debts and rebuilding the salle."

"Hold off on that for a while."

"Why?"

"As long as the Rage continues," Taegan said, "Impiltur is still in danger. People everywhere are in danger. It sounds preposterous, doesn't it, like a declaration from some windy old saga, but it's true, and I have this nagging itch to continue trying to improve the situation. I can't say why, but it's so."

"Then you're going to join Her Majesty's army in the east?"

Taegan shook his head and replied, "They have a vital job to do. So do the messengers the lords are sending to other lands to urge the rulers there to find and destroy the rest of the cult enclaves, before the lunatics can churn out hordes of dracoliches. But chance, in the person of poor Gorstag, chose to plunge me into the secret heart of this affair, and I intend to continue mucking about there. Which is to say I'm going to seek out Dorn, Kara, and their comrades in the north, and aid them in their endeavors. Until I return, I see no point in squandering this wealth on my creditors, or on building a school either. Keep it safe for me, and if I don't come back, it's yours."

"I don't know what to say."

"Don't get too excited. I do intend to survive."

"Do you think you can even find your friends?" asked the halfling.

"One nice thing about flying is you can cover a lot of ground."

"But according to you, the skies will be full of mad dragons attacking anyone they see."

Taegan grinned and said, "That should make it interesting."

It was ghastly to behold the inert spill of shattered bone and scraps of corruption divided by the fortress wall. It was infinitely worse to scramble down into the crypts, find the vault plundered, the phylactery missing, and know that the dracolich, magnificent above all other creatures, as splendid and as terrible as a god, could never be reborn.

Sammaster clenched his skeletal hands and wailed with grief. His desiccated eyes ached and would have streamed tears if they could.

The undead green, slain. His faithful followers likewise slaughtered, their supposedly secret stronghold discovered and overthrown. It was one more debacle in an endless chain. His failure to win Mystra's love or Alustriel's. His accidental massacre of the innocents he'd tried to rescue. The stripping-away of the powers he'd wielded as one of the Chosen. Humiliation on humiliation. Defeat on defeat. He pummeled his own head and clawed at his own withered face in a frenzy of self-loathing.

He might have continued that way for a long while, had it not abruptly occurred to him that if enemies had found his outpost, they'd likely learned of the catacombs in Lyrabar as well. He rattled off words of power, and between one instant and the next, the magic transported him to his study in the tunnels beneath the royal city. It only took another moment to confirm the worst. His notes, which he'd carelessly left there simply to save himself the bother of toting them about, were missing.

Once again, self-hatred, that feeling of being utterly despicable and unworthy, threatened to overwhelm him, but he found the strength to quash it. For after all, he wasn't really to blame for any of the tragedies and misfortunes of his long existence. Jealous, spiteful, deceitful Mystra was—the Lady of Mysteries and her countless groveling lackeys, and they couldn't truly hurt or thwart him any longer, because he finally understood his destiny. If only he could quell his seething emotions and think clearly, he'd see that all that had happened in Impiltur amounted to nothing more than a petty setback.

He reminded himself that he had other servants, other spellcasters laboring in secret to create dracoliches.

And no one could decipher his journal.

Even so, he wished he'd destroyed the artifacts he'd discovered in the course of his investigations. But like all true wizards, he was a scholar, with a respect for archival lore and antiquities. Such a desecration would have troubled him, particularly since he'd believed no one else would ever even try to unravel the puzzle.

And surely that was still true. Certainly no one could do it in time to spoil his grand design.

But perhaps he should hunt down the thieves, slaughter them, and take his papers back, if only to punish them for their effrontery.

Unfortunately, that could take time, and his time was infinitely precious. Only he could rush about Faerûn, temporarily quelling the frenzy in the minds of chromatic dragons, convincing them to accept their eventual transformations into liches and to perform the essential tasks they must perform in the meantime.

So he'd let the thieves live for a while. They couldn't follow where he'd gone, and even if they did, the traps he'd sown in his wake, like the Styx dragon and skeletal wyrms in Northkeep, would account for them. Or the other dangers the meddlers would encounter along the way. Even without knowing who they were, he could make sure there were plenty of those. He'd planned to do it all along, simply because the lands to the north were the gateway to the heart of the power, and thus it seemed a sensible precaution to throw them into chaos.

Finally, suppose that, by some miracle, the thieves did manage to follow the trail all the way to the end. It would simply mean they'd stumble into the grip of Sammaster himself, for that at least was absolutely inevitable.

Though it was both profoundly unlikely and utterly unimportant in the greater scheme of things, he almost hoped they would deliver themselves up for his personal vengeance. Smiling, at peace with himself once more, he straightened his cloak then recited another spell of translocation.

CHECK OUT THESE NEW TITLES FROM THE AUTHORS OF R.A. SALVATORE'S WAR OF THE SPIDER QUEEN SERIES!

VENOM'S TASTE
House of Serpents, Book I
Lisa Smedman

Serpents. Poison. Psionics. And the occasional evil death cult. Business as usual in the Vilhon Reach. Lisa Smedman breathes life into the treacherous yuan-ti race.

March 2004

THE RAGE
The Year of Rogue Dragons, Book I
Richard Lee Byers

Every once in a while the dragons go mad. Without warning they darken the skies of Faerûn and kill and kill and kill. Richard Lee Byers, the new master of dragons, takes wing.

April 2004

FORSAKEN HOUSE
The Last Mythal, Book I
Richard Baker

The Retreat is at an end, and the elves of Faerûn find themselves at a turning point. In one direction lies peace and stagnation, in the other: war and destiny. *New York Times* best-selling author Richard Baker shows the elves their future.

August 2004

THE RUBY GUARDIAN
Scions of Arrabar, Book II
Thomas M. Reid

Life and death both come at a price in the mercenary city-states of the Vilhon Reach. Vambran thought he knew the cost of both, but he still has a lot to learn. Thomas M. Reid makes humans the most dangerous monsters in Faerûn.

November 2004

THE SAPPHIRE CRESCENT
Scions of Arrabar, Book I
Available Now

FORGOTTEN REALMS

R.A. SALVATORE'S
WAR OF THE SPIDER QUEEN

THE EPIC SAGA OF THE DARK ELVES CONTINUES.

New in hardcover!

EXTINCTION
Book IV
Lisa Smedman

For even a small group of drow, trust is the rarest commodity of all. When the expedition prepares for a return to the Abyss, what little trust there is crumbles under a rival goddess's hand.

January 2004

ANNIHILATION
Book V
Philip Athans

Old alliances have been broken, and new bonds have been formed. While some finally embark for the Abyss itself, others stay behind to serve a new mistress—a goddess with plans of her own.

July 2004

RESURRECTION
Book VI

The Spider Queen has been asleep for a long time, leaving the Underdark to suffer war and ruin. But if she finally returns, will things get better... or worse?

April 2005

The New York Times *best-seller now in paperback!*

CONDEMNATION
Book III
Richard Baker

The search for answers to Lolth's silence uncovers only more complex questions, allowing doubt and frustration to test the boundaries of already tenuous relationships. Sensing the holes in the armor of Menzoberranzan, a new, dangerous threat steps in to test the resolve of the Jewel of the Underdark, and finds it lacking.

May 2004

Now in paperback!

DISSOLUTION, BOOK I

INSURRECTION, BOOK II